RESILIENT

ICONIC SONS MC: BOOK ONE

SHE

WILL

NOT

BE

DEFEATED

KAHLANI B. STEELE

Someone once told me that nothing lasts forever.

There is always an end.

Stay strong.

"**W**ould you shut the fucking kid up?" Peter roared from the lounge room.

At eleven years old, Charly, barely able to reach over the top of the crib, quickly lifted the crying baby out of his cot, hugging him close and pressing a light kiss on his tear-stained cheek. He was probably hungry. She sure was. Her stomach rumbled and cramped. Mama had gone out to the store, but that was a couple of hours ago.

Not that she'd be much help even if she were here.

"Hey, hey," Charly whispered to her baby brother, ten-month-old Fabien. His face was blotchy red, and dirty tear marks ran down his cheeks.

Charly sniffed. Fabe needed to be changed, too. "It's okay, Fabe. I'm here," she murmured, bouncing him up and down. It wasn't okay, though, and Charly wasn't sure how to make it all right.

"Where the fuck is that bitch?" her stepdad yelled, too lazy to get out of his recliner to look for Charly's mom.

That could work to Charly's advantage.

Peter was drunk. Surprise, surprise. It would have been more of a shock if he'd been sober. Unfortunately, he was an angry drunk, one of those people everyone in town knew to steer clear of when he'd been drinking.

Charly and Fabien didn't have that luxury.

Usually.

If he stayed in his recliner and didn't come looking for her mom or them, then maybe, just maybe, Charly could get them out the back door and over to the neighbors. If Mrs. McNally were home, she'd let them in. She always did. Charly tried not to go there too often. She didn't want to overstep and end up with nowhere to go, but it seemed like Peter was having more and more of his episodes. This would be the second time Charly had run from the house this week with Fabien in her arms.

Wrapping Fabien up in a blanket, Charly tiptoed out the back door, holding her brother's head to her chest in a protective grip, trying to muffle the sound of his snuffling against her skinny little chest. He was getting so big. His legs dangled down nearly to her knees. She wasn't sure how much longer she could carry him around.

Charly shivered, even with Fabe's warm weight against her. She didn't dare go to her room to get shoes or a coat, but it wasn't far to Mrs. McNally's.

"Charly!" Peter yelled.

That was it. They had to go now. Charly had been on the receiving end of Peter's fury before and had the bruises to prove it. She probably had a few broken bones, too. There was a spot on her ribs where Peter had kicked her that still hurt if she took a deep breath. Despite her pain, Mama never took her to a doctor. If she did, Peter would beat her up, and then both of them would be hurt. Being injured meant being stuck in the house and possibly getting knocked about again.

It was a cycle Charly tried to avoid.

Charly wasn't allowed to go to school if she had any visible injuries in case some nosy teacher reported her bruises. That was the worst. Charly loved being at school. School was safe. It was the only safe place she knew of, other than at her neighbor's, where no one would hurt her and someone would ensure she had enough to eat and warm clothes to wear.

But no one was at home to protect Fabien if Charly was at school. Mama was no better at safeguarding Fabien than keeping Charly safe.

Sometimes, it felt like she couldn't win.

"Charly! Where the hell are you?" Peter bellowed from inside the house.

Charly ran. She scampered up the steps to Mrs. McNally's door and knocked, hoping it was loud enough for Mrs. McNally to hear but not so loud that Peter would.

The door opened, and she was there as if she'd been waiting.

"Charly, come in, dear." Mrs. McNally ushered her and Fabien inside.

She wore a blue sweatshirt with a picture of a bird embroidered on it, jeans, and fuzzy slippers on her feet. Her hair was a fluffy white puff. Charly had no idea how old she was. Peter referred to her as "the old bat." But Mrs. McNally still went to work a few days each week. She couldn't be that old.

Charly slipped inside, sighing with relief at the warmth. She heard the lock click as Mrs. McNally locked the door behind her. She'd made it. They were safe. This time. She wouldn't think about the next time yet.

Charly looked around at the spick-and-span room, with shelves displaying an assortment of knick-knacks. Most were mementos from trips Mrs. McNally had taken with her husband before he'd died. Sometimes, she'd tell Charly stories about the different little trinkets, the café they'd found, or the little town having a parade for something silly. Charly loved the idea of people going places together and not fighting. In the background, soft, twinkly music was playing on the radio. Mrs. McNally always had the radio playing whenever she came over. Charly loved listening to music. It was way better than the shouting, screaming, and blaring of the television at all hours of the day and night, which were the background sounds of her home.

Mrs. McNally took Fabien from her arms and told Charly to sit at the kitchen table. With Fabien balanced on her hip, Mrs. McNally went to the fridge and retrieved a jug of juice, pouring it into a glass. As she replaced the jug, she grabbed a bottle for Fabien. Charly wasn't sure when Mrs. McNally had started keeping bottles and diapers in her house for their "visits," as she called them. She was relieved she didn't have to gather any supplies before getting them out of the house.

Charly watched as she took out a pot, filled it with water, and set it on the stove. Mrs. McNally then placed the bottle in the pot. Next, she entered the pantry and pulled out a container of home-made cookies. Charly's stomach rumbled at the sight of the chocolate cookies. It had been a while since she'd last eaten anything.

Mrs. McNally smiled at Charly as she placed the plate of cookies in front of her. "Eat up, dear."

She returned to the stove, tested the temperature of the milk, and then sat at the table opposite Charly. Fabien greedily sucked on the bottle as Mrs. McNally gently rocked him.

Charly paused between cookies. "Thank you, Mrs. McNally."

"That's okay, Charly. You know you and Fabien are welcome anytime."

Charly's eyes stung with unshed tears. She wished she and Fabien could stay here forever, but sooner or later, she had to return home; otherwise, Peter would storm over here screaming blue murder and causing damage to the house. Last time, he'd shattered the front window because Charly refused to go back home with him. Maybe this time, he'd fall asleep before looking for them over here, or perhaps he'd just be too lazy to get out of the recliner.

A loud bang made all three of them jump. Fabien began to whimper. The door rattled as someone tried to open it.

"Bitch!" Peter yelled from the other side of the door. "Open up, or I'll bust your door in, you old hag!"

Fabien started crying, and Charly's whole body trembled. It

hadn't taken Peter long to come looking for them. He sounded furious. Charly swallowed hard. She looked up at Mrs. McNally, unsure what to say or do. They couldn't open the door. The beating she would get would be monumental. But it would be worse if they didn't open the door when she finally went home.

She wished she didn't have to go home.

"Stay there, Charly. I'm calling the police." Mrs. McNally got up to get the phone, depositing Fabien in Charly's lap.

The banging continued with each blow against the door, louder and more demanding than the last. Charly held Fabien closer and tried to cover his ears, but it didn't help. He began crying in earnest, big, gulping sobs that shook his whole body. The cookies lodged in the pit of Charly's stomach as her anxiety rose. Her hands trembled uncontrollably.

Mrs. McNally returned to the kitchen, still on the phone with the emergency dispatch operator. She put a hand on Charly's shoulder, and Charly leaned against her.

Finally, she heard the whoop-whoop of the police siren.

"Hey, Peter," a male voice said outside. "What's going on?"

It didn't surprise Charly that the police officer knew her stepfather's name. This wouldn't be the first time they'd been called to the house, or the first time Peter had dealings with the police.

"Stupid bitch won't open the door." The door rattled as Peter kicked it.

"It might help if you asked a bit more politely." The officer's voice was even and calm. Maybe this wouldn't get any worse. Perhaps the police officer would get Peter to go back home, and Charly and Fabien could stay here until he sobered up.

"My damn kids are in there. I want them to come home. It's my right. Make her open the door."

"How about we go to the station and discuss who has what rights?" The officer's voice was getting closer to the door.

"Screw you!" Peter screamed.

She heard a fist hitting flesh, a sound she was familiar with. Then, men were yelling, thumps, and nothing but Peter swearing.

There was a polite knock on the door. "Mrs. McNally? It's okay. You can open the door now."

Mrs. McNally unlocked the door and cracked it open. Charly peered around her. Peter was face down on the lawn, hands cuffed behind his back. "Thank you, officer."

The officer was someone Charly thought she'd seen before. "Are the kids here?"

Mrs. McNally nodded and opened the door wider so he could see in.

"Do you know where the mother is?" the officer asked.

Mrs. McNally looked over to Charly. "She, uh, went shopping."

"How long ago was that?"

Charly bit her lip as she thought. "A few hours ago."

The officer nodded and then looked back over to Mrs. McNally. "Can they stay here for a bit? Or do I need to call someone?"

Charly knew who someone was. Foster care. They'd separate her and Fabien, for sure. She wrapped her arms more tightly around her little brother and held her breath, waiting for Mrs. McNally's answer.

"Of course. We'll be just fine here now." Mrs. McNally smiled over at Charly.

Charly slumped into her chair with relief. They were safe, at least for a few days. Maybe all those wishes amounted to something.

ONE

"**J**ess!" boomed Con from the kitchen. "Can you take the rubbish out?"

Charly glanced at her coworker at the Brothers in Arms Bar and Grill. Jess exhaled, squared her shoulders, and headed towards the kitchen, rubbing absently at her left wrist.

Charly cut her off before she got to the swinging doors. "I'll get it."

Jess had been keeping the sleeve of her shirt pulled down over her wrist all day, but Charly had glimpsed the deep purple bruise. She was pretty sure she knew how Jess had gotten it, too. She'd had the "pleasure" of meeting Jess's boyfriend, Sol. Charly knew his type all too well.

Jess stopped. "You don't mind?" She cringed a little as if she thought Charly would hit her, too.

"Nah. It'll give me a chance to get some fresh air." Charly entered the kitchen and grabbed the trash bag. Well, she tried to. The damn thing weighed a ton. She stumbled on her first attempt to lift the heavy bag.

She stepped back, hands on her hips. "Jesus, Con! What have you got in here? A dead body?" The room was like a sauna—well, maybe more like a steam room—with the moist heat from the dishwasher mingling with the heat from the grill and the deep fryer. It smelled like heaven.

Con didn't even look away from where he was pulling clean pots and pans from the drying racks. "Stop whining, kid." His voice was like gravel—rough, low, and gritty. He looked rough, too, with his tattoo-scribbled body, gray hair standing on end, and a face weathered by wind and sun.

It didn't fool Charly. She was well aware of what violent men—abusive men—were like, and Con wasn't one of them. She'd seen the teddy bear beneath the gruff exterior. She'd also had his beer-battered chips and the gravy he made from his grandmother's secret recipe, which he said he'd take to his grave. The man could cook. That was for sure.

"Why'd you ask Jess? Isn't it Maxine's turn?" Maxine seemed to always wiggle out of unpleasant chores like taking out the garbage, and no one ever seemed to notice.

Con turned towards Charly, one graying eyebrow raised. "You still whining?"

"And I'll keep on whining till I get an answer." Charly tried to sound serious but couldn't keep the smile off her face. Talking to Con always put her in a good mood.

"Because I say so. That's why." The fifty-something continued to bang the pots and pans as he put them away.

"See? Now, how hard was that?" Charly laughed as she half-lifted and half-dragged the heavy bag through the kitchen and into the connecting staffroom. Noticing that the outside light was on, she didn't bother to switch on the staffroom light, as the glow from outside illuminated it enough for her to find her way to the door.

She took three more steps into the room and froze. Someone outside the door was moaning. Loudly. For a second, she thought someone was in pain, and then it became clear that they were moans of pleasure. Someone was having a very good time, from the sounds of it.

She knew she should turn right back around, but curiosity got the best of her. Carefully, Charly twisted the door handle, grimacing as it made a soft clicking sound, and peered through the screen. "Damn," she whispered.

A dark-haired woman, jeans down around her ankles, was bent over the picnic table. Charly couldn't see her face, but the tattoo of a heart with a knife through it on her right hip was visible. The man pounding into her from behind was unmistakably Charly's boss, Dominic Price. There was no mistaking the broad shoulders that tapered down to narrow hips or the long, dirty blond hair braided across the crown of his head and down his back. She couldn't see it now, but Charly knew the sides had a number-two buzz cut with a zigzag design carved on each side. It was a one-of-a-kind mohawk, and it suited him. Well.

As Charly watched, Dom twisted the woman's long, dark hair around one fist and pulled. With the other hand, he gave her ass a hard smack. The woman moaned louder. "Yes, Dom. Yes. Harder."

Charly swallowed hard; her mouth suddenly dry.

Dom obliged, letting go of the woman's hair to grasp her hips, keeping her in place as he thrust harder and faster. The woman rocked back into him, rising onto her toes and arching her back as her body trembled, and she cried out in release.

Charly's mouth might have gone dry, but other places were getting wet as she imagined what it would be like to be that woman. A steady throb started between her legs, nearly matching the pounding of her heart.

Dom let out a low growl, and his body stiffened. Then he stepped back, pulled his jeans onto his hips, zipped up, and refastened his belt.

Charly quietly shut the door but lurked around to eavesdrop, trying to get her breathing back to normal. She was panting as if she'd run a mile.

"Okay, babe. Thanks for that," Dominic said.

"Let's go back to the clubhouse, honey. I can show you what else I can do with my mouth," the woman said, her voice honeyed and low.

"No. Just go out the side gate. I don't want my staff to see you." Dom was all business. He'd gotten what he wanted and what he needed. He was done. It didn't mean anything more to him than that.

"Really? That's all I get?" the woman wailed.

Charly nearly snorted. Why did women always get upset when Dom dismissed them? What on earth did they expect? Why did they think they were different from all the other women who were in and out of Dom's bed? What made them believe they were special? Nobody could tame a man like Dominic. But did that deter women from crawling into bed with him? Or, in this case, bending over the picnic table for him? Absolutely not. It seemed to make them more eager to spread their legs for him.

"I told you I only had time for a quickie. I'm busy," Dom said brusquely.

Typical Dom. Brutally blunt. Damn. He'd be coming back this way any second. Charly's face flushed, realizing he would know she'd been listening if she didn't move. She had to leave, return to the kitchen, and take the enormous trash bag.

With all the strength she could muster—strength she didn't know she had—Charly picked up the trash bag and shuffled back into the kitchen. She'd barely made it back when she heard the wire door slam shut as her boss appeared, looking for all the world like he'd done nothing more than go for an evening stroll.

She turned around to make it look like she was heading into the staffroom with the giant trash bag.

"Fuck, Charls. Give me that bag. It's almost bigger than you." Dominic moved Charly aside and lifted the bag as if it weighed nothing, his biceps flexing beneath his shirt. "Hey, Con! Why'd you tell Charls to take the trash out? The bag weighs nearly as much as her."

"I didn't ask Mighty Mouse over there to do it. I asked Jess." Con appeared in the doorway between the kitchen and the staffroom. "Charly just appeared like magic."

Charly whirled around. What had Con called her? "Mighty Mouse?"

Dom chuckled. "Tiny but mighty. It fits."

Charly reached for the bag. "I am capable of taking the rubbish out, boss."

Dom danced back a step, remarkably light on his feet for such a big man, and then he was out the door with the bag as if it held nothing but feathers. She was talking to the air. There was no point in protesting. Charly shook her head and went into the dining area to help Jess wipe down the tables, grabbing a damp cloth as she went.

Jess had worked at the Brothers in Arms Bar and Grill for two years, taking Charly under her wing when she first started. It was a good thing, too. There were many unwritten rules that Charly could easily have fallen foul of without Jess's guidance.

Little by little, Charly had picked up a few "rules" of the club. Firstly, she wasn't allowed to call them a gang. Jess had explained that this pissed the "brothers" off. They were a club, a family. Secondly, they often referred to each other as "bro" or "brother," although most were not blood-related.

Over time, Charly had met several regular members at the bar and grill and knew them well enough to get the occasional chin nod as they passed. She'd nod or wave back, and this usually earned a half-smile. Words weren't necessary for them.

Another rule was no backtalk. Jess explained that it was a sign of disrespect towards the brothers and could have serious consequences, including being fired. Charly didn't get this one because she often heard Maxine backchat Rocky and Dominic. Although they got pissed off when she argued with them, she was still here. Charly herself had stood her ground on a couple of occasions. Despite a firm verbal warning from Dominic, she still had a job.

"Hey, girl," Jess greeted her. Jess was a few inches taller than Charly, with a mop of strawberry blonde hair and a spray of freckles across her pert nose. She was curvier than Charly, too. Something that the close-fitting top and jeans she wore made readily apparent.

Charly shifted the salt and pepper shakers and napkin holders out of the way on a table to give it a proper wipe-down. "Hey, yourself."

"You okay?" Jess had stopped what she was doing to look at her.

Charly glanced over at her. "Great. Why?"

Jess shrugged and went back to her work. "You look a little flushed, that's all."

"Oh, uh, I was in the kitchen. It's hot as hell in there." It wasn't a lie. It just wasn't the real reason her cheeks were flushed. It wasn't like she was going to tell Jess about watching Dom and whoever that woman was have sex in the back of the restaurant. She certainly wasn't going to tell anyone about her secret fantasy. It was embarrassing enough that she'd eavesdropped on them. Her heart was still racing, remembering the salacious scene in the courtyard.

She sighed and went back to wiping down the table. It wasn't like she had a shot at being with Dom. It was obvious that her boss had a type: tall, beautiful women with long, dark hair. Charly had long, dark hair, but at five feet four, she was too short. Besides, Charly's experiences with relationships and men were practically non-existent. Her only sexual encounter didn't count. It had been forgettable at best, leaving her wondering what the big deal was about and not wanting to find out. She didn't have the know-how that the women who serviced Dom had. She wouldn't know what to do if she ever had a chance.

It's too bad that something about Dominic intrigued her from the moment she first met him at her interview two months ago. Charly had trembled as she sat across from him in his office. She'd struggled to raise her voice above a whisper.

"Do I make you nervous?" Dominic chuckled.

She folded her hands in her lap to prevent fidgeting. "Yes. You're intimidating."

A slow smile spread across his handsome face. "Good."

She stiffened. She'd been around aggressive types before—men who blustered and threatened. Fearing someone isn't the same as respecting them. Dom hadn't seemed like that type. She was more set back by his size and the energy that seemed to roll off him in waves. You never knew, however. Some men could turn on a dime. "I'm not sure I want to work for someone who likes intimidating his employees." Charly felt her face heat up. She'd accused her potential employer of being a bully. What the heck had gotten into her? She needed this job.

The smile stayed on his face, but he leaned forward on his desk, and Charly was all too aware of the muscles in his arms. "You have a mouth on you. I'm not sure I want to hire a loudmouth."

"Then I guess we're even." Shut up, Charly! If she didn't stop now, she'd be back on the unemployment line. Dragging in a deep breath, she tried again. "Forget that, will you? How about we start again?"

"I don't know why I should bother." Dominic reclined in his chair and stretched his arms behind his head, looking satisfied.

Smug bastard. Charly gritted her teeth in annoyance, but she reminded herself what her goals were here. She needed a job. "I'm a hard worker, a quick learner, and reliable. I've had experience in the hospitality industry."

"Yeah, I guess working at McDonald's for two months prepared you for dining service." The sarcasm practically dripped from his words.

"Are you mocking my job at McDonald's?" She sat up a little straighter. An honest day's work is an honest day's work and should be respected. She surveyed his desk to see what she could throw at him besides his laptop. She didn't think a pen could do much damage. It'd probably bounce right off that hard chest of his.

"Not at all. You're the one pushing your experience in the hospitality industry." He looked back down at her application.

"You've had many jobs in the past five years: dog walker, babysitter, and pizza delivery driver. You even had a short stint at the post office. You don't have a history of longevity in one place. I want someone who's going to stick around."

He was right. Charly was used to moving around. Most of her childhood had been spent bouncing around in different foster homes. It had gotten to be a habit. She was always looking for something new and different to motivate her, searching for a place where she could settle down. One day, she'd find that place that felt like home-where she fit in and felt safe. Charly was tired of moving around all the time. She didn't know if it would be this place, but she'd never find out if she didn't convince Dom to hire her.

"All that experience means I can work anywhere. Put me in any restaurant section, and you'll see how well I fit in." Charly grasped at straws. She needed this job, or she would end up homeless.

"I'm still worried about that mouth of yours."

Her lips tingled as his eyes zoomed in on her mouth. She resisted the urge to lick them. "I thought we were working with a clean slate here."

"Can't ignore facts."

"What facts?" Charly's brows furrowed in confusion.

"The fact that you don't have a filter for that headstrong mind of yours." Dominic's eyes gleamed with unrestrained humor. He was making fun of her.

Fine. He could mock her all he liked, as long as he didn't dismiss her. "I thought you might appreciate honesty. That's another one of my strengths."

"Honesty's all good, Charls. However, I need someone who can keep their opinions to themselves when dealing with difficult customers." The smug smile had left his face. He wasn't joking anymore. He meant what he was saying.

Charly couldn't argue with his point, but she felt like object-ing to the nickname he'd bestowed on her. She bit her tongue. Try not to be a loudmouth.

"I can keep my opinions to myself." She crossed her fingers behind her back.

"Are you sure, Charls?" Dominic didn't look convinced.

"I haven't said anything about that nickname, have I?"

Dominic studied her tightly closed lips and grinned. "A tiny step in the right direction, I guess." His eyes sparkled with satisfaction.

She let out the breath she'd been holding. "Does that mean I have the job?"

Dominic threw his head back and burst out laughing at her forthright question. The sound carried to her chest, and some-thing strange settled there. "Yes, Charly. You have the job."

A high-pitched whistle cut through her reverie, and her eyes whirled toward the bar. She spotted Dominic motioning her over. Damn, she'd been caught daydreaming. She wasn't sure how long she'd been wiping down the same spot on the table before her, but it was more than clean.

"Charly! Dom's calling you." Jess nudged her.

"So, he has to whistle at me like a dog?" she mumbled, earning her a bit of a side-eye from Jess.

"My office. Now!" His brusque command got Charly's back up, but she swallowed her irritation and followed him.

"Someone's in trouble," Jess said in a singsong voice as Charly approached Dominic's office.

"You're jealous." Charly turned around and poked her tongue out in jest.

"Too right! I wish it were me who was in trouble with him. I'd love to get a spanking from the boss." Her friend sighed wistfully.

Charly thought about the way Dom had smacked that woman's ass while he'd slid in and out of her and the way the woman had moaned. Her face heated up again, and that little throb between her legs beat a little harder.

She wasn't alone. All the female employees had crushes on Dominic. It wasn't just his looks, although those didn't hurt. There was something about him—something primal and charismatic. It was like all the hairs on Charly's arms stood on end every time the man walked into a room.

Their other boss, Rocky, was also easy on the eyes but not as magnetic. Despite his name, Rocky's laid-back nature was no match for Dominic's hard-as-nails reputation.

Both men belonged to the Iconic Sons Motorcycle Club. When Charly learned that her bosses were bikers, she'd contemplated bolting, not wanting anything to do with criminals. Her need to pay the rent, plus Jess's plea that Dominic and Rocky were good guys, convinced her to stay. Besides, she liked her coworkers—well, most of them. She reluctantly tolerated Maxine. The woman was always on her case about something.

Entering Dom's office, Charly sat in the only chair across the desk from Dom while he finished texting someone. When he put his phone down, he raised an eyebrow.

"What's that look for?" Charly frowned.

"You don't know?" he asked.

Charly took a second to review everything she'd done during her last couple of shifts. She wasn't perfect. Who was? But she couldn't come up with anything that would have Dom summoning her to his office like a naughty schoolchild.

"I've had another complaint about you from Maxine." He cocked his head to one side, watching her and waiting for a response.

Of course. Charly blew out a frustrated breath. "What have I supposedly done now?"

"She says you've been flirting with the customers and pocketing their numbers." His fingers drummed on his desk, and he looked at her through narrowed eyes.

This wasn't good. Dominic had a strict "no fraternizing" policy for staff and customers, and he meant it, too. He'd recently fired two employees—Peggy Stanley and Terrence Brooks—whom Con had walked in on in the pantry. Peggy had been riding Terrence like he was a hog she was taking on a test drive while cans of tomatoes and beans rolled around them on the floor. They'd been out the door, pink slips in hand, before they could even zip up their jeans.

Charly hadn't been the one doing the nasty in the pantry. Nor was she the one who was continuously dropping the pen she was using to take orders and bending over very slowly to pick it off the floor, or the one who batted her eyelids at customers and leaned over tables low enough to give guys a good look at her cleavage.

That would be Maxine herself. Somehow, Dominic never seemed to notice that, though. Charly's sense of injustice ratcheted up a notch.

"Is Maxine talking about herself or me?" she asked.

Dominic's lips twitched at Charly's cynical remark. "Probably herself."

Charly threw her hands in the air. "Then what's the issue? Why call me in front of God and everybody when you know she's making this stuff up?"

He shrugged. "Any complaints I receive, I have to address."

"You know I'm professional at all times. I don't even know why we're discussing this. Maxine is always complaining about me. There's *my* complaint, by the way." Let's see him address that one.

Getting up, Dominic rounded his desk to perch on the edge. "Do you know why Maxine's always complaining about you?"

Charly looked at him and said, "I wish I did." The woman had taken an instant dislike to Charly, and nothing Charly did or said seemed to change that.

Dom snorted. "She's jealous."

"Jealous? Of me?" Charly shook her head in disbelief. "I don't believe that. What for? Being the one Con calls Mighty Mouse? Maxine's just a drama queen."

Dominic smiled. Oh, wow. His face went from handsome to drop-dead gorgeous in that moment. Butterflies fluttered wildly inside Charly's chest and lower. "Of course, you'd see it that way," he said.

Whatever that meant. "Are we done? Or do you need to lecture me more about my improper behavior and slap me on the wrist?"

"I could put you over my knee if you like." The smile turned wolfish, and damn if Charly didn't find him even more attractive.

Despite her best effort at resistance, the thought of Dominic bending her over his muscular thighs and slapping her bottom with those strong hands made Charly's stomach clench. She could imagine the way the cold air in the office would feel on her bare ass. The slight scrape of his rough, calloused hand against her skin. Her nipples hardened, and that added to the fantasy that was building in her mind. Maybe he'd slip his hand inside her shirt. Or pause between strikes against her cheeks to slip a finger between her legs. She bit her lip and then said, "Maybe I need to lecture you about improper behavior at work."

"Maybe you do." His answering grin made her toes curl.

She needed to get out of the office quickly before she threw herself at him. She got up to leave.

"Hang on, Charls." Dominic held up his hand. "Don't forget that we're having a barbecue at the lodge this Sunday."

The lodge was Dominic's holiday home by the lake in the countryside. Once a month, all the employees attended a big gathering with their families. Last time, Charly had skipped the event, thinking it was optional, but she'd been wrong. Dominic had firmly told her that she was expected to be a part of the gathering and not to let him down again—one more of those unwritten rules.

Charly rolled her eyes. "I'll be there. Don't worry."

The sudden steel in his look set off Charly's warning bells. His body became motionless, like a panther, ready to pounce. "Did you roll your eyes at me?"

"No," she lied, trying to keep her voice steady.

He took a step towards her, narrowing the gap between them. He tilted her chin so she could look directly into those steel-gray eyes. "Must've been mistaken then." His voice remained deadpan.

She studied Dominic's face. His relaxed demeanor didn't fool her. There had been a veiled warning in his words. Her heart picked up pace, but it wasn't from fear. The feel of his hand was warm and gentle on her chin. The smell of whisky and leather emanated from him. His heat. Altogether, it nearly made her dizzy.

"I can pick you up if you like." He stepped back and became his charming self again. Charly wondered whether she'd imagined the whole thing.

"That's okay. Jess has already offered to go with me. Thanks anyway." Jess had felt bad that she hadn't given Charly the heads-up about the mandatory barbecue and offered to help her get ready and give her a ride this Sunday.

Dominic gave her a brief nod of acquiescence. "Make sure you turn up, Charls, or I'll come and get you myself."

"Got it, boss." It took everything Charly had to turn her back on him and walk out of the office. As it was, she felt the heat of his gaze traveling up and down her as she walked away.

"Charly," he called right before she reached the door.

She turned, keeping her eyes directly ahead. "Yes, boss?" she asked softly.

"Why did you insist on taking the garbage out if Con asked Jess to do it?" His head was cocked just a little to one side.

She hesitated, but she didn't think the truth could hurt. "Jess's wrist hurts her, and she doesn't want anyone to know. She keeps pulling her sleeve down over it. I figured I'd take the garbage out so she wouldn't have to choose between hurting herself more or telling people something she wanted to keep to herself."

"Did she ask you to do that?" Dom raised his eyebrows and crossed his arms over his chest.

Charly tried not to stare at the way his biceps bulged. "No. It just seemed like the right thing to do."

He nodded his dismissal, and she got out of the office as quickly as she could without running.

She returned to the table she'd been cleaning when summoned and had barely finished wiping it off when Jess was at her side. She had a broom to sweep the floor beneath the tables, even though it was already clean. "Come on, birdie. Tell all. What's the hot goss?"

It wasn't exactly hot, in Charly's opinion. "Maxine's made another complaint against me."

Jess made a face and pulled out a chair to get a better angle for sweeping. "Oh, for goodness sake! What was it this time?"

"I've been flirting with the customers and getting their numbers." As if.

Jess scoffed. "You? You wouldn't know how to flirt, even if you tried."

Ouch. Not exactly a compliment. "Thanks, tons!" Charly frowned at her friend.

Jess waved her comment away. "Oh, you know what I mean. Flirting is something that Max does. Not you."

Ha! Charly wasn't the only one who'd noticed that, then. Talk about the pot and the kettle. "I don't think the boss believed her, either." She paused, reflecting. So why had he called her in there?

Jess stopped for a second to lean on her broom. "Dom's way too intelligent to fall for Maxine's crap," she sighed.

Charly could practically see the stars in Jess's eyes. "Your infatuation is showing," she laughed.

Jess snorted. "Name one female in this place who isn't infatuated with Dom."

"Me," Charly replied with a straight face, knowing she wasn't exactly telling the truth. She prayed that Jess couldn't smell the white lie.

"Besides you. Name one."

Charly gave up. Arguing with Jess was pointless because she knew her friend was right. It was impossible to deny the allure of a self-assured man like Dominic.

$$\star\;\star\;\star\;\star\;\star$$

DOM SMILED AS HE watched Charly go out the door. He'd known Maxine was stirring up trouble, something she was a little too good at, in his opinion. That was a problem for another day. He hadn't been able to resist having an excuse to have Charly alone in his office with him or to have her a little off-guard.

She intrigued him. She was a fascinating combination of sass, spirit, and sweetness. None of the women who worked at the bar and grill or the strip club the MC also owned and operated did much because they thought it was the right thing to do. To them, the right thing was what would get them what they wanted, whether it be more money, more attention, or more power.

Stepping in to do someone else's chore because that person might be hurt? Not in their wheelhouses.

He liked her softness, too. Her rounded bottom and ample chest had his fingers itching to trace those curves. He'd gotten a little peek at what that might be like when he'd lifted her chin. The little gasp that had escaped her had his cock getting hard inside his pants, even though he'd just ridden Kyra hard out in the courtyard.

He'd made many women moan and cry out, but he wasn't sure he'd ever gotten that sharp, surprised intake of breath. Most of the women he used to satisfy his appetites were experienced enough that nothing surprised them. He'd thought that was a good thing. He'd thought he liked having women who knew how to please him and how to be pleased by him.

Maybe he'd have to give that some more thought.

TWO

Jess pulled into the pebbled driveway that led to the front of the lodge, twenty minutes outside of the city. Charly had been relieved when Jess had pulled up to her apartment, and Sol hadn't been in the car. She hadn't been looking forward to spending twenty minutes stuck in a car with him. He made her uneasy, and she was sure he knocked Jess around with some frequency.

Charly stared in awe at the magnificence of the old-style country house. She hadn't expected this at all. The two-story house had a wraparound porch of weathered timber. A stone pathway led up to the veranda steps, where antique church pews welcomed the guests. A corrugated iron roof finished off the magnificent architecture. She'd expected something more rustic. Not this elegance.

On one side of the property, large red oak trees surrounded a lake as far as the eye could see. The opposite side had a huge octagonal gazebo. Behind that, if someone looked closely, the glimmer of still water could be seen.

A line of Harleys stood in front of the house, gleaming in the late summer sunlight.

Charly exited the vehicle and slowly made her way up the path. Jess joined her, and they linked arms. The happy grin on Jess's face mirrored Charly's own.

"I didn't realize how grand it was," Charly commented, her eyes taking in the beautiful scenery around her. Acres of lush trees and shrubs spread beyond the gazebo, making her wonder where the property line ended. Did Dominic own all this land?

"It's pretty spectacular. Let's go around the back. Everyone should be there." Jess tugged on Charly's arm, leading her towards the back of the house.

Charly could hear laughter and the blare of rock music. Her nerves got the better of her, and her steps slowed almost of their own accord. Jess had to practically pull her along.

Charly spotted Dominic immediately. At roughly six and a half feet tall, his imposing figure stood at least a couple of inches taller than the other men. Her radar consistently clocked him whenever he entered a room. The energy that bristled around him thrummed her nerve endings without seeing him. The awareness was instant.

Coincidentally, Dominic turned his head in their direction at that exact moment. His eyes tracked their movements as Charly and Jess approached his group. He stood milling around with people Charly had never seen before. The two men had a similar build to Dominic but were slightly shorter. Broad shoulders tapered to narrow waists, and the muscles on their arms were visible without so much as a flex among them. They, too, were covered in tattoos and wore black leather vests identical to Dominic's, with a large red and black emblem on the back and the words ICONIC SONS MC. They must all be members. Brothers, she mentally corrected herself.

With them were three women wearing decidedly less than the men they accompanied. Jeans so tight they might as well have been painted on, and there was a variety of tank and halter tops under which Charly was sure no one was wearing a bra. All of them were tall and thin. Charly had seen the brunette before. She'd been at the bar several nights before, although she hadn't been the one to serve her. As they approached, the brunette leaned back and laughed, the movement imbued with animal grace. It was like watching a cat stretch—and not a little house cat, either. Something more significant and much more dangerous. The sun glinted off the piercings on her face. Charly felt like a little mouse, small and drab. Not mighty at all. She pasted on a bright smile. She wasn't here to compete for attention or become anybody's best friend. She would make sure Dom knew she was here and then find other folks from the bar to hang with.

"Hey, Dom," Jess called, waving as they approached.

"What's up, Jess?" Dominic gave Jess a chin lift.

Then his eyes met Charly's, and his grin grew wider. "Well, look who's here. Hello, stranger."

Charly couldn't help but laugh at his sarcasm. "I wanted to save you the trip of coming to get me. Who knows where I might have been? You'd have been out all day searching for me."

Dominic snorted. "I'd have found you, Charls."

"How? I don't even have GPS on my phone."

Charly had been on her own since she was 18. There wasn't much help once you aged out of the foster care system. Her salary at various jobs had always been at the bottom, and despite her work ethic, she never really stayed anywhere long enough to move up the ladder significantly. She had enough to rent her little one-room efficiency and feed herself. Fancy phones weren't in her budget.

She did have an old flip phone. Detective Shane Carter had given it to her years ago, so she'd always have a way to contact him if she needed him and for him to check in occasionally.

She'd met Shane on the worst day of her life. She'd never forget his calm, caring presence or everything he'd tried to do for her since. She didn't know what it was like to have a father. Her mother hadn't known who her biological father was, and Charly's stepfather hadn't been any version of a parent. Shane was the closest thing Charly had ever had to having a dad.

"Someone's begging for a hiding," Dominic warned with a steel edge, snapping Charly back to the present.

"Why do you always go immediately to a spanking? There's a support group for people with your problem, boss. BDSM Anonymous." Where did that come from? The words slipped out before she thought about them and immediately regretted them. Almost as much as she regretted having the mental image of Dom smacking her naked ass and her unexpected reaction to it.

The woman with the piercings took a small step away from Charly as if distancing herself from her sass. However, the two men standing beside Dominic openly chuckled at her suggestion. Charly instantly liked them, even though they looked scary. Charly knew that looks could be deceiving. These were hard men—tough men—not abusive ones. They didn't have that vibe.

"It looks like you need help, brother." One of the men raised his beer to Charly and then took a long swig, making the tattoos on his neck jump and dance. He had a square jaw and a twinkle in his eye. He was a nice-looking man, for sure, although Dominic overshadowed him.

Dominic drilled her with silvery eyes—startling eyes that seemed to look right through her carefully crafted, tough outer shell. But she did catch a slight twitching of his lips. Good. He wasn't mad—maybe he had a sense of humor after all, and she still had a job.

"Shut it, Gun." Despite Dominic's stone-cold tone, Gun merely smirked, undaunted, and slid an arm around a blonde with big hair and even bigger boobs.

The other badass had a bald head and a muscle-upon-muscle build. He was a dead ringer for Vin Diesel. "Let me see if I can bring the number up." Badass Number Two pretended to search for the support group's number on his phone.

"Give me that, Vin." Dominic went to snatch the phone from him, but Vin quickly stepped back.

"Oh, my God!" Charly blurted out, laughing out loud. "Your name is Vin?"

"What?" Vin stared at her curiously.

"I was just thinking that you looked like Vin Diesel. You know, the guy in the *Fast and the Furious* movies?"

Vin presented his sexiest grin. The man knew darn well he was hot. "I've been told that before."

"I was thinking the same thing," chimed in Jess.

Dominic pushed Vin away. "Get lost, Vin." His dirty look did not faze the handsome man, who just raised his beer in a toast to Charly and Jess.

"Come on, Charly. Let's go mingle." Jess tugged at her arm, and Charly let herself be led away. She could have sworn she felt Dom's gaze on her the entire time.

✶ ✶ ✶ ✶ ✶

CHARLY WALKED OVER TO the gazebo where Jess and Maxine sat, hoping Maxine wouldn't pick at her too much. She was surprised when Max moved over as she walked up and patted the bench next to her. "Take a load off, Charly."

Charly looked at the bench. *In memory of our son, Alfred James Edward Reed, "He will wipe away every tear from their eyes, and death shall be no more; neither shall there be mourning, nor crying, nor pain anymore, for the former things have passed away." Revelation 21:4.*

The metal plaque affixed to the back was old and blackened, but Charly could read it. She wondered who Alfred Reed was. She looked at the other two benches and read the plaques: Dr. James George Alfred Reed and Elizabeth Anne Reed.

"I could live out here," Maxine said, leaning back on the bench as Charly sat beside her. "Away from all the noise and the hustle and bustle."

Jess made a noise of agreement.

Over by the jetty, kids squealed with delight as they cannonballed into the lake, while their parents applauded their derring-do while keeping a close watch on them. Charly smiled, wishing she'd been at the previous month's gathering. She hadn't known what she was missing. She wouldn't make that mistake again.

Charly couldn't imagine living in a place like this. She glanced around, her gaze snagging on Dominic. It wasn't the first time. She couldn't resist sneaking furtive glances his way like he was some magnet that pulled her attention. He knew it, too. He always looked in her direction when she peeked at him. She couldn't be sure she was the one he was looking at from across the vast lawn. Regardless, each time, her heart got stuck in her throat.

This time, when their eyes met, Dom separated from the group he'd been talking to and walked to the gazebo. Maxine and Jess watched his approach, too.

"Hey, Dom. How much rent would you charge to live here?" Max called out as he got nearer.

Eating up the space with his long strides, Dom said, "Dream on." He leaned against one of the gazebo's railings and took a swig of his beer.

Charly swallowed along with him as she watched his Adam's apple move up and down and the way his long fingers held the beer bottle. How the hell did he make everything look that good? Since when did watching a man drink beer leave her nearly breathless?

"You're lucky I let you come here once a month. Be grateful," Dom said to Maxine, but with a smile.

Charly snickered at his retort, and Dominic straightened up at her sass. Charly held her hands up. "I'm quite happy living where I am."

"You don't like the countryside?" His body turned to face hers directly.

"I love it. It's beautiful here, and I'm grateful you invited me." Her eyes twinkled, knowing he'd catch her pointing out that she'd been ordered rather than just allowed.

"You want a tour of the house?"

That was unexpected. She hadn't seen many people going in and out of the lodge; most were scattered over the lawn. Being alone with Dom inside the house made her mouth suddenly dry. "Um, sure." She looked over at her coworkers. "Did you guys want to come too?"

"They've already had the tour," Dom explained. "Been here quite a few times."

He held his hand to her to help her off the glider.

It wasn't some special favor, then. She'd look silly if she refused now. In truth, she didn't want to. She was curious to see what the inside of the place looked like. She noticed Maxine giving her the evil eye out of the corner of her eye; so much for building up some camaraderie.

"Well then. Lead the way." Charly took his hand and let him help her off the seat. Like him, his hand was warm, hard, and rough. She expected him to drop her hand as she walked down the steps out of the gazebo, but he kept it encompassed in his own. Her heart beat fast inside her chest, and she hoped he wouldn't notice her sweaty palms.

When they reached the porch steps, Charly tried to retrieve her hand, but Dominic held firm. The moment she stepped inside the house, she forgot all about it. The walls soared up to high peaked ceilings, and glittering chandeliers hung in the center of each room. None of them needed to be on at the moment because of the light let in by the large windows.

Charly gasped as they turned the corner into a library with built-in bookcases lining each wall. So many books! She wondered what it would be like to spend afternoons curled up in one of the overstuffed armchairs, reading one after another.

He gently guided her into the spacious room. "Dr. James Reed had this room remodeled for his wife, Elizabeth, in the early 1900's."

"Oh, wow! Is this house that old?" Charly exclaimed, her eyes widening with surprise.

Dominic laughed. "Yes, but it's a bit of a sad tale. Do you want to hear it?"

Grimacing, Charly nodded. At the same time, her heart tripped. Although she did want to hear about the house's history, the thought of it holding unhappy memories made her sad.

Sensing her anxiety, Dominic pulled Charly onto the couch to make her more comfortable.

"Dr. James Reed and his wife had a son, Alfred. In 1915, 20-year-old Alfred enlisted in the army while a war raged. Dr. Reed and Elizabeth were horrified that their only son had signed up without talking to them first, but it was too late. Soon afterwards, Alfred was sent to a basic training camp to prepare for eventually joining the fight."

Charly couldn't take her eyes off Dominic as he magically weaved a story of a family tragedy. She listened, enthralled by his strong, deep voice and tragic words.

"As it happened with many of the young men who fought in the war, Alfred was killed in action. Elizabeth was devastated and went into a deep depression. Dr. Reed tried everything he could to help his wife, but all his medical experience failed. He, too, took the news of Alfred's death hard."

Dominic looked out the large window, and Charly's gaze followed his path. Her eyes landed on the gazebo.

"He built the gazebo for Elizabeth so she could sit out there and remember their son." Dominic's light gray eyes zoomed in on her. "Did you notice the plaques on the benches inside the gazebo?"

Charly nodded, finding them even more poignant now that she had some context.

Dominic continued with the story. "Elizabeth spent hours inside the gazebo, reading a book or just sitting there, thinking."

Charly sensed that more heartache would come and unconsciously reached out to grasp Dominic's wrist. Dominic suddenly stopped his narration and stared at the tiny hand encircling his thick arm. Thinking he was annoyed, Charly quickly tried to remove her hand, but as quick as a flash, Dominic's other hand covered hers, holding their connection.

"Sorry, I thought you were about to say something bad. It was a knee-jerk reaction." Charly felt she needed to explain her actions.

"I don't mind, Charls. Unfortunately, this story doesn't have a happy ending. I can stop now if it upsets you." His hand squeezed hers in sympathy.

"No. I want to hear it. I know what's coming, so ignore me if I seem jumpy."

Dominic glanced at her suspiciously.

"It's okay." Charly waved her free hand, urging him to continue. "I want to know what happens. Go ahead."

His features relaxed. "Where was I? Oh yes, Elizabeth in the gazebo."

Charly tried hard to concentrate as Dominic's thumb casually stroked the back of her hand.

"One day, when Dr. Reed returned home from his travels to the outskirts of the town, making home visits to the poor folk who couldn't get to his practice, he found the gazebo empty. Every night, without fail, Elizabeth would sit under the pavilion, where she found solace from dawn to dusk. It was usually the first place he looked for her, but on this evening, it was empty.

"Surprised to find her missing, he searched the house but couldn't find her. He enlisted the help, and they began to search the house from attic to basement, gradually making their way outside to scour the grounds. It was getting dark, so Dr. Reed reluctantly ended the search until morning."

Dominic abruptly reached across to touch her forehead. His thumb rubbed at the spot where her frown had appeared as if trying to erase it. Charly automatically stopped frowning, goosebumps whooshing down her arms.

"Did they find her? Did they find Elizabeth?" she asked breathlessly.

Dominic nodded. "Unfortunately, they did. Elizabeth was floating face-down in the lake. They couldn't determine if she'd drowned by accident or suicide because Elizabeth couldn't swim."

Oh, the poor thing. Charly hoped she'd found joy in her gazebo despite missing her son. "She probably drowned accidentally. I don't want to think of the alternative. It's too depressing."

Dominic laughed at her reasoning.

"What happened to Dr. Reed afterward?" Charly asked.

"He lived a very solitary life after his wife's and son's deaths. Dr. Reed retired soon after and was reclusive until he died in 1936. Unfortunately, they didn't find his body until months later, as he had shut out most of his friends and family after his son's and Elizabeth's passing."

Charly blinked away the tears. What a bleak and heartbreaking tale. Her gaze swept around the airy library, trying to picture Elizabeth relaxing in the room. Her eyes snagged on a large portrait of a beautiful woman with dark hair and sparkling eyes. The picture must have been painted before her son, Alfred, died. She looked so happy and carefree.

"Is that Elizabeth?" Charly got up and walked towards the massive painting without waiting for his reply. She felt rather than heard Dominic standing closely behind her. The hair on the back of her neck stood up.

"Yes, several years before the war."

Charly read the fine print: 1908, seven years before her son died. Alfred would have been thirteen years old at that time—a young teenager.

"I take it that you like it?" Dom laughed and tucked a lock of hair that had escaped her ponytail behind her ear. Surprised by the intimate gesture, Charly instinctively pulled away, but Dom quickly held her hand again. "If you like this room, wait until you see the formal dining room."

He led her farther into the interior of the house.

✻ ✻ ✻ ✻ ✻

AFTER THE TOUR, THEY emerged onto the back porch. Gun, Vin, Jess, Maxine, and the dark-haired woman were already gathered there. "What did you think, Charly?" Jess inquired.

"It's a beautiful house. And the history is pretty riveting, too." Charly threw Dominic a lopsided grin. She'd been touched by the obvious pride he had in the lodge. "Thanks for showing it to me."

She walked over to where Jess stood and leaned against the railing.

The dark-haired woman slid over to stand next to Dom, running a long-nailed finger along the vein bulging in Dominic's bicep. She leaned in to whisper something to him. Dom shook his head and firmly lifted her hand off his arm. "Not now, Kyra. Find the other girls. I'll talk to you later."

A dark flush crept up Kyra's cheeks. Charly figured that Kyra had little experience being turned down for what was pretty obvious she was offering Dom. She stalked off the porch without another word but with a rather scathing sneer in Charly's direction.

Whatever. Charly had nothing to do with why Dom wasn't interested in Kyra. She could glare all she wanted.

"That woman doesn't quit." Gun lifted his head in the direction of Kyra's disappearing figure.

"She's got her claws in you, brother," Vin added.

"The bitch wants to, but that'll never happen." Dominic's mouth twisted with distaste. "Not in this lifetime."

Dom's disgust surprised Charly. She turned to watch Kyra sashay away. She'd spotted the heart tattoo on the woman's hip, peeking above her low-slung jeans. Charly was sure Kyra had been the woman with Dom in the courtyard the other night, the one he'd had bending over the picnic table and crying out for more.

She was gorgeous. Tall and thin and skilled in ways to please a man. Why wouldn't Dom want her? His disrespect didn't mesh with how he'd treated her as he gave her a tour of the lodge. He'd seemed to enjoy her astonishment and delight at the house's splendor, and he'd been witty and charming as he walked her around the various rooms. The complete opposite of the growling man who had rejected Kyra in front of everyone with no regard for her feelings.

Charly had seen Dom be patient and brusque. Even short-tempered a time or two at the bar. He didn't pussyfoot around trying not to hurt people's feelings, but he didn't go out of his way to hurt people.

"She's not going to stop trying, man. You know that." Vin pointed his beer bottle at Dom.

Charly was confused. She had to ask. "What won't she stop trying?"

All three men glanced at her. "She wants to be Dom's old lady," Gun said.

What did that mean? "Is that code for girlfriend?"

Three pairs of gorgeous eyes lit up. "You could say that," chuckled Vin.

Charly still wasn't sure she saw the problem. "And she's not girlfriend material?"

"You ask too many questions, Charls." Dominic shot her a stern look, his lips flattened with displeasure.

Where did the sweet guy who answered all her questions about the lodge's history go? "You weren't complaining about it before," Charly said, feeling a little testy. What was wrong with being curious?

Dominic's eyes turned hard, yet his voice was quiet—a deadly combination. "What I do is none of your business. Got it?"

The sudden chill in his voice made Charly's blood run cold. She would have retreated a step or two if the railing hadn't already been at her back. She felt her face flush the way Kyra's had. He was right. It was none of her business. He was her boss. This was a work gathering. Whom he did or didn't have a relationship with wasn't something that needed to be discussed. Feeling guilty, she apologized. "Sorry. I won't ask again."

Charly turned to Jess. "I see Con and his wife. Let's go say hello." Without waiting for her friend to follow, she marched on ahead.

*****

"I LIKE HER."

Of course, Vin would. Dominic frowned, wanting to give his friend a hard shove and not understanding why.

Dominic felt as if live wires surrounded him. He was amped up with no way of releasing his pent-up energy. He might have to seek Kyra out later, after all. Maybe he should find Serena. She was less clingy. He probably shouldn't give Kyra too many ideas. She was already on his last nerve.

Or maybe it was Charly who was on his nerves.

Damn her and her inquisitiveness. Damn her girl-next-door beauty. Damn her smart mouth. Damn her for everything! He felt guilty for pissing her off. He wanted to go after her and comfort her.

Whenever she was around, he became hyper-aware of her presence. She set his pulse racing and his gut churning, and he constantly found inane reasons to seek her out, like actually listening to Maxine's complaints about her. Charly was unpredictable. He never knew how she might react to any given situation. In his world, that was a death sentence. But with Charly, it was different. It *motivated* him.

Releasing a heavy sigh, he turned to his brothers. "She's doing my head in."

"I can see that, brother," said Vin. "What are you going to do about it?"

"Fucked if I know. Steer clear, I guess." The no-fraternization rules at the bar were there for a reason. While he knew that he could bend those rules for himself as a boss, he'd never really wanted to before. There was plenty of pussy out there for the taking that he wouldn't have to see at work every day or cut a paycheck for.

"How's that working out for you?" Vin bumped him with his shoulder.

Dominic was tempted to give Vin a whupping just to shut the idiot up. "Bloody difficult." He dragged a hand over his eyes.

"It sucks to be you."

Dominic stomped inside the house before he gave in to the need to punch Vin's lights out.

✳ ✳ ✳ ✳ ✳

"THEN HE DARED TO make me pay for my meal!" Maxine exhaled a dramatic sigh.

Charly tried not to groan. Maxine's stories about her love life were a bit of a circular loop. She kept repeating the same mistakes. She'd choose a guy because of his looks and his attitude, then seem shocked when they were losers who treated her like crap.

Max was a good-looking woman. She could have her pick.

"Ever thought of dating a nice guy, Max? Maybe somebody who isn't so handsome but has a job and opens doors for you and stuff?" Charly suggested, tongue-in-cheek. She already knew the answer.

Maxine sent her an incredulous look. "No way! They're too boring."

"Jess!"

Charly jumped at the sudden bellow of rage. She twisted her head around to see Sol thundering across the lawn, his face red and his fists clenched, making a beeline towards Jess. "You bitch!" Sol screamed at Jess, spittle flying everywhere. "You fucking wait till you get home!"

Jess curled in on herself as if trying to make herself smaller and less of a target.

Charly knew that move. She'd seen her mother do it countless times when Charly's stepfather was looking for a reason to beat the crap out of her.

Charly was out of the gazebo and running to Jess before she thought about it. She'd only made it a few steps before a strong arm encircled her waist, pulling her back and lifting her off her feet.

Oh, hell, no. Sol was nearly on Jess. It didn't take much insight to see that Jess was terrified. Charly had to get there. She needed to help her friend and wouldn't let anyone stop her. She threw an elbow back into her attacker's face, struggling to get free.

"Jesus Christ, Charly! What the fuck?"

Charly gasped as she turned to face Gun, who was rubbing his jaw where she'd hit him with one hand while still keeping a grip on Charly with the other. She'd deal with the consequences of having hit him later.

"Sorry, Gun. But let me go! I've got to get to Jess." She tried to pry his arms from around her waist but with no luck.

"Calm down, Charly. Let Dom and Vin handle it," Gun growled in her ear.

Looking up, Charly saw that the two men were closing in on Sol and Jess. As Sol cocked his fist back, clearly ready to throw a punch that might well have broken Jess's jaw, Dominic grabbed Sol's arm and twisted it up behind his back. In seconds, Sol was doubled over and then forced to the ground. Dom's knee in his back kept him there.

"Get off me, asshole! I'm not here for you. I'm here for that lying bitch." Sol struggled against Dom to no avail.

"That lying bitch, as you call her, is my employee on my property and is under my protection," Dom said, his voice cold and calm. "You will not touch her."

Charly stopped struggling against Gun, waiting to see what would happen next. She'd never seen a scenario like this one. No one had ever stood between her mother and her stepfather. No one had ever really tried to help except Mrs. McNally, and the old lady would certainly never have been able to stop the abuse physically.

"That's right," Gun said in her ear. "Calm your ass down."

Sol was calming down as well. Dom had leaned over and was speaking quietly into his ear. Slowly, Sol stopped struggling against him. Vin stood back but was close enough to assist Dom if the tides turned.

Charly grabbed Gun's wrist. "Let me go to Jess. Please." Either her pleading worked, or Gun deemed it safe enough. He released her, and Charly ran the last few yards to get to her friend's side. Gun stood beside Vin, ready to jump in if his assistance was needed.

Jess's whole body trembled as Charly put her arm around her waist. "I didn't tell him I was coming here," Jess whispered. "I thought I'd be home before him, and he'd never even know."

"Why wouldn't he want you to come here?" Charly asked.

"I don't know. He hates Dom. He says he's too full of himself." Jess turned and buried her face in Charly's neck. "He's been after me to quit at the bar, but some weeks, it's the only money we have coming in."

Charly's jaw tightened. More than likely, Sol wasn't crazy about Dom giving Jess a paycheck that might let her escape from under his thumb. Jess had only been 17 when the then twenty-nine-year-old Sol started pursuing her. There'd never been an equal power balance in the relationship, and Jess getting her own money and powerful friends threatened Sol. He thought dominating Jess made him a big man, but all it made him was a bully.

Now that Sol had stilled, Dom stood and took his knee off his back. In seconds, Sol was back on his feet, lunging at Jess. Instinctively, Charly pushed Jess back behind her, putting herself between her friend and the rampaging man.

She hadn't needed to. Vin and Gun were there in a split second, creating a protective wall while Dom pulled Sol back by the collar of his jacket.

"I'll fucking kill you!" Sol ranted like a maniac, sweat pouring down his face. Dark circles under his eyes stood out against the grayish pallor of his skin. His pupils were so dilated that his eyes looked utterly black. He was high. Charly wasn't sure what he was on, but whatever it was, it wasn't calming him down.

Dom yanked Sol aside and half-dragged him back down the driveway. Over his shoulder, he called, "Charls, take Jess inside while I make sure this asshole leaves."

Charly wasted no time obeying that order. Taking her shaken friend's elbow, they headed back up to the house.

Once they were inside, Charly got Jess a glass of water. "Drink this. It'll help."

Jess took the glass with shaking hands. "Oh, Charly. I can't go home." She started to sob.

"You don't have to," Charly said, instantly deciding. "You're coming home with me. You can stay as long as you need to while you figure out what to do next."

Jess's attempt to smile made Charly sad. Hopefully, she will come to her senses now and realize what a dangerous man Sol was. He would not change. He would only pretend to change to make Jess forgive him and then repeat the same behavior. Charly knew this because her stepdad had been the same.

"Thanks. I'm sure he'll cool down in a day or two. It's just that he loves me so much, you know?" Jess looked up at Charly, mascara streaking down those freckled cheeks. "He doesn't mean to hurt me. It's just that I frustrate him so much sometimes."

Shaking her head, Charly turned away. Charly knew that Sol did not love Jess. He loved *controlling* her. There was a big difference.

$$\ast \ast \ast \ast \ast$$

DOM WATCHED UNTIL SOL had driven off his property. Something would have to be done about that one. Dom knew his type—the type that made themselves feel big by making someone else feel small. He wasn't crazy about adding drugs to the mix, either. It made the aggressive man even more unpredictable. He turned to say what he was thinking to Vin and Gun. That's when he saw the bruise forming on Gun's cheek. "What the fuck happened to you?"

Gun rubbed his jaw. "Charly happened to me. She was charging over to get to Jess. I grabbed her to stop her so you could handle the situation. She threw an elbow right into my face."

"Mighty Mouse to the rescue again." Dom snorted. "Come on, let's figure out the next moves."

He strode across the lawn and entered the lodge. In the kitchen, he found Charly crouched before Jess, dabbing away some makeup that streaked her cheeks. Both women looked up at the sound of them entering, Jess with fear in her eyes and Charly looking like she might leap at whoever was coming in.

Dom cocked his head toward Gun. "You roughing up my brothers, Charls?"

A faint blush stained her cheeks. "I didn't know it was him. He grabbed me from behind."

No apology. Good for her. She owned her actions. "What exactly did you think you would do if he'd let you go?" he asked, honestly curious at what this tiny package of a woman thought she could do to stop a raging bull like Sol.

Charly stood and squared her shoulders. "I was going to protect Jess."

He pressed his lips together so he wouldn't laugh because she was serious. "I appreciate the thought, but I'll protect my people on my land."

"I know that now." Charly's stance relaxed, and so did how she looked at him; something softened in her eyes.

Dom felt something loosen in his chest, and for a moment, the two of them stood and looked at each other as if there was no one else in the room.

Gun cleared his throat, and Dom broke the connection. Turning to Jess, he said, "You can't return to your place, Jess." Dominic kneeled and took the place where Charly had been moments before. "Do you have anywhere else you can go?"

Nodding, Jess said, "Charly said I could stay with her."

Dom blew out a breath. Would that put Charly and Jess in danger? Not that Charls seemed to mind a little danger. He made eye contact with Vin and Gun, who each gave him a nearly imperceptible nod. Okay, then. They'd work together to keep the two women safe from Sol.

He stood, dusting off his hands. "Okay," he agreed. "I'll drive you both home."

"Didn't you get here on your motorcycle?" Charly asked.

Dominic's eyes crinkled with amusement. "I did, but I'll borrow someone's cage."

She blinked a few times. "Is that code for a car?"

The men laughed. Even Jess managed a little smile.

✶ ✶ ✶ ✶ ✶

CHARLY HOISTED HERSELF INTO the back seat of Jess's Jeep Cherokee while Dominic helped Jess into the front passenger seat. Charly sat behind Dominic so that she could easily talk with Jess, but maybe also so she wouldn't be forced to look at him. She wasn't sure what that moment in the kitchen had been, but it had left her feeling as flustered as holding his hand on the way up to the lodge had done earlier.

The way he'd crouched down in front of Jess and the gentle voice he'd used when asking about her plans. It seemed completely different to the hard man who barked orders around the restaurant. So had the way he'd led her through the lodge and answered her questions about the house's history.

She realized, belatedly, that she hadn't given Dominic her address, yet he seemed to know where he was going. He pulled up outside her apartment complex. Then, instead of dropping them off, he turned off the ignition and got out of the vehicle.

Charly pulled her keys from her bag and walked to the door of her place. It was a small complex with only eight units, but it was clean. Before she got to the door, Dominic plucked the keys from her hand and unlocked the door himself. She stared at her empty hand for a second, then glanced at Jess, who gave her a weak smile.

Dom let himself into her flat and ordered Jess and Charly to wait outside while he checked her tiny apartment for any bogeymen.

"All clear," he informed them, handing her keys back.

"Thank you." Charly wasn't crazy about keys being plucked out of her hand or ordered around in her home, but she appreciated what Dom was trying to do. He'd put himself out there to keep them safe.

"Hang on, Charls. I need to speak to you for a second." He indicated for Jess to go inside, then closed the door.

He leaned one shoulder against the wall and looked down at her, his features softening. "Are you going to be okay?"

"Yeah. We'll be fine. I've got some wine in the fridge." Her attempt at humor didn't garner a smile from him. Instead, he reached out and played with a loose strand of hair. Charly tried to contain the shiver that swept through her as his fingers grazed her cheek.

"Thanks for letting her stay with you."

"She's my friend. I wouldn't have it any other way." Charly was finding it hard to breathe with him standing so close. It was like he sucked all the air out of the space.

His gray eyes narrowed as he considered what to say next. "Sol's a dangerous man, Charls. Does he know where you live?"

She looked down at her feet. Did Sol know where she lived? Had she said anything the few times she had been with him and Jess? Could Jess have mentioned her address? "I don't think so. Then again, I didn't think you did, either."

He frowned. "I'll have my brothers keep an eye on your place."

She was about to protest and then thought better of it. She didn't much like the idea of being watched, but she also didn't like the idea of Sol showing up unannounced. "Okay. Thanks."

Dominic bent down and brushed a feather-light kiss on her cheek. "Be good." Then he was striding down the hall and the stairs.

Charly watched him go, her hand touching the spot where he had kissed her.

✶ ✶ ✶ ✶ ✶

WELL, THAT HADN'T TURNED out close to how Jess had hoped. She looked around Charly's crappy little apartment, annoyed that she was here and not because of Sol's rampage. Yes, he scared the ever-living daylight out of her, but she'd been safe with the MC there. Jess knew Dominic would protect her. Attacking one of his employees on his property wasn't something he'd turn his back on.

What she wanted was to find a way into the MC permanently. Working for Dom wasn't giving her the recognition or respect she deserved. Jess wanted to be part of the inner circle, not just another employee at the bar and grill. She'd worked hard to position herself to get Dom's attention. Instead, he had a hard on for Charly. What the actual hell was up with that? Little Miss Goody Two Shoes was bland and nothing like the usual women who hung around the men of the Iconic Sons MC. But Jess was. She had the looks and the finesse to charm the rugged bikers, not Charly.

Besides, Charly wasn't interested in any of the brothers that way. On the other hand, Jess wanted to be Dom's old lady. He was precisely the type of man she wanted. Someone good-looking, tough, and highly respected in the club. Then she could kick Sol to the curb, knowing the club would protect her.

Otherwise, he would probably kill her.

She sighed. She could make this work. Keep your friends close and your enemies closer, right? Well, she needed to do something about Charly. It didn't sit well with her that Dom couldn't keep his eyes off her. Anyone who had eyes could see he was somehow bewitched by the stupid bitch. Jess intended to put a stop to that as soon as she could.

She'd stay here with Charly for a bit, just until she could worm her way into the clubhouse. Until then, she'd pretend to be Charly's friend for a bit longer and gather whatever information she could to get rid of her for good.

THREE

Charly bopped to OneRepublic's "Counting Stars" on her iPod while she refilled the condiment bowls in each booth. A firm hand landed on her hip as she stretched to put a ketchup bottle back in place. Purely on reflex, she whirled around, fist cocked.

Dominic grabbed her hand before she could swing. "Whoa, there!"

"Jesus! You nearly gave me a heart attack." She pulled her hand away from him and pressed it to her chest. "Don't sneak up on me like that!"

Dominic pulled an earbud out of her ear and chuckled. "Warning received. You didn't hear me when I called you. I had to get your attention somehow."

She hadn't realized she'd had the music turned up that loud. She turned it off, plucked the other earbud out, and breathed deeply to calm herself down. "What are you doing here anyway? You don't come in on Mondays." Dominic worked Thursday to Saturday, and Rocky did the other days.

"Came to see how Jess is holding up." He sat in the booth so she didn't have to crane her neck to look up at him, and he gestured for her to sit, too.

Ah. There was that protective streak Charly hadn't expected in him after seeing how he treated some of the other women who came through the bar. "She's okay. She's still a little shaken up, but she'll stay with me for the next few weeks until she decides if she wants to move back in with her mom. She'd rather not," Charly added. "She's worried about her stuff, though." She slid into the booth across from him. Jess had been fretting about her clothes and other belongings. She didn't want Sol to destroy it all, but Charly didn't think it was safe for her to try to collect her things herself.

Dom knocked his fist against the tabletop. "Tell her we'll sort that out for her."

"Why don't you speak to her yourself? She's over there." Charly pointed across the room to where Jess was talking to Maxine. She was surprised he hadn't spoken to her first.

Jess looked over as if she'd heard her name being mentioned. Her gaze flicked from Charly to Dom and back again before she turned back to Maxine.

"Don't need to. Besides, I also came to see how you were." He leaned a little closer to her over the table.

Charly's eyes widened in surprise. "Me? Why? I'm not the one with an abusive boyfriend." She leaned in, too, so she could keep her voice low.

"Sol is going to see you as something that's getting between him and Jess. It's a good thing Jess is staying with you, but it puts you in danger, too. I have a bad feeling that he won't hesitate to hurt you if he can."

Their faces were so close now that Charly could feel the heat of Dom's nearness. "I don't particularly like him either. But I'm not afraid of him."

Charly sat stock-still as Dominic reached out to feather his fingers down the side of her face. She felt the imprint of his touch on her cheek. Part of her wanted to shove him away. Another part of her wanted to lean into his hand. "You should be afraid of him, Charls. You need to be cautious. I don't want you to approach him. You have the annoying habit of inserting yourself into fights you can't win. You react. You don't think about the dangers when running headlong into a precarious situation."

"It's not me you should be worried about. It's Jess," Charly muttered. She knew too many warning signs to get involved with someone like Sol.

"You're wrong. You're both at risk. I worry more about you because you're so busy trying to protect everyone else that you forget to protect yourself." Dom leaned back in the booth, his fingers tapping out a rhythm on the table.

"I know how to protect myself." Charly lifted her chin.

He chuckled and shook his head. "I know you do. What I'm saying is that you don't need to. I've got your back."

Those four simple words took Charly's breath away, and she blinked away a quick surge of tears. How long had it been since someone had said that to her? How rare was it for someone to say that and mean it? She remembered that terrible day when her world had come apart and another man, strong and kind, had said that to her. "I've got your back, too."

This time, Dominic didn't laugh. Never taking his eyes off her face, he stood. Then his hand was beneath her chin, lifting her face. She stared in fascination as his pupils dilated, almost eclipsing the light gray.

Ever so slowly, Dominic lowered his head and lightly grazed her lips with his. She held her breath and didn't budge an inch when he whispered in her ear, "Thank you, Charls."

* * * * *

JAX WALKED INTO THE visiting room and immediately spotted his cousin. He was hard to miss. Dom's height, hair, and clothes made him stand out in the crowd, but that wasn't it. There was a bond between them—it had always been since they were kids. Something invisible and indefinable connected them.

Sure enough, Dom's head lifted upon hearing his approach. He stood but stayed back. The guards weren't playing about the no-touching rule, including manly hugs and handshakes.

Jax slid into the chair across the table from Dom, and Dom sat back down. "Good to see you, brother."

Dom smiled. "It's good to see you, too. I'm glad we'll see more of you soon."

Jax was scheduled to be released in five days, and man, he couldn't wait. "I'm coming out locked and loaded."

"I figured. Got a place at the clubhouse for you all ready to go."

The words were reassuring, but two little lines had appeared between Dom's brows. Something was wrong. "So, what's up?" Jax asked. "You look worried."

Dom sighed and ran a hand over his face. "I'm not worried. Maybe confused."

"About what?" Dom was not often confused. He knew what he wanted when he wanted it and how he wanted it, and he didn't hesitate to pursue it. He was smart and tough. Jax couldn't think of a scenario in which his brother would be confused.

Dom leaned back in his chair. "We've got this new hire at the bar."

"Uh-huh." Jax wasn't sure where this was going. The restaurant didn't have a huge turnover, but people generally didn't stay in service positions for too long.

"She's... different." Dom squinted his eyes as if he were looking off into the distance.

A woman had Dom tied up in knots. That was something new. "How?"

Dom shook his head. "You'll meet her when you get out and maybe shake some sense into me. She's an employee, and you know how I feel about fraternization."

Jax did. "That's the good thing about being the boss. You can decide which rules apply to you and which don't. What else is stopping you?"

"She's a bundle of contradictions. She's a tiny little thing."

That surprised Jax. Dom generally went for the long, leggy type.

"She's always jumping into the fray, ready to protect people even when there's no way she could win the fight she's picking. Jess's old man stormed into the gathering at the lodge last Sunday, looking to cause trouble. She ran over as if she was going to be able to stop somebody half a foot taller and probably a hundred pounds heavier than her. Gun grabbed her to try to stop her, and she nearly gave him a black eye."

Jax snorted. "Seriously? How did Gun take that?"

Dom leaned forward. "Surprisingly well. He seemed to think it was funny. She has that effect on people."

"She's affecting you, brother. What's her name?"

"Well, Con started calling her Mighty Mouse, but her name is Charly."

Charly, huh? Jax looked forward to meeting the woman who had captivated his cousin.

✶ ✶ ✶ ✶ ✶

CHARLY AND JESS ARRIVED at the bar around eleven on Thursday to start their shift. Charly had to admit that getting a ride in Jess's car was more convenient than taking the bus. It was a luxury she wasn't used to, and she did her best to remind herself that it was also a luxury that would soon go away. True to his word, Dominic and a couple of the brothers collected Jess's clothes and personal care items from the flat she shared with Sol. Sol hadn't taken it too well, and the broken nose, swollen eye, and missing tooth he ended up with when he tried to stop them probably hadn't improved his disposition.

Still, Jess probably wouldn't stay with her much longer. Her flat was small, intended really for one person. Jess would find her own place soon, and her car would accompany her.

Charly hadn't seen Dom again since he checked in on Monday. He'd been in her thoughts—maybe a little too much. She couldn't stop thinking about how he'd touched her cheek and that sweet, soft peck he'd planted on her lips. She couldn't quite explain her reaction to it.

Charly wondered if it had the same impact on Dominic. Was he thinking about that almost-kiss, too? Replaying it in his mind? Savoring the memory of it? It was highly unlikely. Why would he? There'd probably been a parade of women in the past few days, each taller, sexier, and more experienced than Charly. The thought left a bad taste in her mouth.

It didn't matter. There was a no-fraternization rule, and that was that. Whatever feelings Dom had stirred up in her didn't matter. She needed to stay focused on her work and be the best server she could be to keep this job and maybe finally get a bit ahead. She walked into the kitchen behind Jess, found an apron to wrap around her waist, and got to work, doing her best to avoid Dom. He didn't make it easy, however. Every time she looked up, he was watching her from a distance.

During the busy lunchtime rush, Charly had just finished taking an order and turned around to find a tall man in a business suit. "Excuse me. Would you tell me where to find Dominic Price?" he asked.

Charly bit her lip. She knew exactly where Dom was. It was like she always knew. Even if she wasn't aware of tracking him, they connected. That didn't mean she wanted to go and seek him out. Scanning the room, she spotted Maxine behind the bar.

"Hey, Max, this gentleman wants to talk to the boss. Do you mind letting him know?" Charly got her answer when Maxine's eyes lit up.

She'd known they would. Maxine wouldn't turn down any excuse to be alone with Dom, even for a second or two.

A few minutes later, Dominic came through the doorway behind the bar. Charly had kept her eyes out for him. Knowing where he was would help her keep some distance between them. Although he was striding towards the businessman, his gaze swept the room, searching for something or someone. Quickly averting her gaze, Charly was grateful for the ringing bell, signaling another meal was ready.

Watching his movements, she exhaled deeply when both men disappeared beyond the doorway. Charly knew she would have to overcome her sudden shyness to continue a comfortable working relationship with Dominic. But they needed boundaries. If she needed to speak up, she would. She decided that the next time he touched her in a way she thought was inappropriate, she would tackle the issue. But until then, she needed to put her big-girl boots on and stick to their easy-working relationship.

"Yo! Charly!" Jerked back to the present by Con's booming voice, Charly stepped up to the serving hatch to collect the waiting meals.

Charly stacked the empty plates and took them into the kitchen. As she exited the kitchen, she accidentally bumped into Dominic, who grabbed her upper arms to steady her.

"Whoa!" she laughed as they collided.

Charly tried to pass him, but he stopped her. "Hold on a minute, Charls. I'll speak with Con briefly, and then I need to talk to you."

She waited by the doorway. When Dominic returned, he gestured for Charly to follow him. "My office."

Heart pounding, she trailed after him, ready to play it cool. "What's up?" Charly sat on the chair, and Dominic perched on the edge of his desk. She smoothed a hand over her skirt, ironing the imaginary wrinkles, and waited for him to speak.

"Listen, Gun spied Sol driving past your apartment several times last night. I think you and Jess will be safer at the clubhouse."

"Did Sol come into the building?" Charly's heart pounded at the thought of Sol lurking near her apartment.

"No. But he's stalking you. He knows where you live and must have figured out Jess is staying with you. You're not safe there anymore."

"What's at the clubhouse?" The idea of going there made Charly nervous. She liked her little apartment. It wasn't much, but it was hers, and she'd fixed it up as much as she could on her limited budget.

A soft look changed Dominic's serious expression. "I promise you'll be safe there."

Charly chewed on her bottom lip as she contemplated his offer. Deep down, she agreed it would be safer for the pair to stay at the clubhouse for a while. Without adrenaline surging through her, she knew how much bigger and stronger Sol was. And how much meaner. However, she needed to talk to Jess first. She didn't want to decide without knowing Jess's thoughts. "All right. Let me discuss it with Jess tonight, and I'll let you know as soon as possible."

Dominic nodded. "Good. I want to hear from you sooner rather than later."

There was at least one little problem with that. "How do I get in touch with you?"

Dominic stretched his arm out. "Give me your phone, and I'll put in my number."

Digging into her back pocket, Charly passed him her ancient phone.

Dom turned it over in his hands. It looked tiny when he held it. "What the heck is this contraption, Charls?"

"Hey. That's my phone you're making fun of." She knew it wasn't much, but it had been a lifeline for her more than once. Plus, it was her connection to Shane Carter and, from there, her past. He and his wife, Tessa, were the only ones she was in touch with who knew what had happened to her brother and mother—the only people she didn't have to explain it to but knew how it had fractured Charly's life into a million pieces.

"This is a *phone*?" Dom asked.

"Stop complaining. It does what it's supposed to do." She couldn't help but laugh at his expression.

"And what exactly is that?" He arched a brow skeptically.

"Listen, if you prefer to write down your number, that's fine with me." She called his bluff and was gratified to see him punch in his number. Charly heard his phone buzz and knew he had her number, too.

Possibly in more ways than one.

* * * * *

BY THE END OF her shift, Charly was so tired that she collapsed in a corner of the kitchen. Jess reached out to help her up. "Come on, girl. Let's go home."

She kept her head down as they walked through the restaurant, only looking up when Jess stopped by the front desk.

"Come on, Dom. One drink. Please?" purred Maxine, flashing a sultry smile. She leaned over the desk, giving Dom a big eyeful of her cleavage.

Dom didn't so much as glance at Maxine's chest. "Forget it. You and I are not happening, so get that out of your head. No fraternization, remember?"

His gaze swiveled to Charly. He opened his mouth like he might say something but then shut it and remained silent.

Maxine had not missed the way he had looked at her. "What if Jess and Charly came? Would that appease your moral conscience?" She said the last two words with enough sarcasm to curdle milk.

Shocked at Maxine's blatant disrespect, Charly gaped at her coworker. Undoubtedly, the brazen woman was about to lose her job.

Instead, Dominic reconsidered. "That I'll allow." He turned to Charly and Jess. "How about it? Drinks at Denver's?"

"Sorry, Dom. We're exhausted. Charly's about to fall asleep standing up." Jess poked her playfully, and Charly nodded in agreement, relieved she didn't have to talk her way out of this awkward situation.

"Fair enough. You ladies all right to get home safely?"

"Yeah. I've got my car." With that, Jess nudged Charly out the door.

* * * * *

WATCHING THE LIGHTS OF Jess's car disappear around the corner, Dominic called Vin.

"Y-ellow?" Vin answered on the third ring.

Absently smiling at the familiar greeting, Dominic got straight to the point: "Is there any sign of Sol yet?"

"Nope. Pretty quiet tonight."

"Be extra vigilant. If that bastard lays one finger on—" Dominic clenched his fist at the thought of Sol even touching one strand of hair on Charly's head or hurting Jess.

"I get it, Dom," interrupted Vin. "She's important."

He didn't bother to refute his brother's comment. "She'll talk to Jess tonight. Hopefully, we'll have them safe at the clubhouse soon." Dominic closed his eyes and released a frustrated breath. He wanted them at the clubhouse yesterday.

"What then? Confine them to the dungeon under lock and key?"

Sometimes, Vin's humor irritated Dominic, although locking them away wasn't a bad idea. He kept that thought to himself. He didn't need any more ribbing about BDSM.

Still, Dominic was impatient to have Charly in his territory, finally under his control and within arm's reach whenever he needed to claim her. He hungered for her touch, witty comebacks, candidness, and genuine, gut-clenching laughter. He craved her feistiness and fearlessness, although the latter gave him a coronary.

He had no clue where these feelings had materialized. He only knew that the moment Charly had stepped into his world, it had tilted on its axis. Occasionally, Dominic resented having these emotions and blamed Charly for his sleepless nights and his disinterest in seeking relief from a sweet butt. Kyra had made it clear that she was ready and willing to satisfy his needs, but the thought didn't appeal to him. It even sickened him a little.

Kyra wasn't genuine, thoughtful, or willing to go out of her way to help someone else, much less charge across a lawn to attack a charging bull of a man.

No. He wanted Charly, and only Charly.

It was an unfamiliar and uncomfortable sensation, especially since he didn't want to scare her off. He recognized her lack of sexual experience. Charly was nothing like the sweet butts and club whores. Her rebuffs and tendency to shut down whenever he got too close made him want to pound his chest and, at the same time, take her in his arms and comfort her. All that sass and bravado was covering up some deep vulnerabilities.

Dominic knew she was attracted to him, too. He'd noticed her watching him. She blushed when he caught her staring and quickly averted her gaze. It gave him great satisfaction to know that their chemistry was mutual. Playing this waiting game had to come to an end soon. Dominic couldn't recall when he'd wanted just *one* woman this badly.

Tomorrow, when Charly and Jess were safely settled under his roof, he would begin pursuing her more aggressively inside his sanctuary. It was time to end this torture. He'd make it worth her while. He knew how to please a woman and always had them coming back for more. He'd teach her a few things, and once he got her out of his system, his life could resume as usual. He'd be upfront with her. Make sure she knew his terms.

Then, the fun and games could begin.

✶ ✶ ✶ ✶ ✶

SEATED AT A TABLE in the back corner of the karaoke bar, Charly looked over at Jess, who was gently swaying to Mac's refreshingly hypnotic rendition of John Denver's "Country Roads." The karaoke bar had been a good idea. It was better than staying home and worrying about when or if Sol would show up. It had been fun to get dressed up together. Charly had on jeans, her imitation cowboy boots, and a peasant top that gave a hint of her cleavage but not too much. Jess was a bit sparklier with a sequined tank top and stilettos with her tight jeans.

It was Charly's regular night at the bar. One of the traditions she treasured. She'd made some friends, and the bartenders knew her now.

Charly had yet to discuss staying at the clubhouse with Jess. She was reluctant to ruin her friend's relaxed mood by scaring her with the news of Sol stalking them. She knew she'd have to say something sooner or later, but she decided it would be later when they got home. For now, they'll enjoy the evening and the music.

On Charly's left sat Jim, another regular, tapping his fingers to the beat of Mac's song. Charly had found this gold nugget almost a year ago. Singing was a pastime that gave her absolute joy and confidence. It soothed the constant fears that she tried desperately to hide. Music was the one thing that calmed her.

"Thank you, Mac. And now we have the incredibly talented Charly with 'Diamonds' by Rihanna," announced the deejay.

Charly made her way to the deejay booth amidst the hollering and hooting from the crowd. It was Saturday night, and it was a full house. She passed Mac, who whispered, "You go, girl."

Taking center stage, Charly blocked out the faces. The cheering died down, and a hush came over the crowd. Focusing on the screen, she began to sing as the words slowly scrolled upward.

A deafening applause brought Charly back to earth when the song was over. Passing the microphone back to the deejay, she made her way back to the table where Jim, Mac, and Jess waited.

Jess was gawking at her with an open mouth while Mac and Jim congratulated Charly. "Beautiful, Charly."

Both men had been the reason she'd come back each week. Without their encouragement and friendship, she wasn't sure she would have had the courage to sing in front of a room full of strangers.

"Oh my God, Charly!" Jess gushed. "I didn't know you had such a fantastic voice. That was amazing!" The compliment made Charly blush.

"Are you going to sing, Jess?"

"Me? No way! Your voice puts mine to shame. I'd be embarrassed to sing after that!"

"We could do a duet."

"I'll think about it."

Charly got up to get the song list and placed it before Jess. "Pick a song. And I'll buy a round for everyone while you do that." Charly glanced over at the men. "Same?"

At their nods, she proceeded to the bar to her favorite bartender, Josh. It took her two visits to the bar to collect everyone's drinks. When she sat down again, she turned to Jess. "Have you chosen a song yet?"

* * * * *

BOTH WOMEN WERE SLIGHTLY tipsy when leaving the karaoke bar around midnight. Charly called for a taxi as they shivered in the cold night air. Twenty minutes later, they arrived home. Jess got out first while Charly paid the fare. Thanking the driver, she collected their belongings from the back seat.

A sudden, piercing scream broke the stillness. Charly jumped out of the taxi. Sol was there, and he had Jess on the ground, dragging her by the hair to the side of the building where it was dark. Without thinking, Charly raced towards his large silhouette.

"Let go! Let go of Jess!" Charly screamed, closing the distance between them.

She jumped onto his back and clung to his neck, trying to choke him. With all her might, she reared back, attempting to pull him off Jess but doing little to dislodge him. He brushed her off as if she were no more consequential than a fly. Falling onto the grass, Charly knew Sol would kill Jess if she didn't act quickly.

Blindly aiming for a weak spot, Charly kicked out at his knee with all her strength, hoping her imitation cowboy boots would deliver some damage. Sol's knee buckled, and he lost his balance. Trying to stay upright, he released his hands from around Jess's throat. Jess scrambled away as fast as she could. Roaring with rage, Sol turned his anger on Charly. He pounced on her, inflicting a painful punch to the side of her face. Momentarily stunned, she saw stars.

Suddenly, his heavy weight was lifted off her. Still semi-conscious from the powerful blow, Charly's hand touched her cheek. She could already feel the burning sensation as her cheek swelled up.

She sat up to find Sol lying on the ground, being pummeled by Gun. Where the hell did he come from? Had he been watching the apartment? Charly watched in awe as he delivered a series of devastating blows, rendering Sol unconscious.

In the distance, sirens got louder until police cars were everywhere. Red and blue lights lit up the darkened street. Four police cars were parked in the front, blocking the roadway. A couple of police officers pulled Gun off Sol and led him away in handcuffs. When Charly thought they would arrest him, she stood uneasily on her feet, but two officers held her back.

"Don't arrest him. He was helping us!" Charly tried to pull away, slipping through their grasping hands to rescue Gun. She couldn't bear the thought of him being punished for saving their lives.

"Stop resisting!" an officer shouted, reclaiming a firm grip on her upper arms.

"He didn't do anything wrong." She pointed at the unconscious Sol. "That's the man you should arrest. He tried to kill my friend." She continued to struggle.

"Charly! Stop!" Gun's command halted her resistance. "I'm okay. Stop resisting."

The police officers detained her even though she'd stopped resisting them. She swallowed nervously as they snapped the handcuffs on her.

Charly heard the cacophonous racket of a loud motorcycle. A female officer was cuffing her, but the commotion forced her to spin around. She saw Dominic running past a group of officers. They managed to restrain him, although it took four of them to do it.

He was shouting Charly's name repeatedly. "I'm all right, Dom!" she shouted back. The officers had him handcuffed and were walking him over to a third car.

Dominic never took his eyes off her. "Take the cuffs off her!" When nobody uncuffed her, he growled louder, "Take those bloody cuffs off her!" He then began to fight again, trying to reach her. Someone grunted as Dominic headbutted them in the nose.

"Please uncuff me," Charly begged the female officer. "I need to calm him down."

The officer looked to her partner, who nodded. Charly rubbed her wrists and ran over to Dominic.

"Stand back!" An officer held an arm out to prevent her from getting any closer.

Charly ignored the officer's warning. She stepped closer, speaking softly to Dominic. "I'm uncuffed, Dom. Stop fighting them."

She got within inches of her fired up boss and placed her hands on his chest.

"Come here." Without hesitation, Charly pressed closer. She felt his rapid heartbeat and warm body. Dominic lowered his head until it touched hers. She felt the prickly whiskers of his beard scrape her skin.

"Fuck, Charls," he whispered. "I told you to stay out of it. He's dangerous."

Charly knew Dominic would remain calm only if she appeased him. "I'm sorry."

"Look at me." She lifted her eyes, and Dominic growled when he saw her cheek. "Did *he* do that to you?"

"It's nothing." She covered her swollen cheek.

"Don't piss me off. Did he do that?" Charly could tell Dominic was holding on by a thread from the trembling of his body.

At her nod, he growled. "He's going to pay for putting his hands on you." They spoke in low murmurs so that no one could overhear them. "You know I'm mad at you?" When Charly refused to talk, he gave her a shoulder nudge. "Answer."

Expelling a heavy sigh, she responded. "I know. I've said I'm sorry."

"Sorry doesn't cut it. Not when your life's at stake. You did the wrong thing, but we'll discuss this later. Make sure you get checked out by the paramedics."

The ambulance arrived, and Sol was wheeled into the vehicle. Another paramedic was attending to Jess while she sat inside a second ambulance. Gun walked over to them. The police had finally understood that he'd been the one to save Charly and Jess from Sol.

"Gun, take Charly and Jess to the clubhouse after Charly's been seen by the paramedics. Keep them there till I return," Dom said.

Charly was about to argue, but Dominic speared her with a warning glare. "Don't."

Then Dominic was shuffled into the back of a police car.

✳ ✳ ✳ ✳ ✳

DOMINIC WAS NO STRANGER to anger. It didn't take much to piss him off, and he was well aware of how to channel it into action.

Nothing had prepared him for the rage he'd felt when he'd arrived at Charly's apartment to find her in handcuffs. He knew better than to fight with cops, especially when a dozen of them were milling around. He hadn't been able to stop himself. He'd had a burning need to get to Charly, to make sure she was okay, and to get those fucking cuffs off her wrists.

What had she been thinking? Had she thought she could somehow subdue Sol? She was reckless. Sometimes, being fearless is not a good thing.

He leaned back against the rough concrete wall of the cell, which would most likely be his home for the next few days. Leave it to Sol to get him arrested on a long weekend.

It might be a good thing in the end. It would give him some time to cool down, to get that hot flame of fury banked down enough that he'd be able to look at Charly without wanting to strangle the man who had bruised her cheek.

✳ ✳ ✳ ✳ ✳

THE COPS HAD KEPT Jess, Charly, and Gun at the station for hours, questioning each separately. By the time they were released, Charly could barely keep her eyes open despite the pain in her cheek.

Gun bundled them into the car and drove in a direction that was not Charly's apartment.

"Where are we going?"

"Clubhouse."

She pulled herself upright. "Why? Sol's not a threat to us anymore."

"Dom's request. I plan to comply with it. I suggest you do, too." He threw some side eyes in her direction.

She was too tired to fight. "Could we at least stop by the apartment to get some clothes and stuff?"

Gun had acquiesced to that.

Finally, they pulled up to the clubhouse, and Charly clambered wearily out of the car. Gun got out of the driver's seat and stretched. He was nearly as exhausted as she was.

"Thanks, Gun," Charly said. She owed him her life. Who knows what Sol would have done if Gun hadn't gotten him off her?

"What for, darlin'?" He looked down at her.

"For saving me from a madman?"

He grinned. "It's what I do."

Charly had to chuckle. "What? Rescue damsels in distress from madmen?"

"Yep."

Charly grinned back at him.

Vin and another biker, Achilles—whom Charly learned was the president of the club—bundled her and Jess into the clubhouse. They passed through an open room with a bar, and then both women were directed down a hall into a bedroom. They would be sharing the room for the next few nights.

Even though the men hurried them through the maze of rooms and hallways, Charly still heard the unmistakable sounds of couples having sex. Muffled moans and grunts echoed through the place, and the whole thing reeked of sex. Was this the place that Dom felt was safer than her apartment?

Wide awake now that they'd reached their final destination, Charly took a moment to look around. The double bed occupied most of the room, with a chest of drawers, a television, and a two-seater sofa filling the rest. A door opened into a tiny ensuite that contained a shower recess, a basin, and a toilet—all the necessities.

Were they planning on keeping her and Jess locked up for the entire weekend? She supposed it was only fair. Dom was locked up because of her, after all.

* * * * *

JESS SILENTLY SQUEALED WITH joy. She was finally at the clubhouse. Phase One accomplished. Now for Phase Two: win over Dominic.

Jealousy, like liquid lava, spread throughout her body. Dominic had been so worried about Charly that he'd scarcely noticed Jess. The only reason he'd lost it was because of *her*! The bitch lying next to her in bed.

Jess couldn't understand why Dom was fussing over Charly. Sol had strangled her, not Charly. Didn't that deserve some concern? She'd almost been killed by her abusive boyfriend, but did Dom come over and offer *her* comfort? No!

Gun had helped her to the ambulance and stayed with her for a bit after the cops released him. Although Gun had tried to reassure her, Jess hardly paid attention to what he said because she'd been too distracted by what was happening between Dom and Charly.

Jess's mind exploded, recalling the way Dom had rushed towards Charly while she'd sat in the ambulance, shaking and frightened.

He'd fought with the cops just to get to *her*. It was time to up the ante and lure him away from Charly.

Jess would find her weak spot and then use it to turn Dom against her.

* * * * *

CHARLY WOKE WITH A start. Something had woken her. It was pitch black inside the room, except for the beam of light at the bottom of the door. It sounded like a chorus of laughter that had woken her, and it struck Charly that the sound was right outside the bedroom door.

Dressed in gray tracksuit pants and an oversized T-shirt, Charly got out of bed, trying not to disturb Jess. She cautiously opened the door, enough to see if anyone was there, but only saw an empty hallway. Stepping outside, Charly tiptoed down the corridor to where the noise came from. Sneaking a peek into the room, she caught sight of a group of men giving bear hugs to the male in the center of the circle. When the circle parted, she gasped at the man himself. He was gorgeous.

He wore jeans, a white T-shirt, and a black beanie to cover his head. Like most men around there, he was tall, athletic, and covered in tattoos. His face was beautiful—alarmingly so. Several— primarily naked—women stood around; their eyes locked on the handsome man.

One of the men brought forward a sexy blonde wearing a bikini. She had an angel tattoo stretching across the expanse of her upper back. "Jax, this is Angel."

Sure, her name was Angel. Charly rolled her eyes. It was probably something else entirely—Brenda or Susie.

"She's new at the strip club," the man explained to Jax.

Another biker cackled. "Yeah, and she's been *dying* to meet you." A round of chuckles followed.

Jax sized up the female from head to toe, his gaze lingering on her double-D boobs. "Yeah?" he cooed, his bright blue eyes swirling with desire.

Stroking his muscular arms and brushing her massive boobs against them, Angel purred. "I've heard you haven't had a woman in a long time."

"You heard right, sweet thing. You plan on fixing that oversight for me?"

"Come with me." Her sharp nails lightly scratched his chest.

Jax grabbed her hand and dragged her into the bedroom. "Let's go."

Alarmed, Charly fled back to her room. Hopping into bed, she tried not to think about what Jax and Angel were doing. Why did Dominic think she'd be safe *here*? That was her last thought as darkness once again claimed her.

FOUR

"**M**orning, sunshine," chirped Jess.

Charly groaned. She was not a morning person. "Go away." She tried to go back to sleep.

"Wake up, Charly. Don't make me go out there by myself." Jess pulled the duvet off her.

"Jess!" Grumbling, Charly rose. Wiping the sleep from her eyes, she stretched and yawned. That gave her a good look at Jess's bruised face and reminded Charly of hers. "How are you feeling today?"

Jess sighed deeply. "Still a bit spooked, but I'll be okay."

"You're safe from Sol now, Jess. He can't hurt you while he's locked up." That kind of fear wasn't always rational. There had been things that had triggered her fear responses, even though her step-father was in prison. Even now, angry or threatening voices sent her into a fight-or-flight state. Aggressive men were like ticking time-bombs, and they still had the power to make her heart race.

"I know. I've just been afraid for so long. I wanted to leave him, you know, but he…"

Charly hugged her friend. "I know, Jess. And I'm always here if you need to talk. These guys at the clubhouse will protect you, too." At least, she hoped they would. She wasn't sure how they treated women after the scene she'd seen last night. It wasn't like Angel had seemed less than willing to do whatever Jax might want to do, but there were all kinds of reasons women acted that way.

Jess perked up at the mention of the clubhouse. "I've often wondered what it was like here but never had the guts to ask. I guess I'll find out now!" Jess headed to the ensuite.

After showering and dressing, Charly and Jess apprehensively made their way through the house. Locating the kitchen, they paused in the doorway. Standing at the stove was a slim, pretty woman with a blonde pixie cut. She had on jeans and a light blue tunic top.

"Oh, hey," the woman greeted them with a wide smile. "Did you want coffee?"

"That would be great," Charly sighed. She didn't function well until she'd had her first cup of coffee in the morning.

"I'm Sara, by the way. Sit down." She indicated the kitchen table and then brought two mugs of steaming coffee.

Charly wrapped her hands around the mug and inhaled the aroma.

"Hi, Sara. I'm Jess, and this is Charly. You'll have to excuse her until she's had her morning wake-up brew." Jess and Sara both laughed.

Charly took a sip of her coffee and hummed a little. She looked up to find Sara gazing at her.

"So, you're Charly?"

Charly set the mug down, unsure what the question meant, except that Sara had undoubtedly heard her name before. "That's me," she said warily.

"How do you like working for Dom?" Sara's gaze didn't leave Charly's face.

The question threw Charly for a loop. "Umm. He's okay. Why?"

"Dom's my cousin." Sara leaned one hip against the table.

"Oh, then I'd better watch what I say." Charly laughed, but Sara didn't. "He's a good boss. Really," she insisted when Sara gaped at her. "Although I will admit he's bossy and a tad overprotective." Charly lifted her hand with her thumb and index finger close together.

Finally, Sara smiled again. "You're being nice. My cousin can be a difficult man. But when you earn his trust, he's loyal to a fault."

"Very true." Charly couldn't have agreed more, thinking back to the way Dom had raged against the cops until they'd undone her handcuffs. "So, do you live here?"

"Oh, no! I live in Sutton Park with my fiancé, Chad, and our son, Nolan." Sara smiled when she mentioned her son's name.

Charly's throat constricted with sadness. She knew what it was like to love a little boy that fiercely.

"How old is he?" Jess asked.

Sara smiled at Jess. "He's four. But he's an old soul."

Charly heard footsteps behind her. Turning around, she saw Jax and Angel enter the kitchen. Angel wore a short, satin robe, and Jax wore faded black track pants. His impressive chest was bare, every ripple of muscle on display. Charly stared at the eagle tattoo spanning his chest, its sharp talons clawing at his pecs, and the tips of its wings reaching the edge of his shoulders. It was breathtaking. Charly realized she was staring and looked away, embarrassed. Her eyebrows shot up when Jax kissed the top of Sara's head.

"Morning, sis."

Oh, okay. Sara was Jax's sister and Dom's cousin, so Jax and Dom were cousins.

"Hey, Jess." Jax gave her a chin nod.

Jess's face lit up. "Hi, Jax. When did you get in?"

Charly looked back and forth between the two. Jess had a similar look in her eye when Dom paid attention to her.

"Last night," he answered and then turned to Charly. "Hello."

Charly hadn't been aware a person could put that much sugar into a simple greeting. "Morning," she said, looking down, hoping no one would notice her blush.

Jax stared at her swollen eye. "Who did that?" His voice had lost all its charm, and he sounded angry.

Self-conscious, Charly covered her bruise with her hand. "Just some jerk. Don't worry, he's locked up. Hopefully, also wearing a knee brace." Charly hoped her kick to his knee had done some damage.

Jax caught his sister's eye. Sara shrugged and went back to making breakfast. Jax turned back to Charly.

Angel cleared her throat, clearly unhappy that Jax had focused in on Charly so wholly and quickly. She leaned against the doorframe, letting one shoulder of her short gown slide down.

Sara turned back to the stove, but not before Charly saw her roll her eyes and give a little snort.

Jax, however, wasn't amused. "Get lost, Angel." He pulled out one of the kitchen chairs and spun it around to straddle it, his thick arms resting on the back. "I haven't seen you around here before."

Angel left, but not before giving Charly a healthy dose of stink eye. Charly didn't blame her. Jax's behavior was rude even though she hadn't had a good first impression of Angel. "I haven't seen you before, either," she shot back, head up now and meeting his gaze.

Sara burst out laughing. "Sorry, Charly. Jax can't help himself when he meets a pretty woman."

"Fuck! You're Charly?" Jax appeared utterly blindsided.

Jess slumped a little beside her, giving Charly a twinge. It wasn't like she was asking for any of this attention. She wasn't sure why she was getting it. She'd never met Sara or Jax before and had no idea why they would have heard her name, much less heard anything about her. "Yeah, that's me," she said cautiously. "Why?"

"I've been hearing about you." Jax sat up and stretched.

"Oh?" Charly turned her coffee cup in a circle on the table, not wanting to stare at that broad expanse of chest or the way his muscles flexed. What would it feel like to have those muscles move under her hand? She shook her head. Where did that thought come from? "I hope you've been hearing good things." With any luck, he hadn't been talking to Maxine.

"Well, that's a matter of opinion. Dom speaks about you with a lot of frustration," Jax mused.

Charly sat back on her chair, eyebrows raised. That surprised her. "Dom's been talking about me?"

"Pretty much nonstop." A smile played across Jax's full lips. "I can see why."

"Have you moved back here?" Charly decided it was time to change the subject. She wasn't crazy about talking about herself in the first place, and Jax made her feel a little like an insect under a microscope.

"Moved back?" Jax's brows wrinkled in confusion.

"Well…" *Oh, to heck with it. She was going to say it. Why pretend?* "I saw you come in last night. Everyone seemed happy to have you back." Charly deliberately glanced in the direction Angel had left earlier.

"It *was* a great homecoming." Jax chuckled at Charly's shocked expression. "But I didn't move away, babe. I was incarcerated."

"Incarcerated?" His reply caught her off guard.

"In prison," Jax explained patiently as if she were a child.

Her lips tightened. "I know what being incarcerated means. What did you do?"

"Sent someone to the hospital." He inspected his fingernails as if the conversation bored him.

"Male or female?" she asked.

Jax's head came up, and his eyes narrowed. He stared at her for a long time. "I don't beat women. You'd be wise to remember that." With that said, he pushed back his chair and stormed off.

Charly blinked a few times at his abrupt departure, surprised at how angry her question had made him. An uncomfortable silence enveloped the room.

"You wouldn't happen to have any Panadol?" she finally asked Sara. Her headache was beating against her skull, and her mood suddenly changed.

"Sure, hon." Sara pulled a bottle off one of the shelves and shook out a couple of tablets for Charly.

Charly tossed them back, using the last mouthful of coffee to wash them down. "My head is pounding. I think I'll lie down for a bit," she said.

She returned to the bedroom without waiting for a response.

* * * * *

CHARLY WOKE UP AN hour and a half later, grateful that the ache in her head had subsided. Her eye was still tender, but it had stopped throbbing. Now, she had to worry about the twist in her gut. She felt guilty for jumping to conclusions about Jax earlier. She had to stop thinking that all men abused women because that wasn't the case. She'd struck a nerve when she'd implied otherwise.

She washed her face, pulled her hair back into a ponytail, and searched for him. The kitchen and lounge were empty. She poked her head out the front door. Her stomach rolled when she saw Jax smoking a cigarette near the front gate with Gun and Vin. *Great*. Now, she'd have an audience for her apology.

Charly had no trouble apologizing if it was warranted, but she was ashamed of the reason for her apology. She wasn't thrilled at the idea of rehashing her childhood with anyone. Plus, despite how rough they looked, the guys had been nice to her. She was an idiot—her and her big mouth!

Pulling her ponytail straight, Charly took a deep breath and marched outside. As she did, she heard Gun say, "You seriously should have seen it. She charged across the lawn like an angry mama bear and jumped on his back, beating at him with those tiny fists." He balled up his fists and waved them in the air.

Jax shook his head. "Like a little warrior princess, huh?"

"Exactly." Vin smiled at Jax. "That fits her perfectly."

Even better. They were already talking about her. Whatever. She needed to make this right. What anyone else thought of her was their business.

Charly walked up to Jax. His eyes tracked her approach. He stared at her with stolid indifference, making it difficult to gauge his mood. Charly, on the other hand, knew her guilt must be flashing like a neon sign across her face.

"Hey." She tucked her thumbs into the waistband of her jeans and rocked back on her heels.

"Yes?" Jax blew a cloud of smoke skyward.

Her gaze flicked to the two men standing beside Jax, watching her with interest. "Um, I'm sorry about before."

"I'm not sure what you're talking about, babe." Jax dropped his cigarette and ground it out under his boot.

He was looking down, but Charly caught the ghost of a grin on his handsome face. He was toying with her. "You know what I said. I was out of line."

"I can't recall what you said. Can you repeat it?" He cocked his head to one side and batted his eyelashes at her.

Vin chuckled, and she glowered at him. He covered his mouth and pretended to scratch his chin.

"Oh, for heaven's sake!" Charly grumbled. "When I accused you of hitting a woman."

Jax's grin turned into a chuckle at her discomfort. Then his tone turned serious. "Yeah. You should be sorry. You're in our world now, Charly, so watch what comes out of your pretty mouth, yeah?"

"Dom did warn you she had no filter," Gun commented. Charly hadn't known that. She wondered what else he had said. What had Jax said earlier? That he'd been hearing about her nonstop? With frustration?

"If I recall, he called her a loudmouth." Vin, the funny man, winked at her.

"*She's* right here, guys," Charly said. She looked at Jax. "Do you accept my apology?"

He took a step closer. "Does it come with a kiss?"

The air between them warmed. "No!" Yet Charly couldn't keep herself from glancing down at Jax's lips, imagining them parting invitingly, her lips drawn to his like a magnet, feeling soft but demanding on her own. Goosebumps erupted on her arms despite the warmth of the day.

"Then I'll have to think about it." Jax lit another cigarette.

She rubbed her arms. "You do that." She headed back to the house, trying to shake those images out of her head.

* * * * *

JAX'S GAZE FOLLOWED CHARLY as she flounced back inside, ponytail swinging. That ponytail gave him ideas. She wasn't his usual type. His rap sheet so far included tall, willowy, loose women who would fulfill his every fantasy at the click of his fingers. Charly was none of those things.

That might be one of the things that drew him to her. With most women, his relationship was transactional. He wanted something from them. Usually sex. They wanted something in return. Protection. Power. Standing.

Charly didn't seem to want anything from him. Sure, she was a bit sassy, but there was such a clear sense of kindness and honor underneath it that it was difficult to stay angry with her.

"Bro, Dom has dibs," Gun said.

Jax already knew that. "He doesn't mind sharing." It wouldn't be the first time.

Gun shook his head. "Oh, he will this time. Charly's his kryptonite. You didn't see him ready to knock down every local cop to get to her."

"You're exaggerating." Jax waved Gun's words away.

Jax and Dominic had grown up together in the Iconic Sons MC like brothers, and Jax knew that Dominic was the motherfucking Great Wall of China. Strong. Stalwart. Unmovable. Abandoned at a young age after suffering physical and mental abuse by a tyrannical father, Dominic had been taken in by his aunt and uncle, Jax and Sara's parents.

Deacon, Jax and Sara's father, was a second-generation member of the MC. Retired now, he had been a road captain for many years, often planning runs and leading his brothers in the club formation on the rides. Dominic's pop, Daniel, was Deacon's older brother. From his early teens, Daniel had been a tearaway, too unstable and unpredictable to become a patched member of the MC. Resentful of this exclusion, he'd run away at seventeen but stayed on the fringes of the club, often running back whenever he got into trouble.

Deacon met Sharyn, Jax's mom and Dominic's aunt, when her car broke down along a deserted highway. Fearing she was stuck in the middle of nowhere, Deacon miraculously came along while leading the club on one of their runs. Seeing Sharyn in distress, he signaled for his brothers to keep going while he stopped to help her. The rest is history, although it took several years to get his wife down the aisle to make an honest woman of her.

They adopted Dominic when he was four years old. Social services had shown up on their doorstep with a scrawny, sad, young lad in tow. Deacon had been enraged to learn of his nephew's treatment by his brother. Sharyn immediately opened her arms to the neglected boy and took him under her wing. Dominic was their son, an integral part of their family.

The MC was Jax's family. All the men were his brothers, but he and Dominic had a special bond, closer than two brothers could be. They shared everything, including women. They were good foils for each other.

Dominic was very controlling in the bedroom and often came across as cold and detached. Jax was Romeo, the lover, and the giver. But—like Dominic—when the sex was done, it was over. Women knew the score. If they got too clingy, they were out. They were expendable. It's harsh but a reality in the MC world.

"I guess you'll have to see for yourself then, bro." Vin laughed.

"Fuck off." Dropping his cigarette butt in the dirt, Jax stamped out the burning tip with his boot. He headed inside, wanting to find Charly and tell her he had forgiven her for her insubordination. He grinned, wondering how she'd handle that. He wouldn't mind getting a little pushback from her. Maybe their sparring would create some sparks. Or perhaps he should say more sparks. There'd been some already. He hadn't missed how she'd averted her gaze from his chest when she realized she was ogling. Or how her gaze lingered on his lips when he mentioned kissing her.

He found her in the kitchen, helping Sara and Jess make food for that evening's barbecue. "Okay if I borrow Charly for a minute?" he asked Sara.

"Go ahead. Jess and I have things covered here." Sara brushed her hair back from her face with her forearm.

Charly looked back and forth between them. "Do I have any say in this?"

"No," Sara and Jax said in unison.

Jax held out his hand, and Charly placed her hand in his but with a worried look. She was a little scared of him. Good. She should be.

He led her into the deserted lounge and sat on the couch. He patted the cushion next to him and signaled for her to sit down.

She took a deep breath, let it out, and then sat.

He hadn't missed how her deep inhale made her round breasts rise and fall beneath her t-shirt, and his palms itched with the urge to cup them, to run his thumbs over her nipples and watch them peak. There'd be time for that later. "I forgive you for your insubordination."

"Insubordination?" Her voice rose, and she pushed herself further from him on the couch.

"Bad behavior, disobedience," Jax explained, enjoying how flustered she was getting. The way her cheeks turned pink was cute.

"I know what it means, Jax. But I think 'a slip of the tongue' or 'tactless comment' might be more appropriate. Insubordination is a little strong." She crossed her arms over her chest protectively.

"My apologies." He leaned back on the couch and stretched his arm across the back.

"Well, that sounded sincere." Charly made a face at him.

Jax chuckled. "You're easy to bait." Her emotions rose close to the surface. What else might he make her feel? How else might he make her react? Ideas began to race through his head.

"Are you bored or something?" She leaned back against the couch, relaxing a little now that she realized he'd been teasing her.

"No. I happen to enjoy your company. Is that so hard to believe?" He turned his head to look at her straight on.

"Yes!" She sounded almost indignant. He didn't miss her surreptitious glance at where Angel had disappeared earlier.

He shifted closer to her on the couch, so his arm was almost around her. He could smell her shampoo—something clean and citrusy, with something a little floral beneath it. "Well, it's true. Why else would I be here?" He pulled her a little closer.

She stood, brushing her hands together. "That's what I'm trying to figure out."

Then she was gone.

✳ ✳ ✳ ✳ ✳

CHARLY HEADED BACK TO the room she shared with Jess, feeling shaken. She didn't understand what Jax was doing with her or what kind of game he was playing, and she didn't understand the feelings he stirred up in her, either. She was excited, scared, intrigued, attracted, and repelled all at once.

One thing she did know was that she didn't belong here. She wanted—needed—to go home. They were all ridiculous. She wasn't going to lie. Being assaulted by Sol had shaken her, and she knew it had shaken Jess. It was nice not to have to go back to the scene of the attack right away.

Now, however, it was time to go home. She wasn't a hostage. She should be allowed to leave of her own free will. She found Jess in the room they were sharing.

"Hey." Her friend seemed perkier than usual as well. She was probably sleeping much better than in the apartment she'd shared with Sol.

Charly shuddered at the idea of having to sleep next to the person who was abusing you. "I'm going to arrange for Vin or Gun to drive us home this afternoon, okay?"

Jess hesitated. "Um, do we have to?"

"No, but there's no real reason for us to stay." Her apartment was safe; the MC had taken care of that.

"Well, I'm enjoying myself. I feel safe here." Jess sat on the bed, pulled her knees up, and wrapped her arms around her shins.

Charly sat down next to her. "I know that, but I thought you might want to get back into a normal routine."

Jess bit her lower lip. "I'd rather stay a bit longer."

Charly didn't want her friend to feel guilty or pressured into leaving. "Okay. But I'm going home. Will you be all right on your own here?"

Jess's face brightened. "Yes. I've got Sara to keep me company."

Charly quickly stuffed the belongings she'd brought into her backpack and went to look for Vin or Gun. Finding both sprawled on the porch chairs in front of the house, she approached the duo.

"What's up, sweetheart?" Vin flashed his sexy smile, his white teeth gleaming against his olive skin.

She smiled back. How could she not? "You're just who I've been searching for. Which of you handsome men will take me home today?" Her hopeful spirits wilted a little at their silence.

Vin and Gun looked at each other, and then Vin said, "Sweetheart, it's not time yet. Dom doesn't get back till Tuesday."

Charly waved off Vin's concern. "Yeah, I know that. I'm not sure what that has to do with anything, but I'm ready to leave now."

Neither Vin nor Gun moved.

"Who's taking me?" she asked.

Gun sighed. "Darlin', what makes you think we're taking you anywhere?"

Charly paused. "Because I asked nicely?"

Their low chuckles did nothing to dispel the fear that was rising in her. She wanted to get out of this place.

"Sorry, Charly, but you're stuck with us for a bit longer." Gun didn't look sorry.

Charly glanced at the exit, bewildered by their refusal to take her home. The large, wooden security gate had a thick chain and padlock wrapped through the gap. Walking over, she groaned when she saw that it was a combination padlock.

It wasn't going to be easy to get out of here. She'd have to tough it out.

* * * * *

IT WAS LATE EVENING; daylight had disappeared hours before. Floodlights illuminated the clubhouse's backyard, and the aroma of onions and barbecued sausages filled the air. A table with bread rolls, condiments, and paper plates was set up. Charly and Jess had spent the afternoon helping Sara prepare the salads and side dishes. People were lounging around, laughing, and drinking.

Charly took her plate and sat down next to Sara and her fiancé, Chad, who was also a biker. He was a big guy with a full beard. He reminded Charly of a grizzly bear. There was a twinkle in his eye that made Charly instantly like him. Besides, how bad could he be if he was okay with Sara? Jess, Vin, and Gun had already taken up the spots on the other side of the picnic table.

"And then Nolan said he wanted to be a tiger when he grew up. I said he couldn't, and he said that I'd told him he could be anything he wanted to be when he grew up, and he would be a tiger. Thank you very much." Sara threw her head back and laughed.

"Hoisted by your own petard there." Charly snorted. "Where is Nolan tonight?" Charly asked, taking a bite of potato salad.

Sara gave her a big smile. "He'll be here tomorrow. Right now, he's with his Nan and Pop."

"You like kids, Charly?" Chad asked, leaning forward to look around Sara at her.

She shut her eyes against the emptiness in her chest. She felt it every time she thought of Fabien. She'd loved him from the time her mother brought him home from the hospital. He'd been hers. He'd had her whole heart. It hadn't helped, though. She hadn't been able to protect him. She'd failed him.

Charly closed her eyes for a few more seconds, trying to banish the image of her baby brother being wheeled out on a stretcher in a black bag. At the time, she didn't know what it was. She'd come home from school to find her house surrounded by police cars and ambulances. Luckily, Mrs. McNally spotted her and brought her to her house after letting the police know who Charly was and where she'd be.

Charly had kept asking what had happened and where her mama and baby brother were, and Mrs. McNally kept saying someone would be over to explain soon.

That someone had been Detective Shane Carter, who later gave her the flip phone that Dom had thought was amusing. It might have been old, and it might not do the things a smartphone would do, but it had been her connection to the man she considered a father figure for a long time.

Shane had kneeled so he could be eye-to-eye with Charly and explained that her brother was dead, shaken by her stepfather, and that a children's services officer would be arriving soon to find a safe place for Charly to live.

Since then, Charly has avoided kids. She didn't want the responsibility or the heartbreak when she failed them. Charly swallowed hard and pushed the thoughts away. "I don't have much experience with them, so I don't know. We'll find out tomorrow, I guess."

"Here's a hint: You'll be stuck with him all day if you mention soldiers or dogs. He's a chatterbox," Chad warned.

Charly tucked that little bit of information away. "It could be an icebreaker."

"Or it could put you in a coma," he quipped, cackling at his joke.

Sara playfully slapped his arm. "Oh, stop it. Our child is far from boring."

"Well, his mom is not boring." Chad pulled her close and kissed her neck, making Sara giggle like a teenager.

"Shove over, Charly." Jax had walked up to the table with a plate mounded with food. Without waiting for Charly to move, he wedged himself in next to her, shoving her up against Sara.

"There's an empty chair over there," Charly said, indicating the lawn chair a few feet away.

"I'm comfy here." Jax's thigh pressed against hers, but he didn't seem to notice her attempt to wiggle away. "Hey, Vin, when's Dom's bond hearing?"

"Tuesday." Vin made a face.

Jax frowned. "He hates being locked up. What the fuck happened?"

Charly squirmed. She felt responsible for what happened to Dom. Would this be another black mark against her name? Right next to them all calling her a loudmouth? Would she even have a job when all this was over?

"Keep still, babe." Jax laid a hand on her knee to stop it from bouncing.

His touch sent an electric zing up her leg. An unfamiliar sensation of need coiled inside her belly. She bit her lip to keep from gasping.

Gun set down the sausage he'd been devouring. "We told you what happened, bro."

"Not that part, Gun. What got Dom arrested?" Jax took his hand off her leg to start eating.

Charly could feel her face burning up. She wasn't sure which she was more embarrassed about—being responsible for Dom fighting with the cops or her reaction to Jax's touch. Luckily, no one seemed to notice.

"He assaulted a cop." Vin leaned back and scratched his chest.

"Shit. What the hell for? He's usually smarter than that."

Charly wished Jax would stop pestering the guys for information.

"Charly was cuffed. He didn't like it."

Thanks, Gun.

Jax turned to look more closely at Charly. "Is that right?"

Charly shivered under his steady gaze. "I told him I was okay." Was it her fault he hadn't listened? She wasn't sure anymore. All she knew was that it had somehow always been her mama's fault when her stepfather got angry and that she had often been punished for it. Severely.

Gun reached across the table and put a big hand over her small one. "We're not blaming you, darlin'. Dom's very protective. He couldn't handle seeing you handcuffed, is all."

Charly stared down at Gun's hand on her own. His hand was warm and rough, dwarfing her hand. He kept his touch light and gentle, not trying to trap, hurt, or blame her.

He was trying to reassure her. He was trying to make her feel safe.

Maybe the clubhouse wasn't so bad after all.

* * * * *

THE NEXT AFTERNOON, JAX strolled into the kitchen, where Charly was helping Sara wash up from lunch. "Hey, Charly, there's someone I want you to meet."

"I'm helping Sara," she said, not sure she wanted to go anywhere with Jax or who he wanted to introduce her to.

Sara shooed her way. "Go on. I've got this."

Sighing, Charly let Jax take her hand and walk her around the side of the main house to where the garage was. Several motorcycles with parts missing were stored inside in the process of being restored to their original, pristine condition. Next to the garage was an enclosure that contained a swing, a slide, a seesaw, a child-sized cubby house, and a picnic table. A young boy with brown hair sat there, playing with toy soldiers. Nolan. Next to him on the bench sat Gage, one of the prospects.

Earlier, Charly had asked Jax who Gage was. She had seen him following the orders of some of the men, including Jax, and he did so without ever complaining. Jax told her he met Gage at a local charity drive, where the MC had raised money for a children's benefit several months earlier. There, they'd struck up a conversation, and Jax quickly developed an affinity with the younger man. He offered to be Gage's sponsor and introduced him to the MC.

Gage was a qualified lawyer, but after passing the bar exam, he declined to join his father's law office. This led to a fight between the two men, and Gage had not spoken to his father since.

This information shocked Charly because she couldn't fathom why Gage would turn down an opportunity to work as a lawyer, something he had spent years studying for, and then end up here at the MC.

Jax said that Gage was a prospect, which meant he was at the beck and call of any patched brother. To become a patched member of the MC, prospects were expected to do whatever the brothers needed done, and that included babysitting Nolan.

Opening the gate, Jax waved at the little boy. "Hey, bud." He tousled the young boy's hair affectionately. He gave Gage a chin lift, and the prospect got up and left. Instantly knowing what Jax wanted and instantly obeying.

They sat at the table; Jax was next to Nolan, and Charly sat across from him. "Nolan, this is a friend of mine, Charly."

The boy looked up at her with gorgeous, big, brown eyes. Wise eyes. Then he looked at his uncle. "You don't have any friends that are girls, Uncle Jax."

Charly smiled at the honest statement. "I must be the first." She glanced up at Jax. "I feel so special."

Jax tilted his head to one side. "You are. Maybe more than you know."

Before Charly could respond, Nolan asked, "Do you like soldiers?"

She had been warned, but she couldn't help herself. He was so sweet and so cute. "They're my heroes," she said.

"You asked for it, babe." Jax winked at her. "Listen, bud; you two stay here for a bit. I'll be back with a surprise if you're good."

"Yippee!" the adorable boy squealed with delight.

Jax sauntered off, and Charly couldn't take her eyes off him. His swagger made her stop and take a second—and perhaps third—look. The man was the devil incarnate.

He returned ten minutes later, holding two bowls. Beside him was Jess, carrying another bowl. Charly smiled and gave her a little wave. Jess had been through a lot, and Charly was impressed with how she bounced back after all that had happened.

"And fis soldier has a AK-47. It can shoot a hundred bullets really fast." Nolan was an encyclopedia of information.

"There you go, bud. Your favorite. Banana split." Jax placed a bowl in front of Nolan, whose eyes had grown huge at seeing his favorite dessert.

Jess gave Charly the last bowl. Her stomach growled.

"Learn anything?" asked Jax.

"Plenty." She squinted at Jess. "You're not having any?"

"And pile on the pounds? No way." Jess rubbed her stomach.

"Rubbish! You're perfectly proportioned. It's me who needs to lose weight, but—"

Jax interrupted her. "Don't go there," he warned.

"As I was about to say, I don't care what anyone thinks about my weight."

"You're not even overweight, Charly," Jess admonished.

"You're perfect," Jax said.

Charly wasn't sure what to say to that, so she focused on the ice cream, taking her time and savoring the creamy sweetness. She looked up to thank Jax. Her face burned when she realized Jax was watching her lick the last drops of melted ice cream from the spoon. He'd demolished his ice cream within minutes and had spent the rest of the time gazing at her. Nolan returned to his soldiers, making gunfire noises and telling his narrative.

"I need to go pee," he suddenly burst out, bopping up and down on the bench.

"I'll take you, Nolan," Charly offered. It would get her away from Jax and the attention he was paying to her.

"I'll come with." Jax got up to join them.

"No. You guys stay. He doesn't need an entourage to use the toilet."

Charly's heart stuttered when a tiny hand curled around hers, and shiny, innocent eyes peered up at her trustingly. Swallowing, she closed her hand around his, and they headed to the main house.

Entering the hallway to the bedroom, she took a left to the bathroom and saw Nolan carefully inside. She stepped away to give him a little privacy. Frowning, she heard a disturbing sound coming from one of the rooms nearby. Treading lightly, she listened with her ear against the door. She heard someone choking. Twisting the knob, Charly stopped short at the scene in front of her.

A rough-looking biker held a young woman of about eighteen or nineteen by the hair. She was kneeling, naked, her head roughly pressed against the man's groin. Charly noticed she was struggling; her eyes were watering, and saliva was spilling from her mouth as she grunted in pain.

"What are you doing? Let her go!" Rushing forward, Charly went to pull the girl away.

"Fuck off, bitch!" The biker grabbed the female by her hair and pulled her up.

"Let her go! You're hurting her." Watching the young woman in pain angered Charly.

"Get lost, bitch! I can do whatever the hell I want. Leave, or you can take her place."

Charly tried again to extract the woman from the biker's grip but only succeeded in creating a tug of war. She let go so that she wouldn't hurt the young woman anymore.

"I'm going to get Jax."

"You snitch, and I can guarantee, slut, that she'll be punished."

He gripped Charly's arm painfully and shoved her out the door. He did it with such force that she knocked her head hard against the wall, then slammed the door shut. Tears spilled from her eyes, not only at the pain as she touched her head gingerly but also at the injustice of the situation. The poor girl looked terrified, and Charly felt helpless.

The feeling was familiar. She'd been a little girl then. Even younger than the young woman she'd seen being abused in that room. She'd been powerless.

Well, she wasn't powerless anymore. She was getting out of here, and she was going to take that girl with her.

Nolan came out of the bathroom down the hall. "Whatcha doin' on the floor, Charly?"

"Figuring out how to get back up, buddy." Because that's what she always did, she got back up.

✶ ✶ ✶ ✶ ✶

NOLAN SPENT THE AFTERNOON keeping Charly company. Chad had been right. He could talk the hind leg off a donkey—in an endearing way. They'd played with soldiers and on the slide and swings until Chad showed up to take Nolan and Sara home.

Charly had no idea where Jax and Jess disappeared to, and she wasn't sure she wanted to know, but she spotted them cozied up on the couch at the front of the clubhouse when she walked around the corner. Charly's steps faltered when she saw Kyra and Angel were there, too.

While Jax was happy to see her, Kyra and Angel weren't. She had no clue what she had done to piss them off.

Seeing no more room on the couch, Charly grabbed a chair from a nearby table and placed it next to Jess. Jess was acting strange around Jax, which Charly noticed: twirling her hair and laughing too hard at everything he said. He was eating up the attention. Good. Maybe it would distract him from her, and she wouldn't have to figure out the conflicting emotions he stirred in her. Besides, it would be good for Jess to take her mind off Sol.

"Babe, sit here." Jax moved over to make room for her. Jess's frown was brief, but Charly saw it.

"Nah, I'm good. What did I miss?" she asked.

"Not much. Where have you been?" Jax said.

Jess stiffened, but Jax seemed oblivious to any tension.

Charly decided not to comment. "I've been with my good buddy, Nolan. But Chad came to pick him and Sara up."

"Oh, Nolan's such an adorable little thing." Angel's iciness proved how insincere her comment was.

"He doesn't talk much, does he?" Charly smiled.

"Charly, be nice." Jax hid his amusement behind a stern voice that didn't fool anyone.

Jess glared at her. Stinging from the swift change in Jess's behavior, Charly shut her mouth, not sure why her friend was angry at her.

Jax's phone buzzed, and he got up to take the call, so Charly was left with two and a half frigid women to converse with. She rated Jess a point five because she was usually a good friend.

"What are you even doing here?" Angel asked, turning on her the second Jax was out of earshot. "You don't belong."

Charly agreed with her. "It's not my choice. You'll have to ask Dom when he gets back on Tuesday."

"Dom's not interested in you," snapped Kyra. "You're way too plain and fat."

Okay. The gloves were off. "Who said Dom's interested in me?" she asked nonchalantly.

"No one said it, bitch. But you're thinking about it. Sorry to disappoint you." Kyra flicked her long, dark tresses with her sharp nails. "The brothers prefer women who know how to have a good time."

"That's right. Jax couldn't get enough of me the other night," bragged Angel.

Charly thought it was probably because he hadn't had sex in four months but decided not to voice that opinion. She glanced over at Jess, who didn't meet her gaze. Why hadn't Jess come to her defense?

Resentment boiled up inside her. Time and time again, Charly came to her aid when Jess was being bullied. Why was Jess standing by while these jealous bitches insulted her? Some friend. And that was why Charly didn't trust many people. When it came to the crunch, they bailed. All of them. Always.

Charly was more troubled by Jess's apathy than the women's tirade. She couldn't sit here anymore and deal with her friend's indifference. She got up and left the room.

"That's it, bitch. Run along," sneered Kyra.

That was it. Charly had had it. She was going home. She didn't know what was up with Jess, and maybe she didn't want to know.

* * * * *

JESS FELT TRIUMPHANT WHEN Charly rushed out of the room, upset. Finally, someone else didn't appreciate all the attention the bitch was receiving. It had taken everything she had not to reach over and claw Charly's eyes out when Jax forgot about her the moment Charly interrupted their conversation.

Neither Dominic nor Jax had ever shown the slightest interest in her despite her best efforts. So far, even Maxine's aggressive pursuit of Dom has failed miserably. Yet Charly had only been working at the restaurant for a couple of months, and already she had both men panting after her. What did the bitch have that she didn't? It was good that she now had Kyra and Angel to help further her agenda.

* * * * *

CHARLY PRETENDED TO BE asleep when Jess came in late that night. She didn't want to talk to her so-called friend. She had made a plan, and she was getting out of here.

It was practically dawn before the clubhouse was silent. The men partied hard. That was okay, Charly thought. The harder they partied, the harder they'd sleep.

She slid soundlessly out of bed, careful not to wake Jess. She picked up her backpack from where she'd stowed it near the door and crept out the door, opening and shutting it without so much as a click. She had plenty of experience figuring out how to get in and out of places without attracting attention.

Now came the tricky part—getting that young woman she'd seen out with her. She went down the dark hallway, staying close to the wall to avoid any boards that might creak beneath her feet. Finding the door that had been slammed in her face before, she slid it open as silently as she'd shut the door to her room.

Even so, the young woman's eyes opened when Charly peeked in. She wasn't surprised. Constant abuse meant you were constantly on guard, always vigilant. The girl would be a light sleeper.

Finger to her lips, Charly beckoned to the girl to come with her. The girl shook her head. Charly beckoned her again. The girl's face flushed, but she pulled the sheet down far enough to show Charly that she was naked.

Ah. Embarrassment. Charly was a little shorter and a little wider than the girl, but she could wear Charly's clothes for long enough to get out of there. Charly opened the backpack and pulled up a T-shirt.

Biting her lip and glancing at the snoring man beside her, the girl crept out of the bed and out to Charly. Wordlessly, she slipped on the T-shirt and sweatpants Charly had given her, and the two made their way out of the clubhouse.

Charly's heart raced. She knew what might happen if the man woke up and found the girl gone, but they had to chance it. They had to get out.

Charly led the girl over to the padlocked gate.

Judging the distance between the ground and the gap in the gate to be too high to climb, she spotted an empty chair on the porch. Lifting the chair, she gasped when it proved heavier than she first thought. The girl was at her side in a flash, helping her lug it over to the gate.

"Thanks," Charly whispered. "What's your name?"

"Carrie," she whispered back.

She placed the chair on the ground and climbed onto the seat, slipping her shoe into one of the gaps. Then she swung up and over the gate. Hanging precariously from the top of the high gate, she let go and landed on the other side with a thump.

And directly into the arms of Dom.

FIVE

Dom made his way to the front gates of the clubhouse, barely visible in the early morning light. Leave it to the cops to release him at the butt crack of dawn. If they thought that would keep him from getting out of that hell hole, they had another thing coming.

Then, he saw the shadowy shape climbing over the top of the gate. What the actual hell? He eliminated the distance between him and the gate in two long strides, and Charly fell directly into his arms.

Charly had been the only thing on his mind for the past seventy-two hours. Now, here she was, exactly where he wanted her. Well, maybe not exactly. He wanted her beneath him, gasping with pleasure. He wanted her on her knees before him, his cock between her sweet, plump lips. This would do for the moment.

"Good morning to you," he said.

The relief in her eyes pleased him greatly. "Dom. What are you doing here?"

"I live here." He looked between the gaps in the gate and saw Bolt's woman on the other side, arms wrapped protectively around herself. "What's going on here?"

Charly pushed away from him. "I'm going home and taking Carrie with me."

Towering over her, Dominic pressed her against his thudding chest and cradled her head in his large hands. He frowned when Charly tried to pull away. "What's the matter?"

"Nothing. I just bumped my head."

"Let me see." Immediately, he turned her around, gently brushed his fingertips, and found the swelling.

"How the hell did this happen?" Dominic's anger was reignited; his woman was hurt.

At that moment, Bolt came crashing out of the house, making a beeline for Carrie.

"No!" Charly grabbed the gates as if she were going to try to climb back over.

Dom moved her away and undid the padlock, walking through and bringing Charly with him.

"What's this bitch doing here?" Bolt shouted at Charly.

Dominic stepped up to him. "What the fuck did you just say?"

"This whore thought she could meddle in my business."

Dominic threw back his fist and slugged him. The huge man staggered backward and fell with a heavy thud. Dust clouds exploded around him.

"What the fuck?" he screamed, wiping away blood. "You choosing a whore over a brother?"

"Never speak like that about her again." Rage turned his vision red. He took several deep, long breaths to steady himself and then turned to Charly. "What happened?"

"I saw him assaulting her." She nodded at Carrie. "So, I tried to stop him."

Lights came on in the house. Vin, Gun, and Jax came pounding out the front door, skidding to a stop, when they saw Dom standing over Bolt on the ground.

Jax coaxed the young woman forward. "Has Bolt been hurting you?"

The traumatized teenager nodded. "He hurt her too." She motioned to Charly.

Dominic exploded. It was up to Jax to find out what had happened. "What did Bolt do to Charly?"

"He shoved her out of the way, and she hit her head against the wall. Hard. She looked a bit dazed," said Carrie.

"That bump on your head," Dominic murmured, fisting his hands.

"Get him out of here!" growled Dominic. Vin and Gun hauled the man up unceremoniously and dragged him away.

Jax walked up to him and embraced him. "It's good to see you, brother."

"Never again." Dominic nodded, understanding precisely what Jax meant. He and Jax had not spent this much time apart since they were kids. They were a team. He turned to Charly, who had an arm protectively around Carrie. "You two go inside."

"Dom—" Charly began.

"We'll talk in a minute. I need to consult with Jax."

Charly sighed and walked back into the clubhouse with Carrie by her side.

As soon as the door shut behind them, Jax turned to him and said, "Charly?"

"She's mine." His eyes clashed with Jax's, his focus resolute.

"Yours?" Jax raised a brow, his eyes searching Dominic's.

Dominic narrowed his eyes. "What are you getting at?"

"Sharing."

Dominic shook his head vehemently. "Not Charls. She's different. Nothing's happened yet, but it will."

"She likes me," Jax said confidently.

"What have you done?" Dominic struggled to contain his rage at the thought of his cousin staking a claim before he did.

"Nothing's happened. Cool your jets." Jax raised his hands in surrender. "We do this one together."

"It won't work. Charls is not like that. She's naïve. Inexperienced."

"She's funny and smart, protective and courageous, and she can handle us," Jax insisted.

Dominic was not so easily convinced. "I want to believe you, Jax, but we only get one shot at this."

"Come on, Dom. It's us. We don't fail. We *won't* fail." Jax gave Dom one of his charming smiles.

Dom felt himself soften. He could never say no to Jax. "We *can't* fail, Jax. If she shies away from both of us, I'm staking my claim."

"You plan to claim her as your woman?"

"Not sure. We have chemistry, and I want to explore that. I have never wanted a woman like this before, so don't fuckin' mess this up."

"Not my intention, bro. Not my intention at all."

Dominic went in search of Achilles. They had to do something about Bolt. This was not his first incident of abuse. He was a sociopath and a dangerous predator when it came to women. The club didn't tolerate violent behavior towards women, and they didn't know how old the teenager was. If she was underage, the bastard would pay. Bolt needed to go.

Achilles combed his hand through his hair in frustration. "I heard what happened. Tomorrow morning, we have a vote. How the fuck did no one see this?"

"He does it behind closed doors. Doesn't leave visible bruises. Caused a head injury to my woman. Kill; he needs a lesson." Dominic wanted to be the one to give it to him.

"It probably won't make much difference. He gets off on inflicting pain, and he likely gets off on receiving it, too."

"It'll cause more pain for him to hand in his colors."

Achilles grunted in agreement. "Go see your woman."

✳ ✳ ✳ ✳ ✳

IT SEEMED THE COMMOTION had woken everybody up. Charly and Carrie sat on the sofa with Gun and Vin standing over them.

"Ice pack," Dominic ordered, and Gun hurried to fetch one.

Gun returned with an ice pack, and Dominic sat beside Charly on the sofa, holding it against her bump. She attempted to hold the ice pack herself, but he grabbed her hand and placed it on his knee instead.

"Dom, you're back." Kyra appeared out of nowhere and stood next to him, her bosom inches from his eyes.

She grazed her nails across his nape and leaned in to kiss him. At the last minute, Dominic averted his face so that her lips landed on his cheek.

Jess stood next to Kyra, both women looking disgruntled. It wasn't hard to miss the glares she was throwing Charly's way. What the hell was going on? Dom thought Charly and Jess were supposed to be best friends. What the fuck was Jess's problem?

Dominic paused. Charly had her arms around the teenager, comforting her. He loved that about her—the way she looked after others. It pissed him off that other women were jealous of her. Charly had more kindness in her little pinkie than they had in their whole bodies.

Dominic thought he was a damn lucky sod to have found her. She epitomized all that was good. Charls had the smarts, the looks, the big heart, and the spirit of a warrior.

"Let's go." He gently took her hand.

"Where are we going?"

"Somewhere private."

Dominic ushered Charly to the back of the clubhouse.

"Why are we going to the bedroom?" she managed to croak out.

"Not for the reason you're thinking."

Dominic swept back the hair hiding her eyes. "You don't ever have to be afraid of any of us again, Charly. Bolt won't ever hurt you again."

He grazed his fingers along her cheekbone, then slid them upwards to comb through her hair. Hearing her swift intake of breath, he pulled back.

"Sorry, babe. I didn't mean to hurt you."

"You didn't," she responded shyly, and Dominic's heart kick-started at the thought that perhaps it was his touch she'd reacted to.

"Tell me what you saw Bolt doing to the girl," Dominic asked. The bed squeaked as he sat down next to her.

"He was forcing Carrie—that's her name, and she's nineteen, by the way—to take his…"

Dominic laughed at her embarrassment. "His cock?" he supplied for her.

"Yes!" she cried, blushing profusely. "His cock." Charly studied her hands. "I tried to get him to stop by pulling her away from him. But we only ended up in a tug-of-war. When I threatened to say something to Jax, Bolt told me he'd punish her. He then shoved me out the door, and that's when I banged my head on the wall."

Dominic took Charly's clenched fists and waited until she made eye contact. "I promise you, babe, that neither Bolt nor any other brother will ever put their hands on you again. You should feel safe here. I brought you here to protect you, and I failed."

"It's not your fault, Dom." Charly tried to reassure him, but he shook his head.

"It is. I practically forced you to come here and told my brothers to keep you here until I got released. It's my fault, and I'm so fucking sorry this happened to you, Charls."

"It was my choice to come here."

It messed him up inside to hear her try to make excuses for what happened, to make him feel better. It was up to him to make *her* feel better.

"Don't make excuses for what happened, Charls. It shouldn't have happened to you, and that's on me."

Dominic touched her soft lips when she opened her mouth to reassure him. That was a mistake because now he wanted to kiss those soft lips. Unfortunately, now was not a good time. His woman needed his support, not a hot and heavy make-out session.

"What will happen to Carrie now?" There was that protective spirit. Dominic knew that Carrie would be safer at the clubhouse.

"She's under our protection now. She'll stay here with Sara for a bit. We can always put her up in one of the units at the back if she wants to stay here. Ultimately, it's up to her."

Charly nodded in agreement. Who knows how long the frightened teenager had been used and abused by psychopaths like Bolt.

Her sigh held a mixture of sadness and frustration. "I'd like to go home now."

Dominic's eyes narrowed. "Why?"

"I want to be alone and go back to my normal routine. It's been a stressful few days." She ran her hand along the bedside drawer, brushing away imaginary dust.

"I get that, but I'd rather you stay one more night so that I can keep an eye on you."

Dominic sensed that Charly was at her breaking point. "I told you I feel fine physically. I need some space away from everyone. I'm not used to being surrounded by people twenty-four-seven."

He finally relented and searched for Jax to tell him he was taking Charly home. In the car, Charly insisted on sitting in the back.

"Charly tried to escape this morning," Dom said conversationally.

Jax's full lips curled upward. "Did she now?"

"Climbed the gate."

Jax glanced over his shoulder, throwing her a teasing grin. "Resourceful. Have to watch this one, Dom. And add escape artist to her list of skills. I didn't expect that from her."

"It shows how well you *don't* know me," Charly shot back.

Good. Whatever had happened hadn't dampened her spirit.

Jax twisted in his seat. "Then it's time we got to know you, heh? What do you think, bro?"

"It's overdue."

When the car pulled up outside her place, Charly opened the door. "Thanks for the lift," she said.

Dominic turned off the ignition. He held back a grin at Charly's dismayed look when he and Jax exited the car.

Entering her apartment, Charly told them to wait in the dining room. Dominic ignored her and followed her as she went into the bathroom for toiletries, then opened a closet to grab Jess's clothes. After she'd gathered Jess's lingerie from a drawer, she turned around only to bump into him. The pile of clothes fell out of her arms as she tried to regain her balance. Dominic's hands steadied her.

"Nice bedroom, babe." Jax wandered around the room.

"Can you please not touch my things?" She sounded more irritated than frightened.

His cousin picked up the one-and-only photo from the nightstand. "Is this you?"

Jax passed the photo frame to Dominic, who looked at her questioningly. "Who's the woman and baby?"

Charly snatched the frame from him and held it close to her chest. "My mama and brother," she said shortly.

This was the first time he'd heard about any family. "You've never talked about them before," he said.

She shrugged her shoulders.

"Where are they?" Jax's eyes probed hers.

A shudder rolled through her body. "Dead."

"Oh, babe, I'm sorry," Jax said quietly.

Dominic peered down at her. "Do you have any other family?"

Charly shook her head.

"No one at all?" Although he meant to console her, his words came out harshly.

"Don't feel sorry for me. I'm used to being on my own." She set the frame down on her bedside table.

Dominic cradled her face, forcing her to look up at him.

"Listen up. You're not alone anymore."

Then he boldly claimed her mouth, and time came crashing to a sudden halt. Charly gasped, giving him the perfect opening to deepen the kiss. She moaned when his tongue brushed against hers. His hands held her tightly against his body as he continued to plunder her mouth, his tongue seeking out hers again and again. Charly gripped his arms tightly, and he wondered if she felt the room spinning, too. Just as suddenly, he broke off the kiss with a groan. When Jax attempted to take her in his arms, Charly tore herself away, panting with alarm.

"What are you doing?"

Dominic froze when Charly panicked. "It's okay, Charls. Jax only wants to kiss you."

"Well, that's not happening. I'm not like the others." She stepped back, folding her arms.

Jax slowly stepped forward. "We know that. It's part of what makes us want you so much."

Fear was written all over Charly's face, as Dominic explained. "It's who we are. We share."

"I can't do this." She stepped away from them.

"There's chemistry between us, Charls. Jax and I want to explore that with you."

Charly shook her head. "No." She fixed them with an unwavering stare.

Jax grumbled, "Why the fuck not?"

Charly stormed to the front door and opened it. "You can leave."

Dominic refused to budge.

"Hang on," Jax said. "What's the matter? We're simply having a discussion. That's all."

"No. You want some ménage à trois, and I'm not down for that."

"A moment ago, you kissed me like there was no tomorrow." Dominic's reminder made her blush.

"It's nothing to be ashamed of," Jax reassured her, prompting her to roll her eyes.

"Just be honest with us. Why does the idea of Jax and I wanting a relationship with you frighten you so much?" Dom asked.

Charly spoke softly. "You make it sound like what you're suggesting is normal. It's not. Not for me, anyway. What would people think? Look at you two, and look at me." Charly threw her arms out.

"Worlds apart. I'm not very experienced, and well, you two have a lot of experience, I'm sure."

A long silence ensued. Finally, Jax spoke up. "Then choose one of us."

Dominic pushed Jax up against the wall, his forearm pressed to his cousin's throat.

"What the fuck are you doing?" Dominic whispered menacingly. "We talked about this. She's *mine*!"

His face turning red, Jax gripped his forearm, loosening the pressure. "We should let Charly decide," he wheezed as Dominic let go.

"We had an agreement. If it didn't work, I would claim her."

"I want her, too," Jax argued.

"Too fucking bad! She's mine." Dominic seethed at his cousin's betrayal.

"She's not a piece of property, Dom. Charly can make her own choices."

"Don't be such a hypocrite, Jax. We grew up in the same fucking brotherhood."

"I know that, but Charly's different. You treat her like property; she'll run a mile."

"Hey! Stop fighting, guys." She handed over the bag containing Jess's property.

Dominic frowned. "What's going on between you and Jess anyway?"

Jax clicked his tongue in exasperation. "She's jealous, Dom. She's always had a thing for me. I've been friendly with her because of her situation, and that's all. Jess doesn't like that I like Charly."

"Charls—" began Dominic.

"No. I need you both to leave." Charly stood her ground, opening the door again.

$$\star\;\star\;\star\;\star\;\star$$

THE NEXT DAY AT work, Charly stood to one side of the kitchen serving hatch, peering into the dining room and pretending to load dishes into the industrial dishwasher. She'd scurried back there when Dominic and Jax had come in earlier and was staying there as much as possible to avoid having to talk to either of them. Or, worse yet, both of them together. She shuddered, thinking about the scene in her apartment the day before. Both of them? Seriously? Who the hell did they think she was?

In the household where Charly had grown up, sex was intermingled with abuse, punishment, and power struggles. She'd lost her virginity to a boy she'd worked with at one of her many jobs, more because she wanted to be rid of the burden of it than any desire for him. Afterward, he boasted about it to all their coworkers. She'd gotten so much harassment that she'd quit.

As far as she knew, sex and desire were always something for her to feel shame about.

It wasn't that she *wasn't* attracted to them. They were both handsome, and they could be seriously charming. She hadn't missed how Jax had dealt with Carrie the morning before. How gentle and kind he'd been to the poor girl. Nor had she stopped thinking about how Dom had been ready to fight half the police force to make them take the handcuffs off her and be sure she was okay. Their hearts were strong and good.

She'd had a moment of panic when Jax suggested she choose between them. How could she? She was physically attracted to them both. They were beautiful men. She loved how Dom took up space in a room, not just because of his size but also because of the dominant male energy he exuded. She adored Jax's easy smile and teasing banter. She couldn't deny how Dom's protective streak stirred her, and no one had ever flirted with her like Jax did.

There was no way to choose.

But a threesome? She didn't think so.

She wasn't crazy about seeing Jess, either, since her former friend hadn't said one word to her all day.

A fork slipped from her hand, hitting the floor with a clatter.

Con growled at her. "Charly! What's gotten into you today? And why are you hiding in my kitchen? Get out and set up the tables."

Damn. She wasn't ready to give up her hiding place. "I thought you'd be grateful for my assistance since Joel's not here."

"I can handle myself. Now get!" He hustled her out.

Charly reluctantly left the kitchen and started wiping down some tables. Just her luck—that was when Dominic and Jax came out of the office and headed her way. Had they been watching for her? Her heart thumped inside her chest.

Jess stepped out of her workspace and into their path. They swerved around her. "Excuse us, Jess," Jax said as they brushed by her.

She kept her head down, polishing the already clean table as if her life depended on it.

"Good morning, Charls," Dom said, moving to one side of her as Jax moved to the other.

She could feel the heat coming off their bodies, and her arms erupted in goosebumps. She straightened up and took a step back. "Good morning," she greeted.

Dom propped one hip on the table so he was closer to her, eye-to-eye. "We were just looking at your employee file," he said.

Oh, great. Were they about to fire her for not sleeping with them? So be it. She didn't fancy finding another job, but she'd handle it if necessary. "And?"

"We noticed your twenty-fourth birthday is in a few days. We're taking you out," Jax said.

She didn't miss that it was a statement, not a question. Did she want to fight it? When was the last time someone had gone out of their way to celebrate her birthday? She couldn't remember. On the other hand, she didn't want to encourage them. "Both of you? At once?"

Jax chuckled. "Of course."

Charly inhaled a calm breath through her nose. "Ja-ax, we talked about this."

"Char-lee," he teased. "It's no big deal. Dinner. A nice chat. What's the harm?"

She shook her head in resignation. "You can't take no for an answer, can you?"

"Nope," he agreed with that charming grin of his.

She thought for a second, her toe-tapping on the floor. "Doesn't change things, you know. The answer's still the same."

"That's fine. Pick you up at seven on Friday," said Dominic.

Her stomach fluttered. Was it just her? Alone? With both of them? It wasn't a good idea. "Can we invite Sara? I'd feel more comfortable if she came along."

Dominic's eyes darkened, but he said, "If that's what'll put you at ease, then okay."

✶ ✶ ✶ ✶ ✶

A LITTLE BEFORE SEVEN on Friday, Jax texted to say they were on their way. Charly rechecked her hair, makeup, and dress. She left her hair down rather than up in her usual ponytail. Left loose, it came almost to her waist.

She smoothed down her white, long-sleeved bodycon dress, checking in the mirror to see how it hugged her curves. She slipped on black and white heels to complete the look. Okay, she was ready— at least, she hoped she was.

Inhaling nervously, she went to the door when Jax tapped his signature knock: tap, tap-tap, tap. He repeated the pattern twice.

"Happy birthday, sweetheart." Jax produced a gift-wrapped box.

"You didn't have to get me anything, guys." Despite her protests, she was delighted to receive their gift.

Tearing off the paper, her eyes widened with astonishment. It was a smartphone. Tentatively, she slid the lid off, took the phone out, and studied it.

"Wow. A phone. But I already have one," Charly said, turning the device over. She refused to admit that she had no clue how to use one of these things.

Jax took the phone from her. "Here, I'll show you how to use it."

Jax and Dominic spent the next ten minutes explaining all the features. Charly's mind was confused, trying to remember even half of the information.

"It also has a GPS tracker on it," Jax announced. "It's a safety precaution in case you get into trouble."

She made a face at him. "What trouble am I supposed to get into?"

"You seem to have a knack for it, Charls," Dom said. "You've got some bumps and bruises to prove it." He lifted her chin and ran his thumb over the spot on her cheekbone where the bruise Sol had given her had faded but not disappeared. She shivered a little at his touch.

It was hard to argue with that, but she still felt uneasy. "So, let me get this right. You can check up on me anytime and know where I am?"

At Dominic's nod, she continued. "That's a bit stalkerish, don't you think?"

"I prefer to see it as taking care of one of our own. Jax and I have the GPS tracker app on each other, same with the other brothers," Dominic revealed.

Dominic's explanation settled the matter somewhat, but there was still the issue of money. "I'm not sure I can afford to keep paying for something like this. Aren't these plans expensive?"

Charly felt overwhelmed. She was incredibly grateful for the thoughtful gift, but how practical was it? Although she hated to throw such a nice gesture back in their faces.

"Babe, it has a two-year contract. And we're paying for it."

Oh.

✶ ✶ ✶ ✶ ✶

CHARLY GASPED AS DOMINIC pulled up in front of Stars Align, a fine-dining restaurant where a single meal cost an arm and a leg.

"We're eating here?" she asked, wide-eyed.

"Only the best for you, babe," Jax said as he helped her out of the car.

She spotted Sara waiting at the front, also decked out in a dress and heels. Jax's sister hugged Charly. "Happy birthday, Charly. Thanks for inviting me. I can't wait to see what this place is like."

Charly grasped her hand. "I think you're the one doing me a favor," she whispered. "I was a little nervous about being alone with those two, and that was before I knew where we were going."

The maître d' escorted their group to a table on the balcony. Bronsone Bay spread before them, light reflecting off the water like little diamonds. The maître d' clicked his fingers, and a young man wearing a starched white shirt and black trousers trotted over. "This is Ryan. He will be your waiter tonight." He bowed formally, then departed.

Charly tried not to giggle as she imagined Con introducing her, Jess, or Maxine that way to their customers.

Eyes twinkling, Jax asked, "Something amusing?"

Shaking her head, Charly said, "It all feels a little surreal. I'm usually the one waiting on someone else, and nobody ever introduces me like that."

"It can be a bit pompous," Sara agreed.

Ryan returned with the wine menu, and Jax turned to Charly. "What'll you have?"

"I'll have wine, thanks. A Riesling." She could use some liquid courage.

Dominic whispered something to Ryan, who then left to get the drinks. A few minutes later, he returned with a trolley. It contained a silver bucket full of ice cubes and a bottle of wine.

"I didn't mean for you to bring a whole bottle," Charly teased the young waiter. "A glass would have been fine."

"No problem, ma'am."

"Ma'am? I'm only twenty-four!"

Ryan blushed. He looked so sweet and innocent, so she touched his arm. "It's okay. You might need to carry me to the car when I finish the bottle."

He retrieved the bottle and attempted to unscrew the cork. Charly tried to hide her grin when his attempts failed. "Do you want a hand with that?"

She was in such a jovial mood that she wasn't aware of the tension around the table. The sudden silence had gone unnoticed until Dominic abruptly stood up and snatched the bottle of wine out of Ryan's fumbling hands.

"I got it, mate. You can go." His harsh tone had poor Ryan scuttling away.

Dominic quickly popped the cork.

"That was rude," Charly muttered.

"Too fucking bad. You don't pay these prices to have a moron serve you."

Sara broke the tension. "Did Dom or Jax tell you that I had to break up a fight between them the other day? That reminds me, Jax. You never told me why you were fighting. Care to share?"

"Brothers fight, Sar. It's what men do," Jax drawled.

"Yeah, and I'm the Queen of Sheba. Come on. Tell me the truth." Sara jabbed her brother in the arm.

He grabbed her hand and put it down next to her plate. "When did you become the Queen of Sheba, sis?"

"Stop evading the question."

She glanced at Charly, who was thoroughly enjoying the siblings' banter. "They were probably squabbling about who got to use the toilet first. That happened once when they were teenagers. Dom ended up with a dislocated jaw, and Jax had a black eye. True story."

"I somehow don't think that's why," Charly said.

"It could have been over a girl, perhaps?" Sara surmised, tongue in cheek.

Dominic swiftly changed the subject, and neither ever explained what their beef had been about.

During dinner, Charly noticed a table of women staring and snickering at her. She did her best to ignore them and instead focused on her seared scallops with pineapple and corn salsa. She didn't think she'd ever tasted anything so rich and decadent.

Dessert and coffee demolished, Charly and Sara excused themselves to go to the bathroom.

Reapplying her lipstick, Sara glanced over at Charly in the mirror. "So, care to explain why I'm playing chaperone tonight?"

Charly searched inside her bag and remained silent.

"Is this a date?" Sara asked.

Was it? She hoped not. "No. It's a birthday dinner."

Sara's frown disappeared. "Do you like Dom and Jax?"

"Yes." Charly dug into her purse, unable to make eye contact.

"You like both of them?" Sara pressed, refusing to let the issue rest.

"Yeah, I do." Charly located her lip gloss and uncapped it.

Sara snatched the tube from Charly's hand and turned her around, so they were face-to-face. "Let me get this right. You like Dom and Jax but don't want… what? You're not leading them on, are you?"

Swallowing, Charly glanced away, then immediately brought her eyes back to Sara's. "No! I wouldn't do that." Exhaling roughly, she admitted the truth. "Yes. I like both Dom and Jax. But I don't want a sexual relationship with them because it's out of the realm of my experience."

Sara stared at her, then burst out laughing. "Charly! Do you think the guys care about your lack of experience? They're probably chuffed about it. I'll let you in on a secret. Neither has ever pursued a woman before. Women chase them. So, the fact that they're pursuing you tells me they're serious about this. They're venturing into unfamiliar territory, too."

Sara went back to applying her lipstick, and Charly was left to ponder that thought. She then entered the cubicle to do her business, and Sara did the same.

A minute later, she heard a door squeak open and two females speaking.

"Oh my God, did you see that fat brunette with the pretty blonde and the two hot guys at the table? What an ugly duck!"

"I've no idea what either sees in her. Those guys are way out of her league," mocked her friend.

The women spun around when Charly exited the cubicle and walked to the basin to wash her hands. They put their heads together and sniggered.

After consuming three glasses of wine, Charly's usual inhibitions had vanished. Annoyed at their bitchiness, she flashed a grin at Sara and began singing "Barbie Girl." Their cries of outrage were extremely satisfying as Charly turned and sashayed out of the room.

Linking arms, Sara joined in singing, and they sang all the way back to their table, where the men were waiting for them.

Jax looked at his sister questioningly. She held up a finger, silently asking him to wait.

While waiting for the bill, Dominic, Jax, and Sara had their heads down, busily typing away on their phones.

"You and your toys," Charly sighed in mock resignation.

Once in the foyer, Jax told Sara and Charly to wait, then he and Dominic stalked back into the restaurant. Frowning, Charly took a few steps to see where they went. To her horror, they approached the table where the two bitchy blondes sat. Charly's stomach plummeted. Had they dismissed her already? Were they going to pursue those bimbos right in front of her?

$$\ast\ast\ast\ast\ast$$

JAX AND HIS COUSIN strode towards the blondes, who were watching their approach. Jax smirked when the females started fiddling with their hair, puffing out their chests, and nudging each other. His blood boiled when his sister shared what had happened in the bathroom. He thought what Charly had done next deserved an Oscar. God, he was proud of her. She wasn't going to let anyone keep her down. Nobody messed with her. Nobody. Not even these sluts who thought they were better than everyone else.

"Hello, ladies." Jax used his charm to put them at ease.

"We believe you were talking about the brunette sitting with us." Dominic didn't bother beating around the bush.

"Oh, yeah," one blonde scoffed. "She's no match for you." She played with her hair, unsuccessfully drawing their eyes to her ample chest.

"I believe your exact words were that she's fat and looks like an ugly duck. Is that right?" Jax asked.

The woman's eyes grew wide as she suddenly understood that they were pissed off with her for calling Charly names.

He turned to Dom. "Hey, bro, do you think these women need to get their eyes checked?"

"I don't know, Jax. It could be something more serious. Maybe a neurological condition," Dom answered.

Their stifled gasps amused him. However, Jax wasn't finished. He had a whole lot more to say to these jealous bitches. Dom looked over at him. "They think our girl's fat. What do you say to that?"

Jax glanced towards the foyer and spotted Charly regarding them sadly. She quickly looked away.

"Are they kidding? She's fucking perfect. That ass!" Jax bit his fist.

"Those boobs. A perfect handful. Soft and malleable," Dominic added.

"These idiots said she looked like an ugly duck, bro. Didn't they notice her emerald-green eyes or her cock-hardening smile? What planet do they live on?" Jax shook his head.

"I guess only men like us appreciate a real woman," Dominic replied wryly. "Not some dried-up stick of a bottle blonde."

"All this talk about our girl's making me horny, bro."

"Then it's time for us to take our girl home and show her some love."

Horny as hell but feeling much better after their "talk," Jax and Dominic headed back to an anxious-looking Charly. Judging by Charly's pursed lips and accusing eyes, it was clear she thought they had been propositioning those sluts, and she was pissed off. It was time to set her straight.

Turning Charly to face the blondes on the balcony, Jax said, "Take a look. What do you see?"

Charly peeked in. Both women's chins were trembling as if fighting tears. "What did you say to them?"

Jax bent down and whispered, "How much Dom and I want you."

Her shuddering response pleased Jax. Charly wanted him as much as he wanted her. He was sure of it. They just had to get her to admit it. Eager to get her home and work on that, Jax hustled everyone out.

✳ ✳ ✳ ✳ ✳

SAYING GOODBYE TO SARA, the three of them got into the vehicle. By the time they reached Charly's apartment, she was a bundle of nerves. Charly sensed that the men—especially Jax—were keeping her distracted with general chitchat, but if she were asked to recall what had been said, her mind would have drawn a blank.

Standing outside her door, Charly fiddled with her keys. The last thing she felt she should do was invite them inside, as that would lead to trouble. Instead, she quietly bade them goodnight.

When neither made a move to leave, Charly inserted the key, hoping they would get the hint.

"Wait."

Glancing over her shoulder, she eyed Jax warily. "What?"

"Don't we get a goodnight kiss?" Trust Jax to speak about what was on everyone's mind.

Charly's chest expanded. Did she want this or not? On one level, she did. The kiss she'd shared with Dom the other day had blown her mind. Sensual and commanding, he'd plundered her mouth in a way no one else ever had. She did not doubt that Jax's kiss would be just as devastating. Part of her wanted to find out. A kiss wouldn't hurt, would it? But Charly remembered Sara's earlier comment, and a kiss would certainly come under the category of "leading them on." That wasn't something she wanted to do. She respected them too much for that.

"Thank you for a lovely meal, and I'm sorry, but the answer is no."

Mind made up, she quickly went inside and clicked the door shut.

No one but her needed to know that she had to lean against it for several minutes before her breathing returned to normal and her knees would support her.

✶ ✶ ✶ ✶ ✶

CHARLY CARRIED THE WASHING basket up the basement stairs. She nodded and smiled at the young couple, who lived two doors down the hallway, as she walked back to her apartment. From a distance, she thought she spotted something red on her door. As she got closer, she saw that someone had spraypainted "whore" in large, capital letters.

Shaken, she stared at the word, trying to figure out who would do such a thing and why. If she had to take a wild guess, she'd say Jess. Jess knew where she lived; secondly, her former friend was angry with her. Charly thought about calling the police but changed her mind. She decided to let it go this time. She wouldn't give Jess the satisfaction of knowing that her malicious actions upset her.

Jess hadn't talked about her feelings for Jax. All Jess saw was Jax showing her a bit of attention. If she had tried talking to Charly, Jess would have known that she had no intention of getting involved with Jax, and Jess's path was clear to starting something with him.

Charly understood the attraction. She was attracted to Jax, too, but a relationship with him was a whole different ball game. Charly didn't trust easily. Although she put on a brave front, she didn't have much self-confidence when it came to intimacy. Affection was something that she'd been deprived of during her childhood. Friendships also eluded her, the only exception being the man who had saved her life when she was twelve. Along the way, Charly learned that people didn't always have good intentions, and this incident reinforced that belief.

She spent the rest of the morning scrubbing the paint off the door. She didn't want her landlord to see the graffiti and throw her out. Then again, Mr. Kozlowski was a sweet, old man. He'd most likely offer to clean the door himself. But this was her problem. She'd handle it.

Just like she always did.

SIX

Maxine had been giving Charly dirty looks all morning at work. At first, Charly thought it was because she knew about her birthday dinner on Friday night, but she decided that couldn't be the case. The guys weren't like Maxine. They didn't go around discussing their business with everyone.

Something was up. Maxine and Jess had been huddled together in the staff room, breaking apart when Charly entered.

Dominic and Jax were popular men, and everyone wanted a piece of them. Unfortunately, their interest in Charly had consequences for her: jealousy, envy, and hatred.

Sara had called Charly on her new phone to invite her to a barbecue at the clubhouse. At first, Charly tried turning her down, but she soon realized that Jax's sister was one determined lady. When she put Nolan on the phone, Charly knew she was lost.

"Please, Charly. Please come. I've got two new soldiers to show you," the little boy said.

How was she supposed to say no to that?

Then, to add to her dilemma, Dominic informed her that he and Jax were picking her up after work and taking her to the clubhouse.

"I'll pick you up tomorrow, okay?" When Dominic made plans, everyone followed them.

"Ah," she hesitated.

"After work. Be ready."

"But—"

"Wait out front for me."

"I—"

When Dominic tried to interrupt her again, she stamped her foot. Silvery gray eyes sparkled. "Charls?"

"Would you let me speak?" she asked, waiting for his permission. "How are you going to explain my presence? I don't need protection."

"Babe, if you think for one minute that the brothers don't know about our interest in you, then you're more naïve than we thought you were," Jax said.

Great. Were they all discussing her business? This was precisely what she didn't want. "What do you mean? Did you say something to them?"

Jax cocked an eyebrow. "You would have been safe to go home that night, but Dom insisted on having you at the clubhouse. He's been acting out of character for a while. They knew what was up."

Charly looked for confirmation from Dominic. His lips twitched.

"Oh my God! This is so awkward. Do they know nothing is going on between us?"

"It's none of their business," Dominic declared.

"I'll just get a taxi," she pleaded, to no avail.

True to their word, they showed up as she clocked out and escorted her to the car. Once they got to the clubhouse, Charly hopped out of the vehicle.

"Stay here, Charls. Sara should be here any minute. Stay with her. She'll protect you in case anyone bothers you. Jax and I have church first."

"Church?" The two men had never seemed religious to her.

Dominic's eyes warmed at her confusion. "It's code for a meeting—club business. I did tell you we were meeting up with the brothers. Remember?"

Charly nodded. She looked around the room and worried that the other men might view her in the same light as the club whores. It made her feel ill at ease.

"Relax." Jax felt her stiffen. "Get used to being around the brothers."

A whirlwind of energy bolted out of nowhere. "Charly! Charly!"

Instantly, her worries vanished. Charly braced herself for Nolan's impact. He crashed into her legs, wrapping his arms around them.

"Hey, buddy." She ruffled his hair.

"It looks like we have competition." Jax prodded Dominic.

"Nolan's our secret weapon, Jax. We must remember that."

Charly followed Nolan and Sara out the back. Nolan dragged her to the playground, where he insisted she push him on the swing. Unable to resist the little tyke, she spent the next half an hour in his lively company.

"All right, Nolan. Go and play by yourself. Charly and I are going to have some adult time," his mother called out.

But Nolan put up a mighty, determined fight. "But me and Charly are still playing, Mommy."

"You can play again another time."

"We haven't finished."

Charly stared in amazement as Nolan glowered stubbornly at his mother. He crossed his arms and stamped his foot.

That would have earned her a backhand across the face at his age. "Listen, buddy. Let Mom and I chat for a while, and then I'll come back and spend some more time with you, okay?"

"Okay." He raced off, sounding a war cry.

Charly sat down next to Sara, who didn't waste any time. "Are my brother and cousin treating you well?"

Charly knew what Sara was hinting at. "Nothing is going on, Sara. I'm here because you twisted my arm."

Sara smiled. "You saw how much Nolan missed you. I didn't lie."

Just thinking about Nolan had Charly smiling back. "I know, but I have a sneaking suspicion that you're playing matchmaker."

Sara's face turned serious. "I've never seen either act so possessive over a woman, Charly. I'm waiting for you to take a chance on them."

The thought tied Charly's stomach in knots. It was too much. "You need to let me work this out on my own. If I never take that risk, then that's my choice."

Sara put a hand on Charly's arm. "What's the hold-up, Charly?"

Charly contemplated Sara's question. Although Sara was a keen advocate for such an unconventional relationship, not everyone else was.

"I guess not everyone is as supportive as you are about this thing between us." Her eyes glanced towards the closed door where "church" took place.

"That's true. Some of the sweet butts are not happy because you're essentially stealing the two most coveted brothers from their grasping claws," Sara laughed.

Charly didn't think it was all that funny, especially not after spending a morning cleaning nasty graffiti off her apartment door. "I'm aware of that. I already know that Angel and Kyra don't like me."

"They're clinging on to false hope. Jax and Dom never promised them anything other than sex. These women pretend that they don't want anything more, but the reality is that they do. They want to belong. Being the property of a brother gives them status. They would kill to have that prestige."

Although she was becoming more adept at interpreting biker vocabulary, Charly cringed at the word "property" and the idea of someone killing to be that for someone else.

When the church meeting ended, the brothers poured out of the clubhouse. Dominic and Jax swooped in on Charly while Chad joined Sara.

* * * * *

JAX'S PROVOCATIVE SMILE FILLED Charly's vision seconds before he pressed her up against the wall and kissed her. All her nervous energy evaporated when his soft lips landed on hers. Charly pressed even closer, her hands caressing his upper chest before gliding up his back. His erection pumped between her thighs.

One pair of lips was replaced by another when Dominic shoved Jax aside. Dominic took charge like he always did.

"How about we show you how much we like you?" Jax nuzzled her neck.

Charly's head was about to burst; she felt dizzy. Licking her lips nervously, she nodded.

"Words, Charls. Use your words."

"Yes," she managed to say.

"Good."

Dominic rubbed her thigh, making her shiver with excitement. Jax undid the buttons on her blouse. Charly's breathing quickened.

"Cute bra." Jax pulled on her strap, releasing the catch.

Taking her knee, Dominic parted her thighs. Lifting her skirt, he peered underneath. "You're wearing underwear."

Charly released a burst of nervous laughter. "Naturally."

"Take them off."

Charly stood up and removed her top, bra, and underwear. Self-conscious about her belly bulge, she covered it with her hands.

"Move your hands, babe."

Charly shook her head, reluctant to expose herself.

"Charls." Dominic's authoritative tone made her whole body go taut.

"And the skirt, too." Jax carried on as if he hadn't noticed her apprehension.

It was difficult stripping under the searing heat of their watchful gazes.

"Sit down." Dominic patted the space between them.

Swallowing down her anxiety, she did as she was told. Dominic lifted her knee and placed it over his. "Have you ever been touched here?" His hand slid along her inner thigh until it almost reached her moist center.

"I've had sex before."

"Not what I'm asking."

Charly threw her head back and moaned when a finger grazed her clitoris. "Oh!"

The tips of Jax's fingers swept along her collarbone, down through the valley between her breasts, then up underneath one breast to circle her areola, making her nipples stiffen painfully. A few simple touches had her moaning and panting for more.

Her body was instantly bombarded with the most intense sensations when, simultaneously, a finger penetrated her hot center, and a warm mouth closed over a sensitive nipple. Her body was racked with uncontrollable tremors. When another finger was added to her tight pussy and Jax's fingers tweaked her other nipple hard, her body bucked as she experienced her first orgasm.

Charly tried desperately to close her thighs when the pleasure got too much, but Dominic held them open with an iron grip as his fingers thrust inside her, his thumb massaging her swollen nub. Her hand pushed against his wrist unsuccessfully. Moan after moan passed through her lips. Her heart felt like it was jumping out of her skin. The explosion was nothing like she'd ever felt before.

Charly jerked awake in the darkness, the sheets damp with sweat. Her heartbeat ricocheted inside her chest. Her fingers fanned out along the mattress, making sure she was alone in the bed. Dear God. The dream had seemed so real.

✴ ✴ ✴ ✴ ✴

THE FOLLOWING DAY AT work, Charly couldn't get the erotic dream out of her head. It was like the fantasy had planted a seed inside her head. Flashes of naked bodies, whispers of breathless sighs, and the echo of heartbeats thundering inside her chest consumed her mind and body.

She stacked some plates and cutlery and took them into the kitchen.

"Charly, could you take this outside for me?" Joel held several empty boxes in his arms.

"Sure."

Throwing them over the top of the skip, Charly dusted her hands and went back inside. The sudden clanging of pots made her jump. "Get a grip, Charly," she whispered to herself.

At the end of her shift, she was almost out the door when Dominic whistled for her.

"Yo, Charls. My office." He quickly turned around without waiting for her.

Charly didn't know whether to be annoyed or thrilled, but the sudden flush throughout her body tended to sway more toward the latter.

The instant she closed the door, Dominic's expression turned serious. "Listen. Jax and I are going on a run tomorrow. We'll return on Saturday."

"A run?"

Dominic grinned. "It means my brothers and I are taking off for a couple of days to handle business."

"What business is that?"

"Club business. Not your concern."

"Why are you telling me this?"

Dominic arched a brow. "So you don't worry when I'm not here."

"I wouldn't have been worried. I know Rocky is in if you aren't here."

"You playing me?" Her boss did not look happy.

"Did you want me to worry?" she asked innocently.

"I'm telling you, so you *don't* worry."

"Then I won't."

"But if you miss me while I'm gone, I'm fine with that."

Charly was impressed that the all-too-serious man was able to crack a joke.

"Jax and I want you to meet us at the clubhouse when we return."

"Why?" Charly quickly shut her mouth.

"You know why, Charls. We told you how we felt about you." Dominic stepped out from behind his desk.

"And I told you I wasn't interested in a ménage à trois."

Secretly, Charly felt guilty for lying because her dream featured that ménage à trois. Admittedly, she was warming up to the idea but was too embarrassed to say it.

"I'm not sure it's a good idea. I don't want to give either of you the wrong idea."

"I promise it's just a casual get-together. I want to give you time to get used to being around us. Maybe if you get to know us better and we get to know you better, you might change your mind. If you can't handle both of us, I'm happy to see where you and I could go. And if that's something that you still can't do, then I'll accept that. I won't like it, but I'll deal."

Could she trust him when he said he'd accept her answer, even if it were no? Did she want to say no? After last night's dream, she wasn't so sure anymore. She was tempted to touch him right now, but she resisted the temptation only because she wasn't ready for dominant Dominic yet. Add to the mix the sexy allure of Jax, and it was difficult to fathom how she could cope with the pair of them together.

SEVEN

While Dominic and Jax were away, Charly sensed a radical change in Jess. She'd heard through the grapevine that Jess was living with Maxine. At work, the two of them constantly whispered to each other, their heads bent as if conspiring. Each time Charly passed one of them, nasty names were uttered. She got used to hearing *bitch, whore, slut,* and other vile names. Pretending not to hear them, Charly would continue like nothing had been said. Unfortunately, this didn't stop the harassment.

One afternoon, Charly was returning from her lunch break when she ran into Jess coming out of the bathroom. Charly walked past her without acknowledging her, but Jess wasn't having it.

"How are your boyfriends?" she snarled, ugly lines furrowing her pretty features.

"Cut it out, Jess." Charly attempted to get past, but Jess blocked the doorway.

"Listen, bitch. You're the one who chose to open your legs like the whore you are. How does it feel to know you betrayed Max and me? Does it make you feel good, huh?" She turned the door handle and shoved Charly into the bathroom. "That's where you belong, slut. In the sewerage with all the other scum!"

Rattled, Charly stood on trembling legs, staring at the closed door. She hadn't done anything and was already being bullied for it. Charly knew that if she reported Jess to Rocky, he would tear the girl to shreds—none of her employers would ever condone Jess's actions—but she didn't want to antagonize Jess any more than she already had. It's best to keep quiet for now, and if Jess continued to bully her, she would say something.

People thought she was already sleeping with Dom and Jax. Wasn't that part of her problem with the whole situation? What other people thought?

Well, if they already thought she was sleeping with them, and she was going to be taking the heat for sleeping with them, and she wanted to sleep with them… Why the hell wasn't she sleeping with them?

* * * * *

NERVOUSLY WAITING INSIDE THE clubhouse, Charly paced back and forth, watching for Dominic and Jax to return from their run. She twisted her head around when she heard Sara's soft laughter.

"Charly, come and sit down." Sara patted the empty seat beside her. Nolan sat in front of the coffee table, playing with his soldiers and making gunfire sounds. "You're making everyone nervous."

Charly took a seat next to Sara. Watching her new friend with her man and son made Charly want something like that. She wanted to be part of something bigger than just herself, to belong to a place and the people in it. She'd always thought it would be something more normal, like what Sara had with Chad.

What was normal, anyway? Anyone looking in from the outside would have called her mama's relationship with her stepfather normal: one man, one woman, and a couple of kids. No one saw how trapped and terrified her mother had been or how desperate and frightened Charly and Fabien had been.

If that was normal, Charly wanted none of it. Maybe she wasn't destined for normal. Perhaps she should look beyond what the rest of the world deems to be the right thing.

Charly needed to talk with them and let them know she was ready to take a chance on them. However, it was important for her to take things slowly. Dominic and Jax needed to understand that sex was not something she was prepared to rush into.

The rumbling of revving motorcycles grew louder as they drove through the compound's gates.

Waves of nausea rolled around Charly's stomach, and she took deep breaths to push back the queasiness. Charly couldn't take her eyes off either man as they dismounted their bikes and removed their dome helmets. Her shyness took over, so she moved a little closer to Sara.

Sara erupted into laughter at Charly's flustered state.

"Stop laughing," she muttered.

It only made Sara laugh harder. "You've got it bad, girl, don't you?"

The moment the men entered the room, their eyes scanned the area until they landed on her. Charly's anxiety evaporated when Dominic pushed in front of Jax to reach her first.

"Miss me?" Dominic asked, hugging her. "Good," he stated when she nodded.

"You missed me more, didn't you?" Jax cut in, grinning.

"Fuck off, Jax," grumbled Dominic, elbowing his cousin. "She likes me more."

Charly sent Sara a wide-eyed stare at their bickering, but the woman was too busy showing Chad how much she had missed him. Nolan was jumping up and down, his arms stretched upward, demanding his dad carry him.

"Guys!" Charly shouted over their squabbling. "I missed you both equally."

Their jostling stopped. "We know, babe. We're just antsy because we missed you."

As the evening wore on, Charly noticed the odd looks she was receiving from the club women. It reminded her of Jess and Maxine, who thankfully weren't present, although Sara had informed her that they had been frequenting the clubhouse. Charly wondered if Jess and Maxine had put the moves on Jax and Dominic, but they hadn't mentioned anything, and she was too chicken to ask.

* * * * *

CHARLY WAS TALKING TO Sara when she felt someone brush up against her. Looking up, Jax smiled down at her. When he pressed his hand to her lower back, her toes curled.

"Are you okay?" he asked her. Tongue-tied, Charly could only nod.

Jax looked at his sister. "I'm going to steal Charly for a second." Without waiting for her response, he whisked Charly away.

"Hey," Jax said, leaning in close without touching her.

"Hey," Charly echoed.

"You have something you want to tell me? You've been watching me all night."

Heat engulfed Charly. The fact that he'd noticed her staring at him was embarrassing.

"Maybe later," she replied, straining for air.

"Now, I'm curious. Does it have anything to do with what Dom said before our run?" His fierce gaze belied his soft words.

"Yes."

"Are you ready to talk about it? Are you going to give us a chance?"

Charly licked her dry lips, aware of Jax's eyes following the movement. She nodded.

"Words, babe. I need to hear you say it."

"Yes."

"Come with me."

Taking her hand, Jax spotted Dominic, who was watching them. He indicated that his cousin should follow. Charly saw Dominic put his stubby on a nearby table and stalk towards them.

Jax led her out to the front of the clubhouse, where the motorcycles were parked. A prospect stood guarding the front gate. He jerked his chin at Jax, then turned back to keep watch.

Charly's pulse accelerated as Dominic approached them. "What's up?" he asked Jax, although his eyes remained on Charly.

"Charly has something she wants to tell us."

Dominic visibly trembled. "Okay."

They both waited expectantly for her to say something. She wet her lips again. "Um, I've been thinking about what you said, Dom, about getting to know each other better."

"Okay," he repeated.

"And I would like that too. It's just that I don't want to rush anything. I can only do this if we take it slow." Her anxiety was at an all-time high as she waited for their reaction.

"By taking it slow, you mean…" He leaned in, and she caught his musky mixture of leather and mint.

Charly figured Dominic would want her to spell it out for him. She took a deep breath. "Like you said, take the time to learn about each other and see if we have chemistry. I'm not ready for the sexual side of things because, as you know, I'm not very experienced, and I've never had a threesome before."

"Believe me, babe. There's chemistry," Jax declared emphatically.

"We won't rush into sex, but there are plenty of other things we can do."

Dominic stopped speaking. When his words finally sank in, heat flooded her face. She'd thought about a few of those other things over the past few days.

"Speaking for myself, I don't know what this is yet. It's not something I'm used to. How long this will last, I don't know. But I vow to have a conversation if it's not working for me anymore," Dom said. "I won't just walk away."

"Me too," Jax concurred. "I've no fucking clue how this is going to turn out. All I can say is that I'm fucking relieved that you want this, too."

Charly mulled over their words and realized she felt the same way. As new as it was for them, she had no experience with this type of relationship—something more than a one-night stand. Well, she hoped it was more than that. "I agree to your terms, and I promise also to have a conversation with you if I don't want to continue the relationship anymore."

Dominic stiffened. "That's not—" he began.

"Deal," interrupted Jax, sending Dominic a warning glare.

Her eyes collided with two sets of watchful gazes. Thinking they expected her to say something, she said, "Deal."

When they continued staring at her, it suddenly dawned on her that they expected her to perhaps "seal the deal."

Jax hadn't taken his eyes off her mouth, which suddenly felt very dry. Pressing her lips together, she watched in awe as his pupils dilated.

"Do you want to kiss me?" she whispered.

"I would love to kiss you, babe," he rasped.

Jax gradually lowered his head. With no resistance forthcoming, he took her lips in a slow, gentle kiss. Charly's head was spinning as his tongue flicked teasingly inside her mouth. She had no idea who was making those urgent moaning sighs, nor did she have any control over her body's eager response to Jax's sizzling kisses. He eventually pulled back, leaving her feeling dazed, confused, and breathless. That had been one hot kiss!

Charly jerked slightly when Dominic moved in. He didn't rush her, but he made it known what was on his mind. With her consent, his lips swiftly plundered hers, almost as if he'd waited long enough. The kiss was wet, passionate, and impatient—the opposite of Jax's tender kiss. Dominic's kiss rendered her incapacitated, unable to think or move.

Her brain and body had turned to mush. Charly was disappointed when the kiss was over and belatedly realized she hadn't panicked or screamed in horror at making out with not one but two men. Charly didn't feel dirty or used. She felt on top of the world.

* * * * *

JAX AND DOM INSISTED on driving her home, scoffing at the idea of her taking a bus or a ride-share. Charly wasn't surprised when they walked her to her door. Her hands shook as she tried to get the key in the lock.

Jax took the key from her hand and slipped it into the lock, opening the door. Charly's head buzzed with anticipation and attraction. What would happen now? How did this even work?

"Nervous?" Jax asked.

She nodded.

"Don't be, babe. Let us show you how good this can be." He pulled her close and lowered his head to hers for a kiss. It was more demanding than the kiss she'd shared with him before, but it still had a gentleness to it. He teased her tongue with his. He slid his knee between her legs, and she felt the hard length of his erection press against her stomach.

Then he was gone, and Dom was there, taking both her wrists in one of his large hands and holding them against the wall behind her as he plundered her mouth. Charly arched against him, rubbing along the ridge of the bulge in his pants like a cat in heat. Her groin tingled, creating a cascade of goosebumps along her arms.

Then he moved to the side, and both Jax and Dom slid kisses down her neck. "Let us pleasure you, Charly."

Charly's head spun. The room whirled around her, the whole thing permanent, and still, these two men wanted her for some reason.

Dominic slid his hand up between her thighs, rubbing at her pussy through her jeans. She moaned. Jax slid one button after the other on her blouse until it hung open. He traced the outline of her bra over the tops of her breasts, and she whimpered. Jax reached behind her and expertly released the catch.

Her nipples stood at attention in the sudden chill. She wasn't sure what to do. She barely knew how to be with one man. How was she supposed to be with two at once? She had to try. She wanted them to know how much she liked them, too. She reached for the crotch of Dom's jeans, her hand shaking.

Dominic stopped her. "Tonight is about you."

He undid her jeans and slid them down her legs, kneeling before her as she stepped out of them.

Within seconds, she was naked. Her pussy moistened just from having them look at her.

"You're so beautiful," Jax breathed.

The two men exchanged looks and sat on either end of her sofa. Dominic patted the space between them. "Right here, Charls. You need to be right here."

So many emotions rushed through her, but the desire that felt like a fire inside her burned away the fear, anxiety, and embarrassment, leaving only yearning.

She sat between them, the rough material feeling strange against her bare bottom. The men shifted so they were angled towards her. Jax spread her legs, and instinctively, she tried to close them, but he kept a firm grip on her. Dom's hand caressed her inner thigh. "Has anyone ever done this with you before?"

She wasn't innocent. "I'm not a virgin. I've had sex before."

"Not like this," he said confidently. His finger glided across her slit, giving her clit a tingling sensation.

Charly threw her head back and moaned. "So responsive," Dominic murmured, his scorching gaze burned brightly.

Jax cupped her breast, letting his thumb graze along her nipple. She arched her back, wanting more. He lowered his mouth and flicked her nipple with his tongue as a finger slid into her. She gasped.

Dom's finger slid in and out of her as his thumb circled her clit. Jax continued caressing her breasts with his hands and his tongue. Something coiled deep inside her belly, a tension so strong it was nearly painful with the amount of pleasure she felt. She bucked and arched, wanting it to stop and wanting it to never end at the same time.

"Yes, Charly," Jax whispered against her neck. "Yes."

Dom's thumb moved more quickly, the pressure growing and the heat rising. His fingers were deep inside her, finding and caressing a spot inside her she hadn't known about. He knew her body better than she did and knew exactly what would please her.

A shudder shook her body, and she cried out as the tension released. She felt like she was flying, and the room disappeared. Nothing existed except the waves of ecstasy breaking over her again and again and again.

Finally, she came back to earth, still panting from the earth-shattering orgasm. So that's what all the fuss was about.

Dom slid his finger out of her pussy and slowly licked it.

Then, both men stood up. They stopped at the door, and Jax gave her a grin. "G'night, Charly. Sleep well." Then they were gone.

It wasn't until Charly was climbing alone into her bed that she realized how close their actions had hewed to the erotic dream she'd had of the three of them.

It was like they knew her fantasies without her ever telling them.

$$* * * * *$$

THE FOLLOWING DAY, CHARLY was running late. Sprinting across the street, she glanced at her watch. She had two minutes before the bus arrived.

"Dammit!" It was all Dominic and Jax's fault for keeping her up so late last night. Charly felt lightheaded at the memory.

When she finally reached the restaurant, Maxine's eyes flared with hostility, and Jess's gleamed with malice when Charly stepped through the doors. Last week, one of them had emptied all the condiment bowls after she'd refilled them, and Rocky had growled at her when he noticed her section hadn't been done. Today, they were up to something; Charly felt it in her gut. She'd have to keep a close eye on her station today.

"Hey, Charly." Con was in a jovial mood this morning. Being a chef, he could be cranky at times, but he had a soft spot for Charly, and she'd learned not to take his outbursts personally.

"Morning, Con. Need any help?"

"Nope." He went back to banging pots and pans.

She bumped into Joel. "Can you take this outside?" he asked, handing her a trash bag.

After depositing the bag in the bin, Charly headed back inside. When she reached the top step, the door to the staffroom slammed shut. She tried to open it, but it was locked. She knocked on the door to get someone's attention, but nobody came. She knocked harder. She peered into the window and saw that the room was empty. Charly realized she'd have to go through the side gate and enter through the front door.

It was just her luck that the gate had a padlock on it. She took a step back to judge whether she could climb over or not. It might be possible. Placing a shoe on the fence railing to gain some leverage, she pulled herself up and over. There was nothing to soften her fall, but she jumped anyway.

Charly landed on all fours. She winced as the concrete scraped her hands and knees. She'd have to find the first-aid kit to clean herself up. After dusting herself off, she was heading to the front door when her knee gave out. She must have landed too hard on it. Limping inside, she went to the office to find Rocky.

"Fuck's sake," he muttered when she hobbled into his office. "What the heck happened to you?"

"Long story, boss."

"Let's hear it." He got up to retrieve the first-aid kit from the top drawer of the filing cabinet.

"I was taking out a trash bag when the door slammed shut. I tried to open it, but it was locked. I knocked several times, but no one answered. So, I went around the side gate. That was locked, too. I had to climb over it. I jumped and scraped my hands and knees."

"You're limping." He frowned.

"Must have landed wrong."

"Sit." Rocky was usually an easy-going bloke who liked to regale the staff with stories of his derring-do. Right about now, she expected to hear one of his stories that outdid her accident, but he was discernibly quiet.

While he meticulously cleansed and applied an antiseptic spray and bandages, Charly saw he had something on his mind.

"Okay, I'm calling Dom." Rocky picked up the landline and began dialing.

Charly immediately stalled him. "Rocky, you don't need to call Dom. A door blew shut. What's there to tell him?"

"We both know the door didn't just blow shut." Rocky leveled a look at her. "Have to make the call, Charly. Dom will have my hide if I don't."

Charly grabbed his wrist to prevent him from calling Dominic. "Rocky! No. I'm okay. You can't call Dom because I have a scraped knee."

Rocky wasn't having it. Charly sighed dramatically when the call went through. Rocky spoke to Dominic for a few minutes, then hung up. "He's on his way."

Raising her hands in exasperation, Charly shuffled back into the restaurant. She unlocked the cabinets and placed the condiment packets on her tray, ready to refill the bowls. When she heard the front door open, she quickly refilled the bowls at each table.

Dominic and Jax appeared, displeasure and concern—respectively—on their faces.

"I'm okay," she said. "I told Rocky not to call you. It's a scraped knee, nothing more."

"Office. Now." Dominic's tone of voice brooked no argument.

They met Rocky in the office, each giving a chin lift in greeting. Then, they made her recount the incident again.

"Who fucking locked the door? It's never locked during work hours." Dominic pinned Rocky with a stern glare.

"I don't know," Charly intervened, not wanting Dominic to blame Rocky for something that wasn't his fault. "I couldn't see anyone in the staffroom. I'm sure it was an accident."

"I'll go talk to Con." Jax left the office.

Dom turned to her. "You're not working today, Charls. I'll drive you home."

Now, that would be disastrous. She had bills to pay. "Why can't I work?"

"You're injured." He glanced at her leg as if it were self-explanatory.

"I'm hurt, yes. Incapacitated? No. Would you be saying the same thing if Maxine was hurt?" This was ridiculous.

Dom snorted. "Maxine wouldn't be jumping a gate. She's not that adventurous."

"Funny," she replied sarcastically.

Jax came back into the office. "Neither Con nor Joel locked the door. It must have been one of the servers."

Dominic and Jax exchanged looks. Charly knew what they were thinking because she was thinking the same thing. The girls were on some campaign to sabotage her job or make her life miserable—or both.

"I'm having a word with them." Dominic's anger was apparent.

"Let me deal with them." Charly had to make it clear that she could fight her own battles. Having Dom step in would only make the harassment worse.

"You think you have a say in this?" Dominic scowled, daring her to disagree.

Charly knew when a battle was lost. Her hand swooped in an inviting gesture. "Be my guest then."

While Dominic searched for the girls to give them severe tongue-lashings for their underhanded actions, Jax drove Charly home.

After checking that aliens hadn't invaded her apartment during her brief absence, he gathered her in his arms.

"I would love to stay, but duty calls," Jax said.

"What do you do when you're not at the restaurant?" The question had been brewing in Charly's mind for a while. She had no idea what either of them did when they weren't at the bar and grill.

"I work at the garage."

Charly's finger traced the letters on the front of his leather vest. "What's a sergeant at arms?"

"I bring order to church meetings. I'm in charge of security and protecting Dom and Achilles." He explained patiently, covering her fingers with his hand.

"What about Dom? What is he?"

"Vice president."

"Really?" Charly hadn't realized he held such a high position within the club. "It makes sense."

Charly wanted to know something else, but she wasn't sure if Jax would tell her. She brought it up anyway since he was in a mellow mood.

"Do you have anything to do with drugs or guns?" She'd searched online for information about bikers and had been disturbed by the fact that many clubs made profits from gunrunning and drug trafficking. It was such a violent and unsavory world.

Jax sat up and sighed. "We used to, but Kill ended that a while back. We only deal with legit businesses now."

"What kind of businesses?"

"You know about the restaurant and the garage. We also have several bars, a tattoo shop, a strip club, and a shopping mall."

Charly stared at him, speechless. "A shopping mall?"

She knew some of the club women worked at the strip club, which bothered her, but she didn't say anything. She was grateful that Jax had confided in her and that everything appeared above board.

Jax didn't leave without getting his reward for bringing her home. Her lips tingled after their hot kiss.

"Tell Dom I'll be back at work tomorrow," she told Jax, then firmly closed the door before he could object.

* * * * *

JESS WAS SHAKING WITH fury. Dominic had just finished his tirade, reprimanding her and Maxine over their malicious prank on Charly and threatening them with their jobs. While Maxine had crumbled into a heap of loud wails, Jess silently seethed as he defended the bitch.

Then it was Con's turn. With steam coming out of her ears and nostrils, Jess switched off, seeing only his moving lips, waving hand, and fierce expression. Rage erupted inside her. The men were always protecting Charly. Charly this. Charly that. They thought she could do no wrong.

Jess would make sure Charly paid for the preferential treatment bestowed upon her. The bitch had only worked at the restaurant for a short time, while Jess had several years under her belt. She'd strived to earn Dom and Jax's approval many times over, working overtime and switching shifts so they weren't short of staff, never giving them any hassle. Despite this, they'd never acknowledged her as more than an employee.

Then Charly comes along, and suddenly, the men can't do enough for her. Jess boiled with jealousy. It was unfair!

* * * * *

CHARLY WAS UNSURE WHAT her return to work would be like now that Dominic had spoken to Jess and Maxine. She tried calling him on her new phone last night, but it went straight to voicemail. She'd left a voice message for him to call her, but he hadn't returned her call.

When she called Sara, her friend informed her they'd left on an emergency run last night. Nobody had told her! A text message would have been nice.

They wouldn't be back until Sunday, but Charly wouldn't call or text again because she wasn't going to be one of those clingy women. This relationship was new, and things were going well, so Charly didn't intend to start complaining now. She had to remember that this was different for them as well. When they returned, she'd ask them to send a quick text next time. Easy. After all, Dom had let her know when they were leaving on their last run.

That didn't stop Charly from missing them; the days dragged on. There were no more incidents at work. Dominic must have put the girls in their places. She still got the death glare, but other than that, they left her alone.

Charly caught up with Sara and Carrie. She learned that Carrie had been Bolt's property. Although the young woman didn't go into detail, Charly could surmise the level of abuse she'd experienced. She revealed that she had initially belonged to another club but was "sold" to Bolt when they couldn't repay a debt.

It alarmed Charly to think this kind of exploitation happened inside the clubs. She was confident that Dominic and Jax wouldn't participate in that activity. Their reaction alone to Carrie's abuse told her that. Besides, after Jax shared the details about the MC only dealing with legitimate businesses, it seemed far-fetched that they would exploit young women.

Charly was stirring the spaghetti in her kitchen when her ringtone went off. Her pulse quickened when she saw Dominic's name come up.

"Hey, Dom." Charly couldn't keep the smile off her face.

"Charls. Let's FaceTime."

"Huh?"

"Video chat. Pull up your FaceTime app. I want to see you." Dominic sounded cranky.

Charly stared at the phone, baffled. "You're speaking a foreign language, Dom. I have no idea how to do that."

His impatient growl made her smile. "I'm putting you on speakerphone so Jax can join the conversation."

"Hey, babe. Miss me?" Jax was the polar opposite of his cousin. He sounded cheerful.

"Not really," she lied playfully.

"Bullshit. You miss me. Listen, babe. Why can't you do Face-Time? Everyone knows how to video chat."

"I didn't have a lot growing up. Technology wasn't something I had access to, and even now, I couldn't afford this phone you gave me for my birthday if you weren't paying for it."

"But no young person can live without their phone. It's practically glued to their hands," Jax protested.

"That's them, Jax. Not me. I was shuffled from foster home to foster home. It wasn't unusual for me to arrive at a new home with nothing and leave the same way." She'd be grateful if she had a trash bag full of a few clothes and a toothbrush most of the time.

The silence on the other end grew awkward. They wanted to get to know her better. Well, this was her past. It wasn't pretty, and she wouldn't sugarcoat it, either. Charly decided to change the subject.

"You left without giving me a heads-up." She figured this was a good time to bring the topic up.

"Emergency run, Charls. Did Sara tell you?" Dom said.

Fair enough. "Yes."

"How have the others been treating you?" Dom asked.

"No problem. They've backed off. What did you say to them?" She turned the heat off under the spaghetti sauce so it wouldn't splatter.

"I told them they'd be gone if they didn't leave you alone."

Yep. That was Dominic. There was no pussyfooting around. "It worked."

"Tell us next time they do anything. Don't keep it to yourself. We know you're a warrior princess, but let us handle this. You're under our protection now." Jax all but pounded his chest.

Jax was sweet, but Charly could defend herself. "I'll tell you if it becomes an issue." She would only agree to their demands if it were something she couldn't handle alone.

"No, you'll tell us if they do or say *anything*," Dominic stated firmly.

"What? If they call me a bitch, I have to tell you?" she laughed.

"Yes." Dom wasn't joking around.

Charly was thankful Dominic couldn't see her eye roll. "That seems a bit petty. I've been called worse names. I can deal with a bad name or two."

"Stop. Arguing."

Okay. There was that dominant streak again. "I thought we were having a nice conversation."

"We are. Now shut up," he replied softly.

She couldn't help it. She giggled.

After the initial call, one or both of them called every night. Charly forced herself to concentrate all day at work but couldn't stop thinking about Dominic and Jax, anticipating their calls. They would talk for ages, although Charly found herself mainly talking about *her* day. The guys said little about what they were doing; she only got bits and pieces. If they considered having a relationship with her, they'd also have to share things about themselves.

Sunday night eventually rolled around. Dominic had told Charly to be at the clubhouse waiting for them, where the women had organized a picnic dinner outside. The tables were loaded with enough food to feed several armies.

Angel and Kyra were at the clubhouse, and so were Jess and Maxine. They were all looking at Charly oddly as if they knew something she didn't. Their secret smiles began to niggle at her, but she managed to hold her tongue.

Charly stood with Sara, Nolan, and Carrie. Chad had also gone on the run, and Nolan was running around like a dog chasing its tail, excited to see his dad. Charly knew how he felt. She was excited to see her men.

Several things had dawned on her in the past few days. First, she had to get used to Dominic and Jax being on the road often. Second, she was getting attached to them. Somehow, she had to figure out how to pull back because this situation was supposed to be short-term—only until it ran out of steam. To her, it felt like their relationship was *picking up* steam.

Charly wanted to run screaming to her lovers when they walked in the door. Instead, she stayed at the bar as they prowled towards her. Dominic tugged her t-shirt, causing her to topple off the stool and into his arms. He kissed her greedily, sucking up all the air in her lungs. When he was finished, Jax took over. By the end, she was dizzy with arousal.

"Hi," she croaked, licking her lips.

Charly refused to look in the direction of her rivals, but she felt the chilliness of their stares from across the room.

"Let's get a room." Jax gently pushed her.

"Hold on, guys," she laughed. "Dinner is set up outside. Aren't you hungry?"

"Starving. For you. Let's go." Jax was the impatient one as he dragged her out of the room.

Inside the bedroom, Dominic ordered her to lie down.

"Dom," Charly began hyperventilating, knowing what usually happened in these bedrooms. She wasn't ready for all that—not yet.

"We're not going to do anything you're uncomfortable doing, Charls. I've missed you and want to spend time with you."

He reached out a hand, and Charly slowly took it. Dominic pressed her against his side, brushing loose strands of hair away from her face. He peppered soft, sweet kisses down her cheeks, touching the tip of her nose and landing on her mouth, where he used his tongue to delve inside.

Charly relaxed as he kissed her, his hands staying above her shoulders. Heat warmed her back as Jax positioned himself behind her. She shivered when Jax's fingers trailed down her arms to encircle her waist.

Neither man pushed for more, merely showering her with light kisses and touches. After a while, it was Charly who wanted more. She was aroused. Her nipples were hard and tender, and her pussy throbbed, begging for their touch.

Charly grabbed both of their wrists, one in each hand.

Behind her, Charly felt Jax stiffen. "Babe?"

"I want more," she gasped.

"Fuck!" Jax automatically burrowed his hand under her top and unclipped her bra, releasing her aching breasts.

"Lie back," Dominic commanded.

Charly did so without hesitation, quickly removing her top and bra. She was breathing heavily as if she'd run a marathon. The cold air made her nipples pucker.

Jax latched onto one nipple, and Charly let out a whoosh of air at the pleasurable sensation. Dominic pinched and pulled on her other nipple, startling her. His hand covered her breast, soothing the pain away.

"Charls?" His hand deliberately began to drift southward, stopping at the waistband of her skirt.

Charly read his silent request. "Yes!" she panted, raising her hips to coax him further.

Dominic dipped his head to claim her lips at the same time as his hand tunneled under her waistband and slid inside her underwear. His mouth caught her moan as he pressed down on her clitoris and flicked it several times. Charly's body convulsed as blood pooled at her most intimate core. Just as she thought she was about to explode, his fingers traveled lower and sank inside her wet channel. Dominic started with one finger, then added another and plunged deep.

Charly couldn't hold back the whimpers. Jax got up on his knees and undid the zipper on her skirt, and it fell onto the floor in a puddle. Her underwear soon followed.

"You're sure you're ready for more?" Jax asked.

"Yes. Please." Her voice sounded odd to her ears—breathy and desperate.

He positioned himself between her legs. Dom moved his hand away and slid behind her so she leaned with her back against his chest, his hands circling to play with her breasts. Now, it was Jax's finger, finding its way inside her. Then, pressing gently with his thumbs, he opened her like a flower. For a second, everything froze. Nothing moved. Charly almost couldn't breathe.

Then Jax's tongue touched her clit.

She put her hand over her mouth to stifle her moan of pleasure. His tongue swirled, teasing and touching, finding the exact way that would make Charly moan even louder.

Then he began to move faster, his tongue lashing her, then stopping to suck in her swollen bud, and then back to tonguing her again. She thought what Dom had done to her with his fingers was the best she could ever feel. Now she knew better. She also knew what was in store if she gave herself over to it.

So, she did.

Her body seized with a series of powerful orgasms. Each time she thought she was done, Jax would start up again, and the waves would break over her again.

Charly gradually opened her eyes and stared at the men, reality hitting her in the face.

"Now," she said. "I want to please you."

EIGHT

The following month flew by, and Charly often pinched herself to check that it was all real. She had yet to discover what these two bikers saw in her, but that didn't mean she would pass up on what they were offering. Nearly every night was filled with their touch and their tongues. At first, she'd been concerned that she wouldn't be able to please them in the way they pleased her. Fortunately, she had two highly experienced lovers who were patient and forthright. They didn't hesitate to tell her exactly what they liked and expected the same from her.

Although sometimes it seemed that they knew what she wanted before she did.

Charly knew that one day, when all this came tumbling down around her, these moments would stay with her for the rest of her life, so she gloried in them, trying to push all her worries to the back of her mind.

Growing up with a controlling stepdad and a feeble mother who was incapable of protecting her children, Charly learned early on how to defend herself. She adamantly refused to end up like her weak mother. From a young age, the one rule ingrained in her was, "Don't get too attached. Relationships make you vulnerable, weak, and open to being emotionally and physically hurt." Her mama had taught her that by example.

Charly was on the verge of breaking that one vital rule. It was sinking in that she needed to maintain some independence. The men were so much—so good-looking, such good lovers, so magnetic—that breaking free of their orbit was difficult.

Except, of course, when they were on the road.

Luckily, she'd figured out how to use FaceTime on her phone, and phone sex had taken their relationship to a whole new level.

But not at the ultimate level yet. They hadn't had full-on sexual intercourse yet, and each time they left, Charly ached for them to return. It was time to take their relationship to the next level. They had been gone for ten whole days. They were due back the day after tomorrow.

The bus pulled up outside the clubhouse gates. Charly was going for her weekly visit with Sara and Nolan. Sara worked in the office attached to the garage, so it was easier to get together at the clubhouse.

"Hey, chickie." Sara walked out of the tiny office, locking the door behind her.

"Hi, Sara." Charly bent down as Nolan ran from the playground. "Hey, buddy." Catching him in her outstretched arms, she gave him a big squeeze. "Mmm. You smell good enough to eat."

He wriggled out of her arms. "You can't eat me!" he screamed excitedly and ran back to the playground.

Sara looped her arm through Charly's. "Let's get a drink." Sara uncapped two bottles of Wild Turkey. "Cheers."

"Have you heard from Chad?"

"Yeah," Sara sighed. "Home on Sunday. What about you? Heard from Dom and Jax?"

"We talk most nights." Charly wasn't going to share what else they did. Their sexual life was private.

"What's that smile about?" Sara elbowed her gently in the side as if she knew exactly what the smile was for.

Something caught Charly's attention, and she looked over Sara's shoulder to see Angel enter the clubhouse. What surprised her was that the girl was approaching her—usually, they avoided each other.

Then another figure appeared: Jess. She looked pretty pleased with herself. Something was brewing; Charly could sense it.

"What do you want, Angel?" It was reassuring to know Sara disliked the woman as much as she did. But Angel hadn't taken her eyes off Charly. "What?"

Angel smirked. "You've got no idea, have you?"

"No idea about what?"

"Angel." Charly heard the warning in Sara's tone and glanced at her. What was going on?

"You think you're so important because Jax and Dom are fucking you, but you're not. You're a whore, just like the rest of us."

"What the hell?" Charly was flabbergasted. She had an awful feeling that she wouldn't like what Angel had to say. What else could explain her behavior?

Angel produced her iPhone and tapped on it. "Here. Watch this."

Sara tried unsuccessfully to snatch the phone out of her hand. "Angel. Stop it!"

Holding her breath, Charly watched the video, her stomach lurching at what she saw.

It showed four bodies lying on a bed. A female looked up in the camera's direction and licked her lips seductively. When she pulled back the covers, Charly spotted Jax, another female, and Dominic, all fast asleep. The first woman leaned over Jax and sucked his cock. He stirred, raising his arm over his eyes. It was then that Charly saw the tattoo on the inside of his wrist: the letters WP. *Warrior Princess.*

Jax surprised her about a month ago by revealing his new tattoo. It had meant the world to her at the time, but looking at it now, she felt like vomiting. It had meant nothing to him.

Charly couldn't peel her eyes away from the sickening video.

"Not so superior now, are we?" Jess sneered.

Charly ran into the bathroom. Sara followed her, trying to comfort her, but Charly didn't want to hear it.

"Please go away, Sara," she pleaded. "I need to be alone for a while."

Sitting on the toilet, Charly dropped her head in her hands. Her face felt hot and sweaty. Taking deep, quivering breaths to calm herself down, her body shook with gut-wrenching sobs.

Splashing water on her face, Charly stared at her reflection in the mirror. So, this was what the end felt like? Well, okay. She could deal with that. It hurt, but she'd get past it—like always. Straightening her shoulders, she exited the bathroom and collected her handbag.

"Charly. Let's talk about it. Give the guys a chance to explain." Sara hurried after her.

Sara thought they could explain their way out of this?

"Explain what, Sara? Didn't you see what I saw? I'm going home. And tell Dom I'm giving my two weeks' notice."

"Gage!" The prospect looked up when Sara called his name. He immediately stepped in front of Charly to prevent her from leaving.

"I can't let you leave while you're upset, Charly." He stood in the doorway, blocking her exit.

"Gage, I'm okay. I'm a little rattled, but I've calmed down." Charly tried to get past him but couldn't. "Gage! Let me pass!" She felt so frustrated and hurt. Why couldn't they give her some space to breathe?

Dodging first to the left and then taking a quick right, she managed to slip past Gage. Thankfully, the front gates were open, so she ran across the road to the bus stop.

* * * * *

OBSERVING THE CONFRONTATION FROM the sidelines, Jess cheered as a horrified look came over Charly's face. Phase Two was almost complete: get rid of the competition so the seduction of Dominic and Jax could begin.

Once Charly was gone, Dominic and Jax would need some comfort. Who better to turn to than someone willing and available to fall into their bed?

Angel had screamed and cried when she heard what happened during the club's last trip to the Bridgetown chapter. Eager to rub it in, Meghan sent the video to Angel. Angel and Meghan had been friends until their falling out, and Angel had left the Bridgetown area. After Angel's little hissy fit, Jess knew how to use the situation to her advantage. She casually mentioned the sex tape to Kyra, and this sparked jealousy from the self-centered woman when she eventually saw the video for herself. Both Kyra and Angel hated Charly as much as Jess did, so when Kyra suggested showing the video to Charly, Jess knew her plan had worked. It had been so easy, she thought contemptuously as Charly ran out of the clubhouse.

✶ ✶ ✶ ✶ ✶

ARRIVING AT HER APARTMENT, Charly dropped her keys and bag and flopped onto the bed. Her phone had been ringing nonstop since she left the clubhouse. Ignoring the calls, she turned it off and let her head sink into the pillow.

Charly didn't know if minutes or hours had passed when her eyes flickered open. The room was in darkness, so she guessed maybe several hours. Dragging herself out of bed, she plopped down onto the couch.

Unable to stop herself, she switched her phone back on and saw eighteen missed calls. She jumped when her ringtone buzzed: Jax.

She answered the call, thinking it was better to finish it now than in person.

"Yes?"

"Babe. Thank God! We've been trying to call you all night. Where are you? Are you okay?"

"I'm at home. I'm fine."

"Charls," Dominic said softly.

"What?"

"We heard."

Charly was disappointed when he didn't elaborate further.

"Are you going to give us a chance to explain?"

"Go ahead."

There was a long pause—probably to give them time to spin some sorry tale. "It meant nothing."

That was it? That was Dominic's excuse?

Charly scoffed. "I'm sure it didn't." Had she meant anything to them?

"These women mean nothing to us, babe. They're just pussies available for sexual release. Nothing more." Jax was doing a terrible job of making her feel better.

"And I'm sure you meant nothing to them, either."

"Cut the sarcasm, Charls. It isn't you," Dom sighed.

"Don't tell me what to do!" she spat.

"Let it out, then. Tell us how you feel. We'll listen, no matter how angry you are."

Charly could rant, rave, and get all her anger out, but she wouldn't. No. This had to end. An image of her mama flashed inside her head. There was no way she was going to end up like her. No way was she going to get into the cycle of taking abuse, having the man apologize for it, taking him back, and starting it all over again. Charly had more self-respect than that.

"I thought we were exclusive," she said evenly.

"We are."

Charly coughed incredulously. "Exclusive means none of us fucks anyone else, Dom."

"I know what it means, Charls, but I think it means something different to you."

"What's that supposed to mean?"

"We care about you. We messed up, and I get that. But you have full access to our bodies. Anytime. Anywhere. The whores only get what we choose to give them. And that's not much. To us, that's exclusivity."

Charly listened to Dominic's words with despair. "I see. Well, it was a tough lesson for me to learn, but thanks for the clarification. I've finally got it."

"Have you?"

"Sure. And I think it's only fair that I let you know I'm done at this juncture." She couldn't live like that. No way.

"Hold on a sec. This is not over. We're just ironing out the wrinkles. Nobody said it's over." Jax's charm wouldn't work on her this time.

"I just did. And I meant it, too. I don't want this anymore."

"*We're* not done. This *isn't* over. We'll be back on Sunday. We'll talk about it face-to-face then."

"You guys don't have a say in this. It's my decision. We're obviously on different pages. That's okay. These things happen." She was so full of shit. Her heart was breaking into a million pieces while she spewed forth lies like it didn't bother her.

"Stop fucking saying that. You're pissing me off."

Charly was selfishly pleased. Dominic deserved to feel what she felt.

"Have you forgotten the video I saw? In *my* world, that's called betrayal. It's a moral crime. I don't trust easily, nor do I forgive easily. And I don't forgive what you did to me. I spent the first half of my life watching my mama get beaten down by my stepfather's constant abuse to take him back over and over. I promised myself I wouldn't follow in her footsteps because it eventually led to her drug addiction and her death, and I'm not repeating that."

Charly had just revealed what no other human being knew—a secret she'd kept to herself until now.

As the following silence dragged on, Charly wondered if they'd hung up on her.

"Charls," Dominic said eventually. Charly heard several different emotions color that one word: pity, sadness, regret, and compassion.

"I'm not looking for sympathy. I'm just letting you know where I stand. I don't trust you two anymore. But I get that this is your lifestyle, so I promise you there are no hard feelings. I want to get on with my life." What was so difficult for them to understand?

"Babe, you forget we're venturing into unknown territory with you. We've never wanted a serious relationship with a woman. This is new for us. That means we'll make mistakes. This is the first time you've expressed your feelings to us, Charly. It isn't fair that you shut us out because we did one thing wrong. We're willing to work on it, so why can't you?"

"I have a question. Will you be honest with me?"

"Yes."

Charly grimaced at Jax's immediate response. "Even if it isn't good?"

"Yeah." This time, Jax didn't sound so confident.

"Okay. Is this the first time you have cheated on me?" Charly's shoulders sagged when he took too long to answer. She swallowed down her dismay. "That sucks. I was loyal to you the whole time."

"We're sorry, Charly. But now that we know your boundaries, we're willing to work on them," Jax said.

"Too late, Jax. From Sara's reaction today, she knew what you were doing. I'm sure many of the others did as well. It's mortifying to think how stupid I was. Not only did you cheat on me, you humiliated me."

"You're not fucking stupid. Don't say that. We're the idiots. Please give us a chance." Dominic's pleading wouldn't make Charly change her mind. She was emotionally drained and didn't want to talk about it anymore.

"Look, I'm tired. I've said my piece. Goodbye."

＊＊＊＊＊

ON SUNDAY NIGHT, THE men of the Iconic Sons MC cruised through the clubhouse gates, their engines splintering the quiet peace of the grounds.

Dominic stomped into the front room, anger emanating from every pore. He was on the hunt for one particular troublemaker.

"Where the fuck is Angel?" Dominic growled at Gage.

Gage put down his beer and gestured behind him. Everyone stepped out of their way as Dominic and Jax charged into the back room. They were livid.

Angel was talking to Kyra. She blanched, her eyes widening when she saw the expressions on Jax's and Dominic's faces.

"Get up!" Dominic grabbed her elbow. "Come with us."

"Dom, please!" Her plea went unheard. He was too enraged to listen as he marched her down the steps to the basement.

"I'm sorry!" she cried.

Dominic got in her face. "Why the fuck did you show Charly the video?"

Angel flinched. Tears glistened but didn't fall. "I'm sorry. It was Kyra's idea."

He ignored her attempts to play the blame game. "Who sent you the video?"

"Meghan."

Dominic heard Jax swear. He recalled that she was the faceless whore he and Jax had woken up next to on their recent visit to Bridgetown after a night of partying.

"Why did you show it to Charly?"

"Because *she* gets all your attention. It's not fair to the rest of us!" Her screeching irritated the hell out of Dominic.

"You fucking jealous whore!" He was seething. "Show us the video."

He watched the five-minute video with increasing rage. Charly had every reason to be upset.

Dominic glared at Angel with disgust. "You get out," he snarled. "You're not welcome here anymore. I see your face here again; you won't like the consequences. This is your only warning."

Angel's body shook with her loud sobs, but her begging did no good. He was past the point of forgiveness.

After Angel had gone, Dominic and Jax sat at the bar, downing beers. Neither felt like talking. Sara approached them cautiously.

"Another beer?" At their silent nod, she uncapped two more bottles. "I have something to tell you, but before I do, can I ask that you don't shoot the messenger?"

Dominic's fierce gaze zoned in on Sara. "What?" he barked impatiently, at the end of his rope.

"Charly's giving her two weeks' notice."

"Fuck! She can't quit," growled Jax.

"You still have time to change her mind. Make her see reason," Sara suggested.

"She's already made up her mind, and it'll only make her more determined if we intervene. Charly's stubborn." Dominic hated feeling hopeless; it wasn't his nature to give in so easily.

"Sounds like someone else I know." Sara looked at her cousin. "But you *can* still win her back, you know. Charly's hurt right now, so I don't suggest you go in all gung-ho. Wait a week or so, then start gaining her trust again. I think that's your biggest hurdle."

Dominic agreed. To Charly, trust was everything, and they'd broken it. "What do you suggest? How the fuck do we earn back her trust?"

"Look, I don't think she fully trusted you. It's in her nature to be cautious. She hinted at something once, but I didn't think much of it then. Looking back, I see it now."

"What did she say?" Jax asked.

"We were talking about our families. She mentioned that she *had* a mother and a brother. Past tense. I didn't make the connection at the time."

"Yeah. And we've heard about her stepfather, too," Jax spat, clenching his teeth.

"You still haven't told us how to win her back," Dominic said impatiently.

"Woo her." Sara chuckled at the looks on their faces.

"How the fuck do you woo someone?"

Sara laughed at her brother.

"I don't know. Be spontaneous." Grinning at their incredulous expressions, she elaborated. "Find opportunities to talk to her in a *non-threatening* way." Sara eyed her cousin. "Does she need a lift home? Things like that."

"We can do that," Jax acceded readily. "What else?"

"Be honest and upfront with her. You broke her trust by sleeping around. Give celibacy a try. That would go a long way to gaining her trust."

Dominic kicked himself. The thrill of having sex with whores had long since faded, but he still fucked women out of habit. Having sex with Charly had taken on a whole new meaning for him. He saw her as a person, not just a warm body. He loved everything about her—her laughter, innocence, and feistiness. He loved making her gasp with unexpected pleasure when he did something that had never been done to her before. Charly gave him all the things he wanted and needed to feel like a fucking superhero.

"Anything else?" Dominic was prepared to do anything.

"One more thing. What does she like to do?" Sara asked.

Dominic drew a blank.

Gun coughed behind them. "Sorry. I couldn't help overhearing."

"What?" Dominic eyed him warily.

"Your girl's got pipes. I went to a karaoke bar the night Sol attacked the girls. You might want to check the place out. From how everyone seemed to know her, I suspect she's a regular." Dominic and Jax stared at Gun like he'd grown a second head.

"A karaoke bar?" Dom repeated.

"Oh yeah. She was pretty popular, too. People were banging on the tables, demanding she do an encore. True story."

Jax beamed from ear to ear. "Let's go get our girl back."

"What's the name of the karaoke bar?" asked Dominic. "Although we've got to deal with Kyra first."

Jumping up, Jax followed him. Kyra's face paled when she saw his expression.

"Where's Angel?" she asked, looking around.

"Gone. And you will be, too," Dominic threatened.

"Wait!" Kyra's hand was visibly shaking. "What do you mean, *gone?*"

"She's not welcome back here," Jax spat angrily.

"What's this about?"

That did it. Dominic blew his lid. He couldn't stand listening to her lies anymore. "You know what the fuck this is about! The video. Angel said it was your idea."

"That bitch!" she screamed. "It wasn't me. It was *her* idea."

"Listen, whore. We don't give a fuck whose idea it was. You're both scheming, jealous bitches, and you're both out of here."

"Dom! Wait!" Kyra paused. "I'm pregnant," she blurted out.

"So?" Dominic surmised this was just another ploy to escape trouble.

"It's yours."

The room was silent.

Dom found it hard to accept that Kyra would go to such lengths. "You manipulative bitch! Get out of here. Now!"

"It's true, Dom. The baby's yours." Her words tumbled out in a rush. "The night we fucked in the courtyard at the restaurant, the condom broke. I found semen in my underwear."

No. No way. "You're lying. I would have known if the condom broke."

"Did you check it before tossing it in the bin?" She stood up straighter now.

Fine. Maybe the condom did break. "Doesn't mean the baby's mine. How many brothers have you fucked? All of them?"

"I used a condom every time," Kyra argued, her eyes imploring him to believe her.

"Bullshit! If a brother doesn't want to use a condom, he won't." He'd made similar demands in the past.

"I'm telling the truth, Dom. I'm a hundred percent sure that the baby's yours."

Dominic dragged a hand over his face. "Fuck." Although he was still convinced that she was lying, he had to take action now if there was a chance it was his baby. "How far gone are you? How soon can you get an abortion?"

"Twelve weeks. It's too late."

Dominic calculated the time, counting backward. He and Jax had started their relationship with Charly just over two months ago, so it was possible that the timing was correct. Fuck and double fuck.

$$\ast\ \ast\ \ast\ \ast\ \ast$$

THE NEXT MORNING, DOMINIC called Rocky to see if Charly had turned up for work. After Rocky had confirmed that she was there, Dominic brought him up to speed about her resignation.

"Damn. She's a good employee. Smart. Reliable. Hardworking." He paused. "That came out of left field. What happened?"

Dominic reluctantly confessed.

"Shit, bro. Is it serious between you guys or what?" Rocky asked.

"I wasn't ready to call it quits yet," he admitted.

"Longest I've known you to be with just one woman," Rocky observed.

Dom was well aware of that. "How is she?"

"She seemed fine. I wouldn't know she was upset if you hadn't said anything."

"Charls can be resolute when she needs to be." Dominic could only assume that the wall she had built around herself was a defense mechanism—perhaps conditioning from years of abuse. The thought angered him.

"I'll be in before she leaves. Check on her." After a moment of silence, he added, "Discretion."

Rocky concurred. "Gotcha."

✱ ✱ ✱ ✱ ✱

WORD HAD SPREAD AROUND the restaurant, and the triumphant looks she was getting from Jess and Maxine were doing Charly's head in. She just had to focus on doing her job and get out of there. Two more weeks, and she'd be gone, leaving all this emotional crap behind.

Unable to sleep the previous night, she'd mentally made a list of all the reasons why it was a good thing it was over. She'd found plenty of them. Now, all she had to do was *believe* them and move on. One of the reasons at the top of her list was that she wouldn't have to deal with jealous women. Everywhere she turned, someone wanted to hurt her and make her life miserable, and she was fed up with it.

Charly kept an eye out for any trouble. The girls might be thrilled that she was leaving, but that didn't necessarily mean they would stop bullying her. Their hatred seemed to run very deep. She had had what they desperately wanted: to be Dominic and Jax's number one woman. Not that she'd been their number one; she'd been one of many. And everyone had known that except her.

The day dragged on. Charly kept looking at her watch, waiting for the moment she could leave—there were only ten more minutes to go.

She went into the kitchen. "Hey, guys. Need any rubbish taken out?"

"Yeah. Over there. Thanks, Charly." Joel waved at the bags sitting near the doorway.

"If I'm not back in a few minutes, can you check that I haven't been locked out?" Charly winced, embarrassed that she needed to ask.

"You can bet your frigging sweet bippy that won't happen again, Charly." Con had blasted the girls over it. Neither had owned up, so both had caught his wrath.

After taking the trash out, Charly went to get her bag and clock out. As she was leaving, she froze when Dominic entered the restaurant. *What was he doing here?* She retreated into the kitchen.

"Charls."

He had followed her. She groaned inwardly. She didn't have the energy to deal with him. Charly turned around to face him, a stoic expression on her face.

"If you hang on a sec, I can give you a lift home." He jangled his keys in his hand.

Why was he acting as if nothing had happened? Didn't he and Jax know that they had crushed her heart?

"No, thanks. I'll catch the bus." Charly walked past him out of the kitchen.

"Hold up." Dominic grasped her elbow, turning her around. "I don't mind giving you a ride home."

"Well, I do mind." Anger simmered beneath the surface. "I'd appreciate it if you'd give me some breathing space."

"You said there were no hard feelings."

"There aren't," she lied. "But it doesn't mean I want to be friends with you. And I'd like you to respect my wishes and leave me alone."

* * * * *

IT TOOK DOMINIC EVERYTHING he had to step back. Earning Charly's trust again would take time, so he reluctantly allowed her to leave.

Rocky came up behind him. "That was chivalrous of you, bro."

"Chivalrous, my ass. That was bloody brutal." Dominic watched Charly leave.

"Give her some time, bro. She's hurting."

Dominic knew he was pushing too hard and fast, but patience was not one of his virtues. "I'm trying, Rock. I'm trying."

More than he'd ever tried with anyone before.

NINE

Over the next two weeks, Charly went to the library in her free time to search for a new job online. A few places were looking for servers, so she filled out applications. She got a reply from a café closer to her apartment, called them, and arranged an interview. If she didn't get this job, she'd not only be jobless but homeless as well if she couldn't pay the rent.

Charly didn't tell anyone about her job search or her upcoming interview. She omitted including Dominic or Rocky as references or even mentioning her job at their restaurant. Not even Sara, who had called her several times to catch up, knew about the interview. Charly had tried to dodge her calls, but Sara was persistent. Eventually, Charly relented and agreed to meet her and Carrie for coffee downtown, away from the clubhouse.

✳ ✳ ✳ ✳ ✳

CHARLY WAS ON HER way to meet Sara and Carrie. She was on cloud nine because she had gotten the café job, and it couldn't have come at a more opportune time.

Her last day at the Brothers in Arms Bar and Grill had been anti-climactic, although Con, Joel, and Rocky were sad to see her leave. They made her promise to stay in touch. To get out of there, she agreed, but she knew it was unlikely. It saddened her to leave because they were good people, and she liked her job.

She also liked keeping her heart in one piece.

Charly had avoided Dominic and Jax, but she was ashamed to admit she'd been disappointed when neither had shown up on her last day. Maybe they'd finally gotten the message and would leave her alone. That had been what she wanted, right? Too bad it felt so awful.

"Hi, guys. I hope I'm not late." Charly hugged the women, then pulled up a chair.

"You're fine, Charly. How have you been?" Sara asked.

She ignored their concerned looks. "I'm good. You two?"

"We're good, too," Carrie said with a smile.

It was pleasing to see Carrie's appearance improving. She was looking healthier and maybe even putting on a little weight. She'd been too thin before—far too gaunt for a teenager.

The ensuing silence prompted Charly to say what had to be said. "Listen, can we not talk about my past relationship with Dom and Jax or mention their names? Please." Charly could tell Sara was itching to discuss it. "If it's something you cannot do, then I'll leave. I'm sorry, but that part of my life is over. I'm moving on from it, and it would be nice to have your support."

"Okay." Knowing Sara, Charly suspected she would find a way to bring up the topic later. "What will you have? My shout."

Charly, Sara, and Carrie spent the next hour laughing, joking, and sharing tales about what they'd been up to, although Charly left out the part about her new job. She knew Sara wouldn't hesitate to pass on the information to her brother and cousin.

The conversation lulled, and Sara put her hand on Charly's. "Nolan misses you."

"I miss him." It was true. The little lad had made an impression on Charly. His clever mind and boisterous energy were contagious.

"He'd love to see you again. We should have you over sometime for dinner."

"That would be great."

"Why don't we organize a date now? Tomorrow night?"

Charly wavered. It was too soon. But at the same time, she didn't want to be rude to Sara. "Um, sure. So, just the four of us?" She had to be sure.

"Well, five if we include Carrie."

"Of course. Sounds wonderful. What time, and what do you need me to bring?" Reassured that Dominic and Jax wouldn't be there, Charly relented.

"Seven thirty. And just yourself."

With arrangements made, the three of them said their goodbyes.

✳ ✳ ✳ ✳ ✳

CHARLY RANG SARA AND Chad's doorbell at seven thirty the following evening. She grinned when she heard Nolan shouting her name. He opened the door and leaped into her arms. Charly caught him and settled him on her hips, inhaling the delicious scent of a little boy.

"Hey, buddy. What are you doing?"

"I been helping Mommy set the table." His chest puffed up with pride.

"No way!" she gushed. "Show me."

Nolan dragged Charly inside. "I putted the forks and the spoons on the table, and I putted the salt and pepper on, and I putted the natkins on."

Charly stepped back and pretended to appraise the table with a critical eye. "Wow! This looks fantastic. You have a flair for decorating a table."

Nolan beamed with satisfaction.

Charly was surprised to see Chad in the kitchen. "Hey, Chad. Where's Sara?"

"Hi, Charly. She's still getting dressed." He stirred the delicious-smelling sauce.

"Did you cook all this?" He nodded. "What are you making?"

"Chicken parmigiana, stuffed capsicum, and cauliflower with cheese sauce."

Charly was impressed. "I think Con might have some competition."

"Ha! I'm the better chef," he boasted.

"Don't let Con hear you say that." Charly sat down at the breakfast bar and watched him show off his skills in the kitchen. She turned around when she heard the clacking of heels on the tiles.

"Hi, Sara."

"Hey, Charly. I'm glad you're here. Want a glass of wine?" She opened the fridge door.

"I know you said not to bring anything, but I brought a bottle of wine. We can drink this one if you like." Charly took the bottle from the brown paper bag.

Sara poured the wine and fetched a beer for Chad.

"Is Carrie still coming?"

Sara's shoulders stiffened. "Yeah. She'll be here soon."

Right on cue, the doorbell rang. "Speak of the devil." Nolan and Sara hurried off to answer the door. "Hey, Carrie. Hi, guys."

Charly froze when she heard Jax greeting his sister. Her heart stopped beating, and the blood drained from her face. This was an ambush. A fire ignited in her belly at Sara's betrayal.

Chad watched her reaction. "It's all good, Charly. Carrie needed a ride."

"So, it had to be *them*?" Usually, one of the prospects did the grunt work. "What's wrong with Gage?"

Everyone entered the kitchen, including Dominic and Jax. Charly made a concerted effort to compose herself.

"Hi, Charls." Dominic was polite.

"Hi, Dom, Jax." Her demeanor remained cool.

"Hey, babe." Her eyes narrowed at the endearment. Then she remembered that Jax called a lot of females "babe." It hadn't been unique to her. Maybe nothing had.

Facing Carrie, Charly's face relaxed somewhat. "Hi, Carrie."

"Something smells good. What are you cooking, bro?" Jax broke the tension.

The men went into the kitchen. Sara, Carrie, and Charly entered the living room with the wine. Nolan went back into his bedroom to play with his toys.

Making small talk was killing Charly. Her attention kept straying to the men in the kitchen, and she wondered how long they would stay.

"Sar!" Chad's head popped around the door. "Is it okay if the guys stay for dinner? There's plenty of food."

When Sara consented, Charly got up. "Then I'm going."

Sara rushed after her. "Charly! Hold on. What's the matter?"

"You know what the matter is! We talked about this yesterday. You lied to me, Sara. You're as bad as the rest of them." She fought the tears that were pricking at her eyelids. She'd trusted Sara, and it was just one more betrayal.

The men came around the corner to see what all the fuss was about. "What's going on, Sar?" asked Chad.

"Charly's leaving."

Charly was about to open the door when Dominic and Jax stopped her. She spun around angrily.

"Get away from me!" She brushed their hands off her.

Jax jerked as if he'd been electrocuted, and Dominic scowled.

Using his authoritative voice, Dominic tried to calm her down. "Charly, I need you to calm down. We need to talk."

"We've already had our talk. You're just not listening to me." Charly felt her temper boiling over.

"Let's talk privately." The two men worked in tandem to corral her into the study, shutting the door behind them. Charly sank into a chair and covered her face with her hands.

"We heard what you said, Charly, but we want a second chance." Jax leaned down so they were face-to-face.

"I told you I didn't forgive you for what you did. I refuse to give you another chance. That would be a mistake." Charly was tired of convincing these two that she was done.

"No, it won't be," Jax assured Charly. "We get that we hurt you and are sorry for that. We're assholes." He kept his tone playful, but Charly wasn't falling for his charm.

"You're saying nothing different from what my stepdad used to tell my mama. She always forgave him, but it didn't change a thing. I've seen this play out too many times."

"We're not your fucking stepfather, so stop comparing us to him," Dominic bristled. "We won't cheat on you again. We promise you that."

"I've heard this all before." She looked up at Dominic with sad eyes. "You're set in your ways, Dom. You won't change. You're what? Thirty-something?"

"Thirty-four."

She guessed Jax would be about the same age or maybe a little younger. Dominic had a decade on her, she realized.

"We can take it slower. It all happened quickly once it started. This time, why don't we try getting to know each other better?"

"I thought that's what we'd been doing. No, Dom. You've humiliated me enough. Everyone knew you were cheating except me!" She cringed, thinking about how much satisfaction it had probably given Jess and Maxine, much less Kyra and Angel.

Dominic massaged the back of his neck. Charly sensed he was barely holding it together.

"Charly," Jax said gently, "I know apologizing doesn't fix things, but please give us another chance. We promise it won't happen again."

"I can't, Jax. I don't trust you." She had trusted them, but that had been her mistake.

Dominic swooped in. "Let's take it one day at a time. This time, we'll go even more slowly."

Charly scoffed. She didn't think Dominic or Jax had the

discipline or patience to do anything slowly. Charly regarded the two men closely.

Dominic's forceful and brusque nature often exasperated her, but she secretly craved it because he brought out her feistiness and, surprisingly, her submissive tendencies. To her, Dominic represented strength and security.

Jax was the laid-back charmer. He was someone she could exchange witty banter with—someone who had won her over with his super chilled vibe. He was also a lot easier to read. Jax wore his heart on his sleeve, unlike Dominic, who was more guarded. Jax embodied humor, spontaneity, and tenderness—qualities missing from her life.

They'd filled such a massive hole in her life, one she hadn't realized existed. Could they be telling the truth? Could they change? Would they?

"I need to think about it." Before deciding, she wanted time to examine the pros and cons of starting over with these two. She needed to have her head examined for even *considering* being with them again.

Jax looked relieved. "Take all the time you need."

✳ ✳ ✳ ✳ ✳

CHARLY SILENTLY PATTED HERSELF on the shoulder. She wasn't making it easy for them. First, Jax tried to talk her into taking her job back at the restaurant, but Charly put her foot down. Then Dominic wanted to organize a date for Saturday night. That was her karaoke night, so that was a no-go.

Despite her resolution to stay strong, pangs of doubt consumed her. She missed Dom and Jax. She thought that maybe she was being too hard on them. Charly had only recently figured out that her submissive behavior, especially when she was with Dom and Jax, made her appear meek. In the past, she'd never thought of herself that way. She'd considered herself to be a strong, independent woman. Then again, she'd never been in a relationship before. Being on her own gave her more control over her life. It was different in a relationship—one has to consider the other person as well. In Charly's case, she had to think about the feelings of two other people.

She made a pros-and-cons list. There were more reasons in the cons column, but Charly had rationalized that there were enough arguments on the pros side to give their relationship one more chance. She hoped she wouldn't regret it.

Charly liked her new job at Jeb's Diner. Jebediah, the owner, was an absolute sweetheart—an easy-going, down-to-earth, straight-talking man. She connected with him instantly. Rachel and Donny were the two other servers. Rachel had pink and black hair, a pierced brow, and tattoos. The girl was crazy in a fun way. Donny was goofy. He always made the two laugh with jokes about past relationships.

Charly felt at home after her first week on the job. She hadn't told Dom and Jax where she was working yet, and she wasn't sure she wanted to because she was enjoying her independence too much.

Charly was standing at the cash register, taking a customer's payment, but her eyes automatically went to the door when the bell chimed. Two prominent figures, one with a small child on his shoulders, entered the diner. Charly could only stare in disbelief. How had they found her?

Ignoring her surprise, Jax winked. Nolan bounced on his shoulders, calling her name. They sauntered up to her.

"What are you doing here?"

"Nolan wanted a banana split." Jax's smooth reply irked her. Using Nolan as a cover was a sneaky move.

"There's a café closer to home," she informed them.

"Charls, are you telling us to take our business elsewhere? I'm not sure your employer would be too happy," Dom said.

"How did you know I worked here? And don't say you didn't," she warned.

Dominic didn't bother to lie. "Vin happened to be passing by."

Dammit. Would she ever be free of their control? "Was he following me?"

Jax's tone was serious. "Are you trying to keep secrets from us, Charly?"

"Charly!" Nolan tried again to get her attention.

"Hey, buddy," she beamed at the excited boy. "You want a banana split?"

"Yeah!" His high-pitched voice echoed around the small café, earning a few disapproving looks.

"Keep your voice down, bud," his uncle cautioned.

"Anything for you two?"

She took their orders and told them to find a table. Nolan was busy chatting away to any adult who would listen. Although Dom and Jax pay attention to the little boy, their focus was on Charly.

"Oh my God, Charly! Who on earth are those two gorgeous hunks?" Trust Rachel to notice. Then again, glancing around the diner, most females were gawking—some openly, others discreetly.

"My ex-bosses. They're checking out the competition." Charly laughed at Rachel's horrified expression.

"Are you serious?" she whispered.

Charly grinned. "Yes, Dom's my ex-boss. But no, they're not checking out the competition."

"Where did you work for him? I want to work there!"

Donny approached them, complaining. "Table four is driving me crazy. Can you take over, Charly?"

"Oh, you big baby. Harry's harmless."

"Please?"

When Charly agreed, Donny planted a wet kiss on her cheek in thanks. She went over to check on Harry.

When Jax laid a hand on her waist, Charly was wiping down a table. "We're ready to leave."

They went over to the counter to pay for their meals. Donny stood beside her at the coffee machine, whipping up a cappuccino, and Charly felt the tension in the air as Dominic and Jax pinned Donny with hard stares. They'd seen his kiss, and suddenly, they had to show dominance. It was so ingrained in them—especially Dominic—that it would be impossible to quell that part of them.

After they left, Donny approached her. "Who are they, Charly?"

Charly cleared her throat. "My friends."

"They're more than that. They were both watching your every move. It was kind of creepy."

"Mind your own business, Donny. They're friends of mine, so watch what you say." Despite her doubts about them, no one else had the right to say anything negative about Dominic or Jax.

"Hey!" He took a step back. "I didn't mean to offend." But Charly could tell he was eager to say more. "Wait. Are you involved with *both* of them?"

The way he said it raised her hackles. But instead of yelling at him, she forced herself to ignore him and walk away. Charly understood that not everyone would approve of their arrangement—whatever their relationship status.

$$\star\ \star\ \star\ \star\ \star$$

WHEN SUNDAY ROLLED AROUND, Charly was waiting in the parking lot when two loud motorcycles rumbled up to where she was standing. Dominic had invited her to the lodge, and she'd finally capitulated and agreed to go. Regardless of how much they'd hurt her, her stupid heart didn't have the strength to deny them continuously. Deep down, she yearned to get back what they had before they cheated on her.

"You expect me to get on one of those?"

"Don't see another vehicle, Charls." Dominic dismounted his bike and stepped into her space. She was tempted to step back but stayed put, and he enfolded her in his arms.

"You're riding with me. Hop on." Dominic handed her a black, dome-shaped helmet.

Holding on tight, Charly shut her eyes and leaned into Dominic. She silently screamed when he sped down the road, but it wasn't long before she relaxed and enjoyed the ride. She couldn't believe how amazing it felt as they cruised along the highway.

Charly was disappointed when the ride ended. It had been nice having a reason to snuggle up to Dominic. The familiar smell of leather and sandalwood, the wind in her face, and the soothing vibrations of the engine had put her in a happy mood.

Lifting her leg over the seat, Charly stretched her legs.

"What did you think?" Dominic studied her closely, his lips curving slightly.

Her eyes lit up. "Better than I imagined."

Dominic looked pleased. Taking her hand, he led her into the house. There, she met Sara and Chad, sitting at the kitchen table talking to two older people she'd never met.

Jax urged her closer to the group. The older couple watched with interest. "Ma, Pops. This is Charly."

"Hi, Charly." The man smiled warmly.

Charly couldn't believe she'd been ambushed again. The last thing she'd expected was to meet Jax's parents.

"I'm Deacon, and this is my wife, Sharyn."

She estimated that Jax's father, Deacon, was in his sixties. The long, salt-and-pepper beard matched his long ponytail. His gray-blue eyes shone with curiosity, probably wondering who she was. He wore an Iconic Sons MC kutte, just like his son.

His mother was an attractive woman in her late fifties. She was dressed in a long, bohemian dress that reminded Charly of the hippy era of the sixties. She, too, had long, salt-and-pepper hair that hung down to her waist. Charly noted the sharp eyes that looked at her with suspicion as if she hadn't yet decided what role Charly played in her son's life.

"Our sons have mentioned you a time or two," Deacon offered.

Had they? She wondered what they'd said.

"Sons? You have a brother?" Charly looked at Jax quizzically.

"Dom is adopted. He's family. We're brothers," explained Jax.

They all went outside to join the other guests. Gage and another prospect, Pen, were cooking the meat on the barbecue, and the smell of sausages and onions made Charly's mouth water. The group broke off and mingled. Jax grabbed her hand, and they went over to Vin and Gun, who were flirting with some babes under the canopy of a large, overhanging tree by the lake.

Charly spotted an empty folding chair when Jax pulled her away. He sat down on a different chair and plonked her between his thighs. Charly instantly got up and sat in the other chair.

"What's the matter?" He frowned at her.

"I'm not sitting on your knee, Jax. I'm comfortable here." Charly snuggled into the chair to prove her point.

"Babe." She couldn't tell if Jax was warning her or indulging her.

"Got to get your girl in line, bro."

Charly scowled at Vin, who winked at her.

"Plan to later," Jax said with a nod.

Her cheeks flamed at the intimation.

She glowered at Jax, mouthing the words "stop it." He wiggled his eyebrows suggestively.

"My turn, brother." Startled, Charly stared at Dominic, who'd crept up behind her. He pulled her away from Jax, guiding her up the porch steps to where Dominic's aunt and uncle sat.

Charly hadn't stopped thinking about what may have happened to Dominic as a young boy. Where were his parents? What had they done to him? Why had he gone to live with his aunt and uncle?

"How do you like your new job, Charly?" Deacon asked.

"It's great. My boss is laid-back, and the other servers are fun."

"You didn't like working at the bar and grill?" The question came from Sharyn, so Charly answered with caution. She hadn't quite sussed her out.

"I did. Dom and Rocky were great bosses." Charly glanced over at Dominic.

"Who is she to you, Dom?" Charly stiffened at Sharyn's tone. The woman didn't like her and talked about her as if she weren't there.

"We're friends," Charly said defensively.

"You don't have female friends. So why does she think that you're friends? She doesn't understand the rules of the MC, Dominic," Sharyn said directly.

"She'll learn," Dom said.

Dominic stopped Charly when she attempted to stand, placing a firm hand on her thigh. "Don't move," he warned Charly. Then he glared at Sharyn. "Ma, be nice to Charls, or we leave."

"What about Kyra?" Sharyn asked.

Charly froze at the mention of the other woman.

"Sharyn, shut it!" Deacon's command put a stop to his wife's prying.

"Don't look at me like that," he said, frowning at Charly. "Nothing is going on between me and Kyra," Dom snapped at Sharyn.

Charly squeezed Dominic's hand, but this irritated him. "Come with me."

Dominic steered Charly inside, up the stairs, and into the library. Two brown leather couches were in the center of the room, and a large window, which filled a whole wall, provided natural light. Charly remembered admiring the room during the guided tour.

"Sit." Dominic plonked down next to her.

"What?"

"Ever since you found out that I was adopted, you've been giving me pitiful looks. I can see that you're eager to know, so ask your questions."

It was true; she had so many questions she wanted answers to.

"You don't mind?"

"Ask away. But I don't want your pity."

Charly nodded. "Where are your parents?"

"Dead. My sperm donor was killed in prison, and my birth mother overdosed," he said gruffly.

Charly couldn't believe how eerily similar Dominic's situation was to hers. Although her stepdad wasn't dead, he was in prison, and her mother had died of a drug overdose when she was twelve.

"Is that why you went to live with your aunt and uncle?"

"No. My father was a mean drunk and often flogged me if I got in his way. Sometimes, he locked me out of the house in the dead of winter, so I would end up going over to my neighbors, who then called social services. My mother was hooked on drugs and would forget to feed me. When I was four, I was severely malnourished and underweight. Social services decided I needed to go and live with other family members."

"You remember all that?" The thought horrified her. Thinking about Dominic as a young child, not being cared for the way he should have been, made her sad.

"You cry, and I'll whup you." That stopped the onset of the waterworks. "I don't remember all of it. My parents told me some of it when I was older and began asking questions. Other bits, I do remember, especially my father's floggings."

"I'm so sorry, Dom."

Dominic leaned in, and Charly immediately pulled back. She still hadn't forgiven him or Jax and refused to fall back into their arms so readily. Dominic sighed heavily, sweeping a hand down his face.

Charly knew she lacked the willpower to resist him forever, so she was determined to hold off for as long as possible.

* * * * *

JESS'S SUDDEN APPEARANCE IN the hallway cast a blight on an otherwise enjoyable afternoon.

"Are you back with the guys?" Her lips were pinched, and her eyes oozed animosity.

"Why does it matter, Jess?" Charly didn't refute Jess's belief. It was none of her business. They were no longer friends.

Jess crossed her arms over her chest. "You knew I liked Jax."

"Not before the clubhouse. You didn't say a word." Charly wasn't sure it would have made a difference. She hadn't been the one to pursue them. It had been the other way around.

"Well, you knew Max wanted Dom. Why do you get to have them both?" Jess lifted her chin.

"It wasn't my intention to hurt either of you." Charly's hands fisted at her side.

"You're a whore, Charly. A traitor!" Jess yelled at her, taking a few steps towards her.

A traitor? She'd practically been knocked unconscious while trying to protect her! "How can you say that? I fought for you." Charly realized she'd been backed into a corner by the taller woman looming over her. Something about Jess's appearance scared Charly. Her eyes were bloodshot, her speech was slurred, and her breath smelled of alcohol.

Jess grabbed Charly by the hair, causing her to cry in pain. Charly twisted her head, throwing several open-handed slaps in her ex-friend's face and forcing Jess to back up.

"You need to back off! Jax is mine! You can't have him." A spray of saliva hit Charly in the face.

Charly dove around her and headed for the door.

"That's right, bitch. Run away!"

✶ ✶ ✶ ✶ ✶

JESS LAUGHED AT CHARLY'S disappearing figure. The bitch was weak, always running away. What the hell did Dominic and Jax see in her?

Jess was becoming desperate. She needed protection from Sol when he got out of prison. He would come after her the minute he was back on the street. Jess couldn't run from him forever. She was well aware of Sol's dangerous propensity for violence. He got high on using women as punching bags. He'd done it to her often enough.

Unfortunately, Dominic and Jax kept running back to Charly, not giving her the time of day. Despite her attempts to insinuate herself into their close-knit circle, she remained on the outside.

Even Gun and Vin gave her the cold shoulder. Did they sense her desperation? All she wanted was protection and respect. Didn't she deserve that? She'd even tried testing the waters with Achilles, but he was a tough one. Unless they were lucky enough to be in the right place at the right time, women were insignificant to the hard-as-nails president of the MC.

Having consumed more tequila than she'd intended to, Jess stumbled down the hallway. She opened the door to what looked like a study or library and collapsed on the couch. Her head was spinning, but her mind was turning. Thoughts constantly streamed through her head like a television she couldn't shut off. Faces kept flickering inside her brain. Angry faces, scary faces, and disappointed faces. Sol, her mama, and strangers. Jess slapped her forehead repeatedly, trying to erase the ugly memories. But they wouldn't go away. They never did.

TEN

The weeks flew by, and Charly could tell that Dominic and Jax were becoming increasingly frustrated with the no-touching rule. Charly, too, was sexually frustrated, although her vibrator helped somewhat during the long, lonely nights. It wasn't nearly enough, however.

She missed the sex, sure. Earth-shattering orgasms that left her trembling just thinking about them. Hearing Dominic moan her name. Jax's deep chuckle as she did something that pleased him. The three of them moving together, finding ways to please each other—pleasure Charly had never experienced before. No one had ever cared this much about what she felt and how she felt it. She couldn't remember if she'd ever felt the same way about anyone else.

She'd felt safe with them. Happy.

Unfortunately, it made their betrayal that much worse.

They were trying, and she knew that. They were opening up to her about more than what they wanted from her physically.

Over time, Dominic revealed more devastating details about his childhood. Charly had saved her tears for the pillow because crying or offering him sympathy made him mad. Although Sharyn didn't seem to like her—not that Charly would share her feelings about this with them because she was their mother—she was eternally grateful that she and Deacon had taken Dominic in and cared for him when he needed them the most.

When Jax shared stories about him and Dominic, it always made Charly smile and sometimes cringe, especially when it involved incidents where they fought with each other or got hurt. They fought a lot as kids. Somehow, bloodying each other's noses and blackening each other's eyes were signs of affection between them. One evening, Jax called to say he and Dominic were coming over. It was eight o'clock on a work night, so it surprised Charly that he'd called. Since she'd stopped dodging their efforts to win her over, they'd made excuses to see her every weekend, but they'd let her be during the week. They knew she worked hard and wanted her to get some rest.

Charly smiled at Jax's signature knock. She didn't bother to look through the peephole before opening the door.

Jax and Dom walked in and set a six-pack of beers on the breakfast counter. "Beer?"

Charly screwed her face up. "No. I've got wine in the fridge."

Dominic grabbed his beer and Charly's wine glass and sat on her couch. "C'mon. Sit." He tapped the cushion beside him. "Let's talk." Dominic's directness was a welcome distraction. For some reason, being in the presence of these two still made her nervous—heart-pounding, sweaty palms nervous. It was like the air had an electric charge whenever they were together. She could almost taste the tension along with the leather and sandalwood scent of the two men.

Surrendering, she plopped herself down with a melodramatic sigh. "What are we talking about?"

"Tell us about your real father." Dom fixed her with that steely gaze.

Charly paused for a moment, then nodded. It was only fair that she shared stories about her childhood. Despite the horrible events she suffered, Dominic's early years had been full of tragedy, too. He might be the one who truly understood how her childhood had forged her into who she is now.

"My biological father was never in the picture. My mama got pregnant with me after a one-night stand when she was nineteen.

As far as I can tell, she didn't even know his last name. Her parents threw her out because she often stayed out late, drank, did drugs, and hung around a bad crowd. She'd been in trouble with the law and was an unruly teenager. They'd tried everything to get her in line, and nothing worked. Finding out she was pregnant with me was the last straw." Charly looked down at her hands in her lap. She kept them tightly clasped to keep them from fidgeting. This wasn't a story she shared with many people, and she never felt comfortable talking about it.

"I don't remember a lot about those first few years. It's all kind of a random blur of places and faces. I remember being hungry. I remember being cold. I remember being scared."

Jax made a noise in the back of his throat, and Charly put her hand on his knee to stop him from putting an arm around her or saying something. If he plied her with sympathy, she wouldn't be able to get through this.

"She met my stepdad, Peter, when I was five. He was abusive right from the start. Mama said it was better than living on the streets, especially with a young kid." Charly shrugged. "Maybe she was right. Maybe she wasn't."

"Mama wasn't going to win any Mother of the Year awards. She wasn't the kind to give hugs or make sure I had what I needed. Over time, the drugs got a hold of her, and I had to fend for myself a lot. I didn't even start school until I was seven. Nobody noticed I was supposed to be in school. I've always been small for my age, and most people thought I was younger than I was. Peter was an alcoholic and easily set off. I remember he got angry at Mama once because the kettle was whistling too loudly. He grabbed a broomstick and started beating her with it." She took a deep breath and let it out, trying to get that image out of her head. Her mother had curled into a ball under the table, trying to dodge the worst of the blows, while Peter called her names and smacked her over and over again. Then, when it was over, everyone went on as if that was normal.

"I got good at tiptoeing around the house, keeping myself clean, and raiding the fridge when everyone was asleep or passed out so I wouldn't starve. I loved going to school because that was the only place I felt safe." That hadn't changed much. There were damn few places where Charly had ever felt safe. Between these two men, it might have been one of the only places she'd felt that way.

"Despite starting school later than everyone else, I did well. It was the one thing I was good at. I used to forge Mama's signature on excursion notes and steal money from her purse so that I could join in with what the other kids were doing. Sometimes, our neighbor— Mrs. McNally—would sneak me a few dollars, too."

Charly bowed her head and stopped talking, gathering the courage to proceed to the next part—the part that still haunted her.

"When I was ten, my brother, Fabien, came along. He was born prematurely with drugs in his system, and he spent the first few months on a ventilator. Family services got involved. Mama had to get clean before they would allow her to take Fabien home.

"I remember feeling so sad that I couldn't see my brother. It took a while, but Mama finally got clean. Fabien came home at seven months old, but it wasn't long before Mama was on drugs again. She hid it well from family services.

"Mama and Peter hadn't prepared for how hard it would be to have Fabien with us. He cried all the time and needed constant care. At eleven, I took on that role. I became his mama. I cared for him."

Charly blinked back the tears, choking on her words.

"Fabien was the most beautiful baby ever. I loved taking care of him. He was the reason I was happy to go home. But I came home from school one day, and there were police cars and an ambulance there, and our house was cordoned off. The police wouldn't let me inside. Peter had killed Fabien because he wouldn't stop crying. 'Shaken baby syndrome' was what they said. My brother was only seventeen months old. I failed him. I was supposed to protect him, but I wasn't there when he needed me most." She'd never forgive herself for it. She'd been so happy to go to school that day. They'd been promised a pizza party in math class for doing well on a test. It had been years before she could look at a slice without choking.

"Mama was arrested too, so I was placed in foster care because I had no other family members. Mama no longer spoke to her parents, so I'd never met my grandparents.

"Peter was eventually sentenced to fifteen years in prison for manslaughter. And two months after Fabien was killed, Mama died of an overdose. That's my story." The last few sentences had come out abruptly. Maybe she could hold it together if she didn't let emotion seep in.

Several moments passed in silence until Jax wrapped his arms around her. She could feel his strength seeping into her, and she began to truly understand what the gentleness beneath that strength meant for her. She rarely cried and certainly didn't cry over things that had happened over a decade ago. She'd had to hold herself together. There was no one else to do it for her. Now, though, she could feel someone was there to help her pick up the pieces. She could afford to fall apart. Charly broke down and sobbed. Jax's arms tightened. He gently cradled her head against his shoulder, and nobody said anything for several minutes.

A box of tissues was placed on her knee. She plucked several tissues from it and blew her nose. Once the waterworks died down, Charly felt relief that she'd been able to pour her heart out and speak about the family she'd once had and the brother she'd loved with all her heart.

"Charls, look at me." Slowly, she raised her head. Dominic cupped her cheek. "Thank you for sharing."

＊＊＊＊＊

CHARLY WAS BAFFLED TO see Jax enter the café the following day. He usually worked at the garage during the week. He was carrying a basket, which was even odder. The dainty wicker affair looked funny, dangling from his muscled arm. How could she help but smile at him?

He smiled back as if he couldn't help it, either.

"Hey," he greeted. "Come with me."

Charly glanced at Rachel, who was busy taking a customer's order. Then she peered over at Donny, who was making a cappuccino. Since Charly was between customers, she followed him outside. Jax led her to a bench in the park across the street, and they sat down.

"What's up?" she asked, eyeing the basket. "What have you got in there?"

"Lunch." Jax flashed a sexy grin. "For us."

"Ah… I'm working, Jax." She had a living to make and rent to pay, so she couldn't afford to lose this job. Besides, she liked the cafe and her new friends there.

"I've already spoken to Jeb. He'll keep an eye on things."

Seriously? What was he thinking? "Ja-ax! You shouldn't have done that. I can't be getting special treatment just because you say so."

"Char-lee!" he teased. "It's not special treatment. Jeb said you've been staying past your rostered time, so he was happy to give you some time off."

"Only because it's been extra busy lately. Staying behind for an extra fifteen minutes now and then is nothing." She explained, wondering when he'd spoken to Jeb.

Jax grabbed and held one of her hands, his thumb gliding over her knuckles. "Well, it's something to Jeb. He appreciates your efforts. I appreciate your effort. I admire how hard you work."

Charly bit her lip, studying Jax closer as he set the basket on the bench. "What's the occasion?"

"Does there need to be one? I thought we could spend some quality time together. Just the two of us." Jax unpacked the basket, pulling out trays of sushi rolls, a platter of fruit, and a bottle of wine.

"I can't have any wine, Jax!" Charly admonished. "I'm working, remember?"

"One glass won't hurt." He poured her half a glass of wine.

Taking it, Charly stared at him over the rim of the glass as she took a sip, enjoying its cold crispness and realizing there was no beer in the basket for him.

"You like sushi, babe?"

It was one of her favorites, but she only bought it as a treat. "I do. How did you know?"

"Sara. She said women like this shit. Me, I can take it or leave it." With that, he shoved a whole nigiri sushi into his mouth.

"So, you're willing to eat sushi and drink wine because I like it?" she teased.

"For you? Yes." He wolfed down a couple more sushi rolls, grinning like a fool.

Laughing, Charly bit into her sushi and then moaned slightly at how good it tasted.

"Why aren't you at the garage? Slow day?" she asked after chewing and swallowing.

"Nah. Nobody called in sick today, so I got plenty of guys looking after the garage. Perfect opportunity to grab lunch with my favorite person." He nudged her with his elbow.

"That would be me?" The idea that Jax thought she was his "favorite person" gave Charly a thrill. She couldn't keep the grin off her face.

"Absolutely," he stated assuredly.

"Is this something you do often? Spontaneous picnics with the ladies while they're working?" Charly tried to keep a straight face but laughed at Jax's comical expression.

"Babe, I'm offended."

Charly knew he was pretending. He looked too darn pleased with himself to be offended.

"Yeah! Right!" she chuckled, taking another piece of sushi.

"Honestly, babe. You hurt my feelings," Jax said, pressing a hand to his heart. "I've never done anything like this before." They'd been joking around, but his tone had turned serious.

Charly looked up into his eyes with a bit of wonder. "Then why are you now?"

"I like you, Charly. I want to do nice things for you." Jax smoothed a hand over her crown, sliding it down her hair, and tweaked the end. "This is probably going to sound fucked, but Dom and me, we don't need to try when it comes to women. It's how it's always been. For you, Charly, we want to try. I know I do because seeing you laugh, smile, and look so damn happy makes me happy. I'm not sure I've ever cared this much about how someone else felt or what would please them."

Charly's eyes were bright with unshed tears. When had her happiness ever mattered to anyone? Now, this beautiful man with the sweetest smile only needed to see her happy and be happy himself. How had she gotten this lucky?

* * * * *

"WHAT'S UP WITH YOU?" Rachel asked Charly a week later at work.

"What do you mean?" Charly didn't think she was acting any differently than usual.

"You've been walking on air for over a week now." Rachel leaned in. "Was it because that hunky guy took you out for a picnic lunch?"

Charly blushed. Having Jax take the time to find out what food she liked and bring it to her so he could see her happy was part of it. Another big part was finally telling someone about her past. She knew what people usually thought about people like her, a foster kid from an abusive home with a drug-addicted mother. There was usually some combination of pity and suspicion. Yet neither man had looked down on her, and Dom seemed sincerely grateful that she'd been willing to open up to them.

Charly also appreciated their efforts to step back and let her set the pace of their relationship, even if it was only platonic. She understood that even though they both got frustrated at the lack of physical intimacy, they didn't try to coerce her sexually in any way.

Both of them—but mainly Dom—were used to taking what they wanted when they wanted it. They didn't have to worry about what someone else wanted because the women they usually spent time with only wanted the power and prestige that being with them would bring them.

Charly wasn't interested in power or prestige. While she loved feeling safe, she didn't want their protection.

It hadn't occurred to her before that having her want them for who they were rather than what they could give her might be as new for them as having two such beautiful men want her was to her.

Her phone buzzed in her pocket. She took it out to find a message from Sara inviting her to the clubhouse on Sunday.

"Are you playing matchmaker again?" she said when she called back, not wanting a repeat of the dinner invitation.

"Nope. The MC is out of town. I just wanted to have some girl time," Sara replied.

Charly mulled it over before agreeing to see her on Sunday, feeling almost a little disappointed that it wasn't another one of Sara's attempts to get her back together with Dom and Jax.

Sunday rolled around, and Charly took the bus to the clubhouse. Sara and Carrie were relaxing on the front porch when she walked in. Both women got up to hug her as she walked up the steps.

"Carrie, you look great!" Charly said and meant it. She was almost unrecognizable from the pale, frightened waif that had been cowering on the floor the first time Charly had met her.

"You look pretty good yourself," Carrie replied.

Charly looked down at herself, not seeing any difference. "Really?"

"Really," Sara said. "I'm not sure what it is. It might be something with how you carry yourself these days."

That meshed too well with what Rachel had said to her. It was true. She felt lighter these days—easier in her skin, mind, and world.

Was this another gift Dom and Jax had given her without even meaning to?

Maybe it was time to give them another chance and to give herself another opportunity to be happy. Speaking of happiness, "Where's Nolan?" she asked Sara.

"His Nan and Pop are spoiling him." Sara sat back down and motioned for Charly to join her.

The familiar sound of motorcycles approached. For a second, Charly stiffened. The guys didn't know she was here, and she wasn't sure how welcome she was since putting their relationship on ice, but since they constantly arranged "dates" to see her anyway, she didn't think they'd have a problem with her being here. She'd been invited, after all, just not by them.

Dominic was the first to enter the clubhouse, and when his head swiveled in her direction, their eyes connected. It was as if some magnetic force pulled them together. A rare smile lit up his face as he strode towards her.

"Charls. What are you doing here?"

"Sara invited me over." She indicated Sara with a head nod.

"Girl time, huh?" he chuckled. "I should have known."

"Nothing wrong with that," asserted Sara. "We don't get to see each other as much anymore."

"Not complaining, Sar. Glad you guys caught up." He gazed down at Charly. "Mind hanging out with me?"

Charly wanted to. Her nerve endings lit up merely by being in his presence. However, she was there to hang out with Sara and Carrie and didn't want to be rude to them.

"Go on!" encouraged Sara. "He'll only sulk like a child if you don't." She dodged Dominic's hand as he pretended to swipe her.

"Okay. I was hoping to have a chat with you anyway." Charly cleared her throat.

One eyebrow went up. "Something on your mind?" He motioned for her to follow him inside as he headed to the bar.

Afraid she'd chicken out, she merely nodded.

Jax joined them at the bar, a happy grin lighting up his face. "This is a nice surprise. When did you get here?"

"A little while ago. Sara invited me over." She knew she sounded a little defensive. She didn't want them to think she was like Kyra and Angel, constantly hanging around, hoping to grab their attention.

"It's okay, Charls," Dominic reassured her. "You don't need an invitation to visit. Whenever you feel like coming over, you're welcome. Just give us a heads-up in case there's something already planned."

Charly wondered if he was referring to one of those orgies she'd heard about. As repulsive as it sounded, she kept the thought to herself.

"What did you want to chat about?" Dominic prompted.

Now that she'd been put on the spot, Charly considered aborting the topic altogether. She assumed she'd be able to ease into a discussion about their sexual relationship. She could do this. She felt stronger than she ever had before in her life. She could ask for what she wanted. "I think I'm, um, ready to try again."

Dominic stared at her hard. "Try what again?"

Charly felt their presence strongly. She could cut the tension with a knife. "A relationship," she announced with certainty. "How it was before."

She saw Jax swallow and briefly close his eyes. Dominic stood motionless. "Be more specific, Charls. I don't want to misunderstand the situation here."

"Dom." She released a nervous laugh. "You're not making this easy for me."

"Don't care," he supplied roughly. "Explain. This is important."

Charly spelled it out for them. "I want to have sex with you. I want to kiss you, touch you, and fuck you. I want that so badly; it hurts. But what I don't want is for you to hurt me again." The words tumbled from her mouth.

"That won't happen, Charls. I promise you," Dominic swore. "I'm so damn sorry I hurt you, babe. It's been tearing me up inside that I caused you pain. Never again."

Charly hugged him tightly, then sagged into his embrace.

"What about me?" complained Jax.

Winding her arms around his broad chest, Jax bent down and whispered, "I'm sorry, Charly. I swear, I'll make it up to you. Thank you for giving us another chance, babe."

Charly hoped she wouldn't live to regret her decision. These two men meant the world to her, and she didn't know if she could survive another betrayal.

$$*\ *\ *\ *\ *$$

THE EVENING EVENTUALLY DREW to a close, causing Charly's anxiety to reach "panic mode." Although she wanted to experience what it would be like to have sex with these two dominant males, she was terrified her inexperience would be a turn-off. Deep down, she knew her thinking had to be skewed because Dominic and Jax had already proven that their sexual compatibility was off the charts, even though they'd only gone as far as oral sex.

The sexual tension felt like an invisible predator breathing heavily down Charly's neck. After driving back to her apartment, she started climbing the stairs on jelly-like limbs, with Dominic and Jax close on her heels. She fumbled inside her bag for her keys.

The moment the door closed behind them, they surrounded her. Dominic eased down the zipper at the back of her dress. Feeling the cold, coupled with her nervous state, Charly gasped, her body shivering uncontrollably.

Jax took advantage and kissed her. He opened his mouth and inhaled her every breath, gasp, and moan. She trembled when Dominic tugged her dress down to her hips, revealing two creamy breasts. Jax's hot, wet mouth clamped onto her nipple, the strong suction sending rolling waves of pleasure straight to her pussy.

"She tastes so good," Jax groaned as he peppered kisses along her neck and shoulders.

Dominic got rid of her dress. She stood there, naked except for her heels. He firmly guided her to the bed, and Jax pressed down on her belly until she was lying on her back.

Charly needed to see them naked, too. "Take your clothes off."

Without hesitation, they stripped down until they wore nothing but lecherous grins. Their bodies were magnificent works of art: tattooed, muscled perfection, with not an ounce of fat anywhere.

Lowering her gaze, Charly admired their impressive erections.

"I think she likes what she sees, bro." Jax fondled his cock.

Suddenly remembering the most important thing, Charly opened the bedside table drawer and took out a box of condoms.

Jax laughed. "Someone's been thinking about this."

Blushing, she retorted, "You can't be too careful."

Jax hopped on the bed and stretched out beside her. "I'm teasing." His eyes wandered. "I want to play with these beauties." He cupped her breasts, circling her nipples with his thumbs and watching them rise with his attention.

Dominic got down on his knees at the end of the bed and smoothed his hands over her waist and thighs, making light strokes that sent heat shooting through her. Charly closed her eyes, waiting breathlessly for his touch. He pushed her thighs apart. She groaned loudly when his breath warmed her quivering pussy. Her body arched when he swiped his tongue through her wet folds.

Jax took her hand and enclosed it around his rock-hard cock, guiding her strokes. "That's it. Nice and hard. Yeah, just like that."

Dom's tongue progressively applied more pressure to her clit. She moaned and lifted her hips, opening herself wider as the delicious tension coiled deep inside her.

His tongue moved faster, zeroing in on the exact spot that needed his attention. She began to tremble, unable to track what her hands were doing to Jax. He responded by covering her hand with his again and thrusting powerfully into his fist.

Recognizing that she was close to climaxing, Dominic sucked harder and, at the same time, added a finger to her soaking pussy. The overload of sensations tipped her over the edge, and she came apart. Crying out, her body convulsed and shook as pleasure overtook every nerve end.

"Look at her, Dom." Jax rose above her, watching her explode.

"I'm watching. She's beautiful."

She smiled and began to rise onto her elbows, eyes still closed.

"Keep still," Jax ordered. She forced her heavy eyelids open. They widened in wonder as Jax began to pump his cock harder, releasing a squirt of semen across her chest.

"Rub it in," he whispered, his voice hoarse.

Maintaining eye contact, she slowly massaged his cum onto and around her breasts.

"Turn over, Charls," Dom instructed.

She rolled onto her belly.

"Now up on your hands and knees."

She did as he ordered, her thighs quivering. She knew how exposed she was and how all of her womanhood was now on display. Dom's fingers worked inside her again, spreading her further apart. Tensing, she looked over her shoulder to see what he was doing. Dominic slapped one of her cheeks—hard.

"Ouch," she squealed, attempting to sit up, although the pain had come with a sharp edge of pleasure and anticipation.

"Stay," he growled.

"Don't spank me then."

"Just do what you're told." His voice was cold, but his eyes were burning.

She turned to face forward again to find Jax in front of her, his cock already beginning to harden again.

"Suck it." Jax coaxed her mouth close to the head of his cock.

Tentatively, she licked the head, receiving a satisfied rumble in response. She gripped the base and took him into her mouth, sucking the tip between her lips.

"Jesus Christ!" Jax's hand covered her head, guiding her.

Charly feasted on Jax's cock, on the way her lips glided down his hard length and the way her tongue swirled around his sensitive tip while Dominic's fingers penetrated her pussy, causing her walls to clamp around them. She tried to take Jax deeper into her throat.

A crinkling sound made Charly turn her head. She watched as Dominic used his teeth to tear open the condom packet and easily roll it on his cock. He began to enter her, the walls of her vagina contracting. Charly couldn't contain her shock at the intrusion. Instinctively, she pulled away. He was too big. It wasn't going to fit.

"Easy, Charls. I won't hurt you." But she remained tense. "Relax." Dominic smoothed his hands down her back, relaxing her. After several slow strokes, his cock prodded her entrance again.

Jax massaged her shoulders, distracting her. "That's it. Take a deep breath."

This time, when Dominic pushed inside, it didn't startle her. She felt pressure but not pain. After several minutes, Dominic was all the way in. The vice-like grip he had on her hips steadied her as he slid in and out of her with steady strokes.

Jax steered her mouth back down onto his cock.

Charly's body rocked as Dominic's thrusts increased. "Touch yourself," he barked.

She reached between her legs and massaged her clitoris, slippery and silky with the juices of her previous orgasm. With Dom inside her pussy and Jax in her mouth, she was nearly overwhelmed with sensation. Every sense was filled. The sound of skin slapping on skin filled the room. Her lower body quivered. Dom smacked her ass again, this time bringing only pleasure. The single arm that was holding her up threatened to collapse as another orgasm ripped through her. Charly collapsed on top of Jax, almost comatose.

She was vaguely aware of Dominic pulling out. He leaned forward and whispered, "Still think I need a support group?" before getting up and walking into the bathroom.

"You plan on getting off me any time soon?" Jax sifted his hands through her hair. Charly was too drowsy to respond with anything more than a mumble, but she rolled onto her back.

Jax rolled over her, grabbed a condom, positioned himself between her legs, and hovered above her. "My turn."

He guided his cock inside her a little more roughly than Dominic had done, but Charly was ready for it this time. She arched her back when he began thrusting—leisurely at first but then with more vigor. Dominic re-entered the room and started masturbating, his big hand boldly pulling on his cock.

Charly's body naturally tensed up. She didn't think she could take another orgasm, yet one was building deep inside her, making her shudder until she finally hit the peak.

"Fuck! I can feel her walls squeezing me." Jax's body locked up. "Fuck! Fuck! Fuck!" He let out a roar of satisfaction and then flopped on top of her.

Dominic stepped closer. Jax groaned and rolled off moments before Dominic sprayed cum all over Charly's belly. Lifting her hand, Dominic splayed it over his seed and helped her rub it in.

Then, all three collapsed into a tangle on the sweat-soaked sheets.

* * * * *

CHARLY WAS LATE FOR work. She'd woken up from a sleep deeper than she'd experienced in ages to see that she'd overslept. She rushed into the bathroom to get ready. Dominic, completely naked, walked up behind her as she brushed her teeth. He nuzzled the sensitive spot on her neck.

"Morning," he murmured against her skin. Charly was too busy to acknowledge him. "What's the rush?"

"I'm late for work." Wiping her mouth on a towel, she hurried into the bedroom to put on her uniform.

Jax stretched on the bed, scratching his balls. "Hey, babe," he said drowsily. "We got time for a quickie?"

As tempting as it was, Charly laughed. "No." She checked her watch. "I've got to be at work in ten minutes."

"We'll drive you," offered Dominic, reaching for his clothes.

"Thanks. Are you ready to go now?" Because that's when she needed to leave.

The men got dressed and ready in two minutes and dropped her off in front of the café. "We'll pick you up after work. We'll go to the clubhouse."

Everything that had been warm and fuzzy a moment ago went cold. The clubhouse. It was all well and good when it was just her, Sara, and Carrie, but that wasn't the case most nights.

Dominic noticed her hesitation. "What's the matter?"

"I don't want to run into any of the *mean girls*." She kicked at the sidewalk with a sneakered toe.

"You were at the clubhouse yesterday," Jax said, leaning forward in his seat to face her.

"Sara said the clubhouse was empty," she replied. And it had been until they'd showed up.

"You don't have to worry about Angel. She's gone, and she's not welcome back," said Dominic.

"And Kyra?" she persisted when he didn't mention her name.

"Still there. She won't bother you." Something in Dominic's tone was off.

"Why is she still there?" she frowned.

"It doesn't matter. She's not allowed to talk to you."

"But..."

Dominic kissed her on the mouth, shutting her up. "Have a good day."

✳ ✳ ✳ ✳ ✳

BEING BACK AT THE clubhouse in a crowd was tense. She'd been mortified when Dominic and Jax's betrayal became public; the humiliation of finding out what everyone already knew in front of an audience still stung. Going back wasn't easy, and her stomach roiled at the thought of facing the women again. She knew she was making herself a target by walking in, flanked on either side by Dom and Jax, each with a possessive hand on her lower back.

Giving the guys a second chance was like playing Russian roulette. Her heart could be shot to pieces at any moment, and Charly knew her feelings for them were getting stronger every day.

Charly relaxed when she walked in and saw Sara playing barmaid. Stepping up to the bar, she said, "Do you not have enough work to keep you busy, Sara? You have to take on bartending as well?".

"Working at the garage and looking after a four-year-old keeps me busy enough, thank you. I like to help out." She gave Charly a grin. "What'll you have?"

"A Coke would be good, thanks."

Dom and Jax each ordered a beer.

"Speaking of four-year-olds, Nolan's birthday party is next Saturday. I know he'd be over the moon if you'd come," Sara said. "We're having it at The Playpen, one of those indoor playgrounds."

Charly felt warm inside. "I would love that. Let me know what I can get him, okay?" She reached over to squeeze Sara's hand, happy to be part of the group. It almost felt like a family.

After serving the three of them, Sara came around the bar to sit with them. From the corner of her eye, Charly saw Kyra coming down the stairs from the pool room on the second level.

The bottle paused at her lips. Charly squinted, then turned towards Sara. "It looks like Kyra's got a bit of a pot belly. Has she put on weight?"

Before Sara could say anything, the puzzle pieces in Charly's mind slotted into place. One piece recalled what Sharyn had said:

What about Kyra? Another piece noted Dominic's body language when he mentioned Kyra still being at the clubhouse but not Angel. The final piece understood Kyra's weight gain.

Her gaze flew to Dominic, who was watching her guardedly. "Is Kyra pregnant?"

Dominic clasped her shoulders and whispered, "Let's talk."

Charly allowed herself to be led away. She imagined all eyes on her, once again witnessing her humiliation. Déjà vu all over again.

Dominic shut the door to Achilles's office. He boxed her in, wedging her between the door and a filing cabinet.

"The baby's yours?" she asked softly.

"It could be. I won't know until a DNA test is done, but the timing is right."

She had to credit Dom with not sugarcoating it, although she wished he'd given her some warning. "How far along is she?"

"Four months." Charly worked it out in her head. They'd only started being intimate on any level three months ago.

"Charls? Not while we were together." Dom set his forehead against hers.

She got what he was saying, but with a child on the way, there were many more questions to be answered. "What are you going to do about it?"

"If it's mine, I will be a hands-on dad. He or she will know that they have a father who loves them. It's non-negotiable." He backed a step away.

Charly understood what he was saying. Her refusal to accept the baby—if it were his child—would be a deal-breaker. Well, there were deal-breakers for her, too. "You think I'd have a problem with you being there for your child? I'd have a problem if you *weren't*," she admonished him gently.

His eyes softened, and he drew her closer. "Kiss me."

★ ★ ★ ★ ★

JAX'S POSTURE EASED AS Dominic and Charly rejoined the group. His cousin had his arm around their girl, and she didn't appear upset or angry. He figured the news of Kyra's pregnancy would cause another snag in their attempts to repair their relationship, but it seemed as if Charly had dealt with it favorably. That was his warrior princess.

Vin joined him. "It seems like your girl's accepted the news." He sculled the rest of his beer.

"Thank fuck." Jax's eyes shone with pride.

"You two are putting Charly through the wringer," teased Vin. "Got to ease up on the drama, bro."

"Wait till you meet someone, Vin. I'll happily be a shoulder for you to cry on."

"Never going to happen." Vin shook his head.

"I didn't think it would happen to me. I fucked anything that moved. But you see me fucking anyone else lately?" Jax placed his glass on the bar.

"No. Why is that?" Vin swiveled on his bar stool to face Jax.

It was a decent question. "I can't explain it, Vin. She's everything these whores aren't: caring, honest, and beautiful on the inside and out. I'm getting sick of the fake bitches who only want to be an old lady. It's tiresome."

"But it's pussy twenty-four seven." Vin pointed his beer bottle at him and winked.

Jax shook his head. "I'm thirty-three, bro. Getting a bit ripe for that shit. Besides, sex with Charly is way more satisfying. Don't want to screw up a good thing again."

"Tell me more." Vin rubbed his hands together.

"Fuck off!" Jax elbowed him in the shoulder hard.

"Ouch! What was that for?" Vin rubbed at his shoulder in mock injury.

"Don't think about Charly that way," Jax warned him.

"You're the one who brought it up," Vin reminded him.

"Well, I'm shutting it down now," Jax said, wondering when he had gotten this possessive.

$$\star\ \star\ \star\ \star\ \star$$

DOMINIC LEANED INTO CHARLY while she was talking to Sara. He admired the thickness of Charly's soft, brown hair, which he couldn't resist tugging on. His eyes roamed over her exposed arms and the curve of her breasts. The urge to kiss her was strong, but he chivalrously held back. He could wait until later when they were alone. He might hold back on the kiss but couldn't hold back on touching her. His wandering hand glided around her waist, drawing her up against his throbbing cock. Dominic smirked when he felt Charly squirm. She noticed. Good.

"Leave the poor girl alone, Dom," Sara chided.

"Shut up. I'll do as I please with my woman." Dominic continued to hold her against him. He even planted that kiss he'd promised himself to wait for. Fuck waiting.

When Jax appeared, Dominic saw the identical gleam of hunger in his expression. This ramped up his growing desire to get his woman alone. He bent down to whisper in her ear. Triumph bolstered his need when Charly turned soft and pliant in his arms.

"Excuse me, I have to go to the bathroom." Charly extricated herself from Dominic's arms. The two men followed her down the hall and ushered her into one of the bedrooms.

$$\star\ \star\ \star\ \star\ \star$$

"TAKE OFF YOUR CLOTHES, Charls," Dom said as soon as the door closed.

"No foreplay?" she teased.

He lifted her chin and pinned her with that possessive gaze. "Everything we do is foreplay. Now hurry."

"What's the rush?" Charly began to undress, enjoying their banter.

Jax took over. "You want foreplay?"

Jax stood behind her and lifted her top. He pulled down her bra and squeezed her breasts. Charly sighed blissfully, placing her hands over his.

Dominic moved in, sandwiching her between the two of them. He hungrily took her mouth and ravished it, plunging deeply.

Jax pulled her onto the bed and tweaked her nipples hard, making them sting with pleasure. Dominic slid his tongue into her throbbing cunt. It didn't take long for the tremors to grow. One minute, she held Dominic's head closer; the next, she pushed him away. Jax held her still as Dominic continued to bring her to fever pitch. Her stifled cries echoed around the room.

She was vaguely aware of being repositioned on her hands and knees.

"Anyone taken your ass, Charls?" Dom asked as his hands caressed her inner thighs.

"No." When no more was said, her eyes popped open. "Why?"

"We need to prepare you, babe." Now his fingers slipped inside her still-dripping hole, spreading her moisture up and over her anus.

Charly gulped. They barely fit in her vagina. "You do? I'm not sure either of you is going to fit."

Dominic got up and left the room.

"Where's he going?" she asked Jax, panic edging her voice.

Jax smoothed her hair. "To fetch something to help you take us," he said in a low, soothing voice.

It wasn't working. Her heart raced, and she felt like she couldn't get a full breath in. "I'm not sure about this, Jax."

Jax gathered her into his arms. "It'll be a bit uncomfortable at first, but you're in control. Imagine having both of us inside you at once. You'll like it. I promise."

"How do you know? Have you had your ass taken?" She shot back, not ready to accept empty promises.

Instead of answering, Jax kissed her, momentarily dissolving any apprehension she had. When Dominic returned, her unease doubled. He held up a cone-shaped object and a tube of lubricant.

"When it's time, I'm going to insert this butt plug into your rectum. It'll help stretch you for us. It might feel a bit uncomfortable, but I won't hurt you. Do you understand?" he explained carefully.

She nodded slowly. "Yes."

He smiled. "Good. Now suck my cock."

This time, Dominic sat on the bed, and she positioned herself between his legs. His cock was already at half-mast. She used her tongue to lubricate the head, then dove in. Dominic firmly pressed down on her head, forcing her to take him deeper. She gagged when his cock hit the back of her throat.

"Breathe through your nose, Charls." He stroked her hair.

Beside her, Jax stroked himself while watching them. "Yeah, Charly. So hot. So fucking hot."

Dominic drew Charly away and told her to stand up. Jax reclined back on the bed. "Straddle Jax." With the condom in place, Charly positioned herself over his hips and guided him inside her. She slowly lowered herself down, moaning with pleasure.

Jax clutched her hips to set the pace. Charly laid her hands on his chest, bouncing up and down. She paused when something poked her butthole. Dominic inserted a finger while Jax controlled her movements.

Dominic inserted another finger. "Oh my God," she hissed as the double penetration created the most erotic sensations.

Charly felt Jax's muscles tense up, and his breathing became jagged. Working in tandem, the men took her over the edge until, exhausted, she slumped on top of Jax.

She snuggled against him. His stomach vibrated with laughter.

"Wake up. Dom's getting impatient."

She whimpered when a hand came down on her rump.

"Ow! That stings." She rubbed the reddened cheek.

"Then get on your hands and knees." Dominic's hand glided across her butt cheeks, soothing the pain. "I'm inserting the plug now." Charly tensed. "Relax your muscles. When I push in, you push out." He slowly eased it in. It didn't hurt, but she felt full like there was a big, foreign object inside her.

"Lie on your stomach." Dominic nudged her thighs apart, his cock prodding her opening.

At first, Dominic set a leisurely pace. However, he was not known for taking things slowly, and Charly squeaked in surprise when he rolled her onto her side and raised a knee. His vigorous thrusts rocked her body, setting her on fire. Charly teased her clitoris. Jax lay on the bed beside her, pulling on his cock. He grunted and then showered her chest with cum. A few minutes later, Dominic shouted out his release as Charly's orgasm set off a glorious set of spasms.

The three of them lay sprawled out on the bed, satiated. Dominic asked, "You like the plug?"

"I can feel both you and the plug. It makes it more intense when I climax," she admitted, surprised at both how it had felt and how honest she felt she could be.

"We need you to be ready to take both of us at the same time," instructed Dominic.

Charly tried to picture how that would be possible. "You're way bigger than the plug."

"Next time, we'll insert a bigger plug," he said with a shrug.

Bigger? This one already seems gigantic. "This one's big enough."

"Did it hurt?" Dominic arched a brow.

Charly felt she wasn't going to win this argument. She shook her head. "No."

"Stop complaining," he replied sternly, but his eyes twinkled.

ELEVEN

The maddening sounds of squeaky shoes sliding on polished hard-wood floors and shouts of excited laughter greeted Charly as she arrived at The Playpen on Saturday. Sara waved at her from a table at the end of the large room full of colorful play equipment.

"Where's Nolan?" Charly looked around for the dark-haired boy.

"In the bouncy castle." Sara dipped her head in the direction of the big yellow and red castle.

Charly nodded. Dominic and Jax would meet her after church. It had been two days since she last saw them because they were on one of their road trips. Charly had to quash her insecurities and trust that they wouldn't betray her again; however, it was easier said than done.

Charly placed Nolan's gift on the table, piled high with presents. "How many friends did he invite?" She tilted her head, indicating the pile of gift-wrapped boxes.

"Five. He wanted to invite the whole class, but Chad said no."

"What grade is he in?"

"Pre-primary. He loves school. He's a popular boy, and the teachers say he's very bright," Sara stated proudly.

"I agree."

"Ma and Pops should be here soon."

Charly had expected to see them today, knowing how much they adored their only grandson. It would be a real test to see if she could get through the afternoon and endure Sharyn's hostility.

Behind her, Charly felt a disturbance in the air as two big males sat on either side of her. Her pussy clenched at their familiar smells.

"Babe." Jax smacked a kiss on her forehead.

"Charls." Dominic did the same, curving an arm around her waist and pressing her up against him.

They huddled close, and Charly automatically placed a hand on each thigh. She smiled when both of them covered her hand with theirs.

Sara rolled her eyes, chuckling at their behavior.

"What, sis? We can't be happy to see Charly?" growled Jax.

"By all means." Sara spread her hands wide.

"Then can the eye roll!" Dom snapped.

"Yes, sir." Sara threw up a two-finger salute.

"Your sister giving you cheek again, son?" Deacon's question raised everyone's heads. Charly's heartbeat accelerated. Sharyn was right beside him.

"When does she not?" Jax ducked when Sara threw an empty paper cup at him.

"Hey, Ma. Pops." Dominic tipped his head at his parents.

Sharyn smiled at her son and then swept her eyes across the room. "Hi, sweetheart. Where's my grandson?"

"In the bouncy castle. Chad's with him and the other kids," Sara said.

Sharyn and Deacon sat on the bench, either side of their daughter. Sharyn had yet to acknowledge Charly.

"Hi, Charly. Good to see you again," Deacon said.

Charly appreciated his acknowledgment and inclusion. "Same here, Deacon. Hi, Sharyn." The woman gave her a cursory nod.

"Why don't we go and help Chad with the kids? Leave the women to gossip." Deacon looked around for his grandson.

Dominic squeezed Charly's thigh, offering support. "I'll stay, Pops."

"Yeah, me too." Jax held her hand firmly.

"Go on, you two." Sharyn shooed them away. "Charly can survive without you for ten minutes. Isn't that right, Charly?" Sharyn's challenging gaze held hers.

Something inside Charly locked into place—a new inner strength she hadn't possessed before. Okay then. She could deal with Sharyn on her own. If the older woman wanted a battle, she would get one. Jax didn't call her his warrior princess for nothing. "Of course," she said, never letting her eyes leave Sharyn's face.

"Behave," Dominic uttered softly into her ear. Jax sent her a worried glance.

Charly waved them off. "I'll be fine." She still had Sara to calm things down if the situation got heated.

When the men left, Charly turned to Sharyn. "Do you have something you want to say to me?"

The older woman's eyes were inscrutable. "You're not suitable for my sons."

"What business is it of yours?" she shot back.

Sharyn leaned back and crossed her arms over her chest. "Everything that involves my sons is my business."

"Well, then you need to tell them I'm unsuitable." Charly jutted her chin out with determination. "Go on. See what *they* say. Because they've made it very clear to me that they think I'm more than suitable."

Sharyn's lips pressed together indignantly, but she didn't move.

Charly continued. "What's the matter, Sharyn? Are you afraid of what they'll tell you? You should be. They know what they want, and that's me."

Sharyn waved Charly's words away. "You're too naïve and innocent to keep them interested in the long run. You have no idea what you're getting yourself into."

"What? Am I not trashy enough? Not skinny or beautiful enough? Not obedient enough? Is that what you want for your sons?" Charly kept her voice low and controlled.

"Dominic and Jackson were raised in the MC. They won't be faithful to you, Charly. How will you handle that? They're away a lot. How will you cope with the constant separation? They're going to do and say things you won't agree with. What then?" Sharyn leaned in now.

These were problems that Charly had already encountered. Perhaps Dominic and Jax didn't tell their parents *everything*. "How I react to those situations is between the three of us. *We* deal with each issue if and when it arises."

"You're no different from the women who want to tie them down. And that will never happen with my sons."

Charly scoffed. "I have no interest in being their old lady. I know you don't believe me, but I don't care."

"I suspect you have no clue, but let's momentarily put a pin in that. How long do you expect this to last?"

"Nobody can answer a question like that. Life's unpredictable."

"They're going to let you down, you know. You're nobody special," Sharyn said.

That stung, but Charly didn't react, refusing to indulge the woman. "I never said I was." Charly looked up. "But they're coming back. You can ask *them*."

Three pairs of wary eyes regarded the women.

"How did it go?" Deacon looked from his wife to Charly.

"We're good," Sharyn responded casually.

A chorus of chuckles surprised Charly. She stared at everyone in confusion. "What?"

"Ma approves, babe," Jax informed her.

Charly pursed her lips. "Approves of what?"

"Ma wanted to see if you had the spunk to take us on." Dominic faced his mother. "Are you satisfied now?"

Sharyn reached over and tapped Charly's arm. "You didn't back down, Charly. I admire that. I need someone strong enough to handle my sons."

"Told you so," Dominic declared proudly.

Sharyn smiled at her eldest son. "She also doesn't kiss and tell. I like that too."

Relief washed over Charly. No one knew the emotional toll the confrontation with one of the most influential females in her men's lives had taken on her.

Nolan ran up to Charly, his high-pitched squeal echoing through-out the hall. "Charly! It's my birthday!" Nolan climbed onto the bench.

"I know, buddy. That's why I'm here. To help celebrate your birth-day," she giggled and hugged him.

"Yay!" He jumped on the seat, and Charly grabbed him in case he toppled off. Nolan clung to her neck. "Piggyback!" he yelled. "I want a piggyback."

"A piggyback? Since you're five years old now, aren't you a little old for piggybacks?" she teased.

"Noooooo! I'm still a little kid." He got her in a chokehold.

"Yo! Bud. Ease up on Charly's neck." Jax repositioned Nolan on Charly's back so he wasn't choking her.

"Sorry, Charly." Nolan looked cute with his little boy pout.

"That's okay, buddy. Come on, then. Where shall we go?"

"To the ball pit!"

* * * * *

CHARLY WAS STILL FLOATING in a sea of bliss that night at karaoke. After the party, Dominic and Jax wouldn't leave her until they got rewarded. Happy to oblige, they tried out some new mind-blowing positions. Whenever she thought they'd done every-thing, they surprised her with something new. Each time felt even better than the last. When it was over, she sent them on their way. They weren't thrilled to be kicked out of her apartment and pestered her about where she was going. Charly had to remind them that they often went on the road, and she never knew where they were, so it was only fair that she had her secrets.

"Secrets aren't good for building trust, babe." Jax was taking the whole trust thing seriously.

"Only if they're bad secrets," she rationalized. "This is a harm-less secret. I'm not out having sex with other men."

"You pull that bullshit, and we won't be responsible for our actions." Dominic's lips tightened.

"No bullshit is being pulled, so rest assured."

"You seem chirpy tonight, Charly," Mac said as she joined them at their regular table.

"I'm just happy to see you guys." She gave them a big smile.

Mac and Jim guffawed.

"Oh, listen," Jim called out. "Steve's calling your name."

Charly went up to the deejay booth and grabbed the microphone.

"Ready, Charly?"

At her nod, the music started playing.

Tonight, she chose "Heaven" by Julia Michaels. Charly stared into the crowd and began to sing.

* * * * *

DOMINIC STOOD BESIDE JAX at the back of the karaoke bar, deep in the shadows. Their eyes were glued to Charly, hanging on to every word as she sang, her voice pitch perfect. Gun was right. Their woman had pipes, all right. Dom's eyes scanned the crowd. The once noisy audience was completely enthralled, their eyes riveted to the lone figure singing on stage.

She was magnificent. He'd always loved her fire and fallen hard for how she stood up for anyone she thought needed protection. It gave him satisfaction as he saw her start to stand up for herself more. But this? This was a whole new side of her. It wasn't just that she could hit every note unerringly; it was the emotion in her voice and the way she communicated the feelings behind the song and its melody.

"Fuck me." Jax whistled low and long.

Dominic echoed his sentiment. "Why the fuck would Charls keep this from us?"

Cheers and whistles erupted when Charly finished the song.

"Should we let her know we're here?" Jax asked.

Dominic raised his hand. "Not yet. Hold back for a bit. Let's see what happens next."

✳ ✳ ✳ ✳ ✳

CHARLY WEAVED BACK THROUGH the packed room to Jim and Mac, where a drink awaited her. "Thanks, Mac." She held up her glass and took a sip.

"I never heard that song before. Don't tell me you like bad boys, Charly." Although Jim was joking, the statement was true. She *did* like bad boys. More than she'd ever known.

"Not intentionally," she murmured.

"What's that supposed to mean?" Mac asked.

"Yeah, babe," a voice came from behind her. Charly's head swiveled around. "I'd also like to know the answer to that."

Charly choked on her Bourbon at Jax's question. Mac thumped her back as she coughed and sputtered.

"What the hell?" she croaked, her eyes watering. As she was unable to speak, the four men took it upon themselves to initiate introductions.

After the introductions, Jax and Dominic grabbed a couple of chairs and sat down. Throat cleared, eyes dry, and emotions composed, Charly cautiously observed them. These two had a nasty habit of confronting her at her most unguarded moments.

"Have you been following me?" she asked.

"Happened to be in the area, babe." Jax winked.

"You know these two, Charly?" Jim asked her quietly.

She nodded, scowling at Jax. "You're stalking me; that's what you're doing."

"Why's it such a big secret, Charls? You didn't tell us you could sing. This is something we should know." Dom leaned forward, eyes intent on her face.

Dom sounded hurt, but Charly didn't feel contrite. Experience had taught her to guard her feelings and to protect herself from getting too deep. Her singing was hers and hers alone—it always had been. She opened everything else to them. She needed to keep one little piece to herself. Regardless, this wasn't a conversation to have in front of her friends. "I have my reasons," was all she said.

"You know Charly well, then?" Mac asked.

"Yeah." Dom didn't turn to look at him when he answered. He kept his gaze on Charly.

Charly cringed at Dominic's brusqueness. She hoped Mac's line of questioning didn't get too personal or piss him off.

"Charly needs a man who's serious," Mac continued.

Charly made a face at Mac's overprotective statement.

"We are very serious," Jax said. "Both of us."

Charly's face burned. She was not ready to reveal their relationship, and Mac and Jim's raised brows further intensified her mortification.

She shook her head in exasperation, her eyes flashing a warning. "Enough already, guys. TMI."

"We're only having a friendly conversation. There is no need to be embarrassed. We're all adults here." Jax lounged back in his chair, legs spread wide.

She wanted to throttle him. "Well, this adult would like to change the topic," she said between clenched teeth.

"Fine," Dom said. "Let's get back to why you never told us you could sing."

"No. Choose another topic." She waved her hands like an umpire and changed the topic. "What are you singing next, Jim?"

The deejay announced Jim, and he shuffled up to the stage. Charly sat quietly, fuming because Dominic and Jax had turned up unannounced on the only night she considered her sacred personal time. It was becoming a problem that they didn't respect her boundaries.

Admittedly, she rejoiced in their time together; however, giving each other space to enjoy their separate interests was also important.

Dominic once explained how riding together with his brothers was a fundamental part of being a biker. Speeding along the open road was as essential as breathing. If that was the case, why couldn't she explore activities independently?

She leaned into Dominic and whispered, "I need to talk to the pair of you outside."

He nodded and stood, then followed her out to the parking lot. Jax followed them outside.

Finding a spot on the side of the building, Charly stopped. Hands on her hips, she turned to them. "Guys! Why are you here?"

"What's the problem, babe?" Jax asked, looking honestly confused.

She chose her words carefully. "The problem is that you're here. This is my night. The one thing I get to do all by myself."

"You don't want us to take an interest in what you enjoy doing, Charls?" Dominic challenged.

"No!" she shouted, then changed her mind. "Yes. I don't know."

"Which is it, babe?" Jax asked, his voice a sweet caress.

"Jax, I… it's hard to say." Charly faltered. "Yes, I want you to take an interest, but I don't want you to always sneak up on me. I want to know that I can still be my own person sometimes. You have your time on the road. Let me have my karaoke night. That's all I ask. I'm with you because I want to be with you, not because I have to be or because you control me."

"Why is your beautiful voice such a big secret?" Jax leaned against the wall.

"Because I never know where you go, what you do, or who you're with when you leave. You expect a whole lot of trust from me, but you're the ones who are meant to earn my trust. Instead, what I get is ambushed!" fired Charly.

"I'm sorry, Charls. I wasn't aware you felt this way," Dominic apologized.

"Instead of apologizing, why don't you give me space? I can't ask questions about club business. There's a line drawn between your business and me. Why can't there be a line between my business and you?"

"We heard that you could sing. We wanted to hear it for ourselves. You sing beautifully, Charly," praised Jax.

"Thank you, but could you guys leave now?" Her voice was plaintive, even to her own ears.

Dominic begrudgingly complied with her wishes and had to pull a resistant Jax away. "Fair enough, Charls. I get that you need some 'me' time. Be good." Then he drew her in for a heart-meltingly hot kiss.

"Are you sure we have to leave, Charly?" Jax asked. "Couldn't we stay to hear one more song? Maybe we could do a duet? Or I could sing. I could do Highway to Hell!"

Charly laughed and pushed him toward his brother. "No. Now go."

＊ ＊ ＊ ＊ ＊

"ALMOST THERE, BABE?" JAX'S groan indicated his Herculean efforts to hold back.

He slowed down his thrusts, then came to a dead stop as he pressed his torso against her back. He teased her clit to get her there faster. Dominic continued to thrust upward with heavy grunts.

"Yes!" she cried out, her head thrown back as her release boiled over.

Jax twisted her hair around his fist and resumed his forceful thrusts.

All three finally fell in a heap on top of one another. After a minute or so, Charly tried unsuccessfully to extricate herself.

"Don't move." Jax's slurred command made her smile.

"Dom's getting squashed," she protested weakly.

"No, I'm not," he said from beneath her.

Kissing her shoulder, Jax rolled off, grunting.

Charly went into the bathroom to get ready for work. She was drying her hair when Jax came in.

"We'll give you a lift."

It was a sweet offer, but she was fine on her own. "Not necessary. I can catch the bus. I know you have to leave early."

Dominic and Jax were heading out on the road again. Hopefully, they'll be back later this evening.

"Do you know how to drive, babe?" Jax had to shout over the noise of the hair dryer.

"Yeah."

"So, you've got a driver's license?" He leaned against the doorframe, filling the entire opening.

"Somewhere." Her brows furrowed. "I'd probably have to renew it. Why?"

"Why don't you have a car?" He trailed his fingers down her back.

Charly shrugged. "I can't afford to buy one."

"Ever tried to get a loan?"

She shook her head. "It doesn't fit into my budget. I can barely afford rent, electricity, food, and so on. I need at least a little left to go out and enjoy myself, and I don't like the idea of going into debt." Putting the hair dryer away, Charly faced Jax. "Not everyone has money." It wasn't a sore spot, but she didn't exactly like talking about her lack of money.

Jax pulled her into his arms. "You need a car, babe. I'd feel better if you had one."

"Then I'd better win the lottery," she said against his chest. She pushed him away. "Now, let me finish getting ready."

No more was said about buying a car. Instead, she hopped into their vehicle since they were so persuasive.

"Meet us at the bar and grill after work, Charls. We should be back by around six," Dom said as he let her out in front of the diner.

"Sure." Kissing them goodbye, Charly went inside.

$$\ast\,\ast\,\ast\,\ast\,\ast$$

CHARLY TOOK A BUS to the bar and grill after work.

"Charly!" Con came over and gave her a big hug. "Good to see you, Mighty Mouse!"

She smiled. "Good to see you, too, Con." She'd always had a soft spot for him, and she knew he had one for her, too, even when he pretended not to.

"We could use some help," Joel said, eyeing the spot where dirty pots and pans were stacked on top of one another. "Do you mind?"

She rolled her eyes but still rolled up her sleeves. She looked around the side of the sink. "Where's the dishwashing liquid?"

Con indicated the staffroom. "There should be a bottle in there."

As she set foot in the staffroom, she saw Jess and Maxine. They stopped talking to look her way. Ignoring them, Charly opened the cupboards, found what she sought, and marched directly back out.

She thought she heard one of the girls call her a whore, but ignored them. It still made her mad to think that she'd put her life on the line for Jess when she'd tried to stop Sol from strangling her that night. She thought she and Jess had each other's backs, but it turns out that Jess only cared about herself. Everything else was just an act.

After washing up, Charly sat in the office and waited for Dominic and Jax. She checked her watch for the umpteenth time: six thirty. Deciding she'd waited long enough, she left her bag on the filing cabinet and went to find Rocky.

She found him in the cellar, doing the stock take on the liquor.

"Hey, Rocky. Have you heard from Dom or Jax? They were supposed to meet me here at six but haven't responded to my texts."

"Yeah, about that. They got held up and won't be back till around midnight. I thought they would have let you know." He straightened up, frowning.

"Yeah, that would have been nice." Charly pondered her dilemma for a second. "All righty then, I'm off. I might be able to make the seven o'clock bus."

"They'd kill me if I let you catch the bus. It's getting dark, Charly. Here's twenty dollars. Get a cab."

"Rocky," she grinned. "I'm a big girl. I'll catch the bus."

"I know that Charly, but tonight, you're taking a cab."

Accepting his money reluctantly, Charly entered the office to grab her handbag. She was near the front desk when two policemen entered the restaurant. Charly was surprised when Jess and Maxine approached the officers and pointed at her. She stopped dead in her tracks. What was this all about? A policeman waved her over. She walked to the front desk on shaky legs. Was she in trouble? What had she done?

"She's the one who took my diamond necklace," Jess said.

"I haven't taken anyone's necklace." Fear settled in Charly's belly. This was another stunt they were pulling to get her into trouble.

"I saw her. She put it in her bag." Maxine's blatant lie angered Charly.

"I did not!" Charly cried, reeling from their treachery.

"What the hell's going on here?' growled Rocky. "Let's take this to my office. Stop making a scene in front of the customers."

Charly felt lightheaded. She'd been accused of something she hadn't done, but would the police believe her? Would Rocky?

"Rocky, I didn't steal a necklace," she pleaded with him.

"I know, Charly." Rocky squeezed her shoulder in support.

"Miss, please give me your bag." One of the officers held out his hand.

Charly turned over her bag and instinctively knew the police officer would discover the diamond necklace that Jess or Maxine had placed inside.

When the officer pulled out the necklace, he eyed Charly dubiously. "What's this, then? How did it get in your bag?"

"One of them put it in there. It wasn't me," Charly protested.

"That's not true. It was her. I saw it with my own two eyes," Maxine insisted.

"Why didn't you try to stop her?" the older policeman asked Maxine, regarding her suspiciously.

"I was afraid Charly would tell Rocky that I stole it. She's everyone's favorite little pet!" whined Maxine.

"That's fucking bullshit, Max!" Rocky growled.

"That's your necklace, Jess. Why aren't you wearing it?" Charly looked at her ex-friend skeptically.

"The clasp broke. Look." Jess took the necklace and showed the police officers the missing chain links.

This all seemed too convenient.

"I'm sorry, Miss, but we're going to have to arrest you for having stolen property," the first officer said.

Charly's face turned white. She felt sick to her stomach as the police officer handcuffed her. "Couldn't you dust it for prints? You'll see my fingerprints aren't on it."

"We can, but it takes time," the officer admitted.

"This is rubbish! Charly didn't steal the necklace." Rocky was infuriated. He turned to his two servers. "If this is another one of your schemes, you're fired."

Maxine and Jess shook their heads. "It wasn't us, Rocky. Honest," Maxine said.

"Honest, my foot." It took a lot for easy-going Rocky to get riled up, but they'd managed it.

Before Charly was put into the police car, Rocky took her aside and whispered, "I'll let Dom and Jax know. We'll get this sorted. Okay?"

"Don't tell them, Rocky! I don't want them to know. This is so humiliating." A loud sob escaped her.

"Chin up, Charly," were Rocky's last words as the police car drove away.

✶ ✶ ✶ ✶ ✶

"FUCKING HELL, JESS. WE might be in trouble now. That didn't go the way I thought it would." Maxine had cornered Jess in the staffroom as soon as the police had left with Charly. "That older cop didn't believe us, and Rocky didn't, either."

Jess dismissed Maxine's hysteria. The stupid woman was always overreacting. According to Jess, the plan went perfectly. Charly was going to jail, and she hadn't taken Rocky's threats seriously like Maxine. How many times have Rocky and Dominic "forgiven" Maxine's transgressions? Jess had only stepped out of line once before, so obviously, they would forgive her.

"We're going to lose our jobs, Jess!" whisper-screeched Maxine.

Jess had to rein in her irritation. She had little time for the paranoid harlot.

"We're not going to lose our jobs," Jess reassured Maxine.

At least she wouldn't, Jess thought scornfully. She'd see to that.

* * * * *

DOMINIC SIGHED IMPATIENTLY. ALL he wanted to do was get back to Charls. Unfortunately, their business was taking longer than they thought it would. He took out his phone and tapped on the GPS app.

"What are you doing?" Vin chugged back his beer.

"Checking up on my woman." Dom waited for the app to do its stuff.

"Don't trust her, hey?" Vin teased.

"Oh, I do. But we were supposed to meet her tonight. I sent her a text earlier and haven't heard back. Hope to hell Rock's told her we're not coming back till late." Dom rubbed his chin.

Vin asked, "Think she might be mad?"

"Hope not." Dominic used his thumb and index finger to enlarge the screen. "What the fuck?" He scowled, not liking what he saw. "Jax!"

Jax looked up from talking to Achilles. "Yeah?"

"Check your GPS tracker."

Jax frowned. "Why?"

"Just do it."

"The police station?" Jax barked. "What the hell's she doing there?"

"I'm calling Rocky." Dominic dialed his number.

Rocky picked up on the second ring. "You get my message?"

"What message?" Clearly, something was going wrong with their phones.

"Charly's been arrested. Max and Jess say she stole Jess's diamond necklace, which is bullshit."

"Fuck!" Dominic felt like he'd been punched in the gut.

"What is it, Dom?" Jax asked.

"Charly's been arrested for stealing. Some bogus shit Jess and Maxine have made up. We've got to get back. Now." He stood.

"Hang on, brothers," Achilles interjected. "We haven't finished our business here. You're not leaving."

Achilles's command was met with resistance. Dom felt pulled in half. He'd never put anything before the brotherhood and had never been tempted. But now? With Charls?

"Charly's in trouble," he said.

Achilles's voice grew hard. "Brotherhood before bitches, Dom."

"Kill …"

"She'll still be there when you get back, Dom. This won't. Leave it." He turned his back on them, preventing any further arguments on the matter.

* * * * *

CHARLY SAT ON THE chair in the police station with her stomach tied in knots. She couldn't believe this was happening to her. She wasn't a thief. Even when she'd been hungry, she'd never stolen.

"Charly Sawyer?" Her head shot up when an officer called her name. "I need to take your details."

When the questioning was over, a female officer took Charly into another room to do a body search. A humiliating affair that left Charly close to tears. After uncovering no drugs or weapons, she gave Charly some prison clothes to change into.

The jumpsuit was scratchy and smelled like someone else's B.O. Would she have to sleep in this? For a whole night? Charly froze. She thought she heard a familiar voice. No. It had to be her imagination. She was grasping at straws, creating illusions that someone would save her from this nightmare.

She lifted her eyes and peered down the hall when the person spoke again. It wasn't her imagination. It was him.

"Shane?" He didn't hear her, so she called out again, this time louder. "Detective Carter!" Charly couldn't believe that the fifty-something man who had been her savior after Fabien's death was here.

Detective Shane Carter jerked his head around when he heard his name being called. "Charly? Jesus, what are you doing here?" He came around the desk towards her. "What happened?"

He bobbed down before her, watching her with his kind brown eyes, and Charly could feel the tears ready to escape. Blinking them back, she gave him a crooked smile. He'd gotten down on his knees before her exactly like this on that horrible day when he'd told her that Fabien was dead.

"I've been arrested for stealing." Charly could scarcely get the confession out.

Detective Carter's concern turned to anger. "What the hell?"

"I didn't do it," Charly reassured him. "Some ex-coworkers set me up."

"Why would they do that?" he demanded.

"They don't like me." She chuckled weakly at his look of disbelief. "Nice that you don't believe me, but it's true. This isn't the first time they've tried something to get me into trouble."

"What are you meant to have stolen?" he asked.

"A diamond necklace. The police found the necklace in my hand-bag, which I'd left in the office when I went to help in the kitchen. They must have planted it." Why had she left her bag unattended like that? She should have at least hidden it in the office.

"Planted by whom?" Detective Carter asked.

"It was either Jess or Maxine. They're the ones who called the police. It's Jess's necklace, and Maxine said she saw me put it in my handbag. I don't get it. If she saw me, why wouldn't she stop me then?" Their story didn't make sense. Surely, someone would see that and put a stop to this nonsense.

"Because it's a set-up." He patted her knee and stood. "Listen, Charly. Let me figure out what's going on, and I'll get back to you. It might mean you have to stay in a cell tonight, but I promise to fix this. Okay?"

"Thanks, Shane." Charly was so thankful to have a friend. She desperately needed one right now. She should have known it would be Shane. He'd always been there when she needed him.

A little later, she was led to a cell. The cot was padded with a very thin mattress, a blanket, and a flimsy pillow. Charly tried to find a comfortable position so she could get some sleep. She could hear the shouts and cries of the other prisoners. Some were shouting obscenities, others were saying crazy shit, and a woman even threatened to kill herself. She pulled the pillow around her head, trying to block it all out, and drifted in and out of an uneasy sleep.

Charly was in a semi-conscious state when she heard two famil-iar voices. She pulled the pillow away from her ears as she recognized the voices. They didn't sound happy at all. Charly was worried Dom and Jax would get arrested for arguing with the officers. Rising from the bed, she walked over and peeked through the bars.

"Dom! Jax! Stop arguing!" Her shout quietened the two angry men.

Then, she heard a scuffle and a shout. "Let us see her!"

"Dom! I'm okay. Stop fighting with them." The last thing they needed was for her to get out and Dom to go back in again.

Charly could hear talking. This time, the voices were much calmer. She heard the echo of footsteps approaching. A feeling of relief washed over Charly when she saw Dominic and Jax being led to her cell by a police officer.

Clinging to the bars, she attempted to smile. Each man reached a hand through the bars to touch her in comfort.

"No touching," instructed the officer.

Reluctantly, they pulled away. "What happened, Charls?"

"I didn't steal the necklace. Max or Jess planted it in my bag. They set me up." She knew she didn't have to explain further.

"We know. We believe you," Jax said.

"Thank you. I only wish these guys would, too." Charly indicated the police officer.

The officer grimaced. "Our hands are tied. When an accusation has been made, we have to investigate it. The necklace was in your bag, so we had to arrest you. It's up to the judge in the morning to determine whether you're guilty. You can plead your case then."

"What happened to innocent until proven guilty?" Dominic scowled at the officer.

The officer repeated, "The necklace was found in her bag. It's enough evidence to hold her."

"It was planted there," Jax said.

He shook his head. "Tell it to the judge tomorrow. Your five minutes are almost up."

Charly tried not to let the misery show on her face as they said their goodbyes.

By morning, Charly was exhausted. Expecting a long wait before her arraignment, she was baffled when another officer came in and unlocked the cell. "You're free to go, Miss."

For a second, she didn't move. "Why? What happened?"

"Detective Carter arranged it," the female officer informed her, then put a hand on her hip and said, "Unless you want to stay."

Charly got the hint, stopped asking questions, and followed the officer. Once outside in the fresh air and sunlight, Charly's tiredness evaporated. She crossed the road to wait for a bus. She needed a shower and to brush her teeth. She felt dirty after lying on the filthy cot all night.

Sitting at the back of the bus, away from all the other passengers, she stared out of the window in a daze. She would call Shane later and find out what he did. Whatever it was, she was forever grateful. It wasn't the first time he'd helped her, and she owed him big time.

Leaning back against the headrest, Charly closed her eyes briefly. Images of her baby brother being wheeled out on a stretcher in a black bag took her back to the day she first met Detective Shane Carter.

She'd been sitting on her neighbor's front porch with a blanket wrapped around her shoulders when a tall man in his late thirties, wearing a suit and tie, walked up to her and offered his condolences. Charly was so traumatized by her brother's death that she hardly noticed him.

It wasn't until he bent down and laid a hand on her knee that she finally looked at him. He explained that children's services would be arriving soon, and they would take her down to the station so she could answer some questions.

At the station, he had questioned her in the presence of a children's services officer for over an hour. He asked questions about her mama and stepdad—how they treated her and her brother—and what she had been doing that day leading up to her brother's death. Charly remembered telling Detective Carter everything. He had kind eyes and was friendly. Something about him made her want to share what she'd lived through—the abuse she had suffered at the hands of her stepdad.

When she'd learned from one of her foster parents that her mama had died in prison of a drug overdose, Charly hadn't shed a tear. She had no more tears left for her mama. She didn't deserve them. That's why the urge to cry lately confounded her; it wasn't like her. Something had come unjammed since she told Dom and Jax about her childhood.

A block she'd put up to protect herself was slowly coming down, letting a lot of the old pain out, but possibly also allowing some joy in. Maybe there was more to life than just getting up every day and getting through it.

Charly was almost home, so she wrapped up her memories and filed them away, locking them tight like always.

Dominic and Jax were waiting for her outside her apartment. Before they could speak, she stopped them and said, "I need a shower before anything else."

Neither spoke. They just accompanied Charly to her apartment and waited on the couch. Their willingness to accept her boundaries and put her needs before theirs nearly sent her into another fit of tears.

Feeling refreshed and clean again, she exited the bathroom dressed in fresh clothes with her wet hair tied back.

Jax handed her a steaming mug of coffee. "Thanks," Charly sighed gratefully. It was exactly what she wanted and needed.

"A detective named Shane Carter called us this morning to tell us that you'd been released," Dom said.

"I'll have to thank him later," she replied absently. Sipping the hot liquid, Charly missed the look that passed between her lovers.

"Who's Detective Carter, babe?" Jax asked.

How did she explain who Shane was and all he'd done? "He's the one who helped me after Fabien was killed."

Understanding dawned, easing the tension in their faces. "What did he do, Charls?" Dom asked.

"When? Then or now?"

"Now." Dom's voice got harder.

Charly looked up at him, surprised. "He said he would find out what happened and fix it, which he did. I don't know exactly what he did. I'll speak to him later."

Her answer didn't seem to appease Dom. He remained tense. "We'll come with you."

Their presence would require further explanation, and she wasn't ready for that. "Don't you have to go to work?"

"Jax and I have people who work for us. There's always someone else in charge when we're on the road," explained Dominic. "We want to meet this Detective Carter."

She recognized that tone of voice. Dom had made up his mind. She was too tired and too discouraged to argue anyway. "If you must."

"We must," he confirmed.

"But right now, I have to go to work." Charly slipped on her shoes. "I managed to call Jeb this morning and explain what happened."

"How'd he take it?" asked Dominic.

"He wasn't happy. With them, not me," she assured them. She'd been so relieved when Jeb hadn't, for a moment, thought she might be a thief.

"Right answer," Jax said with a curt nod.

Charly hesitated before asking the next question. "What will happen to the girls?" She loathed pushing the issue; however, what Jess and Max had done was wrong on many levels.

Jax and Dominic exchanged another long look, then Dom said, "We'll speak to Detective Carter first. In the meantime, let them stew on it for a while. They know they'll pay for their actions."

That was okay with Charly. She wasn't sure what she wanted in the long term, but letting Max and Jess agonize for a while was the punishment they deserved.

* * * * *

SHANE CALLED CHARLY AROUND lunchtime, and they arranged to meet after work at a local coffee shop. Knowing that Dominic and Jax would not be too happy if she did this alone, Charly told Shane they would also be present.

"Who the hell are they, Charly? All I heard was that two members of the Iconic Sons MC gave the officers a hard time and that they demanded to see you." Shane's voice was tinged with concern.

"They're friends of mine." Charly could feel the heat creeping up her face and was glad Shane couldn't see her over the phone.

"What kind of friends? Are you in trouble?"

"No, not at all. They're my friends." Charly crossed her fingers and hoped no more would be said.

There was a long pause, and then Shane said, "We'll discuss this later."

Charly hung up the phone, hoping that later would translate to never. It was a conversation she wasn't looking forward to having. Shane was the closest thing she had to a father—and she was uncomfortable telling her father she was having sex with two bikers.

She knew how it looked and sounded. Cheap and tawdry. How could she explain how much more it was than just sex? How these two beautiful men were helping her heal on levels she hadn't known she needed healing. How much joy and meaning they were bringing to her life. She wasn't sure she could even explain it to herself.

* * * * *

SHANE WAS ALREADY SITTING at an outside table, waiting for Charly. She stepped up to him, giving him a tight hug and holding on longer than usual.

"Good to see you, Charly. The circumstances are not so good, but..." Shane pulled out a chair for her.

"You don't know how relieved I was to see you." It was a heck of an understatement. He'd been a lifeline, as usual.

Before either of them could say anything further, her sixth sense alerted her to the new arrivals. They prowled across the road like two leopards stalking their prey, and she sensed Shane watching their approach. He wouldn't become prey so easily.

They staked their claim to Charly possessively, hauling her in for quick, hard kisses. Message delivered, they straddled chairs on either side of Charly.

"They're your *friends*?" Shane's disbelief was written all over his face.

"What's this about friends, babe?" Jax asked.

"We're dating," Dominic said awkwardly.

"You can't even say the word with a straight face." Charly couldn't stop herself from laughing, but she also felt a warmth in her chest. Had Dom ever said that about another woman? Sara had told her that neither Jax nor Dom had ever had to pursue a woman, and Charly knew neither had formed any permanent bond with one. While it might have been one thing for them to make promises to her in private, telling someone else that they were dating was a huge step. To tell a police officer and someone they knew was important in Charly's life. Well, that was more than huge. She turned to Shane. "We're in a relationship."

Shane looked bemused but didn't comment any further.

"So, what have you got for us?" Dominic got down to business.

Shane became all business, too. "I did a background check on the girls you mentioned, Charly. Your coworker, Jess, has a history of framing other women, whom she sees as competition. Three years ago, she accused a woman of punching her in the face. When the police saw her swollen eye, they took the woman in. The next day, CCTV footage was found showing Jess deliberately banging her head against a pole outside a nightclub. Charges were dropped against the woman she accused, and Jess got away with probation but no jail time. Luckily, it stayed on her record and supported what you thought happened, Charly."

Charly listened with growing concern that the woman she'd considered a friend had a history of such disturbing behavior. How could she have been so wrong about Jess?

"I visited her home last night and demanded to know what happened. She wouldn't cooperate, so we took her down to the precinct.

After a couple of hours of interrogation, she finally admitted the truth. Maxine placed the necklace in your bag when you weren't looking. They'd seen you leave the office without your bag and hatched the plan."

There was a heavy feeling in the pit of Charly's stomach. It got heavier and tighter as Shane continued to speak.

"I had the diamond valued today. It's worth eighteen hundred dollars. That would have made this crime a felony, Charly. It's a lot more serious than a misdemeanor and could affect your chances of finding a job in the future."

"How the fuck could she afford something that expensive?" Dominic snapped. "I pay her wages, so I know it isn't within her budget."

"I asked her about it when I started working for you," Charly told Dominic. "I was admiring it, and Jess said Sol had given it to her when they first met." Charly had suspected at the time that it might have been stolen, and Sol had used it to lure Jess into the relationship. She'd been young and impressionable, and an expensive gift like that would have blinded her to many of Sol's faults. Charly almost felt sorry for her.

"They're fired," Dominic growled. "But can they be charged with anything?"

"Yes. They can be charged for making a false statement." Shane turned away from Dom and back to Charly. "Is that what you want, Charly?"

What did Charly want? Revenge had never been her style, but there was more at stake here than her anger at Jess's betrayal. Jess had done this before. She would probably keep doing it if she wasn't punished beyond a slap on the wrist. Who would her next victim be? Would that person have a "Shane Carter" in her corner? Or someone who would scan CCTV footage to see if Jess was telling the truth? And what about Maxine? If she got away with this, would she set up somebody else in the future? This was about more than just Charly. "Yes. I want them charged."

"You'll have to face them in court," Shane said. "Jess will most likely put up a fight. With the prior charge, she'll probably do some time."

"What about Maxine?" Charly asked.

Shane shrugged. "I didn't find any prior criminal history on her, so that'll be up to the courts."

That was good enough for Charly. Dom and Jax nodded their approval.

"Are you okay with getting home on your own, Charls?" Dom asked, standing.

She almost laughed. "I'll be fine."

"Okay. Jax and I have some business to take care of."

Jax stood, and with a quick squeeze of Charly's shoulder, they left. When the sound of their motorcycles faded, Shane turned back to Charly. "Any chance you're free for dinner on the weekend? Tessa would love to see you. She often asks about you."

Like her husband, Tessa had been a massive supporter before, during, and after Charly's stepfather's trial. Shane had promised to stay in touch, so he and Tessa had organized special outings during her stints in different foster homes. On one of these day trips, Shane presented Charly with her old mobile phone so that she could contact him whenever she needed to. The thoughtful gesture helped her immensely, especially when she was having a hard time with some of her foster parents. Shane and Tessa had indeed been her salvation during those dark days.

And here he was, being her rescuer again.

"I would love to come for dinner. Tell Tessa I can't wait."

TWELVE

Jess and Maxine were fired the next day and arrested immediately afterwards. Charly felt like she could finally stop looking over her shoulder. She felt light in her step as she made her way to Tessa and Shane's on Saturday night.

Tessa greeted her at the door with a hug. "It's so good to see you, Charly!"

"It's good to see you, too," Charly said, holding up the bottle of wine and bouquet she'd brought.

"You shouldn't have," Tessa said, ushering her in. "Just seeing you again looking so good is a gift."

They caught up over dinner, with Charly filling them in on her job at the diner and her friends at karaoke. When dinner was over, Charly stood up to help Tessa clear the table.

"I've got it," Tessa said, touching Charly lightly. "You stay here and chat with Shane."

Charly blew out a breath. She was pretty sure she knew what Shane wanted to talk to her about, and she knew it was only because he worried about her.

"Tell me about Dom and Jax," he said.

"They're… Well, I don't know precisely what they are. We haven't really put labels on it, but we're together," Charly said, fighting the urge to fan her flushed face. She'd never been one to do things in the shadows. She'd seen what that had done to her mother. Plus, there was no denying how important they were to her. It felt wrong not to acknowledge them.

"Charly, these men are a law unto themselves," argued Shane.

"I get that, but they would never hurt me. Not on purpose, anyway." It wasn't a lie. They had hurt her, but they were doing everything they could to make up for that, and she trusted them not to repeat past mistakes.

Shane drained the last bit of wine from his glass. "What do you see in them? The way they acted the other day, laying claim to you as if you were their property. What was that all about?"

It was hard to explain to someone who hadn't been around the brotherhood. "They care about me, Shane. I realize they might come across as possessive. I'm not denying that. To them, that's part of how they protect and keep me safe."

"Surely you can't have the same feelings for both of them?" Shane idly turned the empty glass in circles on the table.

Charly could see that Shane was struggling to understand how she could love two men at once. Why would he? She'd struggled with it herself. "I do," she insisted, surprised at how vehemently she felt. "They balance each other out. Dominic makes me feel protected, and Jax brings out my playful side. I like them equally. One doesn't overshadow the other, and their love for each other makes it that much easier."

"What about the MC?" Shane asked. "I'm worried about you being around that kind of illegal activity."

"I'm not. The bar and grill, the shop. They're all legitimate businesses." She didn't bring up the strip club. Even though it was legal, it still made her feel funny. She was grateful for how much Dom and Jax shielded her from that and some of the uglier parts of the club's lifestyle.

Tessa came back in with a chocolate cake that she set in the middle of the table. "It's unconventional," she said, making it clear that she'd been listening in from the kitchen. "You can't deny how well Charly looks, Shane. She's happy. Maybe unconventional is what she needs."

Charly reached over and squeezed Tessa's hand. Maybe she was right. Maybe being unconventional was the right thing for her.

At least for now. Explaining to Shane how important Dom and Jax were to her just brought home exactly how strong her feelings were becoming and how at risk her heart was.

✶ ✶ ✶ ✶ ✶

ON THE DAY OF Jess's trial, Charly stood in front of her closet, trying to decide what to wear. Shane had told her to expect to be called to testify, and she wanted to make a good impression. Most of her clothes were casual. Jeans, sundresses, and the like. She chose a dark knee-length skirt and a blouse with a Peter Pan collar she'd purchased for job interviews.

The courthouse wasn't crowded. Jess's case wasn't the kind of thing that drew much attention from the public. Charly slipped into the back of the room and sat down with her purse balanced on her knees.

Charly insisted that Dom and Jax go to work instead of coming to court with her. Shane was there to support her, and Charly was determined to prove that she wouldn't let Jess intimidate her into hiding by standing up for herself. Dom and Jax weren't happy with Charly's decision but respected her wish to let her go alone, understanding her need for independence.

Right before the judge came in, Shane entered the courtroom and slid into the seat next to Charly. "Are you ready for this?"

She nodded. "I am," she said, hoping she sounded confident despite her nerves.

"Remember," he said. "You did nothing wrong." Then, he moved to the front of the room to be close to the prosecutors.

That helped. She hadn't done anything wrong. None of this was on her. Jess had made her bed and now she would have to lie in it. However, that didn't make the moment they brought Jess in less awful. It took Jess zero seconds to find Charly in the gallery, and she fixed Charly with a look so full of venom and hatred that Charly physically pushed back in her chair.

Fortunately, it all went much more quickly than Charly expected. The prosecution called one of the police officers who had come to the bar and grill, and then they'd called Maxine. She'd pleaded guilty and received an eighteen-month good behavior bond with specific conditions, including having no contact whatsoever with Charly. As part of the deal, she agreed to testify against Jess.

The prosecution led her through a few questions, establishing who she was and how she knew Jess and Charly.

Then he asked, "Please tell us what transpired that day at the Brothers in Arms Bar and Grill."

"Well, Charly came in looking for Dominic and Jax," Maxine said, looking down.

"And those people are…?" the prosecutor prompted.

"Um, Dom is the manager of the bar and grill, and Jax is his, uh, brother. They're both members of the MC," Maxine said.

"Go on, please." The prosecutor indicated she should continue her story.

"Well, Jess said she wanted Charly gone and had a plan for how to do it. She knew Charly always left her purse in the office, but she didn't hide it. Jess had this necklace with a broken clasp. She said if I slipped it into Charly's purse, we could call the cops and claim Charly stole it. The cops would take her away, and Dom and Jax would be so disgusted that she was a thief, they wouldn't want to be with her anymore." Maxine licked her lips.

"Liar!" Jess sprung up from the table.

The judge banged his gavel. "Defense, control your client, please."

Jess's lawyer put her hand on Jess's arm and pulled her back in her seat.

When it was the defense's turn to question the witness, Jess's lawyer tried to poke holes in Maxine's story, but there weren't any to poke.

Then, it was Charly's turn on the stand. As she walked past the defense table on her way to the stand, Jess whispered, "Whore."

Charly held her head high and didn't show any reaction.

The prosecution led her through her version of events, her surprise at the necklace being in her bag, and her arrest. When he asked her why Jess would have targeted her this way, her only answer was, "You'd have to ask her."

Charly didn't stay to watch the rest of the proceedings. Jeb had given her the day off work, but Shane had prepared her for what would come next. There would be a forensic specialist who would confirm that Charly's fingerprints weren't on the necklace, and then the defense would have a chance to find some reason to get Jess off. She didn't need to see or hear any of it but had nothing else to do.

Charly decided to take a bus to the bar and grill to see if Dom was there. If he wasn't, she could say hi to Con and Joel. It was nice to know she could stop by and not have to worry about nasty looks from Jess and Max.

It was mid-afternoon, so the place was pretty empty when she walked in. It was too late for the lunch rush and too early for dinner. It would have been quiet except for the raised voices she heard coming from the office.

"I need more money," a woman's voice said.

Charly paused. She knew that voice. It was Kyra. A DNA paternity test had shown that Dominic was indeed the father. Charly was proud of how he'd stepped up to his responsibilities. He was paying for everything: doctor's fees, clothes, furniture, and other necessities for the baby. He'd even attended some of the prenatal appointments with Kyra.

That wasn't enough for Kyra. It seemed she always wanted more.

"What do you need more money for?" Dom asked. "I already paid your rent and gave you money for food."

"You don't expect me to just sit around that crappy apartment all day and do nothing, do you? I need money for other stuff."

She sounded like an entitled teenager to Charly's ears.

"Here, but that's it for this month. Make it last," Dom growled.

Kyra banged out of the office and stopped when she saw Charly standing in the dining room. Even far along in her pregnancy, she still looked glamorous. Charly felt especially mousy in her court clothes. A sly smile spread across Kyra's face as she reached into her purse and pulled out a packet of cigarettes and a lighter. She made a big show of lighting the cigarette and blowing the smoke into Charly's face as she walked by her.

Charly waited until Kyra had left before going into Dom's office.

"Charls!" he said, smiling that handsome smile that changed his face.

"Hi, Dom." She hesitated for a second. "I saw Kyra leaving."

He sighed. "Yeah?"

"Should she be smoking? It's not good for the baby." She sat down across from him.

The smile left his face, and he glowered. "Stay out of it, Charls. I mean it."

"I will," she promised, but it still made her want to wring Kyra's neck. Didn't she care at all about the baby she was carrying?

"Aren't you supposed to be at Jess's trial?" Dom asked, easing back into his chair.

"I left after I testified. Shane said he'd call me and let me know how everything went. I just stopped in to say hi." She fiddled with the buckle on her purse. This had been a bad idea. "I'll say hi to Con and Joel, then go."

He gave her a dismissive nod, and she left, feeling the strain that Kyra and her pregnancy were putting on their relationship all too keenly.

How much worse would it be once there was an actual baby?

* * * * *

JESS ENDED UP RECEIVING three months in prison. It wasn't much, but Charly hoped it would be enough to keep her from pulling similar stunts again. She tried to push down her worries and fears and enjoy what her life had become.

Charly loved her job at Jeb's Diner and the new friends she'd made there. Life with Dominic and Jax only got better. Their relationship—although it still had no title—was getting stronger by the day. There were moments when Charly felt a flicker of fear at how strong her feelings were becoming and at how much of herself she'd given over to Dom and Jax. There were no promises of forever here. She did her best to stay in the here and now and enjoy what they had while they had it. Still, fears crept in.

Charly caught the bus to the clubhouse after receiving a direct command for her presence, all gruff and growly. Stifling her amusement, she complied. She secretly loved Dominic's bossiness.

She found them in the front room, chugging back beers. Charly was also pleased to see Sara, Chad, and Nolan there. In fact, the whole gang was there: Vin, Gun, Gage, Achilles, Carrie, and even Deacon and Sharyn.

"Hey, what's the celebration?" She smiled at the group.

"We have a surprise for you." Jax wiggled his eyebrows.

"Should you be telling me that in front of everyone?" she teased.

"That surprise is for later. Come with us." Dominic took her hand and led her outside. She frowned when the whole party joined them. She was curious. What was this surprise? It wasn't her birthday.

"Hang on. We're supposed to blindfold her first." Sara came forward and tied a scarf around Charly's head.

She gingerly followed Dominic until he stopped. "Take the blindfold off."

Removing the scarf, she blinked in the bright sunlight. Everyone was looking at her expectantly. She peered up at Dominic, confused. "What?"

"Charls, the car." He tapped the hood of a small car.

Her gaze swung to the white car in front of her. Charly gasped, clamping a hand over her mouth. "Oh my God! Is that car for me?"

"All yours, babe." Jax was grinning widely.

Charly kept repeating, "Oh my God!" She didn't know what else to say. She was speechless. What on earth had inspired these two men to buy her a car? Why would someone spend that much money on her?

Dominic passed her the key. "Are you going to test drive it?"

"I'm a little rusty," she hedged nervously. It had been years since she'd driven. Shane had insisted she learn. He claimed it was a life skill as important as knowing how to do your laundry. She hadn't had a car to practice on since taking her licensing exam.

"There's no time like the present to start practicing. Get in." Dominic urged her towards the driver's door.

Hopping inside the car, she breathed in the new car smell. Dom and Jax joined her. Admiring the interior and familiarizing herself with the different mechanisms and gadgets, she put the key in the ignition. She whooped when the engine purred smoothly, and Dominic and Jax laughed.

Pressing her foot on the clutch, she reversed the gearshift, checking her side and rearview mirrors. It was all coming back to her. Charly drove around the block several times, only stalling the car once.

Her head was still spinning when she got out of the car. She leaped into Dominic's arms and gave him a long, hard hug. Then she did the same with Jax, thanking them repeatedly.

"You can thank us properly later."

She intended to give them the best night of their lives.

She couldn't stop admiring her new car for the rest of the evening, stepping outside several times to touch and smell it. Charly would then go inside to give her lovers more affectionate hugs.

They'd finally had enough and had rushed her into the bedroom so she could show her appreciation fully.

* * * * *

CHARLY MOANED AS JAX slowly eased his cock into her pussy while Dominic took her from behind. She couldn't believe how good it all felt.

They'd been at it for hours, and Dominic had blamed Charly's "bloody happy mood" over the car.

Falling onto the bed, her body twitching with aftershocks, she gave a deep sigh of contentment. "You've worn me out."

"Then get some sleep while you can." Dominic slid his hand down her back, over her rump.

"I might take a shower. I'm all sweaty." She rolled over.

"You do; I'll be joining you," Dominic warned.

She laughed. "You're insatiable!"

He slapped a rounded cheek. "You ought to be thankful I'm letting you rest. I'm ready for another round now, but I'm giving you some time because you're tired."

"How much time should we give her, bro?" Jax asked, pulling on his cock. It looked like he was ready to go again, too.

"Half an hour should do it." Dom fell back on the bed.

"Then you'll have to fuck me while I sleep. I need longer than that!" Charly needed at least a couple of hours.

"Hear that, Jax? She's giving us permission to fuck her while she sleeps."

Fortunately for all of them, they did an excellent job waking her up thirty minutes later.

* * * * *

CHARLY HAD NEVER OWNED a car and had no idea how much more convenient her life would be with one. No more waiting for the bus, checking the timetable, or worrying about how she would get home. It also made it so much easier to do things like shop for groceries. Even Donny, one of her friends at the diner who disapproved of her relationship with Dominic and Jax, had to admit it was a nice car and a more than generous gift. It wasn't just generous; it was thoughtful. They'd looked at her life and figured out what would make it easier. It was about her, not about them.

Still, a tiny part of her was worried. This arrangement was only meant to be temporary. She'd be devastated if either of them suddenly had an epiphany that the relationship had gone on long enough. When the date of their six-month anniversary rolled around, she decided not to make a big deal out of it publicly. There was no need to tempt fate.

Charly drove through the clubhouse gates and parked next to Rocky's Jeep. Nolan raced up to her and threw himself into her arms.

"What are you doing, buddy?" she asked, squeezing him.

Nolan peered up at her, his eyes shining brightly. "I catched a cricket. Come and see." He pulled Charly behind him, keen to show off his new bug collector. And indeed, there was a cricket jumping around inside.

"Wow! How did you catch it?" Charly crouched to get a good look at it.

"I catched it in my hands. It tickled." Nolan couldn't have been more serious.

"A tickling cricket? I never heard of such a thing." Charly tickled his belly.

The little boy giggled and danced away. "Charly! You're bein' silly."

Her handsome lovers sidled up to her as she chatted with Nolan. When the young boy talked her into looking for more bugs, she sent Dominic and Jax an apologetic look.

"All right," Jax relented, kissing her sweet spot. "But we're going out for dinner tonight, so dress up."

Dominic chuckled. "We're taking you on a *date*. See? Straight face."

She kissed him, "Impressed." She jogged after Nolan to see if they could find more crickets.

✶ ✶ ✶ ✶ ✶

JAX AND DOM TOOK her back to Stars Align. The same waiter, Ryan, welcomed them. "Ryan! Good to see you again!"

"Miss," he said shyly.

Dinner was enjoyable: great company, good food and wine, and beautiful views. This time around, Charly disregarded any envious stares she received from women at the other tables. Her men ignored them anyway; their attention was solely focused on her.

"Ready to go?" Jax got up and took the bill with him.

"What's the rush? I'm only halfway through my glass of wine," Charly said, holding up her glass.

"We have a surprise for you. We'll give it to you in the car," Dom said.

Charly sighed, not entirely unhappily. "You guys have to stop giving me gifts. I can never repay you for all that you've done already."

"This one's different. And we don't expect you to repay us," Dom assured her.

"Let me guess. You got me a puppy?" Charly teased.

"You want one?" Dom asked as he stood and offered his hand to her.

She had to be careful! These guys would give her whatever she asked for. "No!" she exclaimed. "Too much work. Plus, I can't have pets where I live."

"You'll like this surprise," promised Jax as he returned to the table.

"I always like your surprises. I'm just saying that I don't need them. You've already given me enough." She followed them out to the parking lot.

No blindfold was necessary this time. Once inside the vehicle, Jax told her to close her eyes.

"Now open," he called out dramatically.

Jax was holding up a leather jacket. She read the print on the back: Property of Dom and Jax. Still not quite comprehending, she looked to her lovers for clarification.

"Property?" she asked, frowning.

"Babe, we're asking you to be our old lady." Jax's eyes sparkled.

"What does that mean?" She'd heard the term bandied about at the clubhouse often enough, but she wasn't sure of the full ramifications.

"We want you to be our girlfriend." Dom nearly tripped over the final word.

Emotions swirled inside her. She ran her fingers over the words on the back of the jacket. "So, we wouldn't be only temporary?" Charly stumbled on the last word.

Dom took her hand. "Charls, what makes you think we're temporary?"

"We discussed it before," she replied hesitantly.

"I think we passed that mark a long time ago." Dom raised her hand to his lips and gently kissed the back of her knuckles.

"Oh." She wasn't a fool. She knew she was in way deeper than she'd ever intended to be. Still, there was a little piece of herself she'd kept walled off, just in case—one little shred she could hold onto when they got bored with her or decided to move on.

"Why the hesitation, babe?" Jax looked unhappy. "You know we care about you."

Care. Not love. She knew the relationship had changed them almost as much as it had changed her, but they had never said they loved her. It suddenly occurred to Charly why she was having difficulty accepting the jacket: it signified an important step in their relationship. It meant that she would fall deeper in love with them. The longer she stayed with them, the harder she would fall when it was over. She knew what her heart held and how broken it would be if they handed it back to her.

She looked up at Jax's beautiful blue eyes, trying to figure out how to explain it to him. "Because I'm scared."

"You never have to be scared again," Dom said. "We'll protect you."

But they couldn't protect her from themselves. Mentally, she made a list of pros and cons. Unfortunately, she had the same number of reasons on both sides, so it didn't help her decide. It was up to her to either take a chance or not.

What would her life be like if she ended their relationship today? The thought completely terrified her. Would it be easier to end it now or later? Definitely now. But how would she feel if she didn't give their relationship a chance? She would be gutted—like she'd missed an incredible opportunity.

She made her decision, breaking the last wall down. "I accept." Charly couldn't wipe the smile from her face as they drove to the clubhouse. The three of them spent the night celebrating their new future.

✶ ✶ ✶ ✶ ✶

UNBEKNOWNST TO CHARLY, IT was customary to celebrate the momentous occasion. Although she did not enjoy being the center of attention, she went along with it when people came up to congratulate her.

"What?" Dominic noticed her change in mood.

"Don't take this the wrong way, but I feel as if we're at our engagement party," she whispered to him.

He chuckled. "Bit early for that."

"Way too early for that. I still have to get used to our new situation. Is this going to change things?" She threaded her fingers through his.

He squeezed her hand. "Since you're wearing our jacket, no brother will approach you. They know you belong to us." Not that any of them ever had.

"And you belong to me." *Have to level the playing field.*

Dominic brushed her lips. "Of course."

Kyra had also turned up at the party, but not to congratulate her. All night, she'd been sending Charly glares of icy hatred. It still bothered Charly to see Kyra with a beer in one hand and a ciga-rette in the other, but Dom had made it clear it was none of Charly's business. At almost eight months pregnant, Kyra looked ready to give birth at any moment, so Charly didn't want to have any con-frontation with the woman. Keeping some distance from her, Charly approached Sara and Carrie. However, avoiding Kyra was a no-go. Kyra stepped into Charly's path before she could reach her friends.

Charly sighed. "What is it, Kyra?"

The beautiful woman brandished an insincere smile. "I hope you don't think you've won over Dom and Jax because you haven't."

Charly looked down at her sleeves. "I beg to differ. I'm wearing their jacket."

"That doesn't change a thing. Do you think they're going to be faithful to you? Are you really that stupid?"

Charly could sense Kyra working herself into a rage; her face con-torting with anger. "Listen, you're not supposed to be talking to me."

"I only have one thing to say to you. I'm having Dom's kid, not you. He wants this child, so who do you think has more power over him? *I do!*" Kyra spat the last two words. "And I intend to claim what's rightfully mine."

"Good luck with that." Despite her calm words, Charly was unsettled by the exchange. It was as if Kyra knew her deepest fears.

* * * * *

JESS CAREFULLY CUT OUT each letter from the news-paper. She'd been released early from prison three days before, determined to pay back Charly for putting her there in the first place. She couldn't believe that little bitch had sat up there in court looking like the goody-two-shoes she was, giving testimony that locked Jess up. She'd thought about nothing else during her time inside.

Phase One of her retribution plan: get the club's attention. A nice little note should do it. Phase Two was the real plan: hire a hitman. Jess wanted Charly dead. Bunny, her cellmate, knew some-one. Mike—if that was his real name—had contacted her yesterday. They'd arranged to meet in a couple of days.

Jess let out a long, quivering breath. She felt intoxicated, moti-vated, and exhilarated.

Getting back to the letter, Jess picked up the tweezers and glued the next letter to the page. This would not come back to her, she thought proudly. She'd taken every precaution: gloves and a self-ad-hesive envelope with a typed address. No Maxine to flip on her. No one knew about her distant cousin, John, with whom she was staying temporarily. Only until she got back on her feet, she promised him sweetly. Jess chuckled to herself. Fools, she mused, disgruntled. All of them were fools. They'd underestimated her.

She was going to put an end to that.

THIRTEEN

Dominic was a dad! Three weeks after confronting Charly at the party, Kyra gave birth to a baby boy. To Charly's great relief, he was underweight but otherwise healthy, weighing a little under six pounds.

Everyone had gathered at the hospital, cramming into the waiting room. There'd been an enormous cheer when Dom came out and said, "I have a son."

He was so happy, and everyone was so pleased for him. Charly was determined that she would be, too. She put on a brave face and joined in the happy hubbub.

"You can come in a few at a time to meet Jacob Dominic Price," Dom said.

Everyone stood back to let Sharyn and Deacon go in first. Dom beckoned Jax over and whispered in his ear. Jax looked down at his boots and nodded.

Jax sidled over to Charly as people lined up for their turn to meet the baby.

"What's up?" she asked as he reached her.

"Uh, Kyra doesn't want you in the room with the baby," Jax said quickly as if removing a band-aid.

Charly felt his words like a punch in the gut. She wasn't shocked. She had a nagging feeling that she would be shunned from this part of Dominic's life—the life he would have with his newborn son.

But rather than getting upset, Charly decided to wait and see how things played out. "Sure. I understand," was all she said to Jax.

Once the waiting room had emptied, she decided to walk outside. Charly found a bench overlooking the gardens and sat down.

Half an hour later, she received a text from Dom: "Where r u?"

She texted back: "In gardens on the east side."

As usual, she felt their approach almost before she saw them. Both Jax and Dom came out and sat on either side of her. "What are you doing out here?" Jax asked.

"Nicer views."

She wasn't fooling Dom. "Don't worry. Once she's out of the hospital, Kyra doesn't have a say in who can be around my son."

She bowed her head. "I don't want to cause trouble between you two. It's okay to separate time between your son and me." She didn't ever want to be the reason someone was not there for their kid.

"No, it's not," he stated firmly. "I want you to be a part of my son's life."

Charly didn't argue the point any further. They were lovely sentiments, but knowing Kyra, she would put a stop to that. The woman hated her. Maybe even more than Jess did. Since getting with Dominic and Jax, Charly had made more female enemies than she had in her previous twenty-four years.

✶ ✶ ✶ ✶ ✶

DOM WAS TRUE TO his word. He asked Charly to meet them at the clubhouse the first weekend he had custody. The second she walked in, he presented her with the baby. "Meet Jacob, Charly."

Charly dropped her bag on the floor and took him from Dom's arms. He was beautiful, with big blue eyes and wisps of blond hair. "Oh, my God, Dom. He's perfect," she gasped.

He laughed. "I know."

She walked over to the couch, sat down, and held him in her

lap, admiring him. She counted his fingers and toes, kissing each one as she went.

"I don't suppose you'd mind watching him for a bit while we're in a meeting."

"Go ahead. Just be sure to leave me with diapers and formula, okay?" She barely looked up at him and Jax as they left.

Carrie sat down next to her. "He's so cute!"

"I know. I suppose I shouldn't be surprised. Kyra's gorgeous, and so is Dom," Charly said, giving credit where credit was due.

"Could I hold him?" Carrie asked.

Charly bit her lip. "Do you know how to hold a baby this little?"

Carrie nodded. "I used to babysit."

"Okay." Charly was reluctant to let go of Jacob, but Carrie held out her arms, and she couldn't think of a reason to say no.

She transferred the baby into Carrie's arms. "Be careful. You have to support his head and neck. And oh! Watch out for the fontanel, that little soft spot."

Carrie shot her a look. "I've got him."

"I think maybe he's cold," Charly said, rummaging in the diaper bag for a light blanket. "Let me tuck this around him."

"Stop hovering, Charly," Carrie said.

But Charly couldn't stop, and finally, Carrie handed him back. Charly sniffed him. "Oh, baby. I think you need a nappy change," she cooed. "Oh, yes, you do. You are a smelly little boy."

She took him back to the bedroom and changed his diaper. "Now, let's make you a bottle. I bet you're hungry."

She rummaged in the bag to find what she needed.

✶ ✶ ✶ ✶ ✶

ACHILLES HAD CALLED FOR an urgent meeting with Dominic, Jax, Vin, and Gun.

"What's up, Kill?" Jax asked, looking around at the small group.

"Have a seat," Achilles ordered brusquely. "We need to talk."

"What the hell's going on?" Dominic demanded.

"This arrived this morning." Achilles wiped a hand down his face before continuing. "It was addressed to you two."

He handed Dominic a piece of paper with letters cut from a newspaper to create a message: *Ditch the bitch or else she's dead.*

The room fell deathly quiet. Then Dominic exploded. "What the fuck? Who sent this?" He handed the paper to Jax, then stood up and paced the room.

Jax's face turned white. "What the hell do we do now?"

"We need to protect Charls," Dom said.

"Damn right," agreed Jax. "But who would threaten her?"

"I've been wracking my brain, trying to think." Achilles scratched his head. "Our last road trip to Brighton didn't go too well. Maybe they want to get back at us."

Dominic shook his head. "They wouldn't know about Charls."

"It could be more personal than that," Gun suggested. "Maybe it's someone closer to home."

"You thinking, Sol?" Vin asked.

Gun nodded. "Or perhaps it's a woman like Kyra or Angel."

"My wager is on the girls," Achilles said. "Sol's still in prison and will be for a while. And he's angrier with Jess than he is with Charly."

"Don't discount Sol. Remember, he threatened Charly as well," said Vin.

"I don't think it's Sol," Achilles speculated. "The wording sounds like it might come from a jealous bitch."

"Jesus Christ! What the hell did Charly do to anyone?" Jax punched the table in frustration.

"There are a lot of jealous bitches out there, Jax. You and Dom were pretty popular around here," Vin pointed out. "Then Charly came along, and neither of you had eyes for anyone else."

Dom sank back into his chair. "So, what's our plan?"

"You're not going to like it," warned Achilles.

"Let's have it." Dominic was prepared to do anything to protect Charls.

"You need to end it with Charly." Achilles looked from one to the other.

"No way!" Dominic and Jax shouted at the same time.

"Hear me out, brothers. Say it is Kyra or Angel—and I wouldn't put it past Kyra because she has more to lose—if you end it with Charly, the threat goes away." He motioned as if flinging away a ball.

"Bullshit! Kyra would still want Charls out of the way. Can't we kick Kyra out of the club?" Dom asked.

"We do that, and she might make things difficult for you, especially with your son," Achilles said.

"We're not giving Charls up." Dominic could be obstinate when he set his mind to something.

"I can put Cole on the case. Get him to do some investigating," Achilles suggested.

"Yeah. That's good, Kill. Do that." Dominic relaxed slightly.

"There's still the problem of protecting Charly," persisted Achilles. "We can't let Kyra think we're on to her. We'll also check out Angel and anyone else we can think of."

"What about Jess? She's a possibility," suggested Vin.

"You're right, Vin," agreed Jax. "She got out of prison a couple of days ago, and she'd be blaming Charly for her being locked up in the first place."

The mood was somber as they planned their next move, and the vibe got darker when Achilles pushed his brothers to terminate the relationship temporarily. Dominic and Jax grew more uncooperative, and when Vin and Gun backed Achilles, the two men became enraged.

"Whose fucking side are you on?" raged Dominic at Vin.

"We're on your side, brother. We're only looking out for Charly. Her safety should be your number one priority, too." The other man wasn't backing down.

"Maybe we could stash Charly somewhere safe," Jax suggested. "Till we find out who's threatening her."

"I'm not sure Charly would go for that, brother," Vin reminded him. "Remember when she tried to escape after being cooped up here after the incident with Sol?"

"You can't tell her about this. Everyone's a suspect until we know who sent the letter. She's too trusting. Remember, she thought Jess was her BFF?" Achilles was right. Charly didn't need to know that someone wanted her dead.

A feeling of dread settled in Dominic's stomach. The more they talked, the more it made sense to break up with Charly to protect her. He looked at his cousin, but Dominic could tell that Jax wasn't on the same page yet. "Jax and I need a moment alone."

When the others had left the room, Jax turned on Dominic. "Forget it. I'm not doing it."

"Jax, we've got to look past our feelings and think of Charls. We'll have someone watching her twenty-four-seven while we figure this out. And it doesn't have to be forever. When it's over, we'll explain it all to Charls." Despite a strange tightness in his chest, he tried to maintain his composure.

"No, Dom. She won't forgive us twice. We hurt her again, and that's it." Jax shook his head.

"I disagree. Charls cares about us. She'll find it in her heart to forgive us, especially when she realizes we did it to protect her." She'd be reasonable, wouldn't she? They'd make her understand.

"I say we hide her away somewhere safe." Jax stood his ground.

"Kill said we can't tell anyone, so how would you explain hiding her?"

"Shut the fuck up, Dom. I can't do it. I won't."

* * * * *

CHARLY LOOKED UP WHEN Achilles, Vin, and Gun exited the back room. She smiled at them while Jacob slept in her arms, but they didn't look happy. Something terrible must have gone down during the meeting. And where were Dominic and Jax?

When they appeared, Charly relaxed. She walked over to them, cradling Dominic's son. Although they seemed stiff, they embraced her warmly.

"Ready to go home?" Jax's voice was jagged. Something had upset him. Charly would get to the bottom of things when they got home.

"We'll drop Jacob off first."

"I thought you had him until tonight?" She'd been looking forward to feeding him and rocking him some more.

"Something came up." Dominic's response made her even more concerned.

Arriving at her apartment after dropping Jacob off at Kyra's place, Charly could sense a change in her lovers' behavior. They were tense and unresponsive.

"What's the matter? What happened in the meeting?" she asked.

"You know we can't talk about club business. Leave it be." Dominic turned away, unable to look into Charly's troubled eyes.

$$\star\ \star\ \star\ \star\ \star$$

THEIR LOVEMAKING THAT NIGHT was different. It wasn't as rough or frantic but more tender and slower. Charly wasn't complaining—she still got her pleasure—but something felt wrong.

When it was over, Jax rolled off and went to the bathroom. He didn't come out for a good ten minutes.

"What's the matter, Jax?" Charly held her hand out to him. Jax shook his head and left the room.

Charly caught her breath at his rejection. Her eyes swung to Dominic, who was getting dressed. She had assumed they would stay the night. What was going on?

"Come outside." Dominic left her on her own to get dressed.

Putting on a dressing gown, Charly followed them into the

kitchen. Jax was leaning against the fridge, eyes downcast and arms folded. Dominic slouched against the breakfast bar.

Something was seriously wrong. Taking a deep breath to steady the sudden need to retch, Charly demanded some answers. "You two are acting strange. Tell me what's going on."

Dominic raised his powerful arms and linked his hands behind his head, flexing his biceps. He let out a gust of air. "It's over."

Charly blinked. Just like that. Two words.

Nothing was said for an eternity while Charly processed Dominic's words. So many different emotions pumped through her simultaneously: shock, confusion, disbelief, and fear. How could they do this to her? She'd given them everything, let all her defenses down, and now that they had her completely, they were breaking things off.

"It's over?" Charly struggled to get the words out. "Why?"

She was staring at Jax, who had remained silent up until now. She desperately needed to hear from him. Did he feel the same way? "Why?" she repeated louder.

Dominic spoke, "Things are different now that I have a son. I need to spend more time with him."

That didn't make sense. "I would never stop you from doing that. It doesn't mean we have to end things."

"It won't work," he said.

"Why won't it work?" She needed more explanation than that.

"Kyra doesn't want you near our son." Dom looked away from her.

"You said you wouldn't allow her to do that." Charly could hear the desperation in her voice. She never thought she'd be one of those foolish women who begged. Images of her mother lying on the floor, begging Peter not to leave her, came back to her. Was she any better than her?

"It's you or my son. And I choose my son." Dom still wouldn't meet her eyes.

Charly turned to Jax. "What about you, Jax? You don't have a son. Is it over between us?"

Jax held his hand up when she stepped closer. "Stop, Charly. It's over. Deal with it."

"What was tonight about, then?" Charly was becoming impatient with Dominic and Jax's unresponsiveness and didn't care if she was making a fool of herself. "Answer me, Jax! Explain yourself. If Dom doesn't want me anymore, does that mean you don't either? Are you only capable of loving me if it's together?"

Jax mutely shook his head, refusing to make eye contact.

"What's this about, Jax?" she demanded softly. "Why won't you answer me? Talk to me. Did something happen in church?" When he refused to say anything, Charly got angry. "Someone talk to me! Tell me what the fuck is going on! I have a right to know."

Dominic and Jax remained motionless and uncommunicative, causing Charly to back off. It was no use. Spinning around so she wouldn't have to look at their stony faces, she pressed the heel of her palms to her eyelids to stop the tears from escaping.

"Go," she whispered, defeated. No one moved. "Go," she repeated, a little firmer.

When the door clicked behind her, Charly let her body fall to the floor. She was going to be sick. Blindly finding her way to the toilet, she threw herself in front of the bowl and vomited.

After brushing her teeth, she stumbled into bed, pulled the covers over herself, and fell into a restless slumber. By morning, Charly felt like death. Calling in sick, she stayed in bed all day, leaving the room in darkness. She didn't want to come out until the pain went away.

Day turned into night. Her phone had been buzzing all day, so she turned it off. She didn't want to speak to anyone or think about anything other than how to get rid of the pain inside her chest. It was choking her; she felt as if she was slowly dying.

The following day, Charly called in sick again. She hadn't eaten, showered, or dressed. Her phone stayed off, and the room remained in darkness. Sleep was all she needed right now.

*****

DEAD TO THE WORLD, Charly didn't hear the knocking at her door or the people calling her name. She didn't hear the key turning in the lock or the sound of footsteps leading to her bedroom. She was unaware of the two men standing over her, their relief evident when they saw that she was still alive and breathing.

They quietly stepped out again, not wanting to wake Charly, and returned to the clubhouse. When Vin told them that Charly hadn't been to work for the past two days, they had to check for themselves that she was okay—physically, if not emotionally.

From now on, there would be twenty-four hours of surveillance on their woman at all times. Nothing would touch a single hair on her head.

Dominic wondered if Jax was right. Would Charly forgive them for what they were putting her through? Telling Charly it was over and that he was choosing his son over her was the hardest thing he'd ever had to do.

Dominic hated lying to Charly. The devastation he'd seen on her face had destroyed him inside. But he'd do it again if it stopped her from getting killed. A dead Charly was not an option.

*****

JESS OPENED THE CAR door and sat in the passenger's seat. She looked at the man sitting in the driver's seat.

"Mike?" At his nod, she passed him a photo of Charly. "This is the bitch I want you to kill."

Mike stared at the photo. "Pretty woman," he commented, triggering a rush of jealousy.

Mike was a big guy with tattoos—just her type. He was in his early thirties, with dark hair and piercing blue eyes. In other words, he was gorgeous and badass. Jess hated that he thought Charly was pretty.

"It's a shame you have to kill her," she said sarcastically.

Mike ignored her sarcasm. "How do you want to do this?"

"I want you to kidnap her and torture the bitch. Make her suffer as much as possible, for as long as possible." A charge of exhilaration rippled through her body as images of a badly beaten Charly flashed inside her head.

"Gotcha. Do you have the details I asked for?"

"Yes." Jess scrounged through her bag, retrieving the paper containing Charly's address and work schedule. She'd spent the past week spying on Charly and watching her every move. "The best time to kidnap her would be when she gets in her car after work. She parks behind the café. Charly sometimes goes straight to the clubhouse instead of her apartment."

Another wave of resentment washed over her. Jess could never go back to the clubhouse. It wasn't fair that Charly could waltz in and out whenever she pleased.

"I will ask you again: do you want me to do this? Once I get the deposit, there's no turning back."

"I'm one thousand percent sure. I want the bitch dead."

Jess handed over a thousand dollars in hundred-dollar bills to Mike. She had to sell the diamond necklace Sol had given her years before. Jess was sure he hadn't obtained it legally because he had had no money to spare. It had all gone on drugs, leaving her to support the both of them. Thank God the bastard was in prison.

FOURTEEN

Charly returned to work on Wednesday. When she turned her phone back on, there were over twenty missed calls and text messages from Sara, Carrie, Jeb, Rachel, and Donny. She tried not to be hurt that there were none from Dominic or Jax. Charly hated not returning Sara's or Carrie's calls, but a clean break was the best way. She turned the phone off and dumped it back in her purse, then made sure her old flip phone was charged and ready to go.

Still in a daze, Charly went about her day on automatic pilot. Take the orders, get the food, clear the plates, and do it again. It was as if the light had dimmed in the diner. Everything seemed a little darker, a little slower, and a little duller. Jax was right. There was only one way forward. She had to deal with it and get on with her life without them or the MC. She had to hope that, eventually, this pain would fade, and she'd feel more like herself again. But who was she now? Her relationship with Jax and Dom had changed her. She was less closed off. Happier. More connected. Could she still be that person without them?

Vin and Gun were smoking by their motorcycles in the parking lot where she usually parked her car when she left work. She walked past them on her way to catch the bus.

"Hey, Charly!" Gun called. "Not driving your car today?"

"Tell Dom and Jax to come and pick it up. I don't need it anymore." She kept walking.

"Slow down, sweetheart. What do you mean you don't need it?" Gun jogged to catch up with her.

She stopped and turned to face him. "I don't want anything from them. They either come and get it, or I sell it."

"Darlin', they got it for you to help you get around. It's safer," Gun said.

"Not my problem anymore, Gun." Charly reached into her bag. "Here are the keys."

Gun refused to take the keys when she tried to hand them over. Charly flicked her hand as if batting away a fly. "Fine. Let them know I'll leave the keys at the front office."

That felt empowering. Letting go of things that reminded her of them would help her get over them. That's what she told herself, anyway.

She marched to the bus stop but was aware that Vin and Gun wouldn't leave until they'd seen her safely on the bus.

* * * * *

THE NEXT DAY, SHE was positive that she saw Chad when she exited the supermarket. She shrugged it off and tried to stay busy. On Saturday night, she headed to the karaoke bar. She joined Jim and Mac at their usual table.

"Are you okay, Charly?" Mac asked.

"Yes. Why?" She took a sip of her drink.

"I don't know. You seem sort of down." Mac looked over at Jim for corroboration.

Jim smiled apologetically. "You're not quite as bubbly as you've been these past few months."

Charly knew they were right. It'd get better. It had to. She just had to make it through the next few weeks. "I'm okay. Really."

Then, it was her turn to sing. She'd chosen "Set Fire to the Rain." She began as usual, on pitch and rhythm. As she got into the song, she heard the raggedness in her voice, but she didn't stop. Not even when she felt the tears begin to slip down her cheeks. When she finished, the room was silent for one beat and then two. She thought maybe it had been worse than she thought.

Then, the room erupted in applause.

As she stepped down from the stage, her heart sank when she saw Vin and Gun at the bar. These sightings were not coincidental. Dominic and Jax were checking up on her, which irritated her. They'd broken up with her. Why the hell wouldn't they leave her alone? How was she supposed to get over them if constant reminders appeared everywhere she went?

Charly stomped over to the two buff bikers. Hands on hips, she glared at the smiling duo.

"Hey, Charly. Fancy meeting you here, sweetheart," Vin said.

"Cut the bullshit, Vin. You're following me. I want you to stop."

Vin shook his head. "I heard about your singing. I had to come and check it out."

She rolled her eyes. "You've checked it out; now go."

"I'm still drinking." Vin held up his stubby.

"Okay, then *I'll* go." She started to turn, but Vin caught her by her arm.

"You want a lift home, Charly?" he offered.

"No! I don't!" she shouted, not caring who was listening. "I want you to leave me alone. If you're worried that I'll kill myself, rest assured, I'm not feeling suicidal."

"Good to know." Vin nodded.

"Tell Jax and Dom that I'm hunky dory and no longer need a babysitter," she fumed. "The gall of them to make you do their dirty work."

Exasperated, she moved further along the bar to where Josh was serving. "Hi, Josh. The usual. Thanks."

"Are those guys bothering you, Charly? I can call security if you like," the bartender said.

"No. Don't bother. They're fine." She brushed off Josh's concern with a smile.

He cast another look down the bar at Vin and Gun. "I can give you a lift home when I finish. To make sure you're safe."

Charly appreciated his offer. Josh was a good guy. "No, thanks. Besides, I won't be here at two in the morning."

"Let me give you my number in case you change your mind," he said.

She nodded and got out her old phone. Suddenly, it was plucked out of her hand.

"Hey!" She tried to snatch it back from Gun's hand.

"What are you doing, Charly?" Gun scowled at Josh.

"Gun! Give that back to me!" Charly clasped his massive fist and tried to pry it open. It was useless; Gun's fist was like a boulder. "What the hell?"

"Can't be taking numbers from strangers, darlin'. You're still grieving and not thinking straight." He lifted the phone out of her reach.

"I'm not grieving, and I'm thinking perfectly fine," she fibbed easily. "And I've known Josh longer than Dom and Jax, so there goes your stranger excuse. Now give it back to me, or I'll get Josh to write his number down."

Vin got into her space. "No. You won't, sweetheart. It wouldn't end well for Josh."

"Did you just threaten Josh? If you lay a hand on him, you'll have me to deal with!" She stamped her foot.

"I was only offering her a lift home," intervened Josh.

Gun glanced at him cursorily. "That's our job. Don't you worry about Charly. She's our responsibility."

"I'm *nobody's* responsibility except my own. And I don't need a ride from anyone. If you don't back off, I'll call Detective Carter," Charly threatened.

"All good, Charly." Vin backed off.

Gun handed her the phone back.

She turned back to Josh. "I'll take those drinks now."

$\star\ \star\ \star\ \star\ \star$

DESPITE CHARLY'S ATTEMPTS TO move on with her life, the men of the MC made it impossible. Everywhere she went, she saw them. Why Dominic and Jax chose to remain on the periphery of her life, she couldn't say.

Charly was surprised to see Dominic and Jax enter the diner one morning. She didn't see them immediately, as she was taking orders and her back was to the door. When she twisted her head around, her eyes widened.

Stiffly, she walked behind the counter to pass the order through the serving hatch. Donny noticed her distress and, with a nod, walked up to the table where Dominic and Jax had sat down. They spoke briefly, but Charly noticed Donny didn't write their order down. When Donny returned, he delivered a message. "They want you to serve them."

Panic-stricken at the thought, Charly vigorously shook her head. "Then they can just sit there and not get served."

"I'm all for it," he agreed, "but Jeb would go nuts. Get it over with, and then they'll leave."

Chewing on her nail, she debated Donny's words before approaching the table.

With her pad and pen in hand, she looked at them inquiringly. Their haggard expressions startled her. Did they have regrets? Or was there something else going on? "What can I get you?"

"Charly," Jax said, his voice rough.

"What will you have?" Pen poised above the pad, she waited.

"How have you been?" Dom asked.

"Do you need more time to think about your order?" she asked as if he hadn't spoken.

They quickly gave their order. When Charly made to leave, Jax grabbed her wrist. Gasping, she tugged it free and stalked angrily into the kitchen. She took deep breaths and waited until her heartbeat slowed before returning to the dining area.

Charly ignored them until she had to serve their meal. Dominic took the opportunity to try again. "We only want to know that you're okay."

"I'm okay," she replied stiffly.

"That's good. It makes us happy to know you're doing well," Jax said.

Charly gritted her teeth. "Does it now? Well, it would be even better if you came and got the car. While you're at it, tell your goons they can cease their babysitting duties."

"That's not happening." Dom shook his head.

"Why not?" she demanded.

"We need to know that you're safe," Dom repeated.

"I'm safe. I looked after myself for twenty-three years before I met you. I think I can manage the next twenty-three years. Why are you doing this? You are the ones who dumped me, not the other way around. You walked away. Do you want me to be miserable? Is that what it is? Do you want them to report back about how sad I am?" Charly kept her voice to an angry whisper, aware there were listening ears everywhere.

"No, we don't want you to be miserable. We care about you," Dom said.

"If you mean it and care about me, Dom, let's cut all ties. You said it was over, so make it over. You guys go your way, and I'll go mine. Let me move on since that's what you wanted."

"That's not how it works, Charls. You're still under our care. Even though we're over, you're still our responsibility. It's how it is." Dom leaned in to get closer.

Charly stepped back, kicking herself for wanting to move closer to him instead. "Well, I'm absolving you of all responsibility."

The stubborn-headed mules refused to concede to her wishes. They didn't seem to understand how challenging the breakup was for her. The only thing Charly knew was that she had to get away from them. She had to go somewhere she wouldn't continually run into reminders of them—somewhere they couldn't monitor or control her. Her comment about moving on planted a seed of an idea. She knew what she was going to do next.

* * * * *

AFTER BIDDING EVERYONE GOODBYE at the end of her shift, Charly took the back alleyway and caught the bus to the police station. Shane had called her into the precinct to share something he'd learned. It would be a good time to discuss her plan. She hoped he'd be able to help her. She knew he would if he could.

Charly kept checking to make sure she wasn't being followed. She didn't want anyone reporting a trip to the police station to Dom and Jax. Her heart tripped whenever she heard a motorcycle go past, but she didn't spot any MC members. Taking the lift to the second floor, she stepped into the hustle and bustle of the crime unit.

Shane was waiting for her as the elevator doors opened, looking grim. No hug. No calling her 'kiddo.'

"What's wrong?" Charly frowned.

"Let's find a room." He turned to walk down the hallway.

Charly wondered what could be so grave that it required privacy. She hoped this wouldn't interfere with her plan.

Shane closed the door and moved his chair next to hers. "It's bad news, Charly."

Swallowing down her fear, she steeled herself for what was to come. She'd had a life full of bad news and plenty of practice. "Okay."

"There's a hit out on you."

"What?" This was the last thing she expected to hear. A hit? On her?

"Someone's hired a hitman to kill you, Charly."

Before moving on, Shane gave Charly some time to absorb the shock. "Do you have any idea who would want you dead?"

"I know people who don't like me, but want me dead? That seems a bit drastic."

"Who doesn't like you?" Shane asked.

"Well, there's Kyra. That's Dom's baby mama. There's Angel, another woman from the MC who was kicked out. I guess she would blame me for that. There's Sol. He threatened to come after me. And Jess, since she's out of prison now." Charly ticked the list off on her fingers. It dawned on Charly that she had a lot of enemies—most of them because of her relationship with Dominic and Jax. She frowned when an idea sprung to mind. "Do you think Dom and Jax know about the hit?"

Shane mused over her question. "Possibly. Why?"

Charly filled Shane in on the breakup and told him the guys had been watching her. Were they keeping an eye on her to protect her? Did Dominic and Jax end their relationship to protect her? The haggard looks on their faces when they came to the diner popped into her head. Were they as heartbroken as she was? If so, why hadn't they told her? She sighed. It would be just like them to decide to handle it their way without telling her anything. They'd all made so much progress towards trusting each other. Perhaps this was too much for them, and they decided they could only protect her by reverting to their old ways.

It broke her heart a little more. Maybe the relationship wasn't everything she thought it was.

They spent the next hour discussing Charly's predicament. Shane was surprised by the news of the breakup. Charly could tell he wanted to voice his opinion, but she was grateful he kept quiet. She told him about her plans. "I need to move. Someplace far enough from them that they can't stumble across me. I want to use a different name, too. Can you help me?"

"You know I'd do anything for you, kiddo," Shane said affectionately, patting her shoulder. "Tessa will hate having you far away, but she'll understand, especially if you agree to have dinner at our place tonight. Now let's figure out some of the basics."

When she got up to leave, Charly felt like a weight had been lifted off her shoulders. At the same time, traces of sadness crept in.

"Thank you for doing this, Shane. Without your help, I don't think I'd be able to get out from under Dom and Jax's control. I must get as far away from here as possible, where the club does not constantly monitor me."

"We'll find a new place for you. Somewhere, they, and whoever else is after you, won't find you."

They walked together to the underground car park. Shane unlocked the door of a police car, and Charly threw him a cheeky grin. "People are going to think I've been arrested again."

He scoffed. "No, Charly. People will now think the police are also a taxi service."

✶ ✶ ✶ ✶ ✶

AN HOUR LATER, CHARLY stood in Shane's kitchen, peeling potatoes. Tessa opened the oven door to check on the roast while Shane finished setting the table. It felt like old times when Tessa and Shane would pick her up from her foster home and take her out for the day. Sometimes, they visited places or went out for lunch or dinner; sometimes, they'd take her to their house to spend the day.

Charly marveled at the way Tessa and Shane did everything together. She couldn't remember a single occasion that her stepdad and her mama had ever said a kind word to each other or shared a simple task. Peter had been too much of a demanding tyrant, while her mama had cowered every time he spoke to her and then shut herself away.

Charly smiled fondly as she remembered Mrs. McNally, her neighbor and guardian angel, during the years leading up to Fabien's death. Her heart contracted with sadness because, several days after her brother's death, Charly had been taken into foster care and had never seen Mrs. McNally again. She often wondered how her neighbor was doing or whether she was still alive.

"Shane told me what happened, Charly. How are you doing?" asked Tessa as the three of them sat at the dining table, eating dinner.

Charly speared a potato and chewed on it slowly before answering. She understood that Shane and Tessa shared everything and had no problem with it. She trusted Tessa as much as she did Shane.

"It's been hard," she admitted. Charly wouldn't lie to the two people who'd always had her back. "But there's a lot to do before I leave, so that will help keep my mind off everything that's happening."

"I'm sorry you'll be leaving us, sweetheart." Tessa patted her arm. "Promise you'll stay in touch?"

"Definitely. I wouldn't be where I am today without you."

Charly was afraid she'd start blubbering like a baby. It tore her up to say goodbye again. Would it always be this way? Would those she grew close to turn their backs on her constantly? Sometimes, she felt her life was like a continuous revolving door, never staying in one place long enough to settle down and feel safe.

In some little corner of her heart, she'd thought that was over. That with Dom and Jax, she'd found a safe place to settle down and be comfortable. The second she'd done knocking down that last wall, they'd turned around and shoved her out the door again.

It was time to put the wall back up.

"We feel the same, Charly." Tessa's eyes glistened.

Shane broke the emotional tension: "This was your first serious relationship, Charly. Of course, you're going to be heartbroken. Although I have to admit you like to take things to the extreme. You couldn't start with a few dates with a boy-next-door type, could you?"

Charly chuckled at his teasing. "Apparently not."

*****

JESS FELT A SENSE of déjà vu as she hopped into Mike's car. "You've got the proof?" she asked, her gut clenching excitedly.

"No," he said. "You didn't tell me she had bodyguards."

"Bodyguards?" Jess asked. What the hell was he talking about?

"Yeah. Everywhere she goes, at least one dude on a motorcycle follows her."

Damn. The MC must have heard about the hit somehow. Jess knew those underground grapevines were efficient, but she hadn't realized how efficient they were. Of course, they all rallied to help out Charly. She didn't deserve any of the attention. "So, what do we do now?"

"I'll figure something out, but it will cost you."

"How much?" Jess asked.

"The thousand you were supposed to pay me tonight when the job was done, plus another thousand."

Jess dug into her pocket. "I don't have the full thousand, but here's three hundred dollars now, and I'll pay you the rest when I get it."

"That wasn't our deal. A thousand dollars upfront and a thousand dollars when the job was done. I want my money!" Mike grumbled. Even pissed off, the man looked hot.

"I haven't got it yet," Jess repeated. "I can always offer an incentive. Give you a blow job if you like."

"Fuck that!" The angry man bellowed. "You're telling me you were going to try to rip me off, and you think sucking my cock will make me forget all about it?"

"You sure?" Jess fluttered her lashes, ignoring his threat. "It's a little sweetener on top of your money. You'll enjoy it."

"Stupid bitch!" He grabbed Jess by the throat.

Jess scratched his hands, trying to loosen his hold, but he was too strong. She tried to reach for his eyes, but he'd anticipated that and made sure he was out of her reach. Her vision began to dim. Gray crept around the edges, narrowing what she could see down to a pin-prick. Then everything went black.

* * * * *

MIKE DROVE FOR OVER an hour before turning off the highway along a dirt track. Then he drove for another ten miles until he reached rugged terrain, which was covered with rocks and low-lying bushes.

He hopped out of the van and then dragged Jess's body out of the back. He grabbed a shovel and started digging. It took a while, and he was sweating hard by the time it was deep enough to be sure it would be a long time before anyone found the double-crossing bitch, if they ever found her at all.

Before he dragged Jess's body and dumped it into the hole, he found the $300 she'd had in the pocket of her jeans. He stretched his aching back. Which girl he killed didn't matter to him as long as he was paid.

Picking up the shovel again, he began the process of filling the hole back in, tossing soil over Jess's dead body.

* * * * *

OVER THE FOLLOWING FORTNIGHT, Charly went about her routine. She felt guilty for keeping her coworkers and friends in the dark. She had spoken to Jeb, who promised not to say anything until after she'd gone. He'd been disappointed she was leaving, saying she was one of his best workers. Where on earth was he going to find another Charly? She'd felt both sad and proud.

The slightest sound—a stranger watching her or someone following her home—caused Charly to become alarmed. Ever since she learned that there was a hitman after her, she'd become more alert to her surroundings.

She started taking a different route to work each day, sometimes taking two or three buses when one would typically do. She asked Jeb to change up her work schedule for the next few weeks so she'd be less predictable.

At night, she'd jam a chair under her doorknob to backstop the locks. It was something she'd learned in foster care—a way to keep people out while she was sleeping.

The day finally arrived. Charly woke up to an overcast morning that matched her mood. She made a mental list of everything that needed to be done before leaving her apartment for the last time. Her luggage was packed, ready for one of Shane's detectives to collect later this morning. She had told Mr. Kozlowski that anything left behind he could keep for the next tenant.

Charly was on high alert at work, her heart skipping wildly as the time drew closer for her escape. She left her phone switched on in her locker, then quietly slipped outside to wait for the skip bin truck to pull into the alleyway. She waited anxiously, sweat soaking her palms.

The truck coming down the alley was the best sound she'd heard all morning. When the driver exited the truck to inspect the bin, she quickly snuck around to the passenger side, carefully opened the door, and hopped in.

The driver hopped back into the truck, lifted the bin, and emptied the contents into the garbage disposal unit. After slowly setting down the bin, he pulled forward and re-entered the streets.

Charly stayed low in the seat, hidden behind the driver, so nobody would see her leave. Even with all the changes she'd made to her schedule and routes, she knew a couple of MC bikers would be watching her. They were tenacious. She had to give them that.

The noisy truck drove several miles up the road and into a parking lot. When the driver got out, Charly quickly jumped out of the other side and ran behind the building to the spot where she had agreed to meet Shane. He was waiting inside an unfamiliar blue car.

"Hey," Charly glanced around the car's interior. "Where did you get this car?"

"It's Tessa's. We will do a car swap, but I need you to sign this first." Shane handed her a piece of paper.

"What is it?" She read the paper. It was a contract of sorts: She was signing over ownership of her car to Tessa in exchange for Tessa's car. The form already had Tessa's signature, so it only required hers. After signing it, she passed it back to Shane.

"Good. I'll get you to drop me off back at the precinct. Then we'll say goodbye." Shane watched her sadly. "For now."

Before Shane got out of the car, he handed her a yellow envelope that contained some papers and a new driver's license with a different name, similar to her real one, but changed enough that the MC wouldn't be able to find her with a simple search.

"The address is written on the keyring. I've also included a map for directions. It's about a two-hour drive away. You'll be fine, Charly. And safe. I'll call you in a couple of days to see how you're settling in. In the meantime, you know how to reach me."

After some hugs and tears, Charly was on the road to her new life. She would call Dominic and Jax when she arrived at her destination in case they panicked and thought something terrible had happened to her. She was already dreading the call. It would be excruciating to say their final goodbyes.

✶ ✶ ✶ ✶ ✶

DOMINIC'S PHONE BUZZED. IT was Vin. "What's up?"

"She's gone."

Dominic's heart stopped. "What did you say?"

"Charly's missing. We can't find her. She's not at the diner, but no one saw her leave, and she's not at her apartment, either."

"How the fuck did you screw this up, Vin? Bloody, find her. Now!" Dominic hung up.

"Let me check her phone." Jax's hands shook as he got out his phone and zeroed in on Charly's whereabouts. "She's at work."

"Vin said she wasn't there."

Both men hurried outside on their bikes. They zoomed out of the compound towards the diner.

Rushing inside, Dominic went straight to Jeb. "Where is she?"

The older man shook his head. "She resigned today. She left a couple of hours ago."

"Where did she go?" Dominic's stomach sank. He had a bad feeling about this.

"I don't know. Home?"

They raced to Charly's apartment complex, climbed the stairs, took three at a time, and knocked on her door. When there was no answer, Dominic had no qualms about breaking in.

They opened cupboards, closets, and drawers. Most of them were empty except in the kitchen.

"Jax!" At Dominic's shout, Jax entered the bedroom. Only one item of clothing was hanging in the wardrobe: Charly's jacket with their names sewn on the back.

"Fuck!" Jax covered his mouth.

"How the hell did she escape from right under our noses?" Dom demanded.

"Charly's pretty cunning when it comes to escape attempts," Jax reminded Dominic.

"Where the fuck did she go? Her car! Is it still here?" They ran out of the apartment to the undercover garage. "It's gone. Did she sell it already?"

Once they had located her car, they revved their engines and sped to the address. They reached the front door, knocking loudly.

"Hold your horses!" A shout came from inside the house.

When Detective Carter opened the door to the two men, he didn't look surprised. "Ah. Charly's friends. How can I help you, gentlemen?" There'd been a slight pause before he said the last word.

"We need to see Charls," Dom demanded, ignoring the slight insult.

Shane leaned against the doorframe, looking very casual. "Afraid I can't help you there, gentlemen. Charly's not here."

"Where the fuck is she?" Dom took another step forward, inching into the man's personal space.

"I don't know," Shane replied casually.

"Why is her car here?" Jax asked.

"I bought it from her. It now belongs to me." Shane smiled, clearly having anticipated that question.

"How long has she been planning this?" Dominic tried to contain his growing fears. This didn't happen overnight. This had been carefully coordinated.

"You're asking the wrong person," Shane replied. "Charly hasn't said anything to me beyond wanting to sell the car."

The man's calm demeanor belied what he was saying. Dom didn't believe a word. "You don't seem too upset about it."

"Oh, believe me, when you leave, I'll be doing my own investigation," Shane said.

Dominic knew he was lying. "If you find anything, let us know." It was an order.

"Definitely," Shane said. "You'll be my first call."

Dom knew that was bullshit.

As they mounted their bikes, Jax grimaced. "He's not going to tell us anything."

"I know. But don't worry. We'll do our homework. Cole will be able to find out where Charls went. He can find damn near anything."

* * * * *

JAX SLUGGED BACK HIS beer and banged his empty glass on the bar, signaling for a refill. Sara obliged without a word. He could tell his sister had a few things she wanted to say but knew better than to do it while both were upset.

Meanwhile, Cole worked his magic on the computer—or at least Jax hoped it would be magic. Cole was good—very good. It took time, though, and Jax had trouble waiting for results. If he could have shaken answers out of the computer, he would have.

Dominic's phone buzzed. His cousin frowned at the number on the screen. "Unknown number."

"Answer it," Jax said. "It could be her."

"Yeah?" Dom said as he put the phone on speaker.

"Dom." It was her.

Jax let out a little breath. At least she was alive.

"Charls?" He made eye contact with Jax. "Where are you?"

"I'm somewhere safe."

"Where?" Dom demanded.

"Somewhere you don't need to know. I'm calling to let you know I'm okay, and you don't need to worry about me."

"That's not good enough, Charls. Tell us where you are," Dom growled into the phone.

Jax leaned over the phone. Maybe it was time for a bit of sugar, something he was better at supplying than Dom. "Charly? It's me. Jax. Tell us where you are, babe. We need to know you're somewhere safe."

"I can judge that for myself, Jax. I promise you; I'm safe," Charly vowed. "I know about the hitman."

The news floored him. "How do you know about that?"

"I wanted to know why you were watching me so closely, so I did some research." She sounded so matter-of-fact as if researching hitmen on the dark web was something she did every day.

"How did you find out about the hitman, Charly? It's not something you'd find on the regular internet." Dom was up and pacing.

"I have my sources."

"Detective Carter." Jax figured that bastard knew more than he let on. "Come back home. We can better protect you at the clubhouse."

There was a tiny pause. "No. That's not a good idea."

"Why not? You'd have twenty-four-seven protection. You wouldn't need to look over your shoulder all the time." It seemed so obvious and reasonable.

"It was time to move on anyway. Listen, I have to go. I'm safe and can look after myself from here on out. I didn't want you to worry."

As if that were going to stop them. "Don't hang up, babe," Jax interjected urgently. "We need to talk about us."

She snorted. "I don't think so. We're over. Remember? Your choice. Your idea."

"That's because we were trying to protect you," he insisted. "We're trying to find out who set you up to be killed. Let us do that, knowing you're safe here with us. Please."

Charly declined the offer. "Why didn't you do that in the first place?" She shook her head, knowing they couldn't see her. It was pointless rehashing the 'whys.' "Our relationship was always going to be temporary. I wasn't happy that you ended it sooner than I wanted, but I've come to terms with it. I'm ready for a new chapter in my life. And if either of you cares about me, you will respect that. You also would have trusted me."

"That's bullshit!" Dominic burst out. "I didn't want to tell you it was over. I didn't mean a single fucking word I said that day. I'm sorry for hurting you, and I promise I'll never hurt you again. Please come home."

"I've heard that before," she said. "I learned a lot from our time together. I know now that I need to protect myself as much as I want to protect other people. I'm sorry, Dom, but the answer is no. Goodbye."

Charly hung up, abruptly ending the call.

Jax stared at the phone. She was gone. There was a dull, hollow ache behind his breastbone. How could he have let this happen? He'd known from the start that she was special—so strong and kind. She'd changed him. She made him look beyond what he wanted and what he needed to think about her. He'd found something new in himself, something tender. Somehow, he'd let her get away.

Dominic threw the phone across the room with all his might.

"Dom! Fuck! What did you do that for? How's Charly going to contact you now?" Jax picked up the shattered phone, staring at it.

Dominic stomped out of the clubhouse. Jax picked up the phone pieces and handed them over to Cole. "Any hope for it?"

Cole shook his head. "I think the SIM card might be okay, but the rest? Probably junk."

"Any chance of tracing that call?" he asked.

"Doubt it. I was trying while you were talking. It looks like it was a burner phone. I couldn't get a location." Cole's look was full of sympathy. "She's smart. It won't be easy if she doesn't want you to find her."

Great. One of the things he liked best about Charly—her smarts—was going to make it hard to get her back.

After a few minutes, Jax entered the gym, where Dom aimed powerful strikes at the punching bag with his bare fists. He watched for a minute and then fetched the first aid kit, waiting for Dom to work out his rage before he tried to patch up his cousin's swollen and bloodied hands.

Afterwards, both men sat in bleak silence for a long time.

"Can Cole fix my phone?" Dominic asked quietly.

"Doubtful. The SIM card's good, and she's got my number. Cole said she used a burner phone, so he couldn't get a location."

"You were right, Jax. Charls is not going to forgive us this time."

For the first time, Jax witnessed Dominic cry.

✶ ✶ ✶ ✶ ✶

CHARLY TURNED INTO THE parking lot at the Waterford Apartments. Climbing the steps, she entered the empty foyer, rang the bell at the front desk, and waited. Service was slow, so she rang the bell again. This time, an older woman came hobbling out.

"Sorry, dear. I'm not as fast as I used to be. How may I help you?"

Charly smiled at the friendly-looking woman. "I'm your new tenant."

"Oh. Right. Let me get the paperwork." She read the name on the form. "You must be Charlotte May?"

"That's right. You can call me Lottie."

"Welcome, Lottie. I'm Shirley Douglas."

Once inside her new apartment on the second floor, Charly looked around at the space that would become her new home. It was sparse but clean.

Charly stood by the window, gazing at the park across the road. She heard several children playing on the playground equipment. One little dark-haired boy caught her attention, and her heart contracted. He reminded her so much of Nolan. As she watched the young boy run to his mother, Charly was unaware she was crying until something wet splashed onto her lips.

FIFTEEN

Jax followed the motion of the blonde's head as it bobbed up and down on his cock. The new stripper at the club had a mouth like a hoover. She was playing with his balls and giving it her all—sucking him deep and hard. Now and then, she would look up at him and flash a seductive glance.

"What's the matter?" she purred, her hands rubbing up and down his semi-hard cock.

Jax lifted his chin towards the other chair. "Go to Vin."

Vin looked over at Jax, frowning. "What's wrong, bro? Sybil's the best we got."

This provoked a reaction from the brunette sucking Vin's cock. The arrogant man silenced her muffled outrage. "Shush, sweetheart. You're a fucking pro, too."

"Not in the mood." Jax tucked his now flaccid cock back into his jeans.

"Listen, bro. I'm happy to take another one. More loving for me. But you're missing out." Vin hesitated. "And it has been two years, Jax."

Angry, Jax got up. "I'm going home." He didn't need to be reminded of how long it had been since Charly left.

What did Vin expect him to do? Forget Charly and move on?

When Charly had first disappeared, Jax had fucked a different whore every single night, trying to erase the memory of her—or maybe he'd been trying to recapture the high he felt when he was with her. Whatever he'd been trying to do, nothing worked. On the other hand, Dominic had buried himself in his role as a dad. His son was his whole world. He hadn't hooked up with anyone, either.

Even more frustrating, they'd heard a bit of gossip circulating about a woman who had tried to double-cross the hitman she'd hired to kill her rival. The woman had ended up dead instead. A few other details had made Jax think that the woman in question was Jess. When he and Dom went looking for her, they couldn't find her. She'd disappeared. It had to have been her who had hired the hitman and gotten killed instead of her intended target. Charly wasn't in danger anymore. She could come home. There was no way to tell her that, though.

Finally, Sara had taken Jax aside. "You miss her," she said.

She didn't even have to say who she was talking about. He knew. "More than I thought possible."

"So, fucking find her. Stop moping. Do something."

"How are we supposed to do that?" he demanded. "Cole has done everything he knows to find her, and you know there aren't too many people better with a computer than him."

Sara looked skyward for a second as if she were schooling her impatience. "Get off your ass and look for her yourself. You and Dom."

"Where? Where do we even start? It's a big country, if you haven't noticed."

"I noticed, but you've got a secret weapon. You know your girl. For the first time, you two took the time to get to know someone. You know what she likes, what's important to her, and what she does for fun. Use that knowledge, Jax." Sara urged. "Please. I miss her, too."

Since that day, Dom and Jax had spent every free minute frequenting every karaoke bar they could find. Sara had been right. They knew Charly would find someplace to sing. Working their way out in concentric circles, they showed her picture everywhere they thought she might go.

So far, they'd had no luck. It didn't matter. Jax wasn't going to stop searching, and neither was Dom. They'd bought a home together, so Jacob had a haven away from the clubhouse. The MC would always be their family, and Jake was a big part of that, but Dominic had made it clear that he didn't want his son around the club whores. Jax suspected that Dominic partially blamed them for driving Charly away. That was why he kept his time with Jake separate from his partying at the clubhouse.

Jax pulled his bike up the driveway. He clicked the remote, and the double garage door slowly lifted. Entering the kitchen via the garage, Jax listened for any sounds coming from the house.

"Dom?" he shouted as he approached the stairs. "You home?"

Jake was with Kyra this week. If they had a road trip during Dominic's week with Jake, he paid Mrs. Pope, the next-door neighbor, to look after him. Jake loved staying with her because she had a chihuahua named Barker. He was a little yapper, for sure.

Dom came down the stairs. "Where are we off to today?"

"Arberton," Jax said. It was in the next ring out.

Dom snorted. "Better not tell Nolan. He'll be pissed if he finds out we were that close to LEGOLAND and didn't take him."

"My lips are sealed," Jax said. "Now, let's ride."

* * * * *

DOM HEARD HER WHEN they walked into the Drop That Mic karaoke bar. He froze. There was no mistaking her voice, its sweetness, clarity, and power. She was singing the song about bad boys—the one she sang the first time they'd heard her.

Jax froze next to him. He'd recognized her voice, too.

Dom surged forward, ready to pluck her off the stage, throw her over his shoulder, and haul her back home, where she belonged. Jax put his hand on his arm to stop him. "No, bro. Let's be smart about this."

Dom gritted his teeth, not liking the implication but knowing his cousin was probably right. "What do you suggest?"

"Let's pull back and watch." Jax led Dom to the empty table in the back.

They retreated into the shadows.

Dom feasted on Charly with his eyes. She'd changed. Not much, but he could see differences. She stood straighter and carried herself with more confidence. She was still curvy and delicious, but anyone seeing her would know there was strength beneath the softness.

She finished her song, and the room erupted in cheers. "Yeah, Lottie! Sing us another one, Lottie!"

Dom looked over at Jax and mouthed, "Lottie?"

"Figures she'd be using a different name. Otherwise, Cole would have found her by now," Jax said.

On stage, Charly bowed to her fans and bent over to talk to the person operating the karaoke machine. This time, she chose a country song about climbing mountains and wanting to move them. The words struck a chord within Dom because they described Charls so well. He settled back and let himself enjoy his woman's talent.

They stayed in the back after Charly finished singing and watched one or two more performers. None of them held a candle to Charly. "What do we do?" Dom asked.

Jax leaned over to speak quietly. "We wait. We watch. We gather information. Then we come back, and we bring our secret weapon."

* * * * *

A WEEK LATER, A few minutes after nine o'clock in the morning, Nolan came racing through the front door. Their nephew jumped up and down, shouting with excitement.

"Settle down, bud." Jax picked him up and threw him over his shoulder, which made Nolan squeal even louder.

"Jesus, Jax," said Sara. "Tossing him over your shoulder will only get him more pumped up. He hasn't stopped talking about Little LEGOLAND since waking up this morning. My ears need a rest."

Jax plonked Nolan back onto his feet. "Say goodbye to your mom, pal. We'll leave just as soon as Uncle Dom is ready to roll," Jax said.

"Bye, Mama!" Nolan yelled, almost pushing Sara out the door.

Once Dom came down, the three of them headed out. "Buckle up, Nol," Dominic instructed the still-squirming lad.

By the end of the two-hour drive, Jax was relieved to arrive at their destination. Nolan had chatted nonstop about anything and everything. The main topic was LEGOLAND: the LEGO pirate ship with real pirates and the LEGO cars kids could ride in.

For the next three hours, they wandered through the theme park. On the pirate ship, Nolan, the daredevil, was the only kid brave enough to walk the plank, landing in a sea of blue foam balls. After that, all the other kids wanted a turn. Jax felt absurdly proud.

They walked to the LEGO cars. Only children up to twelve were allowed to ride them, so Jax and Dominic watched from the sidelines as Nolan pretended to drive a vehicle that moved along a conveyor belt.

"How much longer, do you think?" Dom asked.

Jax checked his watch. "Another hour. Then we're on."

By late afternoon, even Nolan was knackered and ready to leave. As they returned to the car, Nolan blurted out that he was thirsty.

"Perfect. I know where we should go," Dominic rumpled his nephew's hair.

As they were driving down the main street, Jax spotted the café. Dominic turned into the parking lot, and the three walked inside the coffee shop.

✳ ✳ ✳ ✳ ✳

CHARLY PARKED HER BLUE car across the street from the Mean Street Café, where Polly and Avery were waiting for her.

It was two doors down from the Drop That Mic bar, where she did karaoke every Saturday night. When the coast was clear, she jogged across the road.

Searching for her friends, who were also her neighbors, she waved at them. Polly and Avery were mother and daughter. Charly had met them two years ago when she'd first arrived in Arberton, although it had taken some time for her to open up to them as she had still been reeling from the breakup with Dominic and Jax.

The memory of the two men never left her. Charly often woke up from nightmares in the middle of the night, crying and sweaty. They were mostly dreams of her trying to reach her lovers, but they disappeared before she could get to them.

For a long time, any noise or sudden move from a stranger in the street would alarm her. She was terrified that the hitman had come to kill her. Over time, the fear had lessened, and now she could leave her apartment without constantly looking over her shoulder. The fear she'd once had of the hitman might have diminished, but the knowledge that someone was looking for her never went away. The possibility of him finding her was still very real.

Shane and Tessa had stayed in touch and visited her once every couple of months. Spending time with familiar faces was fantastic, but their departure always left a void in her chest.

"Hi, guys. Sorry, I'm late." Charly kissed each woman on the cheek. The three met every week for coffee at this café.

These two women were touchy-feely people, especially Polly and Charly had grown accustomed to their affection. Polly and Avery were nothing like the resentful, bitchy women at the clubhouse or her coworkers from the restaurant. They were like a breath of fresh air. Having friends who showed no petty jealousy or malicious intent made Charly value their friendship even more. She felt like she could breathe when she was with them.

"We haven't ordered yet. We were waiting for you." Right from the start, Polly treated Charly like a second daughter.

The server came over and wrote down their orders. Avery, a second-grade teacher at the local school, regaled them with hilarious anecdotes about her young students. Charly secretly treasured the stories because they reminded her of Nolan, who would be in grade two now.

"And Samuel asks me, 'What's *corrumption*, Miss Stephens?'"

"Charly!"

The high-pitched shout made Charly's head spin. Her face drained of color when she spotted Nolan standing beside Dominic, who looked like he'd seen a ghost.

Heart banging against her chest, Charly sat motionless, indecision clouding her thoughts. Should she say something? Approach them? Invite them over? Run?

The decision was made for her as Nolan broke free from Dom and ran pell-mell to her, already talking before he reached her. "Charly! We went to Little LEGOLAND. It was awesome. You should have come with us. Where have you been? What happened to your hair?"

Charly couldn't help laughing at Nolan's enthusiasm. "I got a haircut, buddy."

Charly self-consciously touched her shoulder-length asymmetrical bob, wondering what Dominic and Jax thought of her new hairstyle. She loved it because it was so much easier to maintain.

Dominic strode after Nolan. "Charls." He struggled to get her name out, his voice thick with emotion.

Polly and Avery both looked puzzled. "Charls?" Polly asked.

Charly managed to gather her wits and explain. "It's a nickname." She watched with joy and panic as Jax approached her table, too.

"We've missed you, babe." His voice sent tremors through her.

Charly found it hard to look Jax in the face. She'd been lost for a long time after leaving them and was only now getting used to never seeing them again. And, of course, here they were.

"Who are your friends, Lottie?" Polly smiled at the trio standing around their booth, even though she was uneasy. Why wouldn't she be? Jax and Dom looked no less dangerous than the day Charly had left them.

"Lottie?" Dominic scowled.

"Short for Charlotte." Charly blew out a shaky breath. The situation was becoming uncomfortable. Polly and Avery knew her as Lottie May. How was she going to explain her deception?

"We need to talk," Dom said.

Charly could tell Dominic was aware of her predicament and was allowing her to explain herself away from her friends.

"For a few minutes, I guess," she said. Charly stood on wobbly legs, and her hands trembled so much that she tucked them into the pockets of her shorts.

Charly almost cried when Nolan pried one of her hands from her pocket to hold. She smiled down at him and squeezed his hand. She let him lead her outside, conscious of Dominic and Jax following closely after. Charly crossed her arms protectively and regarded the two solemn-looking men as they went around the corner.

"Okay, I'm here. What do you want to talk about?" She kept her voice light in front of Nolan.

"Why did you leave?" Dom demanded.

"I couldn't stay there. You know why I left," she replied shortly, aware that Nolan was listening in on their conversation. "We've discussed it before."

A feeling of déjà vu came over her when Jax and Dominic glanced at each other. They still did the ESP thing. Then Jax tugged her forward, and she stumbled into him. He enfolded her in his arms, although Charly kept her arms rigidly by her side.

"Glad to have you back, babe. We missed you. We'll talk later." Just as quickly, he walked off, taking Nolan with him.

"Nolan's gone. Now talk." Dom took up a wide-legged stance.

"I told you…"

"Why did you leave and not tell us where you were going?" he pressed.

She stared at him. Had he forgotten what they had done to her? "We were over, Dom. You broke up with me. There was no need to tell you. We were no longer in a relationship because you chose to end it."

"I explained why I ended our relationship. I did it to protect you. Jax and I still wanted to be with you." Dom gazed at her longingly. "We still do."

Charly's mind was spinning. She'd spent the last two years trying to get over them. She wasn't ready to go back to how things were. "Yet you didn't trust me with the truth. You didn't tell me what was happening. Instead, you manipulated me and tried to control me."

Charly's body went taut when Dominic linked his hands behind his neck. He looked skyward and blew out a frustrated breath. "You don't have to worry about anyone wanting you dead. That's over."

"What?" she gasped, shocked at this new information. "When? How? Who?" Why hadn't Shane said anything? "I need to know everything."

"You will. In good time. First, we need to discuss your coming home."

Nothing had changed. It was still all about his agenda and how he wanted things. "*This* is my home now, Dom. I'm not going back. I have a new life here."

Jax returned, leaving Nolan in the vehicle to watch his iPad. "Gage is coming to pick him up," he told Dominic.

Charly's brows furrowed. "What do you mean? Why aren't you taking him home?"

Jax scowled at her as if she'd lost her mind. "Without you? Not happening. We've been looking for you for two fucking years. We're not leaving without you."

She pressed her lips together. "Get used to living in Arberton then because I'm not leaving."

"Your friends don't know who you are, do they?" Dom asked.

Charly glared at Dominic. "Your point?"

"I bet they'd be upset to know you've lied to them." Dominic's threat was clear. He turned and began strolling back towards the café.

"You want to tell them? Go ahead," she said boldly. "But if you think blackmailing me is the way to get me to come home with you, you don't know me at all."

Dominic came to a standstill and turned to face her.

"Charls, you had to make a new life because you were in danger. But you're safe now. If you let us, we'll tell you everything, but first, we need to know that you're coming back with us."

"Why?" she wailed.

"Because we care about you," explained Jax. "We always have. Everybody misses you. You have family back home."

"I can't do it. I've made a new life for myself here." Charly turned to Jax. "And your family is not my family. Polly and Avery are my family because they don't try to control me. There's no drama or jealousy. They enjoy having me around. Your lifestyle is too much for me. It put me in danger over and over again."

"What do you mean our family is not your family, Charls? Are you saying that Sara, Carrie, and Nolan aren't important to you anymore?" Dom asked.

"It's not that, Dom, and you know it! It's everything else. I didn't have any freedom. You constantly monitored my movements or questioned my actions. It was one rule for you and another for me." She shook her head, remembering all the little frustrations and arguments.

"Cut us a little slack, Charls," Dominic argued. "We went into this relationship as blindly as you did. Of course, we were bound to make mistakes. At least we discussed our problems and tried to meet you halfway."

He wasn't getting away with that one. "Did you do that when you ended the relationship?"

"I told you why I did that, Charls. To protect you," Dominic justified. "That's all I ever wanted to do."

"I didn't know that. All I knew was that I was sucker-punched when you suddenly ended it. Jax didn't even give me a reason why he ended things." Charly's glare was full of accusation.

Jax looked guilty. "It was a shitty thing to do, Charly. I'm so fucking sorry."

"It's too late for sorry, Jax. It's been two years."

"You left us!" Jax bit out. "How the hell was I supposed to apologize if I didn't know where the fuck you were?"

Charly was startled by Jax's outburst. He was usually the even-tempered one.

"Then perhaps you should have told me what was happening," Charly said. "We could have worked it out. Instead, you kicked me to the curb."

"We didn't fucking kick you to the curb, Charls," Dominic blasted, upset at her accusation. "We watched over you to make sure you were safe."

"That's not what it looked like from where I stood. Dominic, we can argue this until we're both blue in the face, but it won't change anything. I'm staying here and don't care whether you stay or go. It's up to you." Charly stood firm.

Dominic's jaw was grinding so hard that Charly thought his teeth would shatter. Jax looked like someone had clocked him in the face.

"Hold on a sec." Dominic grabbed Jax by the nape, and they walked around the corner. She could see them whispering, their heads bent close together. Now and then, Jax would shake his head vehemently, and Dominic would grip his shoulders and give him a gentle shake. When Dominic returned alone, he said they were staying.

Jax walked back to the vehicle, where Nolan laughed at something on his iPad.

"I'm going to come back in with you," Dom said.

Charly's lips twisted in disbelief.

She headed back inside. "You won't even try to put yourself in my place, will you?"

"We'll talk about it later," he dismissed, trailing close behind her as she made her way to the booth where Polly and Avery were waiting patiently.

"Polly, Avery, this is Dominic."

Dominic charmed her friends, and Charly was irked to find that she was still not immune to his appeal.

Her awareness was heightened when he placed a hand on her lower back, guiding her into the booth, then slid across the seat with his thighs pressed against hers. She shot him a warning glance, which he deliberately ignored.

"How do you know Lottie, Dominic?" asked Polly.

Dominic replied. "She worked for me at my restaurant."

Avery looked skeptical. "You own a restaurant?"

Charly saw Avery's glance flick to Dominic's kutte.

"A bar and grill," interjected Charly, trying to distract Avery from any awkward disclosures.

"What brings you to Arberton?" Charly glanced at Polly, grateful for her diversion.

"We promised to take Nolan to Little LEGOLAND."

The older woman smiled. "Your son is delightful."

Dominic chuckled, and Charly's gut clenched at the familiar sound. "He's my nephew," he corrected. "But he's a handful."

Charly said farewell to her friends a while later and promised to catch up with them soon.

"I'm parked across the street," she told Dominic when he started leading her towards his vehicle.

"Come chat with us for a bit before you leave. Say goodbye to Nolan."

She spotted Gage talking to Jax.

"Hey, Charly. Good to see you."

"You too, Gage. How did you get here so fast? You weren't speeding, were you?"

"Course not."

"Don't drive like a maniac on the way home with Nolan in the car."

"I wouldn't think of it."

Charly opened the passenger door. Nolan looked up from his iPad and jumped across the seat, flinging himself at her. "Charly!"

He was heavier than she remembered, but she settled him on her hip. She gave him a big cuddle, and he bounced enthusiastically in her arms. Laughing, she kissed him on the cheek and put him back in the car.

Gage, now a fully patched member of the MC, tooted as he left with Nolan belted up in the back seat. The boy had caused a fuss when his uncle Jax told him to go with Gage. He wanted to stay with Charly.

"Okay, babe. Where do you live? We'll follow you."

"Where are you staying?" Charly dodged Jax's question.

"With you." He made it sound as if no other option was available.

"I live in a one-bedroom flat. There's nowhere for you two to sleep."

"No problem. We'll sleep on the couch or the floor."

* * * * *

JAX GOT INTO THE passenger side of the vehicle, his eyes tracking Charly to her car. He couldn't contain his joy. Once inside the vehicle, he whooped exuberantly.

"We've fucking found her, Dom! I'm still pinching myself. Is this real?"

"It's real. We need to bring our girl home, Jax."

"True, brother. We need to be patient, Dom. We have to do it right this time. If we push too hard, Charly will only resist. We need to choose our battles." Too much of what she'd said resonated with him. She'd been right about a lot of it. What she was wrong about was whether or not he could change. He knew he could. So could Dom.

"We managed to finagle our way into her apartment. Thank God she didn't put up too much of a fight," Dom remarked.

"We were lucky this time, Dom. But let's hold off on putting too much pressure on Charly. We need her to come back willingly." The next few days would determine their future with Charly. If Jax had learned anything about Charly, it was that she didn't like being controlled. It was time to change tactics if he was to win her over again. However, time wasn't on his side.

Jax noticed Dom gripping the steering wheel tightly as he negotiated the heavy traffic, keeping Charly in sight.

✶ ✶ ✶ ✶ ✶

CHARLY OBSERVED THE TWO men as they surveyed her tiny flat. It wasn't much, but for one person, it was sufficient.

"Small," Jax commented, taking in the open design. "Neat." The room contained a single bed, a kitchenette, and a small bathroom. A table and two chairs had been placed underneath the window ledge, and a television sat on top of the drawers.

"No couch," Dominic said ungraciously.

"I guess you'll both have to sleep on the floor unless you prefer the comfort and space of a hotel." Charly was pleased that the guys would be uncomfortable sleeping on the hard floor.

"Got anything to drink?" Jax ignored her suggestion, making himself right at home.

"Wine, orange juice, or water."

They eventually settled on juice as the most tolerable choice. After pouring three glasses, Dominic and Jax sat at the table while she occupied the bed.

"You said you'd tell me everything. Tell me what you know," Charly demanded, mentally preparing herself to hear difficult news.

"What do you want to know first?" Dominic leaned on his knees, absently spinning the glass in his hand.

"You said that I was safe. How do you know this?"

"We're pretty sure we know who wanted you dead. That person

tried to double-cross the hitman she hired, and he killed her instead." Dom's expression was flat.

Charly stared down at her hands. "Who hired the hitman?" She regarded Dominic closely as he swiped a hand across his mouth.

"Jess."

"Jess?" Charly's stomach twisted painfully. It hit her hard to know Jess had that much anger and hatred toward her. "You're sure she's dead?"

"Charly, stop fretting. Jess can't get to you anymore." Jax walked over to her on the bed and sat down beside her. "We didn't see the body ourselves, but everything we've been told matches up."

"I haven't seen anything on the news about it," she said, still not ready to believe them.

"And you probably never will," Jax replied. "The guy knew how to get rid of a body. I doubt she'll ever be found."

Charly pulled her legs up to sit tailor-style. If there was no body, there'd be no police case. No wonder Shane hadn't said anything to her. He probably didn't know himself.

✶ ✶ ✶ ✶ ✶

DOMINIC STOOD OVER CHARLY as she slept soundly. Her hair covered her face, and he tenderly smoothed it away. He wanted to see her beautiful, peaceful face. The moonlight allowed him to drink in the sight of her. Her lips were parted slightly. He wanted nothing more than to lie beside her and kiss her until they were out of breath.

He'd woken with a start, afraid that Charly had disappeared again. He relaxed only when he saw that she was tucked safely under the covers.

Dominic heard a rustling noise and turned to see Jax. "Couldn't sleep?"

"Worried she'd run off again," Jax admitted.

"Same."

"What are we going to do, Dom? She doesn't want to be with us anymore. And I don't want anyone else. I've tried it, and it doesn't work."

Dominic understood what his cousin was saying. He thought about her nonstop. Every day for the past two years, he'd been worried about where Charly was, who she was with, and if she was safe. It was not knowing that was the hardest.

Dominic was aware that Charly's absence had affected Jax, too. He'd just taken a crazier route: fucking every female within arm's reach.

"We have to show her we've changed. We must show her we're the kind of men she wants to be with."

* * * * *

THE SUNRISE BROKE THROUGH the curtains, gently waking Charly. She stretched her arms and arched her back. With a tired groan, she blinked away the morning grogginess.

When she finally opened her eyes, she balked. "Jesus!" she coughed when she caught Dominic and Jax watching her with amusement. She'd totally forgotten about them.

"Morning, sleepyhead," Jax laughed. "Glad you're finally awake."

Embarrassed, she rushed into the bathroom. Feeling refreshed, she emerged twenty minutes later, dressed in her work uniform. It was Monday morning, and she had to be at the supermarket where she worked in forty minutes.

"Where are you going?" Jax asked.

"To work." She quickly and efficiently tied her hair into a messy bun. Dominic and Jax seemed to take great pleasure in the simple action, their gazes watching her every move.

"What are we meant to do all day?" complained Jax.

"If you're worried about being away from the club, you can leave anytime." Charly had her back to them, searching inside her bag for her keys. She expected one—or both—of them to explode at that suggestion. When two arms came from behind her and trapped her against a hard body, she stilled.

Jax whispered against her neck. "We're not going anywhere. Ever."

It felt so good to have him pressed against her back, the deep rumble of his voice reverberating against the sensitive part of her neck. She couldn't stop herself from thinking about the times she'd been sandwiched between them, feeling them both moving inside her, every inch of her claimed by them. She felt herself begin to moisten between her legs, and her nipples began to pucker.

No. She also had to remember how they'd broken her, how they'd tried to control her, and how being with them had turned her quiet, simple life upside down. She stepped away from Jax, twisting out of his hold.

"I'll see you after work, then." She grabbed her keys and left the apartment.

It wasn't so easy to shake them.

Christine, her coworker at the supermarket where she worked, sidled up to Charly as she unpacked apples from boxes and stacked them on the shelves, placing the fresher ones at the back.

"I think you have a couple of stalkers," she whispered, eyeing Dominic and Jax hanging around the front of the store. "Those two hotties have been loitering outside for the past hour. Do you want me to call the police?"

Charly considered the idea for a few seconds to teach them a lesson. Then she reconsidered, realizing she had no heart to get them into trouble. "No. I know them. Let me talk to them." Charly asked Christine to hold the fort while she went out to speak to Dominic and Jax.

"You can't stay here, guys," she warned them. "My coworker is threatening to call the police."

"When do you get a lunch break?" Jax asked.

She only had thirty minutes for lunch and wouldn't spend it

arguing with them. "Find something else to do, Jax. I'm not having lunch with you."

"Babe, give us a break. We want a chance to earn your trust again," he reasoned.

How many times did they expect her to play this game with them? "I already gave you a chance. This isn't going to work. You're wasting your time trying. Go home."

"Charly," began Jax.

"Let's go, Jax," stated Dominic. "We'll see you after work, Charls."

"But," he protested.

Dominic squeezed his shoulder, silently urging him to back down. Jax acquiesced, but not happily.

* * * * *

"WHAT THE HELL, DOM?" grumbled Jax.

"Jax, you need to settle down. Charls is going to fight us all the way. We need to be diplomatic about this. Charls doesn't like it when we always check up on her. She's told us that—more than once. We need to listen. We have to stand back and let her be. It's the only way we can earn back her trust."

"It's hard, Dom." Jax dropped his face into his hands.

Dominic sympathized with his cousin. "I know, brother, but it's the only way. It's part of who we are—being in control—but now we must let go. Every time we push, she pulls back. What we've done in the past doesn't work. You know that."

"What if she never wants to come home with us? It would kill me to leave her behind." Jax sounded almost as grumpy as Nolan when told he couldn't have a cookie.

"Then let's be smart about this. You said it yourself yesterday. We have to choose our battles. Remember? Let's take it one day at a time. Show her that we can be patient and wait for her to decide if she wants to be with us."

Jax frowned and opened his mouth to argue, but Dominic grabbed his shoulder. "Listen, Jax. I'm not saying we'll give up if she doesn't want to be with us. I'm saying to show some restraint. Let Charls see that we care about her and want only the best for her. I'm focused on getting her trust back and not intending to fail. You with me?"

"You know I am."

SIXTEEN

Charly came home that evening to find dinner prepared and waiting for her on the table. It wasn't anything fancy—roast chicken, mashed potatoes, and green beans.

"I didn't know you cooked," Charly said, looking back and forth between the two men. Maybe there were more hidden sides to them.

Jax blushed. "We don't, but we know how to pick up take-out food and put it on a plate."

Charly couldn't help herself. She laughed. "You do it well." She washed up before joining them at the table. There was no discussion of her returning with them, and there was no pressure on her to decide. They asked about her day and what it was like to work at the grocery store. They wanted to know if she wanted to stay at that job or do something else.

She fiddled with her fork on her plate. Long done with the meal but not wanting to break the pleasant spell it had cast. "I've always wanted to attend school to get a degree."

"Why don't you?" Dom asked.

"I never had the time or the money." She'd looked into it. Even junior college cost more than she could afford, unless she was willing to go into debt.

Jax and Dom exchanged one of those looks that seemed filled with information only the two could decipher. "What would you like to study?"

"I always wanted to be a teacher." Teachers had been her heroes growing up. So many of them had stepped up to help her and slip her extra school supplies and the occasional meal when she'd been a kid.

Dom nodded a few times. "Makes sense. You're great with kids."

Then the conversation moved on.

The following two nights were much the same until the end of the meal on the third night.

"Need to head back soon, babe." Jax shoveled several fried chips into his mouth.

That got her attention. "You do? When?"

Jax quickly glanced at Dominic before answering. "Soon. A few days at the most. Maybe tomorrow."

"Oh," she said quietly.

"We can't stay here forever, Charly. The club needs us. We've got businesses to run. The brothers are holding down the fort until we return." Jax put his hand over hers.

"I understand." Charly swallowed her disappointment.

"As much as we want to, we can't make you return with us. If this is where you want to stay, Charly, we must accept that." He took his hand away. "We have to honor it."

"I know." Charly stopped eating. She wasn't hungry anymore. Pushing her plate away, she got up to take it to the sink.

What was wrong with her? Had she thought they'd spend eternity sleeping on her floor and talking about her day when she got home? She was impressed that they'd done it for as long as they had. She was even more impressed with what Jax had said about honoring her wishes. There'd been no attempt to force her or control her.

Maybe they had changed.

Had she?

✶ ✶ ✶ ✶ ✶

THE NEXT DAY, CHARLY was arriving home from work when she spotted two unfamiliar Harley-Davidsons outside her apartment complex. Dominic and Jax stood under the eaves at the front of the building, talking to Gage and Achilles.

Gage was the first to notice her. "Hey, Charly."

"Hi, Gage. You're back," she quipped.

"Like a boomerang," he tossed back.

Charly jerked her chin at Achilles in acknowledgment, and he responded likewise. The austere man intimidated her, and nothing had changed.

"We'll be inside in a minute, Charls," Dominic informed her.

"Take your time."

Charly wondered if the guys had come to talk Dominic and Jax into going back home. The idea of them leaving left her with an uneasy feeling. Did this mean they were leaving today? She suppressed the urge to cry.

Jax and Dominic entered the apartment. They seemed preoccupied and solemn. This confirmed her suspicions. "You're leaving?"

"Tomorrow," Jax said seriously.

"Well," she croaked. "Say hi to everyone for me."

That's not what she wanted to say to them. A tight fist wrapped around her lungs and squeezed, making it hard to breathe. What Charly wanted to do was beg them not to leave. Charly reflected on how, in a couple of days, all the past hurt and betrayal had vanished in the face of being separated from them again. Charly had been uprooted so often that, with people coming and going in her life, she'd had no chance of cultivating stability or healthy relationships. People came and went in her world. Charly was never able to hold onto anything or anyone for long. Everyone walked away from her, or she was pushed aside. The only stable people in her life were Shane and Tessa.

Now, she was in limbo. She could either continue her new life as she had done for the past two years or take a gamble and return to an uncertain future with her ex-lovers.

The answer came to her in the middle of the night. Unable to sleep, she'd spent half the night sifting through her emotions.

Charly knew with certainty that she couldn't be apart from Dominic and Jax anymore. Her heart had suffered enough heartache and loneliness to last a lifetime. She was ready to put aside her misgivings and give them another chance. It was on her if it proved to be another mistake.

Dominic and Jax woke up early the following day to prepare for their trip home. Charly puttered around nervously, waiting for the right moment to make her announcement. It was while the guys hovered by the door, about to leave, that she spoke up.

"I…" Charly cleared her throat and started again. "I'm ready to come home."

The following silence was deafening. Blood pounded inside her head.

"You're ready to come home, and what, Charls?" Charly wasn't surprised by Dominic's question.

"And try again. I'm terrified but more scared of not having you in my life anymore. Please don't hurt me again."

"Babe," whispered Jax, hauling her into his arms. "I swear, babe. I won't hurt you. Ever."

Charly held on tightly. When Dominic's warm hand rested on her shoulder, she went into his arms. He kissed the top of her head. "Thank you, Charls. It means the world to me that you're putting your trust in me. In us. I won't let you down again."

"Some things will need to change, Dom," Charly mumbled into his chest.

Dominic's arms tightened around her waist. "I know," he whispered into her hair.

"You both need to allow me some freedom to go places and see people without any guys following me." Charly didn't let go of Dominic, loving the feel of being wrapped up in the safety of his arms.

"We can do that," he agreed.

"And let me make my own choices about what I do with my life without any resistance from either of you." Charly peeked around Dominic to look at Jax questioningly.

"No argument from me, babe," said Jax, grinning happily.

Giddy with relief, they made plans for Charly's return. Charly was surprised when Dominic revealed that he and Jax had bought a house where they spent most of their time with Jake. She would be staying with them there. Unfortunately, she couldn't leave immediately. First, she had to say goodbye to her two dear friends, Polly and Avery. Then she needed to give her employer at the supermarket and her landlord, Mrs. Douglas, notice that she was leaving.

Dominic and Jax arranged to drive back in two weeks to help her move. In the meantime, they would stay in touch by phone.

Now that she had decided and plans were in place, Charly felt a sense of freedom that had been missing for two years.

Getting out her phone, Charly dialed Shane's number to update him on her situation. She let out a nervous breath, worried about telling Shane that she had reconnected with Dom and Jax because he'd put so much time and effort into helping her escape. Charly also suspected that he didn't know that Jess was dead because he would have said something to her. Placing a hand on her chest, she silently commanded her heartbeat to settle down. She sat and readied herself for a long and serious chat with Shane.

$$\ast \ \ast \ \ast \ \ast \ \ast$$

THE DAY ARRIVED, AND Charly checked her reflection in the mirror. She wore her favorite blue and white, floral, bell-sleeved romper with the sleeves off her shoulders.

Dominic and Jax were ready to go; they had been for forty-five minutes. But when Charly exited the bathroom in her sexy outfit, their jaws dropped. She was so busy folding her clothes that she didn't notice them drooling over her. When she finally did look up, she frowned.

"What? Should I change?"

"No!" rasped Jax, then cleared his throat. "No. You look nice."

"Are you sure?"

"Believe me. We're sure. You look beautiful," Dom assured her.

"Okay, I'm ready." Charly heaved her suitcase off the bed, but Jax promptly got in her space. He firmly moved her aside to take the luggage, and Charly noticed he was staring at her exposed shoulders.

Jax reached out for her car keys when all the boxes were loaded into the back of the Jeep.

"I'm driving your car. You're riding with Dom," he said.

"My car's too small for you. It's better if I drive my car. I'll follow you."

"Humor us, Charls," Dominic said, grinning.

She blew out a breath. It would be easy to fall into their old patterns. They were all going to have to work on it together. "No. If Jax wants to ride with me so you can be sure I'm safe, that's fine. But I'm driving my car."

The two men exchanged a glance, and then Jax dropped his hand. "Let's go, then."

Charly giggled as Jax wedged his large body into her car. It was a tight squeeze. Charly looked over at Dominic in the other vehicle, who also smiled.

Charly was a careful driver and kept her eyes on the road, but every time she glanced over at Jax, he would quickly look away. Her skin prickled when she caught sight of his unmistakable erection. She began to regret her choice of outfit. She wasn't sure she was ready to rush back into their physical relationship right away.

"Are we going to your house? Will Jake be there?" she asked.

Dominic had spoken briefly about his son during their phone conversations, and Charly was eager to see him again.

Jax shook his head. "We're stopping off at the clubhouse first. Everyone's eager to see you. Jake's with Kyra. She'll drop him over at our place in the morning."

Charly felt her insides shrinking. "Is Kyra going to be at the clubhouse?"

"Don't worry. She won't be there." There was something off in his tone.

Charly picked up on Jax's odd mood. "What's wrong? There's something you're not telling me."

"Ma and Pops will be there," he admitted.

Great. So much for an easy homecoming. "Are they angry at me?"

"Pops, no. Ma might be a little upset."

Charly swallowed hard. "Jax, I'm not ready for a confrontation with your mom. I don't need that shit."

Jax reached across the seat and clasped Charly's hand. "I promise you, none of that shit is going to rebound on you. I'll take care of it."

Jax grabbed his phone and made a call. "Hey, Pops. We're almost home. Charly is with me. Make sure Ma is on her best behavior. I won't have her upsetting Charly."

Jax listened for a while longer and then hung up the phone. "It's taken care of." He squeezed her knee reassuringly, then left his hand there. Her skin tingled where his hand rested.

✳ ✳ ✳ ✳ ✳

NOLAN CAME GALLOPING OUT of the clubhouse. "Charly! You're here!"

Charly gladly let him usher her inside, where a crowd of familiar faces welcomed her.

Sara and Carrie were the first to hug her. "You look great, Charly," Sara smiled. "Your hair looks amazing. It suits you."

"Thanks."

Charly stepped back and trod on someone's shoe: Dominic. Jax moved by his side, creating a barricade around her and pushing Vin and Gun back.

"Dom! Jax!" she scolded, trying to create a bit more room.

"What's the matter with you two? You brought me here so everyone could see me."

"Of course we did, babe. The guys don't need to get too close." Charly couldn't help noticing Jax's eyes lingering on her bare shoulders. She felt his gaze like a caress.

The crowd parted, and Sharyn appeared. Charly could tell the woman was trying to be nice, but she sensed it wasn't genuine.

Charly was astonished when she stepped onto the back patio and met a larger crowd. A roar of cheers went up, and Dominic and Jax seemed to revel in the unexpected reception.

A table had been set up, and beer kegs were rolled out. Someone was standing next to an open spit, roasting a pig.

It was early evening when Charly bumped into Serena, another woman from the club, in the ladies' room. Serena finished applying her lipstick then turned to face Charly. "What the hell are you doing back here? Nobody missed you."

"Apparently, they did." Charly was fed up with the drama and knew she had to start sticking up for herself. She gave Serena a saccharine, sweet smile and walked off.

Hearing voices from the front room, Charly paused at the end of the hallway. She recognized Vin's and Jax's deep voices.

"Babe!" Jax yelled.

Charly gave him a quick wave and told him she was going outside to talk to Sara and Carrie.

"I'll come with."

"No. You stay here. I love the mohawk, Vin. Sexy," she teased, ignoring Jax's growl of disapproval.

When Dominic and Jax decided to leave, Charly followed them outside. Dominic put out a hand to help her up into the vehicle. This time, she followed their decision to drive her car since she'd had a few glasses of wine. They got to the house, and Jax helped her out of the car and walked her to the front door, opening it with a grand gesture.

The entrance was magnificent. A staircase led to the second floor. On the left side of the stairs, Charly could make out a breakfast bar. To the right was a doorway leading into the living room.

"Should we get my things from the car?"

"Later. We'll show you your room first." Jax guided her up the stairs, and Charly was grateful she wouldn't share a room with them. She was touched that they made sure she had her own space. Maybe this would work. Perhaps they'd all changed.

"Wow."

The bedroom was huge for a guest room. A double bed sat in the center of the room. On one side of the bed was a door to the bathroom, and on the other was a walk-in closet. There was a desk under the window. Charly walked over to examine the papers. Brochures for the local teachers' college. She held them up and looked questioningly at Dom and Jax.

"You said you always wanted to be a teacher," Jax said. "We think you'd be a great one. There's no need to rush into anything, but we'd help if that's what you want to do. It's just something to think about."

Charly clasped the brochures to her chest and tried not to cry. These men listened to her. They wanted to support her. They wanted to make her dreams come true.

With his arm around her waist, Dominic showed her the other rooms. Dominic's bedroom was at one end; Jax's was at the opposite. Her room was in the middle, along with Jake's. Nolan shared a room with him whenever he stayed over. "You like it?"

"Nope. I love it," she said, leaning into his chest.

After a house tour, Dominic and Jax collected her luggage and boxes. They wouldn't let her carry anything, so she started unpacking while they brought her things up.

Once everything was put away, there was an awkward moment as they all stood in Charly's bedroom. No one wanted to say goodnight, yet no one seemed to know what to do next.

Finally, Jax cleared his throat. "We want you to know that this is your room, and we'll only come in if you invite us."

Charly swallowed hard. She didn't know if she was ready for this, but there was only one way to find out. She undid the back of her romper and let it fall to the floor.

"Well, come on in."

$$* * * * *$$

THE DOORBELL RANG, WAKING Charly. She inched open her bedroom door and peeked through to see Dominic opening the front door at the bottom of the stairs. Kyra held a young boy who reached out his arms to Dominic.

"Daddy!"

Dominic swooped him into his arms and kissed his soft hair. It looked like Dominic and his son had a close relationship. The boy held on tightly to his dad's arm.

"Can you drop him off on Sunday night? Justin and I are heading out early Monday morning."

Dominic handed Jake over to Jax and told him to take his son into the kitchen.

"For fuck's sake, Kyra. You asked me the same thing last week. I'm supposed to have him until Monday morning. Tell your loser boyfriend to stay the fuck away from Jake. I told you before I didn't want him around my son."

"Justin's never done anything to hurt Jake, so leave him out of this."

"You don't think I haven't looked into Justin Klim, Kyra? He's a fucking drug dealer."

"He doesn't sell drugs anymore," defended Kyra, growing agitated.

"That's bullshit, and you know it. Pick Jake up on Monday morning."

Dominic closed the door firmly and disappeared into the kitchen.

Charly went into the bathroom to shower. Feeling apprehensive after everything that had happened last night, she descended the stairs. Walking into the kitchen, she relaxed when she saw Dominic bouncing Jake on his knee. The toddler giggled each time his dad tossed him up high.

When Dominic saw Charly standing by the archway, he set Jake on the floor and went to the breakfast bar.

"Want some coffee?"

At her nod, he got out a mug and poured some coffee. Charly glanced over at the two-year-old, who hadn't moved from where Dominic had set him down. He sucked on his thumb and pointed to her.

"Mmm," he babbled.

Dominic placed her mug on the bar and lifted Jake into his arms. He pulled his son's thumb out of his mouth. "This is Charly. Say hi." He watched his son lovingly as Jake said hello to her.

"Hello, Jake." She gazed at the cute little boy. He had blond hair and Dominic's startlingly light gray eyes.

Charly was delighted when he reached his arms out to her. She looked to Dominic for permission before taking Jake into her arms. The sweet toddler began a monologue of babbling, peering at her with big eyes as if he were making a lot of sense. Charly merely nodded as if she understood everything he was saying. She thought she heard the word park. "Park?" she asked Dominic.

Dominic nodded. "He loves the park. We can go after you finish breakfast if you want."

"Don't you have to be at the clubhouse?"

"We do, but the brothers know this is my time with Jake. We'll be going in later."

The park was a ten-minute stroll away. Charly happily pushed the stroller while Dominic and Jax followed behind her. She named different objects on the way and was rewarded when Jake attempted to say the words.

Charly held Jake's hand at the park as they wandered over to the small slide. He didn't seem afraid of anything, so she spent most of the time with her arms out, ready to catch him if he fell or hurt himself.

Dominic got out a ball and began kicking it with his son and Jax. Charly sat on the bench and enjoyed the play between the three males. She was amazed to see how careful the two giants were with the small child.

Charly was disappointed when it was time to head back home. The guys told her they were off to the clubhouse. They took Jake next door to Mrs. Pope, the babysitter, leaving Charly alone. Charly offered to look after Jake, but Dominic shook his head.

"You need time to settle in. Look around the house, make yourself at home, and relax." Charly nodded in defeat. It would have been nice to get to know Jake.

Charly decided to make herself useful and checked the fridge, freezer, and pantry to see what food there was. She got out the ingredients to make lasagna. While baking in the oven, Charly familiarized herself with the house's layout. After tidying up her room, she went searching for the vacuum cleaner.

By seven o'clock, Charly hadn't received a call or text from the guys. She should have asked them what time they'd be home. Plating her portion of the lasagna and spooning some salad to go with it, she sat at the dining table to eat alone.

She watched television, left a note telling the guys that the lasagna and salad were in the fridge, and then headed upstairs to her room.

It was after ten o'clock when she heard the front door opening.

✳ ✳ ✳ ✳ ✳

OVER THE NEXT FEW days, a routine was established. One or both men would spend some time with Jake in the morning before heading to the clubhouse. On the third morning, Charly had tentatively asked if Jake could stay with her during the day, but Dominic explained that he wanted her and Jake to become acquainted first. It was reasonable, so Charly dropped the subject.

When they'd come home at night, the three lovers did their best to make up for lost time, but it was up to Charly to find things to do during the day. After spending three days alone, Charly decided to make a surprise visit to see her old coworkers at Jeb's Diner. Maybe she could try to get her old job back.

When Dominic and Jax left with Jake, she got in her car and drove to the diner, eager to see her friends again. She was chuffed when Rachel and Donny welcomed her with open arms.

"Charly! Oh my God! What are you doing back?" Rachel had changed her hair color to bright blue, but otherwise, things felt the same.

Donny didn't give her time to reply. "Where did you go?"

"I moved down south for a change. I missed you guys, so here I am." It wasn't a lie, but it wasn't the truth, either.

Charly's heart sank when she noticed a third server delivering plates to a table. "I suppose there are no positions open at the moment?"

"You should speak to Jeb. I'm sure he'd much rather have you back than deal with Shawna's constant drama." Rachel rolled her eyes.

Jeb's reaction was heartwarming. The big man captured her in a bear hug, then stood back and chastised her for leaving. Charly was surprised when he readily agreed to give her the job back.

When she told Dominic and Jax the news the following morning, Jax was the first to protest.

"Charly, you don't need to work. We'll support you."

Charly couldn't understand his objection. They'd hardly seen her in the last three days, except at night.

"I'm bored. There's nothing for me to do here. I appreciate the offer, but I'd prefer to keep busy and contribute financially."

"Not necessary," Dominic argued. "We've uprooted you, and now you need to get back on your feet. We don't need your money."

"You want me to be a lady of leisure? That's not going to happen.

I'd die of boredom." Besides, Charly had seen clearly what it meant when a woman couldn't or wouldn't support herself. Financial independence meant freedom.

In the end, Charly won. It wasn't a decision that the men could make anyway.

SEVENTEEN

When Dominic and Achilles returned to the compound just after midday, Jax stood with Vin and Gun outside the garage, admiring his work on his most recent project.

Dominic removed his dome, wiping the sweat from his forehead. Church would be commencing soon, and he and Achilles had important information they needed to share with the club.

"Our contacts have informed us that Solaris Alvarez, who we know as Sol, Jess's ex-boyfriend, has been released from prison." Achilles looked around the table at the unhappy faces of his brothers. "We need to locate him and have eyes on him at all times. He's threatened several brothers, and that can't be taken lightly."

Dominic snuck a peek at Jax and realized, as usual, they were thinking the same thing: Sol had threatened Charly. An involuntary chill rocked his body at the idea of any harm being done to her.

"Anyone know where he's staying?" Gage's question immediately started a rumble around the table.

Achilles banged the gavel to quieten the men's chatter. "Shut up! We'll get Cole to find out that information. Once he locates Sol, we'll get the prospects to keep a constant twenty-four-hour watch on him."

"How long are we going to do that for? Wouldn't it be easier to get rid of him? I'm sure nobody's going to miss the fucker," suggested Gun. Despite his relaxed demeanor, Dominic could tell Gun was aggravated that Sol was out of prison. He'd been the one to pull Sol off Charly that night, and he knew what the fucker was capable of.

"Let's wait and see what he does before we have another murder on our hands," said Achilles.

After the tense meeting, Dominic told Jax he was heading home.

* * * * *

CHARLY SWEPT THE FLOOR and listened to *Set Fire to the Rain*. Singing along to the lyrics made the menial task a lot more enjoyable. Swaying her hips as she swept, Charly let out a scream when a pair of arms came around her. Her instant reaction was to elbow whoever it was in the face, but her arms were manacled to her sides.

"Charls!" barked Dominic. "It's me."

She scowled up at him. "Why did you scare me like that?"

He removed her earphones. "Because you were too busy singing." He nuzzled her neck.

Her weak body quivered with desire when Dominic kissed her sensitive spot. Squirming in his arms, Charly released a shuddering breath. "Dom," she panted. "What are you doing?"

"What do you think I'm doing?" He spun her around to face him, settled his palms on either side of her face, and kissed her fervently.

Charly responded with an intensity that matched his. Winding her arms around his neck, she reached up to seal their lips together. Dominic reached behind her thighs and lifted her so she could straddle his hips. Then he carried her up the stairs, keeping their mouths fused.

Laying her on the bed, he pulled off her clothes, then his own, not caring where they landed.

Charly moaned when he stretched out on top of her so they were skin-to-skin. She gloried at the feel of his erection digging into her belly and the smooth contour of his abdomen and back. She reveled in his hardness, her hips grinding along his hard cock.

Neither of them could wait. Foreplay over, Dominic thrust deep inside her, and they groaned in unison. Leaning on his forearms above her, Dominic's eyes feasted on Charly's face as he pounded her body. After a few short minutes, he threw back his head and emitted a tortured cry of release.

He collapsed on top of her, and she wrapped her arms around him, relishing the warmth, sweat, and smell of him. His chest pounded heavily, gradually slowing to a regular beat. Charly tightened her grip when he tried to get up. His lips tickled her cheek and neck, working their way up to her ear.

"I owe you an orgasm," he whispered.

Charly eagerly agreed and was rewarded generously. Their lovemaking continued into the evening when Jax returned home. He entered the bedroom half-undressed, ready to join in the fun. It was a long time before any of them bothered to leave the bed.

$$\ast\ \ast\ \ast\ \ast\ \ast$$

SOLARIS ALVAREZ TRIED TO blot out the dark fog as he watched a dark-haired woman hop out of a car. She opened the back door and went inside. Seconds later, she pulled a kid from the back seat and a large bag from the boot.

She strutted up the path and banged on the front door. Sol could hear her calling for someone named Dom to hurry up and open the door.

The bitch was whining about being busy and having better things to do. The fucking whore thought she could speak to a man like that. Sol would be happy to teach her a lesson. Women were supposed to cower before men, not order them about.

A large male pulled the door open, talking some crap and waving his hands around. Sol was sure it was one of the men who'd attacked him. He'd stood between Sol and Jess, and no one kept his property from him. She belonged to him. He intended to find out where Jess was and teach her a lesson. But first, he wanted this one.

The kid's cries muted the doorstep conversation. Sol wished someone would fucking shut the kid up. Kids should be seen, not heard. That's what his pop had instilled in him.

The man grabbed the kid and took him inside, then came back out again to yell at the bitch. Their screaming match lasted a few minutes until a neighbor poked her head out her door. The old biddy needed to mind her own fucking business.

She stormed off and slammed the car door. The wheels of her vehicle squealed as she took off, and the male went back inside. Sol decided to follow her. He'd make sure she never spoke to another man like that again.

He stayed several car lengths behind her and parked a few houses away when she entered the driveway. Sol got out of his truck to study the complex's layout. She lived in the end unit—perfect. But he'd wait until it was dark before breaking in.

✳ ✳ ✳ ✳ ✳

WHEN DARKNESS CREPT IN, Sol climbed the fence in the laneway and landed in the backyard. With few places to hide, he stalked around the side of the house, checking the windows for accessibility. Seeing that one was open a few inches, he cut the fly-screen and slid it across.

He was inside the main bedroom, which was a complete shambles. She didn't believe in doing housework. In Sol's opinion, bitches were made for fucking and cleaning, and this one needed to learn that.

A calmness settled over Sol as he snuck through the house. Hearing the television blasting, he stealthily approached the living room. When a male voice spoke, Sol stopped in his tracks. Annoyed that the man had interrupted his plan, an idea came to mind. Retracing his steps, he climbed out of the bedroom window and ran to the front of the unit. Scrounging around, he lifted a solid rock from the garden and threw it at the window, causing it to smash.

Hiding behind a dense bush, Sol waited for someone to come out. He froze when a stocky male exited, shining a torch. The man was built, but Sol was bigger and stronger. Sol waited for him to pass before pouncing on him from behind, sticking the knife into his neck repeatedly. Blood sprayed everywhere, and the man went down immediately, choking on his blood. The bastard was collateral damage. Maybe he should have taught his woman how to behave, and then Sol wouldn't have to do it for him.

Dropping the heavy body on the ground, Sol waited and listened for creaking doors, footsteps, or lights being switched on. It remained dead silent until a faint whisper echoed in the dark.

"Justin? Are you there, Justin?" She sounded terrified, and Sol's ego swelled with pride.

He stepped out from behind the bushes like the Grim Reaper. She screamed and tried to run back inside and lock the door, but he was instantly on her. Closing the door behind him, Sol had to summon his control as a wave of bloodlust racked his body. He intended to take his sweet time killing this one. He wanted to savor each painful, brutal moment.

Killing men didn't give him the same rush as killing women. He craved the sounds of their screams and enjoyed listening to them plead for their lives. They were willing to do anything to stay alive. What they never knew was that death was inevitable. Sol never wavered on the outcome. It's what gave him the incredible high.

The screaming banshee ran down the hallway and locked herself in the bathroom. Sol laughed maniacally. Did she think that a locked door would keep him out? He was a big man and had kept in shape while in prison. Even the other inmates had kept their distance, sensing that he was dangerous. Sol feared nothing.

Aiming his boot, he drove the heel into the door, splintering the wood. His hand reached through the hole to unlock the door. She stood in the middle of the bathtub, cowering and trembling. She wasn't running her mouth anymore; she was too fucking scared to speak.

Sol dragged her out of the tub by the hair. Heading for the bedroom, he threw her onto the bed like a rag doll. She tried to scramble away, only to be dragged by her ankle back to the middle of the bed. Raising his fist, Sol punched hard, knocking her out. He roared with pleasure as blood gushed from her nose.

When the bitch woke up, all four limbs were tethered to the corners of the unmade bed.

"Please!" she begged. "Don't hurt me. Please!"

He relished the look of terror in her eyes.

Sol spent the night savagely attacking and degrading the petrified woman. He viciously raped her over and over again, never achieving an orgasm but enjoying the sense of power nonetheless.

At the crack of dawn, the once loud, disrespectful whore was reduced to a nearly lifeless corpse. Straddling her, Sol wrapped his hands around her neck and stared into her glassy eyes as her life slowly ebbed away. She'd been a coward, not a fighter.

* * * * *

CHARLY JERKED AWAKE AND crawled over Jax to get out of bed.

"Where are you going?" he mumbled, still half asleep.

"I hear Jake."

"He's not crying. He's just babbling to himself." Jax reached across to grasp her wrist, but Charly skipped out of the way.

"But he's awake."

Charly opened the door, eager to see Jake. He was sitting in his bed, playing with his toy motorcycle.

"Hey, Jake," she whispered, leaning over the rail.

Jake stood up and showed Charly his motorcycle. "Bike."

"That's right. Motorbike. Bbbrrrmmm! Bbbrrrmmm!"

Jake giggled at her impression of a motorcycle. Charly couldn't resist picking him up and kissing his soft, downy hair.

Dominic and Jax blocked the doorway, both men grinning indulgently. Since Kyra dropped Jake off four days ago, Charly has hovered around him like a protective lioness.

Jake pointed. "Daddy! Jax!"

"Yes, baby. That's Daddy and Uncle Jax." She kissed his warm cheek.

"It's a shame you have to go to work."

Charly frowned up at Dominic. "Why?"

"You could have looked after Jake today."

"So now I can look after him? Suddenly, I'm a suitable babysitter?" She pursed her lips. "Perhaps I could pick him up from Mrs. Pope's after work?"

Dominic nodded. "Sounds like a plan." Charly rewarded him with a smile.

Charly fed and dressed Jake, then got ready for work.

The only downside to their arrangement was Kyra. When she spotted Charly's car out front, she confronted Dominic about it. They'd had a pretty loud argument, making poor Jake cry. Dominic had passed the distressed toddler over to her while he went outside to deal with Kyra, and then he'd returned looking harassed. Kyra had threatened to take full custody if Charly stayed. Dominic—angry that she was trying to blackmail him—had retaliated, shouting about Justin, Kyra's boyfriend, who wasn't exactly squeaky clean. Kyra's response had been to take off in her car, tires squealing, leaving skid marks on the driveway.

✶ ✶ ✶ ✶ ✶

CHARLY COUNTED DOWN THE minutes until she could leave to pick Jake up. Everyone noticed her nervous excitement.

"What the heck is up with you today? You're like a fidgety puppy," Rachel said.

"I'm picking Jake up after work."

"That explains it. You're like a fierce mama when it comes to that boy. What made Dom change his mind?"

"I don't know. He mentioned it this morning."

Rachel looked at her watch. "It's five o'clock. You'd better go pick up your boy."

Charly didn't need to be told twice. After saying goodbye to the others, she hurried to her car. She unlocked the door, tossed her bag onto the passenger's seat, and entered.

She stilled before turning on the ignition. The hair stood up on the back of her neck. Her intuition told her something wasn't right. Fumbling with the door handle, she tried to escape when something covered her mouth.

✳ ✳ ✳ ✳ ✳

CHARLY GROANED AS SHE woke, feeling disoriented. Opening her eyes, she couldn't see anything. It was pitch black. When she tried to get up, something stopped her. Realizing her hands and feet were bound, she panicked. Where the hell was she?

Taking several deep, quivering breaths, she focused on the last thing that had happened before she ended up here. She remembered being excited about picking Jake up from Mrs. Pope's house. She'd gotten into her car, but something had been wrong. Someone had pressed a cloth over her mouth. They had kidnapped her. Who? Kyra? No, it had been a large person; she knew that much. Was it Justin, Kyra's boyfriend? She'd never met the guy, so it was a possibility. But why? To keep her away from Jake and Dominic?

Did they plan to leave her here to die? Would they hurt her or maybe kill her?

Charly's eyes gradually adjusted to the darkness. She could make out a window and a door but nothing else. She touched the ground, and it felt dirty and gritty. Sitting up, she tested her bindings. Whoever had tied her up had used cloth. Bringing her hands to her mouth, she used her teeth to undo the knot. Sand coated her mouth, but it didn't stop her from gnawing at the material until it loosened. Tugging at the cloth, she eventually freed her hands. She then untied the restraints around her ankles. When she was free, Charly rose on unsteady legs.

Charly used the wall for balance and made her way along the rough surface until she reached the door. Her fingers felt around for a light switch and found a hole in the wall where it should have been. Jiggling the doorknob, she thumped it when it refused to open. She had nothing to pry the door open with, so she followed the wall to the window. The faint moonlight offered little light. Stretching her hands, she ascertained that the ledge was too high and narrow to climb.

Charly heard the jangling of keys. Alarmed, she flattened her back against the wall and waited. A light bounced across the gap in the doorway. Then, a large, familiar figure appeared, almost like an apparition. Sol.

Sol lunged forward with his torch raised. Charly managed to dodge his swing. She tried to run, but strong arms lifted her from behind and threw her to the ground. Winded, she didn't have time to deflect the punch that knocked her out.

Before everything went dark, her last thought was that if she could wish for anything right then—other than being rescued—she would want a chance to tell Dominic and Jax that she loved them.

EIGHTEEN

"Where the fuck is Charly?" growled Dominic, rechecking his phone. "She's over an hour late."

"I'll give her a call." Jax got out his phone and found her number. It went straight to voicemail.

"Let me call Jeb." Dominic tapped his fingers impatiently, waiting for Charly's boss to answer. "Hey, Jeb. Is Charly there?"

The news wasn't good. Jax checked the tracker they'd put on her car. Scowling, he enlarged the map.

"Fuck! Where is she?"

"What is it, Jax?" Dominic peered over his cousin's shoulder, studying the map. "Where the fuck is Greenville? How far away is it from here?"

"Forty miles."

A commotion outside distracted them. When Achilles led Detective Carter inside, the men glanced at each other, their apprehension intensifying.

"Dom. Jax," Detective Carter greeted them somberly. "I'm afraid I have bad news."

"Charls?" Dominic choked out, terror gripping his heart.

"No. It's Kyra."

His shoulders sagged with relief. "What about Kyra?"

"She's dead."

"What? How? When? What happened?" Dominic fired off each question, disbelief written all over his face.

The brothers gathered around. "Can we discuss this somewhere else?" Detective Carter eyed the crowd.

"No. We have no secrets from our brothers. They need to hear this, too."

"Okay then. She was found beaten to death in her bed this morning. It appears the body had been there for a couple of days. Her boyfriend, Justin Klim, was also killed. Stabbed in the neck."

"Fuuuck!" Dominic swept a hand over his crown. "Do you know who did this?"

"Not yet. Why did you think the news was about Charly?"

"She's not answering her phone, and she's late."

Shane noted their distress. "Is she at work?"

"No. I called Jeb. He said she left at five." Dominic couldn't keep still. He got up and started pacing. "Also, the tracker shows her car is in Greenville. Do you know the area?"

"Yeah," Shane replied. "It's on the outskirts. Many houses there have been abandoned and vandalized."

"Fuck!" whispered Jax. "We need to get out there now." He didn't bother waiting for the others to follow him.

Dominic was not far behind as they revved up their engines. Shane called dispatch, requesting immediate backup to the location. Seven motorcycles, followed by two police cars, navigated their way to the outskirts of town.

Fading daylight would hinder their search, but Dominic and Jax refused to let that stop them from finding Charly. Shane received a radio announcement informing him that a blue car had been found at an abandoned petrol station.

"Is she with the car? Is she okay?" Dominic held his breath, fearing the worst.

"She's not in the car. We checked the boot. It's empty."

"We need to check the abandoned houses."

"It's getting dark now. That means it's going to take longer to search each house. But I'll get my men on it." Shane rushed off to assemble the other officers.

* * * * *

WHEN CHARLY CAME AROUND the next time, she discovered she was handcuffed to an old radiator. Her head was pounding. Scanning the area, she saw that it was dilapidated. There were holes in the walls and a huge gap in the ceiling. When she peered through the beams in the roof, she was surprised to see that it was already the crack of dawn.

Wood and broken furniture were scattered all over. She must be in an abandoned house. How would Dominic and Jax be able to find her? Where was her phone? Was Sol still around? Would he return to kill her?

Charly looked around the room. She had to be able to use something here as a weapon. She could tell that Sol had continued hitting her after he'd knocked her out the night before. Her head pounded, and she had trouble seeing out of one eye. There were bruises everywhere she could see. She might not survive his next visit if he returned, and she was certain that he'd come back.

She was still breathing. He wasn't done with her yet.

He was so much bigger, stronger, and meaner than her. She wouldn't be able to overcome him with brute force; she would have to be smarter than him.

Her eyes lit on a piece of wood fractured to a sharp point. She stretched out as far as she could go, reaching with her foot, and was able to get the edge of it. She kicked it towards her and tested it against her finger, satisfied when a slight jab formed a bead of blood.

She slid it up the sleeve of her shirt, hiding it between her arm and the side of her body. She'd have to choose the moment she used it wisely. She'd only have one chance.

She huddled in the corner and waited.

✴ ✴ ✴ ✴ ✴

WITH A POPULATION OF fewer than fifty residents, Greenville had a lot of empty buildings to navigate.

The MC and the police worked together until dawn, scouring each abandoned building for Charly. Although exhausted and frustrated, Dominic and Jax continued to comb the area when the sun came up, refusing to stop. They refused to give up until they found Charly.

Dominic called Mrs. Pope occasionally to check in on Jake. He also received a call from Sara, wanting an update on the situation.

It was mid-morning, and they stopped for a short break with no sign of Charly. "What now?" Dom asked Shane.

Shane shook his head. "I don't know. There's still some area to cover, but she's been missing more than twelve hours. That's not good."

Dom's heart sank.

✴ ✴ ✴ ✴ ✴

FINALLY, CHARLY HEARD THE jangle of keys again. Sol was back. She scooted down and pretended to be asleep.

"Wake up, bitch," he growled, punctuating his words with a kick to her ribs.

She didn't have to fake that moan of pain.

"Yeah. That's right. Get up. We have to relocate. Half the freaking police force is out there. I'm going to have to move you." He crouched down to undo the handcuffs.

Now? Was now the right time to jam the sharp piece of wood into his throat? No. She couldn't get it out of her sleeve and jam it into him before he realized what she was doing. She'd have to wait a little longer. The idea that the police were out looking for her was encouraging, but would they even know where to go if he moved her?

Sol hauled her to her feet. Everything hurt. For a second, the room swam around her.

"Walk." He shoved her, and she stumbled forward, just narrowly catching herself on the door frame before she fell.

"Keep going." Sol shoved her again.

* * * * *

DOMINIC OVERHEARD A MESSAGE on the police radio. One of the houses had signs of someone having been there recently.

The men raced to the vacant house, where they found a pair of handcuffs attached to a radiator. On the floor and wall was blood spatter—evidence that some assault had taken place.

Shane told everyone to clear the building and called in the forensic team.

"Whoever was here has been moved. We'll find out if it was Charly, but it will take a while," he warned them.

Outside, more evidence was found: shoe prints.

"These are fresh," Shane said. "Let's be very quiet. They could still be nearby."

* * * * *

CHARLY HAD STUMBLED SEVERAL times as Sol shoved her along. He hadn't been able to bring his car close to the house—there were too many cops—so they had a long way to walk.

This time, when he shoved her, she tripped over a hillock and went down on her stomach.

"Get up," he said, kicking her.

Charly slid the piece of wood out of her sleeve under her body, making it look like she was trying to get up. "Can't. Hurt."

"No, you're not. Get. Up." He kicked her again.

It hurt so bad, but she needed him to lean down to get his neck closer to her.

She went limp on the ground, hoping he'd think she'd passed out.

"Oh, for fuck's sake," he growled. He leaned down, expecting to grab her by her collar and drag her through the brush.

Charly's heart pounded so hard she thought it might leap out of her chest. *Wait for it. Wait for your moment.*

Finally, Sol leaned over far enough that his face was practically by the back of her head. In one quick movement, she rolled over and jammed the sharp part of the wood into the side of his neck.

He reared back in surprise. "You bitch!" Then he made his fatal mistake. He pulled the piece of wood out of his neck.

Blood spurted everywhere.

✳ ✳ ✳ ✳ ✳

THE TRAIL ENDED IN an open field next to the main road. Shane ordered his men to do a line search of the field. As they formed up, a guttural yell cut through the morning.

Dom shoved past the police officers, running as fast as he could towards the sound. When he reached Charly, he almost couldn't believe what he saw.

Charly stood over Sol, blood soaking the ground around them.

"Charly!"

She looked up, confusion on her face. "Dom?"

"Yes. Yes. I'm here. We've got you." He quickly closed in on her before she fainted.

"Oh, good," she said. Then she collapsed.

Shane ran up to them, panting. He took one look, turned, and shouted, "Get the medics. Hurry!"

Stepping closer, Dominic reached Charly. He was horrified to see that she'd been badly beaten. One eye was swollen shut. Several nails had broken off. She'd fought, and she fought hard.

"Dear God," Dominic said roughly, wanting to gather her in his arms. "Charls." His hands shook as he stretched his arm out to touch her.

"Don't touch her. We don't know what's broken yet." Shane ordered an officer to stand guard. He squeezed Dominic's shoulder, prompting him to step away.

Shane turned to check on Sol. He held his fingers to his neck and shook his head. "He's gone," he said.

The brothers of the MC huddled together when the ambulance arrived. Their faces were solemn as the paramedics checked her breathing and pulse, lifted her onto the stretcher, and rolled her into the back of the ambulance.

"We're taking her to Royal Hospital," the paramedic told Shane.

Shane and the MC followed the ambulance to the hospital. When they arrived at the emergency entrance, they were told to stay in the waiting room until a doctor could speak to them. Dominic paced the floor, consumed with guilt and worry for Charly, when a middle-aged man in a white coat appeared, looking tired.

"Detective Carter?" He approached Shane.

"How is she?" Shane asked.

"She's stable. But she was severely beaten. She has a broken nose, ribs, and fingers. We've sedated her, so she'll be out of it for a while."

Hearing this, Dominic and Jax grabbed each other's shoulders in comfort. Shane thanked the doctor. "Can we see her?"

Walking into the room, Dominic was shocked again to see the severity of Charly's injuries. What hell had his woman gone through to survive? Dominic stood beside Charly, simmering with both rage and anguish.

Jax bent over Charly, kissing her forehead. "We're here, warrior princess. Everything's going to be okay. You're going to be okay. We won't leave your side," he whispered into her ear.

Dominic couldn't hold back anymore. Clasping her uninjured hand, he squeezed it. "Charls, it's me. I'm here, sweetheart. You rest and get better."

* * * * *

SHANE STOOD AT THE foot of the bed, looking down on the young woman who'd captured his heart from the moment he met her. Charly was a strong girl. He knew without a doubt that she would pull through.

Although he'd initially had misgivings about Dominic and Jax, he didn't anymore. They had proven how much Charly meant to them over the past two days. They'd tirelessly fought to find her, and their devastation at finding her unconscious, beaten, and broken further enhanced his belief that they cared deeply for his girl.

* * * * *

SHANE HAD TO LEAVE when he got another urgent call. Dominic and Jax refused to go, so the nurses brought in a fold-up bed. Dominic slept on the chair by Charly's side while Jax took the bed. Dominic didn't get much sleep—he was too troubled about the woman lying unmoving in the hospital bed.

By morning, he looked drawn. Resting his head on his forearm, which was nestled against Charly's, Dominic started when he heard a soft groan. Glancing up, he saw Charly staring at him.

"Charls," he said hoarsely, taking her small hand in his larger one. "I'm here, sweetheart." Unable to stop himself, he brushed back her hair, needing to touch her. "You're going to be fine."

Dominic felt, rather than saw, Jax's approach. "Babe."

"Sol?" Charly mouthed.

"Dead, babe. You killed him." Dominic leaned in closer so he could hear.

Charly nodded, then winced and put a hand on her head. "Good," she whispered.

Dom couldn't help himself. He laughed. "That's our girl."

"Damn straight," Jax said.

Jax alerted the nurse to tell her that Charly was awake. She told them her headache was getting worse, so the nurse gave her a sedative that put her straight back to sleep. Dominic and Jax remained by her side, not daring to leave the room in case she woke up again.

* * * * *

CHARLY ROUSED FROM A deep slumber, slowly adjusting to the unfamiliar surroundings. Blinking to clear away the cobwebs, she was relieved to see Dominic and Jax whispering to each other. Charly gazed at the two most remarkable men in her life.

"Our girl's awake." Jax nudged Dominic.

"Hey," he greeted. "How do you feel?"

"Headache's gone."

"Good." Dominic picked up her uninjured hand and kissed her knuckles. "Any other pain?"

"No. Whatever they gave me is working."

Something pushed at Charly's memory like an annoying buzz. She frowned, trying to remember what was bothering her.

"What is it, Charls?" Both men hovered close.

Then Charly remembered what was so important. "Kyra."

Jax frowned. "What about Kyra, babe?"

"Dead?" Sol had taken great pleasure in seeing Charly's fear as he told her in detail all the terrible things he'd done to the "other bitch." Sol said he killed her. When Sol cruelly relayed how he'd used pliers to rip out every piercing from her face, Charly instinctively knew he was talking about Kyra.

Jax sighed. "It's true."

Despite not liking the woman, Charly felt terrible. She was, after all, Jake's mother. "I'm sorry."

"You've nothing to be sorry for. I'm sorry I even let Sol get near you."

Charly didn't like that Dominic blamed himself for what Sol had done to her. "This isn't your fault. It's Sol's."

"Realistically, I get that it's not my fault. But it doesn't change the way I feel. I'm supposed to protect you."

Charly placed her hand over his. "Dom, you don't need to protect me. Neither of you do."

Jax took her other hand. "We know you're our warrior princess. You've proven that time and again."

Charly swallowed. She thought about the promise she'd made to herself when she thought she was going to die. Now that the opportunity presented itself, she was afraid. They cared about her; she knew that. What did it matter that they didn't love her the way she loved them?

Jax frowned as if sensing her internal conflict. "What is it?"

"I need to tell you something." This was harder than she thought it would be. "I love you," she whispered, holding her breath and waiting for their reaction. However, because of her nerves, her mouth took over. "I should have told you before, but I was worried you didn't want to hear it. Then, when I thought I might die, I promised myself I would let you both know how I felt. I love you." This time, she said the words with more conviction.

Charly stared at the two silent men. She'd surprised them with her outburst, and when they remained speechless, she started to fidget. "I don't expect you to say it back. Just knowing that you care is enough," she mumbled.

Deeply disappointed that her declarations of love had been met with a wall of silence, Charly requested a glass of water. Dominic eagerly got up to hunt down a nurse while Jax coughed nervously and fussed about ensuring she was comfortable.

Vin and Gun arrived later, happy to see her up and talking. They were to take over babysitting duty. Dominic and Jax kissed her and told her they'd be back later.

＊ ＊ ＊ ＊ ＊

"FUCK, DOM. SHE SAID the L word. What the fuck do we do with that?"

"I've got no fucking clue, Jax. But it's a good thing, isn't it?"

"I guess so. What does it mean?"

"Should we ask Sara?"

Jax agreed. His sister would know what to do. He mentally kicked himself. He should have said something to Charly. Instead, he'd stood there like a moron, incapable of responding to her declaration of love.

Heading back to the clubhouse, he sought out his sister.

"Hey. How's Charly?" Her eyes shone with concern.

"She's doing okay," he replied. "She's sedated, so she's not feeling any pain at the moment."

Sara hugged him and Dominic. Jax shuffled his feet, and Dominic rubbed the back of his neck.

"What's the matter? Is something wrong with Charly?"

"No. She'll be fine. It's just that she…" Jax looked to Dominic for support.

"She told us she loved us," Dominic stated.

"That's fantastic! Did you say it back?" Sara clicked her tongue. "You didn't say anything, did you?"

"We didn't know what the fuck to say. Nobody's ever said they loved us." Jax dodged his sister's slap. "Except family," he added.

"Not even the million girls who fought over you? That's a surprise."

"That's different. They love us because of our status. Charly doesn't care about that." Jax knew, without a doubt, that Charly's feelings were genuine.

"Why couldn't you say it back? It's obvious you both love her." Sara laughed at their look of confusion.

"Why do you say that?"

Sara gawked at Dominic. "You've just spent twenty-four hours nonstop looking for her. And, despite your exhaustion, you've not left her side since. That's one example. When she left, you both became empty shells of yourselves. You're different when she's around. You're happier and more alive. You're constantly checking your phone to see where she is, even though you already know. Everything you do, you're always thinking about whether Charly might like it or need it. You bought her a car because you didn't like that she had to catch a bus at night. That's love."

Jax stared at Sara in awe. He had no idea that, all along, he had loved Charly. Sara's words were a revelation.

Swallowing back his dismay at not recognizing his feelings earlier, Jax glanced at Dominic. "Fuck! I knew we should've said something."

Jax was overcome with relief that the newsflash did not upset him. Instead, he felt a sense of happiness that his feelings had a name, and those feelings were reciprocated. "We have to tell her."

✳ ✳ ✳ ✳ ✳

CHARLY WANTED TO GO home. It had been six days since they'd found her in the field. Dominic and Jax had visited her every night, but the tightness in her chest grew each time they left. Not once had they mentioned anything about her admission of love. Nothing had changed—only now they knew that she loved them, and she knew that the feeling wasn't mutual.

She thought she could live with the knowledge that her love was unrequited. Sadly, the truth was much more heartbreaking. On the one hand, she was glad she had told them because if she died tomorrow, at least she could rest in peace. On the other hand, she most likely wasn't going to die tomorrow, so now she had to deal with the depressing fact that the best she could hope for was that they cared about her. She guessed that caring was better than not caring. If she kept thinking like that, maybe she could pretend they'd have a happily ever after. Breaking up was not an option. Two years without them had been painful enough.

Charly received many visitors during her hospital stay. Sara,

Nolan, and Carrie came by several times. Each time, Sara would bring her little gifts from the house to make her feel more at home—books, magazines, clothes, and toiletries. Charly appreciated her thoughtful gestures. The first time Sara brought him, Nolan entered the room, jumping on the bed for a cuddle. She almost cried when he gently hugged her and settled on the covers next to her.

Tessa and Shane also came with little surprises, such as hot cups of cappuccino, a new nightie to replace the uncomfortable hospital gown she was given, and flowers to brighten up the room.

Vin, Gun, Gage, Chad, and even Achilles stopped by, too. Charly saw a softer side to the president of the MC, altering her opinion of the stern man.

Two weeks later, Jax pushed a wheelchair into the room. "Let's get you into the wheelchair. It's time to go home."

As they helped her into the chair, she tried to hide the sharp pain when she sat down.

"Are you in pain, Charls?" The two continued to fuss over her. It was becoming annoying.

"I'm okay. I will be sore for a while, but I can handle it."

"We know you can. We don't like seeing you in pain." Dominic bent down to kiss her forehead. "Let's go home."

Charly had to admit that she was nervous about resuming her everyday life. She was still experiencing a lot of pain and needed medication to control it. She worried that her badass bikers would treat her like a China doll, which was the last thing she wanted. Did she still have a job at Jeb's Diner? Would the nightmares ever stop? When would she be ready to have sex again? Would Dominic and Jax be patient enough to wait or seek attention elsewhere?

As Jax wheeled her through the corridors of the hospital, her anxieties took hold of her. For several moments, Charly panicked as she struggled to breathe. Without warning, she leaned forward and dry-retched.

"Charls!" Dominic caught her shoulders to steady her. "Jesus Christ! You're as white as a ghost. Nurse!"

Charly was embarrassed that people were staring at her. She looked down at the floor as a nurse attended to her. Eventually, her vision cleared, and she could sit up again.

The slight breeze cooled Charly's hot cheeks as they passed through the sliding doors. With the unsettling incident over, she pushed her gloomy thoughts to the back of her mind. It would do her no good nor help her situation with her ever-watchful protectors.

Pulling into the driveway, Charly was disgruntled to see a row of motorcycles and cars parked along the verge. They had visitors—a lot of them, by the looks of it. All she wanted to do was go back to sleep, but now she'd have to put on a happy face and deal with all the attention. Charly wanted to cry.

Deep down, she knew that everyone had been worried about her disappearance. They'd been gracious enough not to exhaust her while she recuperated in the hospital. She wished they'd be courteous enough to let her be while she recuperated at home.

Pasting on a smile, she tried to appear happy to see everyone. One by one, they stepped forward to welcome her back home.

"Charly, welcome home." Sara bent down to hug her, careful not to squeeze too hard.

"Looking as beautiful as ever," Vin teased, only to be shoved aside by Jax. "Settle down, bro. I'm only showing your girl some brotherly love." Charly smiled at their banter. She suspected Jax wasn't threatened by Vin at all.

Everyone said their hellos, including a surprisingly sweet embrace from Sharyn. "You're tougher than you look, little warrior princess," she whispered in her ear.

Dominic told everyone to give her some space. Her eyes glistened with gratitude.

A loud clanging disrupted their conversation while Charly enjoyed a quiet chat with Shane, Tessa, Jeb, Rachel, and Donny. Jax was banging on the breakfast bar with a wooden spoon. Charly was caught off guard when he and Dominic surrounded her. She wondered what in the world they were up to, as Dom appeared to be hiding something.

Jax whistled sharply and told the crowd to shut the fuck up and listen. Horrified by his rudeness, Charly glared at him. Thank goodness Nolan wasn't here.

"It's all good, babe. They need to listen because me and Dom have something important to say."

When a hush fell over the crowd, Dominic spoke up. "As you all know, we're fucking thankful to have Charly here with us. We almost lost her—not once, but twice. It's not something we'd ever wish on anyone. Charly's one of us. She's family."

At this, a chorus of "All for one and one for all" echoed around the room. Tears threatened to spill.

"A couple of weeks ago, Charly told me and Jax that she loved us." Dominic's eyes swept around the room, landing on Charly. His eyes softened when he noted her red cheeks. "Foolishly, like the idiots we are, we kept our traps shut." Charly frowned in confusion. "No one, apart from our family, has ever said those words and meant them. It threw us for a loop."

Jax took over. "We're sorry, Charly, for not telling you how we felt. We chose to wait and tell you so that you'd believe us, considering we've got plenty of witnesses." Both men got down on their knees on either side of her wheelchair, each taking a hand.

"I love you, Charly," Jax said seriously.

"I love you, Charls." Dominic echoed his words.

No one breathed or said a word, and some women openly wiped their eyes. Charly sat speechless for five seconds before covering her face and bursting into tears. Everyone in the room remained quiet, and Dominic and Jax appeared poleaxed by her tearful reaction.

Lifting her eyes, her voice jagged, Charly allayed their fears. "If you can say that when I look like this," Charly waved over the still visible bruises on her face, "I guess you really must love me. I love you, too."

A deafening roar broke out, and the brothers swooped in on the duo, pounding them with slaps on the back and bear hugs.

"One last thing," Dominic announced, holding up the familiar leather jacket that declared her the *Property of Dom & Jax.*

Charly proudly put the jacket on, her eyes brimming with joy.

EPILOGUE

"**I** now pronounce you husband and wife," announced the celebrant. He looked at Chad. "You may kiss your bride."

"Fuck, yeah!" Before the old man finished the sentence, Chad lifted the veil from Sara's radiant face and kissed her passionately.

The brothers of the Iconic Sons MC whistled and hollered in celebration.

Charly grinned as a glowing Sara and Chad turned to face the enthusiastic crowd, with an excited Nolan jumping up and down between them. The ceremony had been short and sweet, with the audience tearing up and laughing simultaneously at Sara's and Chad's hilarious speeches.

The group made a beeline for the bar on the back porch at the lodge. Only family and friends were in attendance. No club whores or sweet butts were present—not on this special day. Everyone spent the rest of the evening eating gluttonously, drinking excessively, and laughing uninhibitedly.

Darkness had fallen, and Charly stood nestled within Dominic's strong arms as Jax approached them, Nolan slumped on his shoulders. The eight-year-old was already beginning to nod off, and now and then, his eyelids would droop.

"Ma and Pops are taking Nolan home. Any minute now, it'll be lights out for him," chuckled Jax. "And Jake is staying over at Mrs. Pope's for the night. Are we ready to head upstairs soon?" His bright blue eyes lingered on Charly's chest, making her nipples hard.

Dominic burrowed his nose along her neck. Charly knew exactly what was on their minds. Her body instantly reacted, her pussy clenching with sudden need. Oh yeah, she was ready.

✶ ✶ ✶ ✶ ✶

CHARLY RELAXED ON THE front veranda, warming her hands with a steaming cup of coffee. The three of them had spent the night at the lodge, along with several other members of the MC.

Charly rose before daylight. These days, she found contentment in the simple things, including watching the sunrise. Spending time with her family also gave her a sense of peace—not only with Dominic, Jax, and Jake but also with the MC.

Her lovers had stayed faithful to her, gradually regaining her trust. More importantly, they showed that they trusted her. She made decisions for herself, and they respected and supported them. Because of their unwavering belief in her, she'd started taking classes at the junior college. It was only part-time for now, but she had big plans. Their loyalty meant the world to her and finally freed her from years of anxiety and repression.

Charly heard the front door squeak. Dominic stepped outside and joined her on the bench.

"Morning, Charls," he said, kissing her upturned lips.

"Hi. Did you sleep well?"

"I didn't get much sleep."

Charly nudged him. "It was your fault. You're the one who kept waking me up."

"You weren't complaining." He wrapped his arms around her.

"Have you heard from the newlyweds?" Charly asked.

Sara and Chad were flying out that morning to spend their honeymoon in Bali, so Deacon and Sharyn were looking after Nolan for the next week.

"Not yet. But Ma rang to say she picked Jake up from Mrs. Pope's. She offered to keep him for the day."

"What did you want to do?"

"You have to ask?" Dominic arched a brow.

Charly laughed. "No."

The door squeaked open again, and Jax came outside, followed by Vin and Gun.

"Move over, babe," he said, wedging himself on Charly's other side. "Give us a kiss," he demanded.

Charly gladly obliged.

"Where's my kiss?" Vin teased.

Vin quickly jumped out of the path of Jax's foot. "Fuck off!" Jax grumbled. "I haven't seen Clark in a while. About time I stopped by."

This wiped the grin off Vin's face. He scowled at Jax. "You keep your dirty paws off Clark."

Charly watched the play between the two men. She didn't take Jax's comments about seeing Clark seriously. He'd only said it to rile Vin. The two of them often goaded each other.

Ever since the younger woman started working for Vin and Gun at their tattoo shop a couple of months ago, it had become apparent that the feisty employee had gotten under the men's skin. Jax had jokingly said that Clark was their kryptonite.

"What's the plan?" Jax asked Dominic.

"Ma's got Jake for the day."

"Yeah? Are we staying here?" Jax massaged the back of her neck, sending shivers down her spine.

At Dominic's nod, Jax flashed a sexy grin. Charly let out a shaky sigh.

"We're off." Gun gave a brief wave as he and Vin walked to their bikes.

"Poor Clark," Charly laughed.

"Don't worry about Clark, babe. It's them you should be feeling sorry for," said Jax, tweaking her hair.

"Why's that?"

"Let's just say it's karma. Those two have no fucking clue what's in store for them."

"You're terrible." Charly elbowed Jax softly.

"You want to reconsider that? Let me show you how 'terrible' I can be." Charly let out a squeal as Jax suddenly tugged her off the bench. Then she followed Dominic and Jax up the stairs, eager to show her men how much she loved them.

Kahlani B. Steele was born and raised in Perth, Western Australia, where she also pursued a degree in Education focusing on Early Childhood Education. Kahlani now resides in a small town called Kalgoorlie. Her passion for reading was ignited at a young age when she fell in love with *Anne of Green Gables* by L. M. Montgomery, a book that sparked her imagination and set her on the path to becoming a writer and educator.

Kahlani B. Steele used a pseudonym under which she published her debut novel, *Resilient*.